SEARING NEED

STEELE RIDGE: THE KINGSTONS

TRACEY DEVLYN

TEAM STEELE RIDGE
Edited by Gina Bernal
Copyedited by Martha Trachtenberg
Proofread by Annie Sarac
Beta Reads by Amy Remus and Isabel Hofmann
Cover Design by Elizabeth Mackey
Author Photo by Lisa Kaman Kenning, Mezzaluna Photography

Print Edition, January 2026, ISBN: 978-1-940677-23-1
Digital Edition, January 2026, ISBN: 978-1-940677-19-4

For more information contact: tdccreationsinc@gmail.com

DISCOVER MORE STEELE RIDGE

STEELE RIDGE: THE STEELES

STEELE RIDGE: THE KINGSTONS

STEELE RIDGE: THE BLACKWELLS

Flash Point, Book 1

Smoke Screen, Book 2

Cross Roads, Book 3

Crash Course, Book 4

End Game, Book 5

STEELE RIDGE CHRISTMAS CAPERS

The Most Wonderful Gift of All, Caper 1

A Sign of the Season, Caper 2

His Holiday Miracle, Caper 3

A Holly Jolly Homecoming, Caper 4

Hope for the Holidays, Caper 5

All She Wants for Christmas, Caper 6

Jingle Bell Rock Tonight, Caper 7

Not So Silent Night, Caper 8

A Rogue Santa, Caper 9

The Puppy Present, Caper 10

For the Love of Santa, Caper 11

Beneath the Mistletoe, Caper 12

ALSO BY TRACEY DEVLYN

NEXUS SPYMASTER SERIES

Historical romantic suspense

A Lady's Revenge

A Lady's Temptation

A Lady's Secret

A Lord's Redemption

A Lord's Bargain

BONES & GEMSTONES SERIES

Historical romantic mystery

Night Storm

TEA TIME SHORTS & NOVELLAS

Sweet historical romance

His Secret Desire

SEARING NEED

STEELE RIDGE: THE KINGSTONS

TRACEY DEVLYN

WWW.TRACEYDEVLYN.COM

For my talented editor, Martha Trachtenberg,
whose keen eye, humor, patience, and advocacy of a certain
character's continued existence
made Riley and Coen's story immeasurably better.

1

An animal's scream pierced the moist North Carolina air.

As she'd heard all manner of screeches, cries, chirps, ribbits, and howls, Riley Kingston's radar barely blipped at the minor disturbance. She swiped at a bead of sweat on her nose before entering the GPS coordinates for the precious patch of *Panax quinquefolius* she'd located.

American ginseng, also known as seng, thrived in shaded, moist, well-drained slopes located across the middle and eastern United States. Many believed the root, resembling a windblown parsnip, cured diabetes, boosted energy, and managed sexual dysfunction, making it a coveted commodity across the globe, especially in Asian cultures.

Kneeling, Riley concentrated as her fingers wended their way between the compound prongs in search of the thick sympodium rising out of the rich black soil. "One, two, three..." She counted each plant with painstaking precision, careful not to miss a single one. In the growing shadows, she relied more on touch than sight.

Although she still had quite a bit of the Steele Conservation Area to survey, she was growing concerned about the scarcity of *Panax* she'd logged so far.

"Riley, you there?" barked a familiar, staticky voice.

She closed her eyes and drew in a deep, frustrated breath before resuming her counting. "Four, five, six, seven—"

"Riley, it's Britt."

No duh.

"Eight, nine, ten, eleven, twelve—"

"Answer the damn radio, Riley, or I'm coming out there to find your scrawny ass."

"Gahrrr!" She dug into one of the many pockets of her field vest. "Can't a girl get some freaking alone time?" Being a female in the Kingston-Steele family was a royal pain in the butt sometimes.

Walkie-talkie in hand, she asked in her calmest voice, "What can I do for you, boss?"

After her Costa Rican research trip abruptly ended, she'd returned home in utter misery. Noticing her struggle, her cousin Britt offered her a much-needed distraction. A job.

At first she'd refused his offer, unable to bear the possibility of another failure, especially one where her strong, got-it-together cousin was concerned. But Britt's annoying and persistent texts and the enticement of getting back into the field lured her into acceptance.

"Are you headed back?" Britt asked.

"Not yet. I want to finish this transect first."

"Look around, Riley."

"Okay." She scanned her immediate surroundings. Patches of jewelweed intermingled with sprigs of Solomon's seal and mayapples on the forest floor. Great canopies of oak, hickory, and maple darkened the landscape above. "Am I searching for anything specific?"

A very male, very big sigh preceded, "Daylight—or lack of it. You need to get out of there before nightfall."

Riley blinked several times, only now realizing she'd been squinting into the shadows. "Um, right. I'm on my way."

"Straight back," he warned. "No distractions."

"Did you miss the part where I grew up and became an adult?"

"No, but I think you did. Hurry up. Randi's taking me out to dinner."

"You don't have to wait—"

"Chop-chop, Riley."

The whole alpha-male thing was downright suffocating. So much testosterone surrounded her that it was a wonder she hadn't grown a set of balls yet.

Clenching her teeth, Riley dropped her walkie-talkie back into her vest and stowed away her handheld GPS unit. With the coordinates marked, she would be able to return tomorrow and finish inventorying *Panax*.

If she didn't love Britt so much, she would've taken the long way back just to piss him off. But no matter how much she'd like to kick his shins, he'd saved her in ways even she didn't comprehend when he offered her this job.

Following her internal compass, she set off for where Britt awaited her at the wildlife research center. Rather than retrace her steps, she made a sharp ninety-degree turn, opting for a shortcut. She knew this land better than anyone. Well, maybe not Britt, but she was gaining ground on her cousin.

She'd spent hours traipsing these hills, conducting vege-tative surveys and observing Britt's beloved red wolves.

Watching the emergence of a new pack of pups this spring had been amazing. Calypso and Apollo demonstrated as much tolerance of their babies' antics as Ross and Sandy Kingston showed their five children.

The importance of the survey and the knowledge that Britt trusted her to do a good job went a long way in repairing her battered ego. But lately a restlessness had settled into her bones, scrambling her thoughts and feelings into a million different directions.

She needed... something more.

Another scream arrowed through the trees, sending ice shards down her spine.

"That was no animal."

Riley sprang forward before her brain could catch up. Ascending a steep rise, she grasped small tree trunks as the toes of her hiking boots dug into the loamy earth.

Once she reached the crest, she spotted a creek cutting along the hollow, creating a shimmering dark ribbon in the gloom. Stands of towering silver-barked beech trees and glossy-leaved rhododendrons fanned out from the rushing water. Not a single bird fussed at her nor did a mosquito buzz at her ear. Every creature in the vicinity held its breath, anticipating.

What?

Another scream, more guttural, more wounded, barreled into her, stripping away her breath and shoving against her heart.

Sweat snaked down her temple as she stalked the ridge-line, searching for the source of so much torment, so much pain.

Time slogged by, though her pulse ticked away each nerve-racking second.

Another scream. No. A man's roar of anguish and hatred and fear.

This time she caught movement up ahead. She sprinted the short distance, her chest near to bursting with anxiety. Below, a small two-person tent, the color of muddy grass, sat amid a blanket of ferns. The domed structure shook as if it straddled a seismic fault line.

Her instincts urged her to rush down the hill. But her too-stupid-to-live meter was clicking off the charts. What if someone was being attacked? Or murdered? Or...

Riley threw her imagination in neutral and reached for her walkie-talkie.

That's when the tent's occupant flung himself out of his shelter and clambered to his feet.

His hair disheveled.

Eyes wild.

And body buck-ass naked.

2

RILEY'S THUMB HOVERED OVER THE TALK BUTTON ON HER walkie-talkie. All thoughts of calling Britt had been obliterated by the panting, sweat-slicked brickhouse of a man below.

His short, military-cut dark brown hair stood out in direct contrast to the several days of growth covering his square jawline.

Lord, have mercy. His body could rival any gladiator's physique. Broad shoulders rolled down to thick, rippling biceps. The slope and depth of his pectorals gave a whole new definition to the term man chest, and the deep ridges of his abs could send even the most enthusiastic thrill seeker into a bout of motion sickness.

A line of sleek, dark hair arrowed downward from his navel to his groin. She stared in astonishment at the sight of him until something began to stir deep in her core. When heat crept up her neck, she forced her attention to the thick muscles that stretched across his thighs to the tops of his bare feet.

Even through the deepening gloom, she could make out

every bunching muscle, every laboring breath, every shaking limb.

When she zoomed out and took in the whole of him, she noticed him scanning the area while he rubbed the back of his neck. He appeared... vulnerable. How could someone so powerfully built seem so lost?

Had he awoken from a nightmare?

Surely not. The sun was only now setting.

She assessed his campsite, his naked body, his physical reaction to whatever emotion he was riding. Riley's stomach slowly folded into itself, clenching and squeezing and then roiling as realization stretched to the surface.

Had the guy been... *masturbating*?

She craned her neck forward, squinting at the area between his legs. "Oh God," she whispered.

The universe couldn't be that cruel.

Well, at least no one had been murdered.

Shaking off the last tentacles of panic, she gave the camper one final disgusted look before turning away—and that's when her walkie-talkie crackled to life.

"Riley," Britt called in an exasperated voice. "Where the hell are you?"

She fumbled with the device, stuffing the speaker into her armpit. With slow, precise movements, she peered down at the naked man, praying he hadn't heard her cousin, and found his gaze zeroed in on her.

His eyes were no longer wild and disoriented.

They were savage.

3

Coen Monroe blinked hard. Images from his nightmare faded in and out, overlaying the woman on the bluff. His pulse hammered against his skull, making his vision blur.

Who was she? What was she doing here? Spying on him? Or passing by?

Looking beyond her at the rapidly darkening sky, his heart sank. She could get off course, lose her way. Fall into enemy hands. Be tortured. Be bru—

No!

He shook his head. *Focus, Monroe. Focus.*

He forced himself to concentrate on a pair of wide, wary eyes outlined by dark frames. She had her hair pulled back in a ponytail, revealing a pale, heart-shaped face. It glowed on the ridge like an angelic beacon. A beacon he ached to follow, to touch, to protect.

A white T-shirt beneath an open, long-sleeved beige shirt and matching cargo pants hugged her tall, slender body. Binoculars and something small and round hung from her neck. She wore an encased Leatherman or some other multi-tool on her belt.

A lost birder? An Indiana Jones wannabe? Her bold assessment of him didn't waver. Someone from his past?

Intent on getting some answers, he ripped a pair of underwear off the line, slipped them on, and stalked toward her. But like Indy, she recognized danger and bolted.

Something primal flipped on in his head, and he gave chase.

He charged up the hill, his bare feet digging into the leaf-littered ground. By the time he hit the crest, Little Miss Indy had melted into the forest. Quieting his breathing, he cocked his head, listening until he caught the distinctive sound of desperate feet crashing through the underbrush.

If he'd been in a rational state of mind, he would've allowed her to flee and not have given her a second thought. But he was far from rational. Kendra's screams still hollowed out his mind, and Paul's, Freddy's, and Miller's mutilated bodies still burned his eyes.

Bloodlust fired into his veins, and a deep-seated compulsion forced his pursuit. Like a dog chasing a cat, he acted on instinct. Every cell in his body commanded him to seize.

Even with night full upon them now, her undisciplined flight left a highway full of clues for him to follow. He increased his speed, his night vision clear.

Red wolves prowled these woods. Although they would more likely scurry out of the woman's way, they were still wild and unpredictable. Like him.

Brambles soon tore into his unprotected thighs, signaling the forest's edge was close. Slowing his pace, he picked his way through wild raspberry vines until he broke through the tree line. And froze.

A short grass meadow opened before him. Trees and dense shrubs lined the entire perimeter, providing a thousand shadowed places where a sniper could hide to pick off his target.

He eased back until the prick of thorns halted his retreat. She was two-thirds of the way across the field when he spotted her.

Arms pumping, ponytail swinging, the woman sprinted toward a large glass structure. A greenhouse sat in the distance with a metal storage shed at its rear and a utility cart parked in the front. A gravel service drive cut through the trees, toward safety.

He scanned the meadow's edge again. With a new moon in the sky, he had no hope of catching the glint of moonlight on a scope lens. But the flash from a muzzle would be unmistakable. And he'd be too late.

A cool breeze kicked up, buffeting his bare flesh, chilling the sweat on his body. Something clicked in his brain like a light switch. On, off. Black, white.

What the hell was he doing chasing a woman who'd wandered upon his campsite? Almost fucking nude, no less. If anyone saw and reported him, he'd have far more things to worry about than a hiker's safety and a sniper's bullet.

Despite his newfound clearheadedness, he couldn't leave. Not yet. The fleeing woman jumped into the cart and flew down a service drive.

Safe.

Who was she? He shoved the question away as soon as it surfaced. He wasn't in Steele Ridge to make friends—or to get entangled with a too-curious, too-reckless woman. No matter how beautiful she might be.

He was here to purge his demons.

Something he was doing a shit-ass job at so far.

With one last sweep of the meadow, he melted into the darkness, into solitude.

Into the emptiness of his life.

4

———

"YOU'VE GOT A SQUATTER." RILEY FLUNG OPEN THE SIDE entrance door to the Steele-Shepherd Wildlife Research Center.

Adrenaline blinded her to the educational displays on red wolves, bats, and a number of other projects Britt had in progress. In remembrance of his mentor and Randi's mother, Barbara Shepherd, Britt had named the center in her honor. Even after a year, Randi still got weepy every time she read the sign above the door.

"What the hell took you so long?" Britt Steele asked, eyeing her. "Did you run?"

Chest heaving, she jabbed three fingers into the stitch at her side. "Did you hear what I said?" She pointed toward the woods. "There's a man camping on Steele property, au naturel."

"Naturel—"

"The full monty, birthday suit, johnson flapping in the wind—"

"I got it, smart-ass." His voice turned low, menacing. "Did he... touch you?"

She rolled her eyes. "I didn't get *that* close."

The stiffness didn't ease from her cousin's shoulders. "What were you doing in that area? You were supposed to be surveying Transect K."

"I finished K and moved on to L."

"I told you to stay out of L."

"No, you didn't."

"Yes, I did."

"No, you—" Riley took a deep breath. "Forget it. Stay out for how long?"

"Couple of weeks." He flicked off the lights. "A month maybe."

She narrowed her eyes. "Do you know him?"

"No."

"But you knew he was squatting."

"Camping."

"What's his name?"

Britt motioned for her to precede him out the door.

Arms folded, she waited for him to set the alarm and lock the building. When he brushed past her and climbed into Old Blue, his ancient pickup, she pushed her face into the open driver's side window.

"His name?"

"Riley, you've got plenty of work to keep that whirlwind you call a mind busy. Forget about the camper."

"Why are you protecting him?"

His truck roared to life. "Let's go. I've got a date."

"You know secrets are my catnip."

"For once in your ever-loving life, listen to me and forget you saw the soldier."

Riley perked up. "Soldier?"

He closed his eyes and sucked in a harsh breath through his nostrils.

"Do you want me to stay away because he's dangerous?"

"No." His hard gaze locked on her while he mulled something over in his mind. "All he wants is some solitude. The last thing he needs is the Kingston Menace buzzing around his ears."

Riley coiled her fingers, her nails digging into her palms. "Do you know what makes no sense to me?"

"I'm backing up."

"Boys pull practical jokes all the time and don't get slapped with insulting nicknames." She kept pace with his truck. "What did I do to earn the title 'Menace'?"

"For one, your shit bomb cost me my favorite sleeping bag."

"That's it?" She raised her eyebrows, incredulous. "What about the cockroaches you unleashed in my purse? That stunt made me pee my pants. In front of Tommy Whittaker."

"Revenge for when you doused my car seat with vinegar. That I sat in."

"Because you wouldn't give me a ride to the library." She pushed her glasses up on her nose. "You were way too cool to be seen with me."

He shoved the gearshift into drive. "Stay away from L."

"Why does he need solitude?"

"Stay away, Riley. He's not one of your lab experiments."

He drove off but only so far as the exit. There, he waited. And waited. For her.

Riley blew out an irritated breath, knowing, *knowing*, he wouldn't budge until she left.

"Damn overprotective men!" She stormed over to her Jeep Wrangler, following in his wake.

A disembodied arm shot out from the driver's side window of Britt's truck and waved her forward. Setting her jaw, she rolled to a stop beside him. She didn't lower her window.

His fathomless brown eyes met hers, and he mouthed "stay away."

She stretched her lips into a sickening sweet smile and murmured, "I hope your Willie falls off before you get laid tonight."

Although he couldn't have heard her through the window, he still sensed the threat to his manhood and pierced her with a payback stare.

Unfazed, Riley sped toward the small bungalow she now called home.

Safe.

Sound.

Suffocated.

5

Costa Rica
10:28 p.m.

CAMILLA WAITED AN ETERNITY FOR THE SENNA TO TAKE effect. She hated having to poison Eduardo and the other security guards, but she couldn't come up with a better way to access the cold storage unit without them finding out.

Guilt speared through her as she recalled Eduardo's smile when she'd handed him a decanter of his favorite hazelnut coffee. She pushed the feeling away. Much more was at stake than the comfort of a few men.

Ten more minutes passed before the first guard peeled away from his post by the Restricted Area door, holding his cramping stomach. The second guard followed his shift leader a minute later.

She counted off another two minutes, hoping Eduardo's gut was no stronger than his companions'. With him sitting in a small monitoring room down the corridor, she would have to have faith that her concoction did the trick.

Forcing a deep, calming breath into her lungs, she flipped up her hood and stepped out of her hiding place. Her soft-soled shoes whispered down the stark white corridor. The only sound came from the battering ram that was once her heart.

The image of Eduardo curled up in the fetal position tore at her conscience. Despite his tendency to boast about his duties, Eduardo was a nice man. She'd spent days cultivating his friendship while pretending interest in his duties. The combination had enticed him into giving her a tour of the monitoring room, including details about the cameras' limitations. Like blind spots.

Keeping her face down, she edged toward the control panel. Too caught up in his boasting, he'd failed to shield the panel when entering the monitoring room yesterday, giving her a perfect view. She prayed the same code would work in the restricted area.

Punching in Eduardo's four digits, she stood frozen until the telltale *click* broke the silence. The moment she stepped inside, overhead lights flickered on, revealing Dr. Young's untidy desk and rows of stainless steel tables. Her heart sank.

Crowded on the tables sat hundreds of specimens that shouldn't be here. They belonged in the wild where God intended them to flourish and provide sanctuary for some and nourishment for others.

Not... this. This demonstration of wanton greed.

Swallowing back her sadness, she rushed to the temperature-controlled metal tray and pulled it open. Wisps of frosty air whirled upward, chilling her face. Inside sat two vacuum-sealed silver canisters.

Removing her backpack, she spread it open and slipped on her gloves before placing both canisters inside. Zipping up her pack, she closed the tray and beelined for the door, certain she would be caught any second.

A dark object on the doctor's desk caught her eye. *"No es posible."*

Even though her internal clock begged her to run, she veered toward the desk. Her shaking fingers fluttered over her discovery with near reverence. This could not be what she thought it was. It just couldn't.

But after peering inside, she couldn't deny the object's identity. "Holy Mother."

Slamming it closed, she shoved it into her backpack and ran. Panic and exhilaration flared through her, almost causing her to forget to protect her face from the camera.

She rounded several corners before slowing her pace. It took two more before she pushed back her hood and stopped peering over her shoulder every two seconds.

When the exit door appeared, she released a tension-riddled breath. She'd done it. She'd stolen back her people's heritage *and* brought the doctor's horrid scheme to a halt. Excitement smothered her fear—until the reality of her situation set in.

"What have I done?" Her whispered words echoed down the corridor.

The whole thing was too big and complicated. Who would ever believe her story? Believe a nobody who had been scraped off the street by a kindhearted stranger? A nobody the authorities could easily dismiss as a disgruntled former employee.

If *he* ever learned of her betrayal, he would kill her. She wouldn't survive a battle with such a powerful man.

Absorbed in her rash stupidity, she missed the warning scrape of boot heel against the tile as she came upon the final intersection. Strong hands shot out, stopping her before she rammed into a large, uniformed body.

"*¡Cuidado!*"

"*Perdóname,*" she mumbled, keeping her head low.

"Camilla?"

Balling her hands into fists, she lifted her head and met Eduardo's dark, penetrating gaze. His face was flushed, and blood-red veins streaked the whites of his eyes.

The senna hadn't incapacitated him like the others. *Oh God.*

"Why are you still here?" he asked, swiping beads of sweat from his upper lip. "I thought you left after you gave us the coffee."

"I—" Camilla searched her frozen brain for the ready-made excuse she'd devised before setting out on this insane mission. "I had hoped to catch up with Dr. Young."

"*¿Por qué?*"

"To see if he would write a letter of recommendation for me."

"The doctor left for San Juan this morning."

Heat spread into the tips of her ears. "So I heard, too late."

He clamped a hand over his stomach. "W-why didn't you call or email him? Could've saved yourself a wasted trip."

"I had nothing better to do." She forced concern into her eyes. "Are you all right?"

"Stomach's not right."

"A couple of my friends came down with the stomach flu a few days ago." She touched his arm. "Be careful. Don't let yourself get dehydrated."

His face contorted as another roiling wave hit his gut. "I'm going to check on my m-men, then head to the barracks."

"Is there anything I can do for you?"

"No, but you should go before someone sees you."

"*Adiós,* Eduardo. I hope you feel better soon."

She stepped around him, and the metal canisters in her backpack shifted, clinking together.

"What was that?"

When his attention narrowed on her backpack, terror rippled through her body.

She searched for a viable answer, but her mind remained blank. "Huh?" she asked in a lame attempt to stall for time.

"Something rattled in your pack."

Shaking off her paralysis, she said, "It must have been a noise down the hall. You know how sound travels in this place." She tossed him a wave over her shoulder and headed for freedom, keeping her steps measured and unhurried.

"Open your pack, Camilla," he commanded in a voice she'd never heard before.

She picked up her pace.

"Stop!"

Tightening her grip on her backpack strap, she ran. Her shoes slapped against the tile floor, drowning out the rush of blood to her head. When a heavier set of footsteps echoed behind her, she thought her heart would explode into a thousand tiny pieces.

Not slowing for the door, she hit the push bar at a dead run. But it wasn't enough. A strong hand slammed into her back, forcing her to the ground. Rough fingers yanked her pack off.

On hands and knees, she scrambled after him, straining to snatch the precious cargo back. "Give it to me!"

Kicking her hand away, he unzipped one of the many pouches and found it empty. "What did you steal?"

"You should ask Dr. Young that question." Using her head like a battering ram, she plowed into his stomach. They landed in a heap on the ground.

Eduardo's eyes rounded as a wash of humiliation, then fury contorted his face. "Fucking bitch!" Holding his midsection, he staggered to his feet and ran back to the building. A dark stain blossomed at the back of his pants and down the inside of his left leg.

The sight caused her a momentary pang of regret until she probed her pack and found the canisters and journal were still inside. Determination lifted the guilt from her chest and dumped it on the ground.

Every hair-raising moment had been worth it. She had given her cargo a second chance. Now she had to find someone to help her, someone she trusted with her life.

The door slammed behind Eduardo, propelling her into action. She had only a short period of time before *he* came for her.

Fear crackled through her body.

6

_____

BEFORE THE SUN ROSE THE NEXT MORNING, RILEY HAD TAKEN matters into her own hands regarding Monty. As monikers went, Monty wasn't great, but given the camper's state of undress yesterday, it seemed fitting.

After Britt had let the "soldier" comment slip, she'd realized that her cousin Reid or his best friend Gage probably knew the camper. There was a good chance Jonah knew about him, too, since he owned the land and, more importantly, seemed to be aware of everything that went on in Steele Ridge, especially anything involving his family.

Typical male shortsightedness. Tell everyone about the strange man hanging out in the woods except for the woman mostly likely to come upon him.

When she got nowhere with Britt, she'd asked the others about the mysterious camper. Surprise, surprise—the Steele boys and Gage had closed ranks and refused to give up the goods. Although she'd expected it, the shutout, the lack of trust, still hurt.

High above her, a woodpecker hammered away at the side of a tree. Something dug into her hipbone. Frowning, she reached down and found a broken acorn shell wedged between her and the ground. She tossed it away and resumed her vigil.

Fuck 'em all. She hadn't been kidding when she told Britt that secrets were her catnip. She couldn't stand not knowing something.

Just ask her dad. When she'd been eight years old, he'd caught her unwrapping her Christmas gifts, peeking at what was inside, then pressing the tape back into the exact same spot. Maybe if she'd stopped at her own presents, she would have escaped detection that night, but her insatiable curiosity had her peeling open her siblings' presents too.

From that moment forward, Riley's presents had shown up under the tree as if Santa had placed them there himself. Christmas became a slow, torturous crawl to the big reveal.

But her dad's silent censure hadn't curbed her appetite for knowledge, especially the forbidden kind. The kind that involved a naked, screaming gladiator who made her insides tingle all over.

Propping her chin on her stacked arms, she stared down at the sparse campsite from her perch on the cliff above. The two-person tent stood shuttered against any annoying, biting insects, and the small round fire pit sat cold and smoke-free.

A large log lay alongside the pit, acting as a rudimentary chair. Behind the tent stretched a sturdy line between two giant trees. A green T-shirt, boxers, and a pair of camouflage pants hung over the cord like limp noodles.

"That's a lot of green, Mr. Monty," Riley whispered. Why would anyone wear that shade of green while on their own time? Not that she was a fashionista like her cousin Evie, but she possessed some sense of what didn't make the eye bleed.

Riley flicked a large black ant off her wrist.

A vision of the camper's dark brown hair, stubbled cheeks, and hair-dusted chest clouded her mind's eye.

Black, she decided, would suit him much better. Closing her eyes, she imagined the color of midnight cradling those powerful, sun-kissed muscles, stretching and contracting to accommodate their every movement. In the shadows of the forest, as the sun set, the shade would make him invisible to his enemies, to his prey, to her.

Except for his eyes.

Those crystal-green rings would penetrate the gloom, cleave through the night, and awaken unspeakable longings.

A stirring low in her stomach made her legs restless. Where did *those* thoughts come from? At this distance, she hadn't been able to make out his eye color, so why had she imagined them green? Like a cat's. A big, dangerous cat.

The sound of a zipper ripping open drew her attention to the campsite below. Mr. Monty emerged shirtless, sweaty, and disheveled. His chest heaved, and something unspeakable haunted the chiseled planes of his face before his hands scrubbed the surface.

When his head dropped between his shoulders and his fingers gripped his skull, Riley knew another nightmare had snapped him from sleep again. After giving what she saw last time more thought, she'd discarded the idea that he'd been pleasuring himself. His "mood" didn't match the action.

Leaning farther over the bluff's edge, Riley forced calm into her thundering chest and willed herself to observe without emotion, without judgment, without speculation.

She mentally cataloged details—*male, white, upper twen-*

ties or lower thirties, close-cropped, military-style hair, no visible tats, knee-length, gray jersey shorts, bare feet. Possible scar along left rib cage and right shoulder. Too far away to be sure—

"*Fuuuuck!*" The soldier bellowed, his fists extended to the heavens.

The hammering woodpecker stopped.

Any comfort she'd derived from her cataloging observable facts vanished in that one agonized word. Why did he come to this place, alone, to fight whatever memory waged war in his mind?

She'd read enough about post-traumatic stress to recognize the signs. He didn't need solitude. He needed someone to help him process his memories. What sort of tragic events had he survived?

He ducked back into his tent and came out carrying a towel in one hand and a scrap of soap in the other. When he followed the meandering creek bed, she frowned, wondering why he didn't freshen up outside his campsite. Then she recalled how the creek grew deeper farther downstream, and about a hundred yards from here, right before a small waterfall, the water pooled into a natural bathtub.

Riley's pulse reverberated through her body, as a horrible, reckless thought struck.

No. It was a terrible idea.

Her fingers curled into the loose leaf litter covering the ridge.

Worst plan she'd ever devised.

She dragged her flattened feet upright until her heels pointed to the sky and dug the toes of her boots into the forest floor.

Wait.

Oh my God. Was she really going to do this?

The moment his bare shoulders disappeared from view,

Riley popped up from her sprawled position and rushed to the least death-inducing slope. Grasping a tree to steady her balance, she angled her right foot until it was parallel with the slope and set it down, allowing it to slide over the leaf litter. Once her momentum slowed, she shifted to her left foot. She alternated gliding steps—right, left, right, left—her heart racing as the speed of her descent increased.

She hit the bottom of the hollow, jarring every bone in her body. Keeping an eye on the spot where Monty disappeared, she sprinted to his tent, dropping to her knees before the closed flaps.

Her fingers grasped the zipper, and she tugged it down an inch—and stopped.

Wrong, wrong, wrong.

Observing him from afar was one thing, even though her conscience twitched like a half-squished worm. But she remembered the rage shooting from those piercing eyes.

She needed to understand who he was and why he was here. Even if she stayed out of Transect L, who's to say that he'd stay in it. Knowing more about him would help her gauge his character. What would he do if he came across her, alone in the woods?

Better yet—what caused his night terrors?

Filling her lungs with air, she entered the soldier's lair.

Coen dropped his shorts and towel on the gray rock jutting out over the creek before striding into the center of a small, natural pool. He stopped when the gentle waves lapped at his hips, the chilly water doing nothing to cool the inferno raging beneath his flesh.

Acid raked his throat raw, and a tremor had taken root in the pit of his stomach.

He sank into the water, submerging until the current flowed over his cheeks, eyelids, lips. Tilting his head back, he opened his eyes and focused on the blurry patch of light pushing through the canopy high above his watery grave.

God, he was so tired. Tired of reliving his last mission, tired of not living a full life. He needed to move on but feared what that said about him as a human being.

His body bucked from air deprivation, and a bubble escaped his mouth.

Just a little longer.

When the echo of Kendra's screams finally gave way to his fight for air, he exploded above the surface, heaving in several hard breaths.

All he wanted to do was return to his unit. But the thought of being responsible for another's life made the tremor worsen.

Who was he kidding? He had no team. No one to lead or protect.

He swept a hand over his face, wishing he could wipe away those three days as easily as he brushed away droplets of water.

The sound of a motorcycle revving up its engine rang through the clearing. Coen waded over to the rock and pulled his phone from a front pocket of his shorts.

Colonel Walsh.

His grip tightened, and he came close, so close, to chucking the device into the water. But years of training and answering the call, no matter where he was or what he was doing, had him hitting Answer.

"Good morning, Colonel."

"How's the mountain treating you?"

"I've had my fill of fresh air and cold baths. I'm ready to return anytime."

"How are your... headaches?"

He squeezed his eyes shut and rubbed his knuckle against the center of his forehead. He should be grateful that his commanding officer knew of his night terrors and, as of yet, hadn't stripped him of his security clearance and reassigned him.

But his pride hated that his weakness was laid bare before a man he respected. A man who had seen far more action and suffered many more losses than he had. To Coen's knowledge, the colonel had never needed a leave to "get his head on straight."

Opening his eyes, Coen's attention wandered upward to

the hole in the canopy and the spray of sunshine diving through. "The head's good."

"Have you spoken to her?"

Fuck no.

His throat closed, barring the kill-your-career response. "Not yet."

Silence radiated on the other end of the line for several uncomfortable seconds before the colonel spoke again. "When? It's imperative that the two of you talk."

"Soon."

A heavy sigh blew into the receiver. "You have twelve days, Sergeant First Class. Twelve days left of R and R and twelve days to make contact. Take care of this. That's an order."

Or don't bother coming back.

He flinched, knowing before he even began that he would fail at this mission.

Who was he, if not a soldier?

JUST A QUICK PEEK, THEN BEAT FEET.

Riley toggled the button on her watch to start the timer. She'd give her scientist's mind seven minutes to assess the reclusive soldier's character. A lot could be learned about a person's proclivities by spending a few minutes in their personal space.

On all fours, Riley inched inside the small tent, bracing herself against any unsavory male smells that might waft her way. The camper had been out here for at least a week, though she suspected longer, given the amount of trash she'd seen him bear-proof up in a tree.

But body-odor-ridden shirts and multiday-worn underwear didn't assault her nose. The scent of pine needles and polyester and musty paper swirled around the small space.

His sleeping area wouldn't meet military standards, but it was tidy enough to make any mama proud. A bedroll rested against one side of the tent, and neat piles of clothes lay on the opposite side. Books upon books lined the head of the tent. How many trips had it taken him to tote all those out here?

An e-reader might have been a better choice. She glanced around for a power source. Then again, maybe not.

Careful not to disrupt anything, she crawled toward his little library, curious about his reading tastes. She guessed that she'd find an overabundance of political or military mysteries and thrillers with a few nonfictions about cars or motorcycles or boats thrown into the mix.

What she found was a surprising variety of genres—sci-fi and fantasy, historical mysteries, postapocalyptic young adult, and even one lone paranormal romance. Not a single true crime, political thriller, or otherwise modern-day novel to be found. All his reads involved other worlds and realms and eras and beings.

A small, battered tin with the initials CJM engraved in the center sat atop one stack of books. When she popped the top open, the sweet scent of ginger wafted to her nose. Smiling, she reached for one of the candied treats but stopped her curiosity in its tracks. She would not steal, no matter the enticement. She was there only to observe. Ignoring her watering mouth, she returned the tin.

A zippered black pouch shoved behind the books caught her attention next. Her heart released a hard thud, the reverberation rattling her eardrums.

With careful fingers, she drew the nylon pouch from its hiding place, half waiting for the snap of a triggered booby trap. But nothing lurched out of the shadows to chop off her fingers, so she opened the pouch and scanned its meager contents. A picture of three men and one woman, resting shoulder to shoulder against a dusty Humvee and holding a long gun across their laps, sat on top. The quartet wore fatigues and satisfied but tired-looking grins. They leaned into each other with a camaraderie that made her eyes sting.

The sight made her think of the evenings when she

and Maggie, Kris and Emmy McKay, and Evie Steele would huddle around a bottle of wine and board game well into the wee hours of the morning. She couldn't remember the last time their schedules allowed for a girls' night out.

The soldier sitting in the middle, next to the woman, looked a lot like her mysterious camper. He wore a stocking cap, and dirt smudged his face. His penetrating eyes were the same yet... different.

They carried a casual softness, a roguish joy for life. None of the hardness and anguish he'd displayed minutes ago.

Next she came across a small, fat, unopened envelope. By the feel of it, several folded sheets of paper were trapped inside. The sender's name—Maria Delarosa; recipient—Coen J. Monroe.

Coen.

Strong. Beautiful. Unique.

Coen.

Riley pushed up her glasses and read the date stamp—July 2. Two weeks ago. Why hadn't he opened her letter?

Flipping the picture back over, she studied the female soldier. Could she be Maria? Or was the letter from an old flame gone wrong?

A quick peek at her watch showed she had little time left. But she couldn't stop her finger from brushing over his name as if she could find her answers buried deep within those four sturdy letters.

Beep, beep, beep.

She hit the dial on the side of her watch. *Time to go.*

After rearranging his belongings back into the order she'd found them, she slid the pouch into its precise, former location. She scanned his spartan quarters, taking in every detail and making sure she'd left none of her presence behind.

Relief followed her out of his tent, thankful she'd found nothing weird or incriminating among his belongings. Yet the mystery surrounding him hadn't diminished. It had intensified.

With feline slowness, she pivoted toward the stream, followed its winding path to the bend where Monty—Coen —had disappeared. A relieved breath *whooshed* from her lungs when she found no broad-shouldered man striding her way.

Fingers shaking, she closed the tent's zipper and stood, mapping the layout of his campsite in one thorough sweep.

Tick tock, tick tock, her inner clock screamed.

Giving herself a good shake, she surged into a half run— and that's when he appeared.

Ice poured into her muscles, locking them into place. Air ceased to move in and out of her body, as if it too feared the slightest movement would mean discovery. Shame blanketed her like a vat of molten tar.

Then self-preservation kicked in, and she evaluated the best route to the ridge. Her heart free-fell into her stomach at the scarce amount of vegetation. He would see her before she could make cover.

Her attention darted back to Coen, and her breath caught in her throat at the sight of him storming toward her.

Fury tightened the cords of his neck and burned the whites of his eyes. His bare chest rose and eddied like a violent tidal wave smashing against a rock-stacked shore. The skin over his face, neck, shoulders, and stomach stretched tight over sinew and bone as if a beast writhed beneath, warring for control. Scars did indeed mark his body.

But none of those things were what set her boots into motion.

It was the jagged, eight-inch knife jutting from his fist that made her choose flight over explanation. But she knew, just *knew,* before she took a single step that she wouldn't outrun him.

And no one would hear her screams.

9

"DID YOU TAKE ANYTHING?" COEN DEMANDED, UNABLE TO calm the fury flowing through his veins. Had he been wrong about her? Had something besides curiosity brought her to his campsite? Had she been scoping the place out?

"W-what?"

"From my tent. Did you take anything?"

All color bleached from her face. "I would never—"

"Then I have to assume you were waiting for me." He shifted closer.

"No! I was just"—guilt flushed her cheeks—"curious."

"Curious," he repeated. "About what?"

She swallowed hard, though her back straightened. "You."

"Who are you?"

"I'm conducting plant surveys in the area."

He closed the distance. "Try again."

"*It's true,*" she all but screamed, stumbling away from him. "I'm a botanist. Well, ethnobotanist, to be exact. I study plants and their impact on human culture. No one has ever heard of an ethnobotanist, so I keep it simple by using the term botanist."

He blinked at the onslaught of information. With a flick of his wrist, he embedded the knife in his log chair. "Did you run out of plants to botanize?"

Her striking gray-blue eyes grew wide as they peeled away from his knife. "Pardon?"

"Why are you snooping around my campsite?" He pointed behind him. "In my tent? I could've mistaken you for—" He bit off his comment.

"Who?" she asked.

His jaw tightened, and he bent to pick up his empty canteen sitting on the log chair. If he hadn't forgotten to take it with him, he would have missed her. "I'm not one of your shamans or whatever. Just a man who wants to be left alone."

Rather than apologize and beat a hasty retreat, the damn woman took a step closer and assessed him like a fucking petri dish. "Why?"

"That's none of your business."

"Where did you learn to turn *Asarum canadense* into candy?"

"Asarum?"

"Wild ginger." She flopped a hand toward his tent. "The tin of sugared treats."

Annoyance made his tone sharp, his words crude. "Did you rifle through my sex toys too?"

"No, I didn't see any of... those." She stared up at him, waiting. For an answer. Did she have no fear? No common sense?

Without conscious thought, he slid into a decades-old habit. Evasion.

"It's not smart for you to be alone in the woods with a strange man."

"I don't have anything to fear from you."

He ran through the number of ways he could kill her—all before she had a chance to scream. "Then you're a fool."

"If you were a murderer or rapist, you would have done the deed by now. When your anger was high and your bloodlust engaged. You wouldn't have stood here, wasting your time on uninspired intimidation tactics."

God, she was naive. The world harbored monsters who enjoyed nothing more than to toy with their victims. For days. Weeks. Years, even.

But the government created men like him so women like her wouldn't be subjected to such evil. The image of a long blade searing through smooth, feminine flesh and tendon and bone pulsed behind his eyes. His palms began to sweat, and a familiar tremor started at the base of his spine and began a slow crawl upward.

Left arm.

Left hand—

"You don't know me." He widened his stance and dropped his voice. "And you obviously know nothing of men."

She flinched as if he'd slapped her. A moment later, she opened her mouth to explain or contradict him or God knew what. He held up a staying hand. The forest began to cave in on him. Time for her to leave. Now.

"Go," he bit out. When she didn't move, he infused steel into his voice. "*Get out of here!*"

Before sprinting away, she studied him like a general working through her next battle plan.

He hadn't scared her. No one damn bit.

Which meant she would be back. *Son of a bitch.*

Despite his irritation, he followed her ascent up the steep hill, marveling at her unbound energy. She paused to snatch a backpack from the top of the ridge, knifing her arms through the shoulder straps. Even with her hurried pace, her movements were smooth and matter-of-fact, as if she'd performed the act a thousand times.

Glancing over her shoulder, over the ridge, she peered at him one last time.

"Don't come back here," he warned, his voice projecting across the distance.

From one blink to the next, she was gone. He ignored the stab to his conscience. If any woman ever needed a lesson in self-preservation, it was that one.

Gritting his teeth against a fresh blast of memories, he swiped away the bead of sweat snaking down his cheek and stood helpless as the darkness ate away at what little was left of his sanity.

10

Costa Rica
8:47 p.m.

CAMILLA'S GAZE SHOT TO THE DOOR FOR THE HUNDREDTH time, certain that armed men would burst inside any second. All day today she'd had the sensation of being... stalked. But she hadn't noticed anyone out of the ordinary.

She shook off her paranoia, reminding herself that she was safe. For now. After being orphaned at the age of twelve, she'd spent years fending for herself, years that had taught her the art of caution.

Only a small group of people from the research center knew her true address, and they were now thousands of miles away. A deep ache of longing splintered her chest, as it always did when she thought of her friends.

Pacing the length of her small apartment, she couldn't shake the feeling that something bad was coming. That *he* was coming.

"Get on with it, you silly, sentimental girl," she scolded herself.

Rushing to the airtight container, she unlatched the heavy lid. Inside rested a bulky, sandwich-sized bag. She removed the bag and carried the precious cargo to the kitchen table housing a large rectangular tray. With trembling fingers, she sprinkled the bag's contents over the pulpy liquid, covering the tray's surface until the last piece sank into its new watery home.

She glanced at the door again, straining to detect any unusual sounds. Silence echoed against the walls of her tiny home.

Lifting a fan to the table, she clicked the speed to low and set about finishing her preparations. Although her apartment contained only three small rooms—a bathroom, a bedroom, and a living room-kitchen combo—it was a palace compared to her prior living arrangements.

Sleeping on a thin, bumpy mattress was far preferable to a nest of blankets on the floor. She would still be laboring away at mindless tasks, stealing for food, if not for an unexpected opportunity.

The past three years had been a blessing beyond imagining—and it was all about to disappear like a wisp of smoke on a breezy day.

She swiped the moisture from her cheek and jammed two sets of clean clothes into her backpack. Opening the drawer of her bedside table, she retrieved a tiny wooden box with a single flower carved into the top by a loving but amateur hand. Her fingers caressed her father's work before she peered beneath the lid to assure herself that the simple circlet of silver still rested inside.

Inhaling, she imagined she could still smell her mother's favored orchid scent. When her vision blurred, she snapped the box shut and dropped it into a zippered pocket of her pants.

Her hand disappeared inside the drawer, and she ripped a taped parcel from the underside of the table's top. Unclasping the metal container, she pocketed her passport and counted the money inside before divvying it up into smaller amounts and stashing it into different pockets on her person and in her backpack.

She hadn't known it at the time, but every spare cent she'd saved the past couple of years had been in preparation for this moment. For years her existence had been about survival, then gratitude. Now she would make a difference. Protect her people's way of life and give her friends one last opportunity to stop others' suffering.

Once she finished packing, she grabbed the items she needed from the small shelving unit and returned to the kitchen to check on the contents of the tray. Satisfied that the batter had firmed up enough, she separated the large piece into four smaller ones and placed them on drying racks in front of the fan again.

Then she set about cleaning up every trace of her activity tonight, just in case *he* found this place.

With as much care as her speedy fingers could manage, she finished preparing the dried rectangles and slid each one into an addressed, stamped envelope. Her fingers brushed over the names in her bold, childlike penmanship.

After losing her mom, she'd had to quit school. But her lack of education hadn't stopped her savior from trying to teach her English in addition to her other duties. If only she'd had more time to finish her lessons, she could have perfected her letters, built upon her lessons. But she hadn't, and she prayed the packages would make it to their destinations without delay.

It took her several attempts to write short notes to include in the envelopes. When she finished, she stared at them with tears of humiliation in her eyes. They would have to do. In a few days, she would call each of the recipients to explain in more detail.

Drawing in an unsteady breath, she stashed the envelopes in her pack and reached for the second canister and the leather-bound journal she'd spent hours trying to read the night before. Although she had failed to decipher the doctor's ramblings, she knew something of value lay within the covers and would not chance mailing it.

With her cargo secured at her back, Camilla strode into her bedroom and opened the window. She scanned the area before lowering herself to the ground. When she made to close the window, she paused to survey her small yet humble apartment. Her home. An ache welled up in her throat, blocking off words and air.

Already she missed this place. A place where she would never be able to return.

Hardening her heart against the anguish, she lowered the sash and left her future behind.

11

"Sweetheart, we're running out of reusable bags," Ross Kingston said. "Can you fetch more from Wilbur?"

"I'm on it, Daddy," Riley said.

She climbed into the back of the truck, also known as Wilbur, parked behind their tented booth at Steele Ridge's Farmers' Market. The action was as familiar to her as brushing her teeth.

The truck received its notorious name when her dad had decided to turn his passion for organic gardening into organic farming. One of his first purchases had been a used moving truck. He'd had the vehicle repainted in what was supposed to be a light tangerine color but wound up being creamy pink. Four-year-old Riley had told her dad it looked like the piglet from *Charlotte's Web*.

Charmed, her dad kept the color and dubbed the truck Wilbur. Although their original market truck had died a slow and painful death many years ago, each one since then had been painted pink and named the same.

Wending her way through the crates of pesticide-free kale, cilantro, onions, carrots, and a dozen other vegetables and herbs, she reached the shelf holding the reusable bags and various other operating supplies.

Although neither Riley nor her siblings had any interest in running her father's business, they all participated in the weekend market during the summer and took shifts at the family store whenever their day jobs allowed.

Finding the box of reusable bags, she grabbed an armful and returned to their stall. Her dad gave her a grateful wink while swiping a customer's credit card through their portable reader.

She gave the petite, brown-haired woman in her midthirties a welcoming smile. "Do you have your own bag, Mrs. Callibaster?"

The woman gave her five-year-old son a pained, side-long glance. "No, sorry. Sammy was screaming bloody murder over the dog tearing up his toy. I left my bag at home."

"No problem." She placed the harried mother's purchases into a small, perfect-for-the-market-sized bag and handed it over. "I threw in a couple of pieces of our home-made peanut brittle." She nodded at the cherub-faced boy watching the crowd of shoppers. "To take off the sting of losing a toy."

"Thank you." Mrs. Callibaster's attention shifted to her dad. "You've got a sweet daughter there, Ross Kingston."

Humor twinkled in her dad's eyes. "She improves with each year."

Mrs. Callibaster laughed. "As parents, that's all we can hope for." She grasped her son's hand. "Have a good day."

"You too," Riley and her dad said at the same time.

"Good morning," a rich, baritone voice said.

Riley glanced up, a smile of welcome on her face, and

froze. Nick Landry stood before her. Easily the most hand-some and intelligent scientist she'd ever met.

Eyes the color of molten gold, skin the tone of sun-kissed sand, and hair the hue of a winter night. He was staggering in his perfection. His heritage was a complete enigma, especially since he could speak a number of languages with precision.

All of this he understood about himself with uncanny clarity and awareness. He used his natural born gifts as lethal weapons. A person felt special and cherished until they weren't any longer. He was equal opportunity in where he directed his affections—male, female, young, old.

Before she'd deciphered his character, she'd fallen prey to Nick's allure, once. A kiss. An all-consuming kiss that had knocked down her defenses and turned her into a clinging idiot. She'd been his perfect victim—alone, uncertain, a little homesick.

To this day, she couldn't recall why she'd pulled back and stopped the most arousing moment of her life, but she was glad her warning bells had kicked in and she'd listened. Or she would've become a Landry Casualty in that camp. Another statistic. Another forgettable conquest.

For all his faults and male idiosyncrasies, though, she liked the dog.

"Morning, Nick." Reaching across the table, Riley gave him a hug and did her best to ignore his deep, appreciative inhalation. She eased out of the embrace, and Nick's consid-erable attention rested on her mouth. "What brings you to my neck of the woods?"

"A conference in Asheville." His golden eyes roamed down her body, assessing, appraising, calculating. "I remem-bered your fondness for your hometown's farmers' market. I hoped I'd get lucky and find you here."

"Why not call? My phone number hasn't changed."

"And miss your look of surprise?"

"Sadist."

He smiled, not contradicting her. His attention drifted to her dad.

"Sorry. This is my dad—Ross Kingston. Daddy, this is Nick Landry."

The two men shook hands.

"How do you know my daughter?"

"Costa Rica. We worked on Project Endurance together. Riley was our most talented ethnobotanist."

Her dad squeezed her shoulder. "I don't doubt it."

"Don't preen too much, Daddy. Nick's only saying that for your benefit. I was the study's *only* ethnobotanist."

A twinkle lit Nick's eyes, making them even more compelling. "My comment still stands."

"Should I leave the two of you to get caught up?" Dad asked.

Riley nodded, and he moved down the table to chat up the vendor next door.

Her attention snapped back to Nick. "What are you really doing here?" She didn't for a moment believe he'd sought her out for no reason.

"I told you." Something flicked across his features. "To check in on an old friend."

"Friend?" she teased. "I considered us more along the lines of companionable colleagues." He'd been courteous to everyone, though he placed people into two categories—sex and knowledge. *Friend* didn't have a place in Nick's world.

"Not for my lack of trying." His gaze traced every contour of her face. "Endurance alone held your heart."

As it did yours.

"Not enough to make it a success." When he didn't reply,

she took his silence as confirmation of her failure and changed the topic. "Can I interest you in some homemade fudge?"

"Absolutely."

Using a set of tongs, she lifted a small, dark square from a floral-patterned platter. "It's my grandmother's recipe."

He popped the sweet into his mouth, chewing with a sensual grace that only he could pull off. He licked his fingers, one by one.

Riley swallowed, unable to look away.

"Delicious." Bracing his fingertips on the table between them, he leaned forward. "Allow me to repay you by joining me for dinner tonight."

"Dinner as *friends*?"

"Of course, what else?"

"Tempting, but I have a date with a plant."

"You'd turn me away after I've come all this distance— just to see you?"

"See that's the thing, Nick." She pushed into his personal space, lowering her voice. "I hear voices in my head. One of the voices has the absolute best radar for detecting bullshit." With her nose, she caressed the air between them, sniffing. "And you've got it smeared all over you."

His bark of laughter echoed through the market. Heads turned in their direction—just in time to see him grasp her face with both hands and plant a kiss on her mouth. She tried to pull away, but the bastard held on. And despite her mortification, Riley's muscles clenched against a stirring deep in her stomach.

Lifting a shaking hand, she dug her thumb into the soft, fleshy part at the base of his neck.

He gagged and released her.

"Goodbye, Nick."

Rubbing his neck, he winked. "Later, Riley." Hands in his pockets, Nick Landry sauntered off. Eyes of every flavor followed him from the market.

Including her father's.

"Did he hurt you?" Ross Kingston asked in a harsh voice.

"No."

"What was that all about?"

"Trying to prove that I'm not immune to his magnetic self, no doubt."

"I don't find guys manhandling my daughter funny."

She linked arms with him. "I'm sorry, Daddy."

"Are you going to see him again?"

"Not likely. He's only in town for a conference."

"Good." He kissed her forehead, then went to gather more product from Wilbur while she refilled the containers set out on the table. They completed the process without a single word, having worked as a team many times in the past.

Once their inventory was replenished, he asked, "How's your survey work going?"

Rather than a list of scientific names drifting through her mind, an image of Coen, naked, hard in all the right places, and angry as hell, surfaced.

What did he do all day? Read? Hike? Sleep? Did he get lonely? Does he have family nearby? How did he come by the sugared ginger?

"Where'd you go, Riley-girl?" Her dad's hand waved in front of her.

She shook Coen out of her head.

Clearing her throat, she said, "Slow."

"I know you'd rather be off in some foreign land finding a miracle cure, but sometimes our greatest achievements can be found closer to home."

"I enjoy the survey work. I've already discovered and documented several rare plant communities." She tossed a wicked smile his way. "Plus the conservation area is vast enough that I can go a whole day without seeing or speaking to another person."

"My little hermit. I've never been able to reconcile how such a lively, vivacious, and ornery young woman could be so content with her own company."

"I'm only ornery when provoked." She sent him a sidelong look. "Which tends to happen a lot with so many men in our family." She smiled. "Present company excluded."

He chuckled. "Well, try to be patient with the surveying. It's a good job until something more to your liking crops up."

Guilt tore through her. She didn't want to worry her dad. Meeting the demands of a successful family business was stressful enough. He didn't need his adult children's problems added to his plate.

She wasn't *unhappy*. But survey work was typically reserved for undergrads needing experience or grads developing their theses. She'd moved beyond those needs. Now she wanted to make a difference, a positive, culture-altering impact.

Costa Rica had been the answer to a long-burning need.

Until it all collapsed.

"Daddy, don't give me another thought. What I'm doing at the conservation area is important work." She wrapped an arm around his solid torso. Despite nearing Medicare age, Ross Kingston could run marathons around most twentysomethings. She gave him a squeeze and stepped away. "What I don't need is the boys getting into my business."

"They love you, Riley-girl. When your mom and I moved out west, I made them swear to look after you and Maggie."

"Somehow I doubt my sister, the soon-to-be sheriff, needed protecting."

"Everyone needs protecting, even the boys. Call me sexist, but I couldn't bring myself to ask Maggie to keep an eye on them while your mom and I were out west."

"I'm sure Maggie kept them in her sights, even without you asking." She brushed off bits of dirt and leaf litter from the table while memories of all the ways her strong sister had diverted disaster over the past few years flashed through her mind. Incidents Maggie had kept from their parents so as not to worry them. Ms. Fix-it.

"What's up? You have that look."

"What look?"

"The one that means you're thinking—or about to unleash hell."

Riley slanted him an aggrieved glance before sharing a sister's fear. "Sometimes I worry that the burden of keeping this town and its residents in check will crush Maggie one day."

He wrapped an arm around her shoulders and pressed a kiss to her head. "There may be times when your sister's responsibilities will be too much for her to endure alone. But as you've said, she has Jayson now to help keep her grounded." He squeezed her against him before returning to business. "If and when her duties become too much, she's smart enough to recognize when it's time to pass on the responsibility. No different than any other high-profile job."

"I hope you're right."

"Of course I am. I'm her dad."

She chuckled. Somehow he always found the right words to make her feel better.

"Back to the boys," she said. "I don't need them hovering

over me all the time. I just turned twenty-five. Time for them to cut the umbilical cord."

"I'll talk to them," he said. "But I suspect their instincts are driving them far more than any promise they've made to me. At least until you're married."

She groaned.

"Hello, Menace."

Speak of the damn devil.

Riley glared at her brother Shep. "Don't call me that, *Harris*."

Avid country music fans, her parents had honored their favorite musicians by giving their children crazy first names —Mandrell, Kristofferson, West, Harris, and Wynette— Riley's personal cross to bear. Shep's first name was Harris, after Emmy Lou Harris. If he wasn't her brother, she would've felt sorry for him. At least she'd been named after a female singer, not a male.

If she didn't know better, she might have accused her parents of smoking weed during the naming process, but they hadn't experienced a brain fart just once, they'd been afflicted five times.

Peering over her shoulder, she murmured to her dad, "Love me, do they?"

She stretched a hand out to scratch the broad, red-gold head of Shep's service dog, Puck. His long, fanlike tail created a dust storm as it brushed back and forth across the ground.

"Deep, deep down, they adore you." Her dad grinned before infusing the same gentle sternness he always employed with Shep. "Son, you know Riley doesn't like to be called that."

"Cash calls her Menace," he replied without guile or

guilt before he consulted his watch and shifted topics. "My shift starts in thirty seconds."

She smiled. It was impossible to stay upset with Shep. "Do either of you need anything before I leave?"

"A cream puff from the Mad Batter," Shep said.

"Do you even eat sweets?"

He shrugged. "I had a weird craving."

"I was thinking of something more practical."

"Be more specific next time."

"Can you stop by the house and get the power cord for the iPad register?" Dad asked, ever the mediator. "I forgot to charge it last night, and I'm not sure there's enough juice to make it to the end of the day."

"Sure. I'll be back in two shakes."

As she edged around her brother, he took the opportunity to flick her ear—as he'd seen Cash do a million times.

She ducked at the last minute, his middle finger hitting air. "What's the matter, Shep? Your inflatable girlfriend spring a leak again?"

A sharp cough drew her attention. Her dad nodded to a group of gray-haired ladies who were staring at her and muttering to themselves. "Sorry, Mrs. Hester, Mrs. Landon, Mrs. Thomas."

The latter two ladies moved on to the next booth. Mrs. Hester winked before following her friends.

As she strode away, Shep said in his matter-of-fact way, "I don't have a girlfriend."

12

A SCREAM TORE FROM COEN'S THROAT, JOLTING HIM AWAKE.

His gut roiled, and he leaned over the side of his sleeping bag to heave the phantom contents from his stomach. Sweat—or tears—he didn't know, dripped off his nose, and a headache split his skull in half.

After several more bouts of organ-clenching misery, Coen fell back onto his makeshift bed. He rubbed his raw, scratchy eyes with the heels of his hands, trying hard to banish the images that wouldn't allow him to close them for more than a few hours at a time. Exhaustion weighed down every cell in his body like an anchor plunging deep into the sea.

Throwing off the damp sheet, he stabbed his legs into his rumpled shorts and threw on a pair of running shoes. He didn't bother with a shirt. It would be one less thing to clean when he returned.

He crawled into the cool, misty morning air. Shadows floated in the hollow like benevolent specters, roaming through a forgotten time. His chest expanded, drawing in cleansing, deep breaths. The rhythmic action did nothing to calm the war that raged in his mind, his heart, his damned soul.

Run, his body demanded. *Run, run, run.*

So he did.

His long stride cut into the rich soil as he ascended the ridge, weaving between trees, shrubs, and jagged rock outcroppings. Once he reached the crest, he loosed himself into the forest, pushing his muscles to their limit, ignoring the shafts of purple and pink and molten red forcing their way through the dense canopy as the sun crept into an azure clear sky.

All the while, his mental compass kept track of his location, mapping the distance and landmarks along his invisible, frantic path.

He ran until he came upon an unfamiliar ridge, one he hadn't found during his previous explorations. He ran until flames licked inside his chest, igniting his labored breaths. He ran until his leaden legs refused to take another ground-eating step. He ran until exhaustion smothered the pounding and the screaming and the awful silence consuming his head.

He ran into *her.*

Coen staggered to a halt, his body swaying and his exhausted mind clawing for clarity. Out of all the thousands of acres he could've run through, how had he managed to intersect the botanist's space? Some might call it fate, but he considered it one more rock in an avalanche of bad luck.

"Who the hell *are* you?"

The botanist whipped around from her crouched position, eyes wide and wary.

Slowly, as if she were afraid of spooking a wild animal, she eased into a standing position. How long they stood there, staring at each other, he didn't know. But from one heartbeat to the next, her gaze unlocked with his and began a slow, thorough progression down his face, along his neck, over his bare chest.

Her inspection lingered at the spot where his shorts rode low on his hips. Hunger pushed away the wariness in her eyes before they continued their meandering journey.

Searing need arrowed through his gut, awakening a part of him that had been dormant for far too long.

Nearly as tall as his six foot two inches, she had long limbs encased in khaki-colored protective clothing, and she wore thick-soled hiking boots. Her long-sleeved shirt hung open over a white, scoop-necked top that hugged her generous breasts and flat stomach.

Coiled energy sparked along every ridge and hollow of her body. She was a sleek thoroughbred, bucking at the starting gate.

He opened his fists he hadn't realized he'd clenched and took one dangerous step forward.

His movement snapped her gaze up to his. Whatever she saw there caused her to take a stilted step backward. He smelled her fear, and it sickened him.

"Who are you?" he repeated.

"Riley Kingston. My cousin owns this land."

Billionaire Jonah Steele was her cousin? Then that meant—

"You're related to Reid."

"Yes, God help me."

All thought of sleek thoroughbreds raced right out of his head.

Rolling his shoulders, he demanded in a low, guttural voice he didn't recognize, "What are you doing here? I warned you not to return."

Annoyance flickered across her features like a fluorescent light bulb blinking to life.

"I didn't return," she said. "You're a long way from your campsite."

The bone-deep fatigue that rode his shoulders hit him hard, and he remembered his need to flee. Flee the memories that had become his living nightmare.

Humiliation barreled through him, and he couldn't bear to meet her penetrating eyes again. Swiveling toward the direction from which he'd come, he stalked off without another damning word.

"Wait," she called.

He ignored her.

"Please, wait." Something in her voice pinched a nerve in his chest.

Leaves rustled behind him. He didn't pause.

She slid to a one-footed halt in front of him, extending a staying hand.

He veered around her.

"Coen, stop, please. I need your help."

Help.

His steps faltered.

"Please, there's an animal trapped in a hole."

He angled his head to look over his shoulder. Worry lines etched her brow.

"You don't want to tangle with a cornered animal."

His statement sat between them for several heartbeats.

"I have gloves."

"What's down there?"

"A juvenile red fox."

He considered her long, lean body again. "If you can't reach it, there's little chance I'll be able to get a grip on it."

"All I need to do is lower myself into the hole another

foot or so. If you hold my feet, I should be able to grab the scruff of its neck."

"Before or after it scratches out your eyes?"

"I can't leave it to die. If you won't help me, I'll figure out something else."

Help me.

Swiping the sweat gathering in his eyebrows, he released a sigh. "Fine, but I'm the one going in."

"With those shoulders? No way."

He frowned at her.

While eyeing him, she made geometric shapes in the air with her hands. "You're too broad for the opening. As it is, I'm going to have to wiggle a bit to fit."

"Show me," he said.

She led him to the place where she'd been crouching upon his arrival. Sure enough, a foot-and-a-half-wide opening yawned beneath the canopy of an ancient oak tree.

Stepping to the edge, he peered inside. He saw nothing but bottomless black.

"How do you know there's anything down there?"

She tossed him a penlight. "See for yourself."

Lowering to one knee, he clicked on the small flashlight, and an oddly bright beam illuminated the pit. A pair of glowing yellow eyes stared back. The fox huddled in a ball against a wall scored by dozens of claw marks.

"Did you try angling a branch into the hole so it could climb out on its own?"

"I couldn't find anything sturdy enough."

He turned the light off and stared into the darkness.

"He'll turn on you the moment you touch him."

"I know."

"You're not afraid?"

"I'd prefer to avoid blood and pain." Her eyes remained

steady on him. "But I understand he'll be reacting out of instinct, not a desire to hurt me. I'll be prepared."

He took in his surroundings, searching for something he could use to widen the opening. The only thing within reach were a few rotting branches.

"I recognize the calculation in your eyes," she said. "Even if we could open up the hole more, there's no way I could haul you out. I'm strong but not that strong."

She was right. He'd wind up toppling headfirst into a pit with a wild animal. And wouldn't that be fun.

Catching the resignation in his eyes, she smiled her victory.

His eyes narrowed.

Turning away, she wrenched off her outer shirt, revealing a tight-fitted tank top that showed off toned arms and a strong, finely muscled back.

"Do you think that's a good idea?" he asked. "The long sleeves would give you an added layer of protection against claws and teeth."

"I'm well aware. But I can't afford my shirt getting snagged on the roots and dirt. My bare skin will help me breach the opening."

Lowering her into the hole, unprotected, raked against every nerve, every instinct he possessed. But with the tools they had at their disposal, he failed to devise a viable alternative.

A familiar tingling sensation started at the base of his spine and wended its way up each vertebra, one by one, an odd combination of heat and cold misting in its wake.

Someone or something watched them.

His hand reached for the knife he kept sheathed at his calf, but his fingers latched onto nothing but bare skin. He almost groaned aloud when he recalled his mad flight from his campsite. All he'd wanted to do was escape into nothingness. He hadn't stopped to consider his weapons or safety, only freedom from his memories.

With a surreptitious tilt to his head, he scanned the openings between trees and shrubs, searching for a gun nozzle or a shadowed figure.

Noticing his attention had shifted to their surroundings, she asked, "What's wrong?"

He held up a silencing hand and continued his search. Just when he began to wonder if his instincts had been testing him, he spotted their stalker.

Low to the ground, half tucked behind a wide tree trunk, a narrow face with unblinking, greenish-yellow eyes stared back. The red fox's long, fluffy tail did not twitch nor did its muscles bunch to leave at its discovery.

Given its size—that of a medium-sized dog—and proximity to the juvenile fox, he guessed their observer had to be one of the kit's parents.

"How aggressive are foxes?" Coen asked.

"They're not." Following his gaze, Riley paused in putting on her gloves. "Unless they're protecting their young."

The fox continued to watch them with unnerving stillness.

He swore. "Let's make this quick."

She nodded, flexing her fingers inside her leather gloves. Kneeling at the pit's edge, she crooned to the frightened, trapped kit. "It's okay, little one. We'll have you out of there in a blink." Looking up at Coen, she asked, "Ready?"

"I'm not the one going into a confined space with a rabid animal."

"Not every wild creature is rabid. Sometimes they're just scared."

He studied her for the space of a breath before motioning to her to get into position. "What do you need?"

"Hold my ankles until I signal that I've got the kit, then pull like hell." She placed the butt of the penlight between her teeth, and without another word, the botanist lay on her stomach, arrowed her arms into the hole, and slid beneath the earth's surface.

Scrabbling to grasp her ankles, he couldn't decide if she was one of the most fearless people he'd ever encountered or one of the most reckless.

She lowered her entire torso into the pit, which left him with a perfect view of her firm, well-rounded ass. Heat speared into his gut.

Reid's cousin, Reid's cousin, Reid's cousin.

He forced himself to look away.

While he'd been preoccupied by the botanist's assets, the adult fox had moved several feet closer. He tightened his grip around her ankles.

"Hurry up," he demanded.

He received a garbled reply in return. Then the muscles in her calves tautened and her body jerked.

"Do you have it?" he asked.

More garbled words. She couldn't speak with the damned penlight in her mouth.

"Do you have it?" he pressed.

She must have removed the flashlight long enough to bark out a loud whispered, "No."

His attention whipped back to the adult sentinel. The fox now sat no more than ten feet away. Way too close for his comfort.

"Ten more seconds and then I'm pulling you out."

He began the countdown in his head while he kept one eye of the fox. Once he hit ten, he said, "Time's up."

Riley began to struggle in his grip, but he dragged her out of the pit, inch by inch, his muscles flexing and straining. When her head cleared the opening, he held his breath, hoping he'd given her enough time to secure the kit.

She spit the penlight out of her mouth and used her free hand to raise herself into a kneeling position. Slowly her other hand cleared the pit and a small, red ball of fluff dangled above the ground.

The adult fox stalked closer, its black-socked paws taking measured steps toward its offspring.

"Set the kit down, Riley."

"I need to first make sure it's okay."

"Set it down."

She must have picked up on the tension in his voice, for she did as instructed.

They both watched as the kit shuffled away, panicking, before noticing the adult nearby. Body low, the kit beelined for the safety of its parent. The two touched noses before sprinting into the woods.

Watching the two foxes reunite helped banish the remnants of his nightmare. He looked to where Riley sat on the ground. Wisps of dark hair framed her flushed face, and dirt streaked her white tank top. Her breasts rose high with each excited breath.

Pushing her glasses up, she gave him a broad, joyful smile.

Something in his chest cracked.

13

I'M HERE.

Riley hit the Send button before dropping her phone into the console's cupholder.

After numerous text messages with Nick, each one more outrageous than the last, she'd finally agreed to meet him for dinner. Actually, pick him up, eat, and then drop him off at the airport.

Not wanting any misunderstandings, she'd made it clear that this dinner was between colleagues—not soon-to-be lovers.

Bahh-ling.

She glanced at her phone's display.

On my way down.

As much as she balked at giving in to Nick's request, she admitted that it would be nice to catch up on Endurance news and hear about his conference. Besides her interactions with Britt, she hadn't talked about plants with anyone in weeks. Not that her "I think we should do so-and-so" and Britt's "Go for it" could be construed as botanical discussions.

Britt wasn't a plant guy. Although he understood the importance of having a diverse native plant community, he kept his focus on maintaining healthy wildlife and left flora management to her.

She should be flattered by his trust—and she was—however, she longed to brainstorm ideas and techniques with other like-minded professionals. Nick would give her the intellectual fix she needed.

So why did apprehension curl in her stomach?

A hard rap of knuckles on her vehicle made her jump. Peering into her rearview mirror, she found Nick's roguish smile filling the frame. He motioned for her to pop the cargo door.

"Hey," he said, sliding his suitcase inside.

"Got enough room?"

"More than enough." He grinned, slow and sexy.

"Do nonsexual thoughts ever cross your mind?"

"I don't remember."

She shook her head. "Get in. I'm hungry."

"Thanks again for picking me up."

"I still can't believe you've been Lyfting or Ubering or whatever it is you've been doing since you've arrived. Why didn't you just rent a car?"

"Not in the budget." He tossed her another wicked smile while clicking his seat belt into place. "Besides, if I had rented, I couldn't have begged a ride from you."

She cast him a warning look. "Keep your hands to yourself tonight, or I'll dump you at my brother Way's doorstep."

"Can I help it if I answered the call of your irresistible lips?"

"Stop it, Nick. Your manhandling upset my dad."

His roguish smile disappeared. "I'm sorry, Riley. I took

our joking too far." He pulled out his cell phone. "What is your dad's number?"

"Why do you want his number?"

"So I can apologize."

"I don't think that's a good idea."

"Why not?"

"Because he likes to hash things out in person, and you're headed out of town. Just let it go."

"Will you pass on my apology?"

"Why is his forgiveness so important to you? You don't even know him."

He studied her face for a blush-inducing moment. "Because he's your father. And who knows when I might be in the area again."

Unsettled, she shifted into drive and redirected the conversation. "Have you eaten at Tupelo Honey Café yet?"

"Not yet." He rested his hand on the shoulder of her seat. "You can take me there some other time. I made reservations at Varsonas."

She considered her pale blue tee and capris alongside his red button-down and black slacks. "I'm not dressed for a place like Varsonas."

"Don't be ridiculous. You look great."

"I'm way underdressed." She maneuvered out onto I-26. "Tupelo is casual and has a great vibe." And no candlelight or soft, jazzy music.

His attention flicked to the passing scenery a moment before returning to her. "Tupelo it is."

They chatted about the weather, traffic, and Asheville's bustling downtown on the short drive from his hotel to the restaurant. When Nick saw the line leading into Tupelo, he balked. "I'll miss my flight."

"Hold on, let me see if I can wheedle us a table."

"Or we could walk to the restaurant where I already have a reservation."

"Just give me two minutes."

He gave her a short nod and followed, looking every inch of the put-out date.

Riley nudged her way through the pillars of people until she reached the hostess podium. Keeping her voice low, she said, "I have a seven o'clock reservation."

"Your name?"

"Kingston."

"Y'all's table's ready. This way."

When she motioned for Nick to follow, his eyes widened. "What'd that cost you?"

"Nothing but a little luck." She didn't know why she kept the fact that she'd made dinner reservations from Nick. She didn't like taking chances or depending on other people. That way led to disappointment.

So she'd taken it upon herself to secure a place at one of her favorite restaurants. Just in case. Having a backup plan helped curb her tendency toward restlessness when she didn't have all the details of an outing.

The hostess led them to a cozy bar and stool section that overlooked the kitchen. Nick eyed the bustling staff and flinched when a pot clanked against the stovetop.

"Do you have a table available in a less active location?"

"Afraid not, sir. Would you like to wait until something else comes open?"

"No, thank you," Riley said, interrupting. "This will do just fine."

Nick's golden eyes, normally sparkling with mischief, leveled on her, flat and inscrutable, before he dropped onto the barstool beside her. "Why do I get the feeling that I've just been replaced by people-watching?"

An astute observation. Any time she came here, she would sit on this exact same stool and watch the kitchen staff zing back and forth between cooking and plating and calling out orders.

Their interactions with each other, the waitstaff, and their customers who dared to sit too close was a fascinating lesson in human social skills. Facial features, tone of voice, body language—they all altered and adapted to whomever was in front of them. Sometimes they changed midsentence.

"Good evening, y'all," a young woman with an infectious grin and curly brown hair said. "I'm Heather and I'll be taking care of you tonight." She slid a plate of steaming biscuits onto the bar between them. "Have you eaten with us before?"

"I have." Riley nodded at Nick. "He hasn't."

The server's smile broadened. "Welcome." She pointed to the biscuits. "These are Tupelo's signature pepper-flaked biscuits and blueberry preserves."

"They're delicious." Riley lifted a biscuit from the plate and tore it in half.

"What can I get y'all to drink?"

"Water's fine," she said.

"Cabernet," Nick said.

"Be back in a minute."

While slathering dark purple goodness on each half of the biscuit, Riley followed the movements of the kitchen staff just a few feet away.

"Do you ever take a break from observing?" Nick asked, preparing his own biscuit with far more finesse than she did.

Releasing a dramatic sigh, she admitted, "Afraid not."

"I guess it's good that I'm fond of that particular trait in you."

"What trait? That I enjoy gawking at strangers?"

He leaned close, tracing a fingertip along her temple. "Your mind. It's forever curious."

Gratitude clenched her chest, even while she was drawing away from his touch. Most people didn't understand her need for knowledge. And when they did, they had no patience for it.

But Nick got it.

She studied him out of the corner of her eye, struck once again by his masculine beauty. She waited for the flurry of awareness she always felt in Coen's presence to kick in. It didn't.

"Here you go," Heather said, setting their drinks down. "Are you ready to order?"

Once they made their selections and were alone again, she said, "Tell me about your conference."

"Conference?"

"The one you flew in to attend." She cocked her head to the side, studying him. "Or so you told me." Always interested in learning more about her field, she had poked around on the internet to see if registration had closed. The closest thing she'd found to a conference was a botanical lecture series at UNC-Chapel Hill.

Chagrined, he said, "Sorry, your abrupt change of topic threw me." He took a healthy swallow of his wine. "As it turned out, *conference* didn't adequately depict what I attended. It was poorly organized, and the keynote presented on concepts I learned two years ago." He bounced his shoulder against hers. "But I don't consider this a wasted trip."

She tamped down her disappointment. She'd hoped to learn something that would shatter her academic world.

"Did you experience any problems while shutting down Endurance?" she asked.

His smile faded, and he shrugged. "Pretty routine."

"How did Camilla adjust to her new duties?"

"Not well, I'm afraid."

"What happened?"

"Dr. Young caught her stealing."

"Stealing what?"

His golden eyes studied her. "Dr. Young's journal, for one."

"His journal?" she asked in astonishment, giving Heather a distracted smile as she delivered their dinner. "Like *the* journal?"

"No other."

"How? Why?"

"By befriending one of the guards. She got his security code and then spiked the security guards' coffee with a large dose of senna."

"No. She would never—"

"I can assure you, she did."

"Stealing." She floated the word through her memories of Camilla. "I find it difficult to believe. Camilla had a strong work ethic and went out of her way to please those she worked with. For her to betray the foundation—" She shook her head. "I don't understand."

"Didn't you find her on the streets?"

"Homelessness doesn't make someone a thief."

"But it ups the likelihood. I imagine that she, like many homeless, had to do a lot of unsavory things in order to survive."

She couldn't argue the point. After all, Camilla's abysmal attempt to lift her backpack purse was what put her on Riley's radar.

"I know it's hard to accept—the two of you seemed close —but the doctor caught her in the act."

"Did he have her arrested?"

"No, but only because we failed to catch her."

Relief swept through her. She dropped her gaze to her plate, to the mound of collard greens. But she stared through the steaming vegetables, the plate, the counter, all the way to Costa Rica until she found a set of forever smiling eyes framed by a thick mass of black-brown hair upswept into a messy knot. To a young, intelligent girl who helped her win the trust of the locals and kept the project organized.

Guilt burned like acid in her stomach. She should've checked on Camilla after she returned to the States. Made sure she had settled into her new responsibilities.

"Where's Camilla now?"

"No clue. She's disappeared."

"How do you know?"

"I stopped by her apartment to drop off some things, and she didn't answer the door. After two days and several attempts to reach her, I asked her landlord to check on her." He stabbed a broccoli floret with his fork. "The place was empty."

"Who gave you her address?"

"Security, why?"

"Camilla was very protective of her private life. I didn't think many knew where she lived."

"I'm not sure how hiring works in Costa Rica, but I assume the foundation would've had her fill out paperwork."

"I'm sure you're right." She dug into her collards, disturbed by their conversation for reasons she didn't understand. "From the first moment I ran her to ground, I was convinced all Camilla needed to turn her life around was an act of kindness. Something to help her regain her footing in the world."

"Locals are great resources for our research. But beyond that, I've found it best not to intermingle. Scientists wind up transferring their thoughts of right and wrong onto the cultural DNA of the people they're studying, which might be very different than their own and could lead to hurt and disappointment and confusion."

The way he framed his comment set her teeth on edge. But the essence of his message made sense—every culture had differing beliefs and value systems.

Even so, she'd worked alongside Camilla for nearly three years. If her former assistant tried to steal something, Riley had to believe she did so out of desperation. It was the only possible scenario that made sense.

"Given your response, I take it that you haven't heard from Camilla since returning home?" Nick asked.

"Not a word." She rapped her nails on the bar. "If Camilla had stolen a piece of equipment, I could more easily accept the situation. What I don't understand is why she would bother taking the journal. Picanula proved not to be a cure for psoriasis, like we'd hoped."

Nick's eye twitched, and he reached for his drink.

A dark foreboding engulfed her. "What?" she demanded. "What are you not telling me?"

"Riley, I—"

"Spill it, Nick."

Bracing his forearms on the counter, he closed his eyes a moment before delivering the best, most wonderful, most horrid secret.

"Project Endurance didn't fail."

14

"Say that again."

"Endurance didn't fail," Nick repeated, eyeing her uneasily. "Well, it did, but it didn't."

She pushed her glasses up, trying to make sense of his gibberish. Since his verbal communication normally emerged perfect and polished, this jumble of words alarmed her even more.

"I'm not following. The project either failed or it didn't."

He released a harsh breath and raked a hand through his perfectly producted hair. "Sorry, I had hoped to avoid this whole thing. I tried to get them to bring you into the circle."

Circle?

"Dr. Young's team did prove that Picanula *treated* psoriasis."

"We were researching a cure, not a treatment. Did Dr. Young test the other two specimens with *Timbroma subvolanum*?"

"His team didn't get that far."

"What do you mean?"

"They found that *Timbroma* had a more prestigious, more profitable use."

"Which is what?"

"The cure for impotence."

"Cure?"

"Can you imagine? Men can now pop a monthly pill and get a hard-on into their nineties."

"Why did he even test the plant for that use?"

"From a comment you made in your field observation notes."

She searched her memory. "I never mentioned—" Then a single word floated to the fore of her mind.

Virility.

A handful of the women she'd spoken to had joked about their men's interest in sex increasing after using *Timbroma.* She'd logged virility in her notes, along with a dozen other observations. But she'd thought their increased sex drive had more to do with them feeling better as their psoriasis abated. Not that *Timbroma* itself caused the reaction.

Her stomach roiled as her role in Project Endurance's demise became clearer. "So Young decided that ensuring boners for ninety-year-old men was more prestigious than curing people of an unbearable skin and joint disease?"

Nick snorted. "Young is a tool, not the decision-maker."

"Who made the decision to shut down the research station?"

"Technically, it never shut down. Simply rebooted with a new team." His attention shifted to the kitchen staff. "Mostly new."

"I take it you stayed on."

"A few of us did, yes."

"Did Young make the impotence discovery before or after I left Costa Rica?"

His jaw clenched.

"Was Dr. Hathaway involved in this?" *Please say no, please say no.*

"He's the one who directed the closing and reopening of the lab."

Every cell in her body deflated, and she caved into her seat. Nothing sparked in her mind, her questions silent.

"Can I interest y'all in dessert?" Heather asked, glancing between her and Nick.

When she said nothing, Nick shook his head. "Just the check, please."

The server set the bill facedown beside Nick's elbow. "No rush. Whenever y'all are ready."

In the silence that followed, Nick said, "I'm sorry, Riley. I wish you didn't have to hear it like this."

Sitting forward, she rubbed her temple. "I'd rather hear it from you than from a stranger months from now."

He picked up the check.

"What do I owe you?" she asked.

"My treat."

"That's not necessary."

"Consider it a thank-you for chauffeuring me around."

And a consolation prize.

By the time she rolled up to the passenger drop-off area at Asheville Regional Airport, the shock of his revelations had worn off. Mostly.

"Are you headed home or off to Costa Rica?" she asked, opening the cargo door.

"Both." He studied her a moment, and a flicker of uncertainty flashed across his handsome features. Then it was gone. "When I finish my next... assignment, I would like to come back and spend more time with you."

"Nick, I don't think—"

He gripped the back of her neck and pressed his cheek against hers. "Don't give me your answer now," he said in an urgent whisper. "Think on it. I'll call you when I'm free." Angling his head, he brushed a tender kiss to the corner of her mouth, inhaling deeply before releasing her.

She stood frozen at the back of her Jeep, following Nick's broad back as he disappeared behind the sliding glass doors.

A volatile mix of emotions warred for control.

One question rose in her mind, again and again.

Why hadn't Hathaway chosen her *to stay?*

15

PEERING OVER HIS SHOULDER, NICK FOLLOWED RILEY'S JEEP AS it zipped by the sliding glass doors. He stared at the empty space, experiencing an unfamiliar tightening around his chest before he shook it off and straightened his spine.

He dug out his phone, selected a ride-sharing app, and requested a driver. Ten minutes later, he was on his way back to Asheville where he'd left his rental car.

Unlocking the silver vehicle, he slid inside and eased out of the parking stall.

16

Riley turned off the Jeep's engine and slung her backpack over her shoulder. Any other day, she would've jumped into the utility-terrain vehicle that Britt kept parked in the wildlife center's storage shed around back.

But she had no wish to have her ears assaulted by the roar of the UTV's engine. Setting off down the gravel service drive, she bit into the pear she'd liberated from the fruit basket at her parents' house. A stream of sweet liquid drenched her tongue and dribbled down her chin. She swiped it away with the back of her hand, savoring the contrast between the velvety smooth juice and the gritty coolness of the pulp.

Phoebe. Phoebe. Phoebe.

She paused to locate the plump, white belly of the eastern phoebe. She spotted the songbird on a bare branch overhanging the drive, her narrow tail wagging down and up, as if to say good morning.

Did Coen stop to enjoy a beautiful butterfly or interesting beetle or flowering plant? Or did he stomp through nature like so many others?

What was he doing now? Washing his clothes in the stream? Still brooding about her plunge into the pit?

After he'd helped her save the kit, he'd lectured her about how long it had taken her to secure the animal. He seemed unable—or unwilling—to understand the complexity of grabbing a frightened, trapped animal in a manner that ensured she would emerge with all her digits and flesh.

Despite his bluster, she'd thanked him and asked if he knew the way back to his camp. He'd given her a disgusted look and stormed off. In the right direction. She'd considered trailing after him for her peace of mind but forced herself to stay, to look away, to pray for his safe return.

He was a big boy. Had likely traversed far worse than the mountains of North Carolina without her assistance.

Ahead, sunlight glinted through the trees like hundreds of sparklers peeking between the leaves. The sight never failed to bring a smile to her face and a giddyup to her step.

As if on cue, she increased her pace until she stood on the small concrete stepping-stone leading into the most amazing greenhouse in Haywood County.

Twenty feet wide and forty feet long, the building's massive interior was split down the center by a wide aisle. On each side, eight rows of rectangular, multishelved metal tables held native plants in various stages of propagation.

At the end of the aisle, a small section had been carved out for an office, housing a metal desk and chair, a two-drawer filing cabinet, and her mama's old patterned couch.

Several workbenches lined the exterior walls, each complete with all the implements needed for potting and repotting. Above the tables, giant ferns overflowed their hanging baskets, swaying in a gentle breeze produced by a trio of large fans marching down the spine of the ceiling.

The mid-July air was heavy with moisture. But it couldn't out-humidity the interior of a glass structure full of plants. Well, it could, but not today. She stripped off her long-sleeved shirt, revealing a pale yellow short-sleeved top.

Long ago, she'd learned about layers. Layers of clothing couldn't save a person from every misery awaiting them in nature, but they certainly evened out the odds.

From her backpack purse, she withdrew her laptop and stack of mail and set them on the desk. While she waited for the computer to grind to life, she dug into a side pocket of her pack for the Cutie she'd stashed there earlier.

In between peeling back strips of orange rind, she began the arduous process of sorting through her inbox, a task she hated more than liver and onions.

"Damn solicitations."

Delete. Delete. Delete...

She continued obliterating the little buggers until she got down to a handful of legitimate messages. Britt asking for her monthly report, her mom gushing about her current culinary disaster, er, masterpiece, and... She swallowed hard, fighting against the sudden cramping in her throat.

Her professor-mentor, Dr. Genosee, asking about the progress of her dissertation.

Three-quarters finished.

She sat back, staring at the screen with burning eyes, the sweet fruit in her mouth turning to dust on her tongue. How could she finish it? Hathaway aborted her research project.

Rubbing her chest, she stretched forward until her index finger hovered over the keyboard. She let it fall.

Delete.

Sick of her computer, she pushed it away and reached for her phone and found three text messages. One from her college roommate wanting to get together for drinks, another from her former assistant asking her to call ASAP, and the other from her mom, reminding her about their upcoming family dinner.

She tossed her phone onto the table. Not feeling sociable all day, she'd come to the greenhouse to get away from people, both in person and electronically. She just didn't want to be what others wanted her to be today. Today she would be Riley in all her non-glory.

Why she'd even opened her email or text messages, she didn't know. Habit probably. A long time ago, she'd learned she had to get rid of the admin stuff first before she could concentrate on the technical, scientific side of her job.

The stack of snail mail she'd picked up from her parents' house stared at her. And stared.

At the bottom of the stack, a large manila envelope looked as though it had traveled every back alley and dusty country road, bumping and falling its way from one post office to the next. Dirt and ink smudges decorated the surface, and a triangular gouge obliterated part of her zip code. Underneath, someone from the postal service had filled in the mystery numbers.

Uneven rows of foreign stamps marched along the upper right-hand corner, and a familiar, shaky hand had scrawled out her address. Her heart squeezed tight as a wave of longing washed over her. The handwriting, the stamps— the package could've come from only one place.

"Costa Rica."

Camilla. It had to be.

The young woman's penmanship hadn't improved since Riley had left that beautiful country. She shook her head. Had Camilla stopped practicing? During the time Riley had worked with her, she'd been so eager, so earnest, so determined.

Her fingers slid over the address again as if she could divine the scribe's secrets over the tight, bold slant of the letters. No, it hadn't been lack of practice that made Camilla's words difficult to read. At least not entirely.

She'd been in a hurry. But why?

A paralyzing sense of joy and dread consumed her. She'd spent three years of her life in that beautiful, environmentally diverse country. Two years learning the people's use of their local plants and one year convincing the people and government to allow her to do a deeper study on a few particular plants and to get funding for the project.

Because she didn't have a PhD, every step of the way was a struggle except for the funding. The Hathaway Foundation had heard about her discovery through her professor-mentor, Dr. Genosee, and had committed to funding the rest of the study without a single meeting with her.

In some ways, she'd never been happier than she was in Costa Rica. A starry-eyed, save-the-world scientist plopped down in a country the size of a shoebox but with the biodiversity of a thousand countries.

However, the beauty and freedom and excitement had been overshadowed by failure and humiliation and despair.

She set the package aside, unable to face a reminder of the place she'd burned so many brain cells to forget.

Grabbing a nearby garden hose, she turned on the water and made a systematic circuit around the greenhouse.

The northern border of the Steele Conservation Area, rich with plant diversity, used to be owned by Randi Shepherd's family. The Shepherds never farmed or timbered the land, leaving it pristine and unchanged for decades.

But the rest of the plant communities in the conservation area—at least the half she'd surveyed—could benefit from a helping hand. When Jonah overheard her and Britt discussing their plans to contract with a local grower, her billionaire cousin had presented her with a set of plans for a greenhouse.

She'd squealed—actually squealed—before launching herself into his arms.

Had Jonah understood what a private greenhouse would mean to a botanist? Or had he thought only of making his family—even extended family—happy?

Knowing Jonah, she suspected he'd considered both, but the latter had held more weight with the kindhearted billionaire of the Steele clan.

The manila envelope drew her attention. It was so thick. Too large for a catch-up note or status report. Not that Camilla had any reason to send either of those to her anymore. When Riley had left Costa Rica, she'd severed all ties with Endurance, including the people.

However, before she left Costa Rica, she'd extracted a promise from Dr. Young, the lead scientist for the lab, to keep Camilla on payroll until they finished tearing down their makeshift lab. She'd hoped the two- to three-week extension had bought Camilla enough time to find another job.

A flare of guilt burned her chest. Caught up in her own emotional turmoil, she hadn't checked in with Camilla since arriving home. What a horrible way to treat someone who'd been such an invaluable member of her team. She'd taught Riley the local language and customs and helped her win over the trust of the village elders and healer. What would have taken most ethnobotanists five years to accomplish, Riley had done it in two.

She forced her attention back to her watering duties.

For someone so young, Camilla'd had an uncanny ability to anticipate Riley's needs—well before Riley knew she needed anything. When she had left Central America, she'd had no inkling of where the rocky road ahead of her would lead.

Then Britt had swooped in and offered her a much-needed job, and now she had this glorious greenhouse to manage. A task too big for one person to juggle.

Would Camilla come here to work, to live? The girl had confessed to having no family and few friends. Would she travel to a strange, foreign land to toil in a stuffy glass building?

What would it take to bring a Costa Rican worker to North Carolina?

Next time she saw her sister Maggie, she'd broach the question. Maggie knew everything, and if she didn't, she'd know whom to ask.

Riley found herself standing before the envelope, the hose forgotten at her feet.

She tested the weight of the envelope in her hand. Heavy.

Unable to deny herself any longer, she hooked a thumb beneath the envelope's flap and ripped it open. A musty scent *whooshed* out, forcing her to rear back.

She pushed the sides together to create a large enough opening to peer inside. A crease formed between her brows.

Reaching in, she removed the item that had traveled over five thousand miles and placed it on the worktable.

"Why did you send me a book, Camilla?"

A protective covering that reminded her of the recycled elephant dung paper she'd seen in bookstores and other specialty shops was wrapped around the tome. Without putting her nose to the speckled paper, she knew where the musty scent had originated.

With careful fingers, she flipped it open and read, "That

Sam-I-am!" She stared down at the familiar illustrations of one of the most popular children's books of all time. A book she'd gifted to Camilla a while ago to help her with her English.

Hurt lanced through her chest.

Why would Camilla return a gift?

17

Dusk settled over the mountain like a cooling blanket. A bird chirped in the distance, its mellow, constant rhythm a sign of the end of a busy and productive day.

But Coen's day was anything but productive. After his run-in with Riley and the foxes, he'd been unable to sit still. He'd roamed the boundaries of the Steele property for hours, only to wind up back at the pit.

Or what used to be the pit. Riley had filled the hole with leaves and rocks and other debris.

Some people around here would've snapped the kit's neck, taken its pelt, and monitored the hole for its next victim.

But not Riley Kingston. She'd gone headfirst into the damn thing. He still couldn't decide if she was the bravest person he knew or the most foolish. Possibly a bit of both.

He shifted his weight and leaned more fully against the tree that hid him from view. Shadows shrouded the area, blinking out the final breaths of daylight.

The massive glass building before him glowed with life. Plants of various shapes, sizes, and colors marched up and down the length of the interior and hung like green waterfalls from metal rafters.

In the midst of it all stood Riley. She chewed on her bottom lip while reading a book, a deep furrow etched in her brow.

He traced the outline of her profile, slipping over the smooth plane of her cheek to the too-long-to-be-perfect nose to the plump fullness of her abused lower lip.

What was he doing here? If he was going to emerge from his self-imposed exile for someone, there were a thousand other, less frustrating women in Steele Ridge.

She stood among her beloved plants at a time when all others flocked to be at home with their loved ones. What drove her to this place, night after night, day after day?

Her hand rose to cover the bottom half of her face. It was the kind of movement a person did while their brain was absorbing a new reality. A reality of good fortune or of unbearable realization.

When she dropped the book and jerked away, he stepped out of the shadows and strode forward several feet before checking himself. What kind of comfort could he offer?

A stranger.

A man who'd sworn off contact with others.

A man who'd chased her away at every opportunity.

A damaged soldier who didn't trust his own mind any longer.

Out of the corner of his eye, he caught the shift of shadow against shadow. He focused on the area, but staring inside the brightly lit greenhouse had blown his night vision.

Peeling away from his surveillance of the botanist, he went on a hunt.

18

Confusion roiled in Riley's stomach.

Why had Camilla returned her gift? Why hadn't she included a note of explanation?

Something was out of whack. First she steals Dr. Young's journal and now this?

No matter how she tackled the mystery, she couldn't come up with a logical reason for Camilla's behavior. She wasn't scatterbrained or unstable or prone to dramatics. She was a caring, incredibly smart, and intuitive person.

After her mother had died, she'd left her small village and moved to a larger town to find employment. She'd done every menial task thrown her way, even pickpocketed to fill the gaps.

When Riley had given her an opportunity to return to her village, Camilla had cried tears of gratitude.

Why would she have stolen the doctor's research journal? Riley loved the young woman, but Camilla wasn't a scientist. Even if she had managed to decipher his writing, she wouldn't have known what to do with the data.

She rubbed her temples. Worry gnawed there. She was missing something.

Something vital.

The sensation of fingernails scraping up her spine had her lifting her head and glancing around. Leaves shifted in the light breeze created by the ventilation system, and hard-bodied June bugs threw themselves against the overhead lights.

Her gaze drifted to her right, toward the forest beyond the greenhouse. But night had fallen, and the only thing she could see was her own reflection looking back.

Even while she stared at her mirror image, the feeling of being watched didn't abate. It intensified.

Her attention shifted from the window to the book to the window again. A cloud of isolation pressed upon her chest. For the second time in a week, she wondered... Who would hear her scream? How long would it take for someone to find her broken body? Besides Britt, few ever bothered to venture this far from the center. And if her cousin didn't have something to pester her about, he stayed away.

A sputtering sound cut through her growing unease. She peered down to find water spitting out from between the hose and nozzle.

She reached down to tighten the nozzle before turning off the water. By the time she rolled up the hose and returned to her desk, her spine no longer felt as though a thousand spiders skittered over the ridges.

But the desire for isolation had vanished, so she closed her laptop and stowed it in her backpack. She grabbed the book, intending to do the same, when a slip of paper broke free of the pages.

Frowning, she bent to retrieve it, wondering how she hadn't seen it before now. She turned it over.

EP not ded. Keep fort safe.

Ded? Fort?

"Camilla," she whispered, "what the hell are you trying to tell me?"

She read the note several times, each pass getting her no closer to the meaning behind the message. She blew out a breath before jamming the note and book into her pack.

Flicking off the lights, she locked the door behind her, then paused on the threshold.

Full-on dark had arrived, and she was a quarter mile from her vehicle. The situation had never bothered her before.

But she'd never had the sensation of being watched before. All in her mind? Or the result of a mysterious package?

Voting for the latter, she set off toward the center. She barely made it ten feet before a figure split from the shadows.

19

Riley's heartbeat skidded to a stop at the sight of Coen stepping into the moonlight. The swift realization that her sixth sense had been correct didn't make her feel any better.

Because when it came right down to it, she knew next to nothing about this man, this soldier, who preferred the company of bears and birds over humans. If not for the Steele boys' endorsements and his reading preferences, she would've marked him as a total creeper. With enormous biceps.

"What are you doing here?" she asked in a calm yet authoritative voice.

"An evening stroll."

She cataloged a wicked-looking knife sheathed at his side and a rifle slung over his back. "Looks to me like you're on the hunt."

His gaze made a slow, lingering glide down her body and back up again. "I'm always on the lookout for my next meal."

Warmth flooded her core, and her breath caught in her chest. Had he just made her *lust* after him with one glance? Her inner muscles clenched.

"Well." She cleared her throat. "Point your bullets that way"—her finger indicated the opposite direction of the center—"until I reach the parking lot."

She set off down the access drive, aware of her every movement, certain that his all-seeing emerald gaze had zeroed in on the slight tremor in her hand.

Gravel crunched behind her, then beside her.

"What are you doing?" she asked.

"Strolling with you."

"Are you *trying* to weird me out?"

"I'm not the one who sat on a cliff for hours to watch someone camp."

Ears burning, she said, "Please tell me this isn't your male protective instinct kicking in."

"And if it is?"

"I'd say knock it off. I've got enough testosterone dogging my heels already."

"Being protected isn't a bad thing."

"Protected and smothered are two different things."

"Ah."

They lapsed into an easy silence while listening to cicadas ratchet up their evening song.

"When do you sleep?" he asked.

"What?"

"Plant surveys during the day and plant propagation at night. You don't seem to have an off button."

Kingston Farms in her spare time.

She shrugged. "I sleep when I'm tired."

"Did you receive bad news tonight?"

She halted and stared up into his too-handsome face. The onset of a full beard coated his cheeks and chin, and his long eyelashes seemed to go on for miles. He was so damn compelling—until you reached his eyes. Those beautiful gemstones were hard and haunted.

"For someone who prefers to commune with nature, you're rather chatty tonight."

"I assumed talking made you feel more comfortable while being alone with me. I'd be happy to stop."

That he would recognize her wariness and try to assuage it did funny things to her insides.

"The news I received caught me off guard, and I can't quite figure it out."

"Maybe I can help, if you care to share."

"Not tonight. I need to think on it some more." She changed the subject. "Are you from around here?"

"Bryson City."

"Beautiful town. My brother, Shep, used to spend a lot of time there. He's into rock climbing, kayaking, zip-lining, all the adrenaline junky sports."

"Shep," he mused. "Shep Kingston?"

"Yes. You know him?"

"He and I used to work for the same outdoor adventure company. Good man, your brother."

Not everyone got Shep. Only a special few tolerated his quirks, and fewer still accepted his Asperger's. That Coen did both spoke loads about his character.

"Shep's a pain in the patoot, like the rest of my brothers. But no one, including me, can resist his genuine frankness."

"I'll take frankness over bullshit any day."

She studied him out of the corner of her eye. "I bet your family was glad to have you back home."

His eyes shuttered.

"They don't know you've returned to the States."

"My family is dead."

Her chest clenched. "I'm so sorry, Coen. I didn't mean to bring up bad memories."

"They've been gone a while."

When she opened her mouth to ask what happened, she shoved her water canister against her lips and drank until the compulsion disappeared. He already thought her too curious and would probably tell her to mind her own business if she dared to pry.

She rerouted to a safer topic. "What about hometown friends? Extended family?"

"If I could go home, hug each of them, eat a home-cooked meal, reminisce about the old days, and sleep in a soft bed, I would've visited days ago."

She counted to five. "But?"

"They'll treat me like I'm a damn hero. Parties, calls for war stories, requests to see my scars, adoring looks."

"You don't like to be the center of attention?"

"Once, I would have preened like a peacock." He rubbed a hand back and forth across his neck. "Now I can't. I just—can't."

Question after question after question churned in her mind like a spin top out of control. If she'd been having this conversation with one of her brothers, she would've probed deeper. Probably the same way Coen's friends would've pushed him for information.

But an ill-used and rusty sense of social grace kept her mouth shut. She tried to view the world through his eyes. Eyes that had likely seen far too much pain and fear and hopelessness. All the horrors of war. Were those the images that haunted him? That ripped him from sleep? That would make him lift his fists to Heaven?

When they hit the outer edge of the parking lot, she paused. "Thank you for the *stroll*."

"No admonishment for not visiting my hometown?"

She pushed up her glasses. "I think you've earned the right to put yourself and your needs first."

His gaze sharpened on her a moment before his attention drifted down to her mouth, lingering there for a breath-stealing eternity. Then his eyes roamed back up to meet hers, and she saw his intent. Saw his unmasked, raw need.

Swallowing down her answering desire, she forced her body to break away from his visual hold. "Good night, Coen."

He said nothing, just stood there and watched her walk away.

She peered into her rearview mirror, expecting to see a wall of darkness where he last stood. But the warrior hadn't moved. Not a single inch.

A shiver skittered down her neck, and she wondered what kind of sleeping bear her curiosity had awoken.

SMACK!

Kendra's head snapped to the side from the force of her interrogator's blow.

"What are you doing in Ecuador?"

The corporal spat a mouthful of blood on the dusty floor before leveling one half-swollen eye on her captor. The other eye was already swollen shut.

"Birdwatching," she said in a scratchy, defiant voice.

Another blow.

Sergeant First Class Coen Monroe fought against his bindings. A fist hammered him in the ribs, doubling him over.

Their captors thought forcing them to observe each other's torture would break them. But they had no way of knowing he and his team had been trained for this exact scenario. Kendra knew he would not save her by providing information to their country's enemy, as he knew she would not.

Now three days into their torture, he prayed for strength.

"What is your mission?"

Her lip curled. "Counting snakes."

The interrogator's eyes sharpened, and he seemed to be mulling over her words. Not all cultures grasped the fine art of American snark, especially not Kendra's.

At six feet, Kendra stood level with most of the men on their team. Add in graduating cum laude from the University of Illinois and street smarts gained from growing up on the south side of Chicago and the Army had one lethal Delta Force operator.

He tested his restraints once again. But the plastic ties at his wrists and ankles held tight. He locked eyes with Kendra, sending his strength down their visual line.

For all his tactical abilities, he couldn't find a way out of this hellhole. He couldn't even get out of this motherfucking chair. Three days without food, water, or sleep. They sat in their own filth.

Soon the interrogator would tire of Kendra and he would come for him. Soon she would get a break.

But not yet.

The bastard put his knife against her cheek and sliced.

"No!"

Coen's face hit the corner of something hard, and his outstretched fingers slid against a cool, silken surface. He tried blinking open his sleep-drugged eyes, but the nightmare's scarlet fingers wouldn't release him.

Slick with sweat, his contorted body lay heaving, gasping, aching to end it all, when a hushed feminine voice filled the night air.

.   .   .

"Charlotte's brisk pace slowed. A man was slumped on the pavement between her shop and the boarded-up bakery next door. He sat with one leg stretched out across the walkway, the other bent at an angle. The brim of his hat protected his face from identification. So, too, did the long black woolen coat and matching muffler around his neck."

Steadying his breathing, he concentrated on the familiar, soothing voice and dragged himself closer to its comforting net.

"The tension in Charlotte's shoulders returned in full force. Even though she could not identify him, she knew what he wasn't—a beggar. Everything about him was too refined for him to be living in the streets. She glanced around, checking the evening shadows as best she could with only lamplight to aid her. Anderson's lending library, Patterson's coffee shop, Gertrude's lace boutique, Tilly's former bakery—they all stood silent and free of loitering troublemakers and customers. If she cried out for help, would the shopkeepers hear her from their snug, upstairs apartments?"

Images of Kendra and the guards faded back into a shallow pocket of his mind. But the guilt of Coen's failure sat like a vise across his chest. His eyelids fluttered open once before shutting again. Tired. He was so damn tired.

He reached out, resting his fingers against the tent, close to the voice, and listened.

"Good morning."

Riley peeled her eyes away from the box she was stuffing with this month's selection of fresh vegetables to find her brother, Way, entering the farm's cold storage building.

"Morning."

"What's wrong with your voice?"

"Too much talking yesterday."

"Too much talking or too many questions?" he asked in an annoying tone that only a brother could master.

"Is there a difference?"

"For you, yes. You're not a conversationalist. More of a listener and asker-er."

"I don't think that's a word."

"It is now." He pulled folded cardboard from a shelf and moved to a workbench behind her to assemble it into a shipping box. "Don't you normally come here in the afternoons?"

"Not today." She took a sip of water, having no intention of sharing her late-night activities with Way. Although she had always felt a greater kinship with him than her other brothers, she would keep this story to herself.

After spending several hours reading to Coen, her throat hurt, her eyes were gritty, and her butt was sore. Thank goodness she'd had the presence of mind to bring a mosquito net, or she'd have to add itching to her list of morning-after complaints.

Even so, she would do it all over again. Who was Kendra? What had happened to her? What had Coen witnessed?

"What can you tell me about PTSD?" she asked.

The air stopped moving behind her, and she waited for him to redirect the conversation like he always did when confronted with questions about his military experience.

"It exists."

Keeping her back to him, she said, "I know it does. I've read enough about it online to fill a book. But I wanted to know what *you* thought about it."

"Why the curiosity?"

She sent him an incredulous look over her shoulder. "Are you serious?"

"Good point. Stupid question." He picked peppers and cucumbers from slanted, square bins and set them in his box. "Why so curious *now*?"

If she told Way about her encounters with Coen, he would forbid her from seeing him again, which she would ignore, which would force him to confront Coen. Way might even compel him off the property, without consulting the Steeles, if he thought it was the only way to protect her.

No, she wouldn't tell him about her time with Coen.

Way sighed. "Post-traumatic stress affects every combat service member to a certain degree. Sometimes bad things happen to them, and other times they're the ones seeing and doing bad things. A blessed few can compartmentalize their experiences and move on with their lives. The rest—" He cut off for several aching seconds. "The rest cope with their memories in destructive ways."

Riley half turned to stare at her brother's back, wondering which category he fit in.

"I'm not a doctor, but the way I see it is that post-traumatic stress only becomes a disorder when you allow it to rule your life."

"How do you mean?"

"Drinking and fighting too much. Losing your family, friends, and job to unchecked anger."

"What if the memories attack when you're at your most vulnerable?"

Way slowly turned to face her. His penetrating gaze studied her as if she were a topographical map and he was charting out the best route to take.

"Vulnerable how?"

She assessed the answer and deemed it safe to share. "While sleeping."

His attention sharpened, creating a deep V in his forehead. "What happened in Costa Rica?"

The question hit her like a shovel to the head. "What?"

"You never explained why you returned sooner than anticipated."

"That's not true. The experiment failed— I came home."

His expression turned skeptical. "You spent years in a mountainous jungle and have yet to share a single fond memory about the experience." He leaned against the table and braced his palms on the ledge behind him. "I find that odd."

"What I find odd is your selective memory. I've shared plenty of stories of my time in Central America."

"When you came home for visits, yes. But not one story since you've returned for good."

She opened her mouth to contradict his statement, but she couldn't come up with a single example.

Her brother wasn't done.

"For years, you work your ass off, day and night, studying hard and saving money so that you could one day run off and study a group of prehistoric people and their plants."

"Indigenous people."

He waved off her correction. "You achieved your goal and appeared happier than I'd ever seen you. So why did you clam up?"

Unable to withstand his too-perceptive regard, she resumed filling her box. "What's left to tell? I don't have anything to show for my time in Central America, except my ability to speak fluent Spanish."

"Did you witness something distressing?"

"No. My time in Costa Rica was near perfect."

A small hole was burned into the back of her head by his considerable, focused attention. She'd made a mistake in asking him about PTSD. But she'd needed to better understand Coen's haunting cries of torment.

The thought of him alone while warring with his memories each night had propelled her into those woods. She'd only intended to check on him, but after she'd arrived, she couldn't bring herself to leave.

So she'd pulled out her mosquito net and latest reading material, a historical mystery about a mismatched pair of sleuths, from her bag and began reading by book light.

An hour later, his first whimper carried through the nylon tent. A muffled thrashing followed, and then his first heart-wrenching plea.

Kendra.

Riley had read enough articles about combat veterans nearly killing their significant others when they attempted to shake their loved ones out of the throes of a nightmare. So she'd remained frozen and unsure, hating that she didn't know how to help him.

When his screams intensified, her helplessness became a physical pain. Staring down at her book, she'd alternated between prayer and tears until the pages blurred and wobbled.

On the verge of storming into his tent, consequences be damned, she heard her dad's words with eerie clarity.

"Sometimes your mother's work would leave her so stressed out by the end of the day that the only way she could silence her mind was by listening to me read. Something about the cadence of my voice lulled her to sleep in a way no sleeping pill could."

Drying her cheeks, she had begun to read aloud. Tentatively at first, and then her voice had grown in volume as her spine straightened with determination.

When the tent's side had bulged outward near her head, she'd swallowed back a shriek. Her breaths had scraped against her throat as she stared at the imprint of his fingertips against the thin nylon barrier.

Readjusting her book light, she had resumed reading, keeping her voice low and calm and measured. Silence had extended over the tent, so she'd slowed her words until they faded into nothing.

A guttural growl had preceded metal crashing against metal. Picking up where she'd left off, she read to him. Read to him until her words had been nothing more than a rusty whisper. Read to him until she heard him stir just before dawn broke over the ridge.

Way interrupted her thoughts. "If not something in Costa Rica, who has you curious about PTSD?"

Way's question pulled her back to her box of vegetables.

Glancing over her shoulder, she wondered how he'd coped with the "bad things" he'd seen, done, and experienced while in the service. Even before he'd gone off to war, he'd always been her larger-than-life brother.

People followed him. Their age, experience, or socioeconomic status made no difference. From his preschool friends in the classroom to his high school football teammates on the field to his mowing crew on his first job to his military unit inside the battle zone, he had led and inspired countless individuals. Individuals who loved him for his decisive but fair nature.

Family, friends, colleagues, small children, elderly adults, animals—he had an effect on them all. When he was here.

His frequent work trips took him away from Steele Ridge. She had never questioned her brother's absences before, but Coen's situation cast a whole new light on Way.

Did he suffer as Coen suffered?

Had his stress turned into a disorder?

"Are you good at compartmentalizing?" she asked, holding her breath.

His hands stilled. "Yes."

She waited for him to say more. When he didn't, she went back to her task. Questions hung in the air like a thick, choking fog. For the first time ever, she experienced a lengthy, awkward silence with her favorite brother.

If only she could come up with a witty comment to reestablish their easygoing bond. But her mind remained stubbornly stupid.

She was about to blurt out an apology when Way finally spoke.

"Whoever he is, Riley, he's not a wounded dog who'll mend with a few clean bandages. He'll need years of care—professional care—if he's brave enough to seek it out."

Throat thick with emotion, she nodded.

A large arm wrapped around her shoulders, and she turned into her big brother's hug.

"It'll take an equally brave and determined woman to weather the storm. At the end—"

"I'll find a rainbow?" she whispered.

"No, Ry."

"What then?"

"I don't know." He rested his chin on her head. "Reach for the rainbow, if that's your thing. But I'd recommend setting smaller, more attainable goals. Then maybe, just maybe, your rainbow will appear."

She closed her eyes, wishing Way would've dug deeper into his inspirational repertoire. But it wasn't his style to hand out false hope. Being a realist was as much a part of his makeup as being a born leader.

"Would your mystery man happen to be Coen Monroe?"

"How do you know Coen?"

"I don't. Not really. I overheard Reid and Britt discussing him." His chest rose on a deep inhalation. "The brother in me wants to warn you to stay the hell away."

"What does the Marine in you want?"

"For you to fight like hell to save him."

The pressure on her chest eased, and she drew in a shaky breath. Way nudged her chin up until she met his gaze.

"Make no mistake, little sis. Coen's reliving a scene that

no man—no matter how well trained—should ever have to live through once, let alone dozens of times."

"You know what happened to him? Can you tell me? Please."

The brother warred with the Marine for a good long time. In the end, his duty to country won. But his loyalty to family didn't completely jump into the back seat.

"If he's having night terrors about one of his missions, he'll be dangerous and lethal during those moments. Don't ever touch him. Do you understand?"

She nodded, glad she'd followed her instincts last night. "I understand. Thank you, Way."

His arms tightened a second before he stepped away. Rather than finish packing his box, he strode toward the door.

"You're leaving?"

He swiped a hand over his cheeks, pausing at the door. He didn't turn around. "Be careful, Riley. With both your person and your heart."

"You said a strong woman—"

"Some wounds are so deep that they can't be repaired."

She stared after her brother long after he was gone. His ominous words tearing into her heart.

22

THRUMP!

Coen's blade landed in the outer rim of the bull's-eye. Good, but not where he'd aimed.

He lined up again and sent the knife flying.

Outer rim.

Two more knives followed.

Same result.

"Dammit," he bit out. "Pull it together, Monroe."

Rolling his shoulders, he prepared to send another blade down the forty-yard lane when he caught the whisper of a boot heel against the grass behind him.

He whipped around, weapon raised—

"Whoa!" Reid Steele held his hands in the air. "It's just me."

"Son of a bitch, Steele." Coen lowered his arm. "You know better."

"I wasn't sneaking up on you; you weren't paying attention, Sarge."

"Drop the sergeant bullshit, or I won't check myself next

time." He'd achieved the rank of Sergeant First Class only weeks after hitting his twenty-fourth birthday and had earned his Ranger tab the year before. He was damn proud of both accomplishments. But neither compared to making selection as a Delta Force operator.

He hadn't thought anything could be more grueling than Ranger training. But Delta Force selection challenged the mind and body in ways that few could handle. Of the 159 men who started selection, only ten became operators.

His friend nodded to the target. "How long's it been?"

"Obviously too long."

"Wanna up the stakes?"

"What'd you have in mind?"

"The first person who hits dead center wins a Triple B steak dinner."

Blues, Brews, and Books—known as Triple B by the locals—did many things right. Owned and operated by hometown girl Miranda "Randi" Shepherd, the shop had a great, down-to-earth vibe, promoted local artisans and brewers, and catered to a wide variety of customers' desires. But nothing topped Randi's prime bone-in rib eye.

Reid had treated him to a rib eye dinner on his first night back in the States. Although the meal had been delicious, he hadn't returned to the B.

His mouth watered. He came close to saying yes but forced himself to remember what had happened last time. Randi's bar and restaurant was one of the major gathering places in in the area. Folks came from several towns over to grab a coffee, sit on one of the cushioned couches and read a book, or wrap around a table with a bunch of friends and shoot the bull.

Laughter and conversation pulsed within those walls, making his nerves fire like rockets beneath his skin. He wasn't ready for that kind of socializing. Didn't know if he'd ever be again.

"Thanks, but I'll pass."

"You've been back close to three weeks. Time to get your ass out of the woods."

In some ways, his last mission felt like a dozen lifetimes ago. In other ways, it seemed like his boots only touched down on American soil yesterday.

"I'm aware."

"It's not going to get any easier."

"Probably not, but I'm not ready to make nice with everyone."

"Then fucking compromise."

"That doesn't sound like you."

"Believe me, I know. Wait until you're engaged. Compromise will become your middle name."

"Not a chance." He waved his fingers in a *bring it on* movement. "Shoot."

"If I win, we eat steak at Triple B. If you win, we'll have steak by your campfire."

He stared at his friend, trying to locate a loophole in Reid's wager. He knew Coen was the better thrower. So why suggest a fool's bargain?

When no obvious pitfall came to mind, he gave himself a mental shrug. If Reid wanted to eat his dinner by the fire, who was he to stop him? He would normally balk at carryout steak, but he'd take Triple B's rib eye any way he could get it.

"Deal."

Reid picked up a throwing knife and flipped it in the air. He caught it with ease and smiled. "Let the pummeling begin."

"Pretty girls first."

"I won't be the one whimpering when this is over."

Coen raised a brow. "Stalling?"

A second later, Reid's first throw landed dead center—in the ring outside the bull's-eye.

Coen whistled. "If only you were two inches higher, the bet would be over."

"Warm-up strike. How many throws?"

"Your game, your choice."

"Best of seven then."

Coen loosed a blade. It thudded into the outer rim, next to Reid's.

"Looks like we found our G spot." Reid's second knife slammed into the target. One inch closer to the bull's-eye.

Coen's next throw found its mark a quarter inch below Reid's. Concern fluttered to life in his chest. Some maggot had punched holes in his hand-eye coordination.

They took turns, back and forth, pausing only long enough to replenish their stock of knives. A weight slowly lifted from his chest. How long had it been since he'd enjoyed himself without enduring bone-crushing guilt?

Without hearing Kendra's screams?

At that sobering thought, he said, "Thank you."

"For what?"

"For talking your brother into letting me camp in his woods. For allowing me to have free rein of this facility."

Reid's state-of-the-art training academy sat on the southern edge of the Steele megacomplex, which also contained several family homes, the wildlife research center, and the conservation area. The training academy attracted law enforcement and special operations units from all over the world as well as pro athletes.

Reid shrugged. "It's worth the steak dinner I'm about to win."

Realizing this was their last throw, with three wins each, Coen steadied his breathing and concentrated on the target. Visualized his knife sinking into the onyx center.

Extending his arm back—

"You know," Reid said at the exact wrong time, "my sister, Evie, talked me into introducing yoga into the training program."

Coen aborted his throw and sent the pecker a kill stare.

Unaffected by his imminent death, Reid continued, "I admit, I laughed at her at first. Downward dogs and tights didn't exactly fit the vision I had for this place."

"She won the battle?"

"Yeah, the little twerp recruited Brynne and Gage. No way to win against those odds."

Not understanding why Reid was sharing the story, he said, "Never hurts to try new things."

"The instructor"—Reid's tone turned more hesitant—"she specializes in post-trauma. Gives the trainees coping tools."

Realization dawned. "You want me to sign up."

"Couldn't hurt. According to Gage, it's more about calming the internal chaos than contorting your body into animal poses."

As good as Reid made it sound, he couldn't bear to sit before another stranger and pour his sad story into her hands. Every other time had been a huge disappointment, and the aftershocks were more disturbing than the trauma itself.

"Thanks, but no sense getting started with something I can't finish."

Reid studied him for a dissecting moment before nodding. "If you change your mind, let me know."

Focusing on the center again, Coen let loose his blade on a slow exhalation.

Bull's-eye!

He couldn't hold back his smile of triumph.

"Too early for smug, my friend." Reid held up a knife. "Prepare for defeat."

Coen curled his arms together and braced his feet apart. His smile didn't waver. He could almost feel the warmth of the fire on his face while he savored his first bite.

His stomach growled. Loudly.

"Trying to distract me?" Reid asked. "Not gonna work." His knife went flying and zinged into the target.

Dead center. Not slightly to the left like his.

Reid swung a shit-eatin' grin his way.

Son of a bitch. The bastard would never let him live this one down.

"Meet me here tomorrow night at five. I'll take you back to my place for a proper shit and shine before heading to the B."

The thought of a hot shower kept his smart-ass retort behind his teeth.

Reid started cleaning up, and Coen waved him off.

"I'll take care of this."

"After you practice some more?" Reid winked and barked out a laugh before striding away. "Remember, tomorrow. Five o'clock. Stand me up and I'll hunt you down and beat your ass."

Still at a loss for words, he responded with an upraised bird to his friend's back. Not at all satisfying, but it was the best he could muster with his gambling debt now looming over him.

The prospect of being in an enclosed space with all

those loud, ask-a-thousand-questions townsfolk milling about made his throat close.

A pair of gray-blue eyes flashed through his mind, and he wondered if he'd see Riley there.

He picked up a knife and sent it flying.

It knocked Reid's bull's-eye shot to the ground.

A *perfect* throw.

23

Costa Rica
11:59 a.m.

CAMILLA STRODE INTO THE LARGE STORE AND YANKED A CART from a long line of its friends. She meandered through the aisles, inspecting articles of clothing and household knickknacks while making steady progress toward the back, where they kept the electronics.

Once she reached her destination, she halted before a modest display of Try Me and Take Me Home phones and tablets. She tested a few out and waited.

A minute and a half later, a baritone voice that hadn't reached its full potential yet asked in Spanish, "May I help you?"

She smiled at the young clerk. "*Gracias*, no. I am only browsing today."

"If you have any questions, let me know."

Nodding, she slid to the next device, following the clerk's movements out of the corner of her eye. When another customer caught his attention, Camilla tapped on the tablet's browser and pulled up a social media site.

Clicking on the search field, she typed in a name. The wheel of death churned at the top of the screen. Tension weaved across her shoulders, and she glanced around to find the clerk. She found him removing one of those activity trackers from beneath the counter.

Several agonizing seconds later, the display refreshed, but none of the available options was her smiling blond-haired, blue-eyed friend.

Frowning, she typed in Lauren's name again. Same result.

She entered a second name and tapped her fingers on the counter through more spinning, refreshing, and scrolling.

A picture of Leo standing on a rock formation in front of an endless blue sky and a sea of trees, his powerful arms outstretched as if to embrace every challenge thrown his way.

Leo the Lightbringer. Somehow he managed to bring smiles and warmth into every room he entered. She read the caption.

It is with great sadness that we announce the death of our beloved brother, Leo Giovanni, who died in a tragic accident yesterday...

Ice seeped into her blood and spread like wildfire through her body.

Her fingers flew across the keyboard, typing in another name. A deafening drumbeat took root in her chest. The only one of her senses that appeared to be working was sight, though it grew blearier by the second.

An image appeared of a dark-haired woman holding a

large red flower in front of her face, obscuring the bottom half of her features. Knowing black eyes peered over the flower, daring the observer to lean closer, learn more.

Camilla's throat ached as an odd sense of homesickness swept into her heart. Odd, because she'd never had a true home, not until the past couple of years, when a scientist who understood more about plants than people had plucked her off the streets.

Wrenching her gaze away, she scanned for news on her bright-eyed colleague. A ball of dread rammed her in the gut, forcing the air she'd kept pent up for the last minute from her lungs.

The scientist's last entry was a selfie of her and Camilla, the day she'd left Costa Rica and returned to India. Not a single post in weeks. For some, this might not be unusual. But Farha used social media to chronicle every minute of her life.

Entering one last name, she held her breath until the next page loaded. She scrolled down the newsfeed, stopping on an image of blue-misted mountains in the background and laughing, blue-framed eyes in the foreground. Time-stamped today.

A tear tracked down her cheek, and she forced back the relieved sob that welled in her throat. With trembling fingers, she closed the social media site and deleted the browser history and cookies before returning to the tablet's home screen.

She gripped the cart and, with an unhurried gait, made her way to the front entrance, where she dumped her prop and exited.

Her world clouded more with each mechanical step. It wasn't until she plopped into a seat at the back of the transit bus that she allowed the tears to fall in silent rivers down her cheeks.

What had she done?

What had she done?

Killed them, that's what.

Killed them all.

But one.

24

Riley stabbed her fork into the mound of spinach leaves, bacon bits, boiled eggs, and warm vinaigrette dressing. She shoveled the heap of goodness into her mouth while trying to listen to her favorite band, Scarlet Glitterati, playing in the background.

But her loudmouthed brothers kept overshadowing the music as they carried on about some testosterone-laden activity they were going to try out at Shep's adventure company—Prime Climb Tours—that weekend. If it had been any other time, she would've participated in their conversation.

But tonight the sting of Nick's revelations about Endurance and Hathaway's rejection still burned.

She rinsed down her bite with a gulp of ice-cold water and dug her phone out of her purse. "If you knuckleheads spent as much time expanding your minds as you do your bodies, you'd all be freaking Einsteins by now."

"Someone's in a foul mood," Cash said, his penetrating brown gaze skimming over Triple B's evening crowd. "Do you think all it takes to become a firefighter and paramedic is muscle?"

Way poked at Cash's bicep. "Are you calling those puny things muscle?"

Cash threw a wadded-up napkin at Way's head. "Don't make me whup your ass in public, little bro."

"How about I show you what a real bicep can do to your perfect nose?"

"Not if I—"

"Oh, for the love of God," she cut in, scowling at her brothers. "How have y'all managed to secure gainful employment when you're stuck in adolescence?"

They grinned like idiots.

Brothers. *Kill me now.*

"Find anything cool this week?" her slightly better behaved brother, Shep, asked, absently rubbing Puck's side. The golden retriever leaned into his master's touch.

A pair of green eyes filled her vision, and something warm curled low in her belly. What was Coen doing now? Sleeping? Hunting? Reading? Screaming?

How did he fill up the hours of his day? Was he bored? Content?

Lord, when would she stop obsessing about his daily activities?

A large hand waved before her face. "Hello?" Cash crooned. "Shep wants to know if you found a carnivorous, bilobed, trapezius fuchsia green thing?"

Shep frowned. "No, I don't."

She smacked Cash's paw away. "Would you like me to give its scientific name or common?"

A shudder racked Cash's body. "A simple yes or no works for me."

"How supportive you are, dear brother."

"I don't speak geek."

Shep waved at someone over her shoulder, but she didn't turn around. If she sought out everyone her brothers waved at, she'd get motion sickness. The combination of her dad's business and living in the same town for decades meant their clan knew most of the town's residents and quite a few of its frequent flyers.

He half rose to shake the newcomer's hand. "What brings you to the B tonight?"

"Same as you, I suspect."

Riley recognized the voice over her shoulder and groaned before setting her phone safely on the table. Easing back in her seat, she braced herself.

Two seconds later, her chair tilted backward and she expertly hooked her ankles around the legs to keep herself in place. Her world continued to roll until she stared up into her cousin's ruggedly handsome face.

"Hello, Reid."

"Menace."

She crossed her arms. "Who's terrorizing whom?"

He kissed her forehead. "If you're going to ignore me, how else am I gonna get your attention?"

"Would you like me to list the ways? In alphabetical order? By order of priority?"

"Hell, no." He released her chair. "Your lists terrify me."

Her body catapulted upright and her teeth clanked together. She turned to deliver a verbal punch to her cousin and caught a familiar pair of emerald eyes locked on her. A long, clear vortex opened up between them, drying up the harsh words. Nothing existed beyond that narrow opening.

The ceiling lights reflected off Coen's close-cropped, damp hair. The beard he'd been sporting had been trimmed to a sexy, dark stubble. His black T-shirt stretched across a broad torso that sported an impressive amount of contours. Contours she'd studied for hours. Blue jeans hugged his lean hips, and hiking boots capped his ensemble.

Fresh from the shower, he was breathtaking in a different way than the feral jungle cat vibe she'd grown accustomed to. She'd been right—black was his color.

Silence floated around her like a heavy morning fog, though she would swear later that she could hear his pulse pounding in his veins. Or maybe it was hers.

Reid set a hand on the back of her neck at the same time Way rose to stand between her and Coen.

She blinked, and the tunnel disappeared.

"Way," Reid said in a careful tone, "this is my buddy, Coen Monroe."

"Coen?" Recognition lit Shep's face. "How have you been?"

"Busy."

At Way's raised brow, Cash added, "Coen, Shep, and I worked together at a guide company before he enlisted in the Army." To Coen, he said, "Way's a Marine."

Coen held out a hand to her brother. "Active?"

Way's fingers wrapped around Coen's, and she saw their knuckles go white.

"My tour ended last summer. You?"

"On leave."

"For how long?"

"Until the end of the month."

End of the month. Her heart clenched.

"Grab another chair and join us," Cash said, disrupting the warrior smackdown. "We're just getting started."

She gave Way a what-the-hell-was-that? look, and he merely stared back. After their conversation at the farm, she assumed he'd welcome Coen with open arms. She would never understand the male mind. It avoided logic like a cat avoids water.

A wooden chair banged into place beside her, and a jean-clad leg slid onto the seat, stopping a mere inch from hers. Then his scent hit her. Pine and fresh air and male.

Tempting male.

Would he tell her brothers about her visits to his camp? About their late-night reading session?

Lord, she didn't even want to think about the catastrophe that would cause. Her brothers would never, ever let her out of their sights.

Alpha-male bullshit.

Dropping her attention to her plate, she closed her eyes and prayed her heart out.

COEN PEERED DOWN AT THE STONY PROFILE OF THE WOMAN beside him. Color crept its way back into her pale cheeks, though it appeared to be taking its sweet time.

He understood her shock. When he finally saw who Reid was teasing, he'd been glad to have been standing in the background. Every other time their paths had crossed, she'd seemed part of the landscape. Confident and blessed with an easy grace, even while being curious but wary of the madman in her cousin's woods.

Tonight, steel still anchored her backbone, yet she appeared smaller, more breakable somehow.

Reid said, "This is my cousin, Riley, or Kingston Menace, whichever you prefer. Riley, make nice with my friend, Sergeant First Class Coen Monroe."

Coen shot a warning glance at Reid before turning to the woman beside him. He could taste the burn of fear she tried hard to suppress. Did she think he would divulge their previous encounters?

He probably should. She'd been unwise in her dealings with him, a stranger camping in a remote area. He could've killed and buried her days ago, leaving her family to mourn the loss but never have closure. A situation he was all too intimate with and would never wish on another.

"Nice to meet you, Riley," he said.

Stunning gray-blue eyes lifted to his, and he detected a hint of gratitude before her shoulders squared and she picked up her phone. "Fair warning, Sergeant. Call me Menace and I'll skewer you."

Her brothers and cousin barked out a laugh.

"Tell you what," Coen said. "I won't call you Menace if you don't call me Sergeant."

She gauged his sincerity for a moment before nodding. "Deal."

"Now that we got all that out of the way—" Cash motioned to a server. "What have you been doing on your leave?"

Coen's stomach muscles heaved inward. This was the exact reason he'd been avoiding people and their incessant questions, placating expressions, and morbid curiosity.

His fingers curled into a fist on his thigh. "Nothing much. A little fishing and hunting."

Out of the corner of his eye, he noticed Riley shifting her attention from his lap to his profile.

"What kind of fish?" Shep asked.

Shep Kingston had changed little in the past decade. Same inquisitive nature and blunt conversation. He'd always liked the adventure-seeking boy, and he suspected he'd feel the same about the man.

"I'm partial to bluegill."

Cash jumped in. "Got any plans—"

"If you're going to grill the poor man," Riley cut in, "at least buy him a drink first."

Cash gave him an apologetic grin. "Sorry, it's just been a long time."

"Evening, y'all," said a pretty, petite server with a purple braid woven into her jet-black hair. "What can I get y'all to drink?"

Cash nudged Shep. "You want another?"

Shep downed the last of his beer and shook his head.

"One more," Cash said.

"Two," Way chimed in.

"I'll have my usual, Kris," Reid said. "Plus two of Randi's prime rib eyes, one for me and one for my friend. Who, incidentally, is buying since I beat his ass yesterday." He glanced at Coen. "Medium rare?"

He nodded.

"You got it," Kris said.

Noting Riley's half-eaten salad and near-empty glass of water, he asked, "Need a refill?"

Her finger paused its scrolling over her phone's screen. A colorful plant etching remained visible at the top of her screen.

Blinking, she smiled at the server. "Another water, when you get a chance. Thanks."

"Coke and Jim, easy on the ice," Coen said.

"Did you ever find out who set Mr. Johnson's storage shed on fire?" Reid asked Cash.

"Mrs. Johnson."

"No shit," Way said, grinning.

"Seems Mr. Johnson spent one too many hours in the shed with his porn magazines."

All the guys at the table laughed. Riley looked at the lot of them as if they were fools.

"Would you burn down your husband's shed?" he asked in a low voice that only she could hear.

"Now why would I burn down a perfectly good building for a guy who wasn't happy with my tits? *Hasta la bye-bye, jerk.*"

His smile broadened.

The next round of drinks arrived, and the conversation flowed from one subject to the next. Then the second round arrived with the food. When no one seemed inclined to nose into his business again, the tension eased from his joints.

Before long, Riley set aside her phone and bantered with the guys, giving as good as she got. It was then he realized that she really had been waiting for him to out her on their previous meetings. He probably should have—for her own safety—but for some strange reason, he wanted to keep those exchanges between them.

The conversation, the joking, the meal... It was all so *normal.* So carefree. For a time he allowed himself to live in the moment, in this bar. He enjoyed the company, the food, the alcohol. Lots of alcohol.

At some point, Shep and Puck left. One minute they were there, the next gone.

But around ten o'clock, the atmosphere changed, became more charged. The tempo of the music pounded, and a group of women took to the small dance floor, their heels clicking against the hardwood. Voices rose to a deafening decibel. A high-pitched laugh pierced the air.

Screams from another time and place trickled into mind. Images wavered in and out of his vision. Explosions shook the ground, and gunshots zinged inches away. Then the smell of death slammed into him, knocking him back in his seat. The acrid scent bled into his nostrils, drowning him in a sea of dismembered bodies and haunted faces and whimpers of loss.

His past became a sword, slicing through his pleasant, alcohol-induced blanket of guilt-free hours.

"Do you need some fresh air?" someone whispered beside him.

He threw back the rest of his beer and held up the empty bottle to the perky, purple-haired waitress. Leaning his arms on the table, he stared at his lap, willing *normal* back. But the room was too loud, too hot, too everything. Sweat rolled down the side of his face. He brushed it away with his shoulder.

A small hand appeared on his thigh, and someone whispered near his ear again, "Do you need some fresh air?"

He leaned into the gentle voice, the comforting touch. The sweet scent of oranges washed away the putrid tang of death.

"Kris, can you bring our checks?"

Familiarity jarred him out of his head for a split second. Long enough to blink, to feel the wooden chair beneath him, to sense the woman beside him.

The voice. *Her* voice.

The one that had read to him in the dead of night. The one that had saved his sanity, if only for a few hours.

Had she been outside his tent? Or had his subconscious conjured her when he needed her most?

He shifted his burning gaze to the botanist and found her peering up at him. Not a trace of her trademark curiosity, irritation, or wariness was present. Tonight, only concern clouded that beautiful face.

Had she noticed the war he waged with his mind? Had she realized the room was closing in on him, suffocating his reason?

What had given him away? Most people had no clue

what to do when he got lost in his head, so they usually just stared at him with wide, cautious, or empathetic eyes.

Not his botanist—ethnobotanist. She might not be treading with her usual take-no-shit attitude, but she was definitely in action mode.

Behind her blue-rimmed glasses, her attention shifted to Way. Something passed between them. Then Reid's head swiveled sharply in Way's direction, as if he'd been kicked.

"Ladies, it's time for me to cruise," Reid said, rubbing his flat stomach. "I've got an early morning."

They had been in the midst of silent communication. About him. He nearly choked on his humiliation.

Coen pushed out of his chair and threw a crisp Ben Franklin in front of Reid. "I'll meet you outside." He forced himself to catch the eye of every man at the table, avoiding Riley's before marching out of hell.

Why hadn't he listened to his gut and stayed the fuck away from this place? Why did he have to slip gears in front of *her*?

Stopping next to Reid's truck, he scrubbed both hands over his face. It was time for him to move on. Ever since he'd caught the botanist spying on him, his sojourn had become less peaceful and more complicated. He didn't do complicated right now.

When he dropped his hands, he noted a silver Audi parked two stalls away. A lone figure sat in the vehicle, unmoving, with the sun visor down—at night. The visor obscured the top half of his face.

Coen's spine tingled and his shoulders sharpened. He slowed his heartbeat down as he scanned the area. When he found nothing else that looked out of place, he returned his attention to the Audi.

Long ago, he'd learned to trust in his training and

instincts. Both told him this guy was up to no good. Most people wouldn't give him a second glance, assuming he was waiting for someone to emerge from the bar. But Coen saw the tension outlining the man's jaw, and his utter stillness was unnatural. No texting, no surfing, no scrolling through the radio stations. Nothing but focused attention on something or, more likely, someone inside Triple B.

Before he realized it, he found himself stalking toward the Audi. He approached the vehicle from the rear, hoping to catch a glimpse of the guy's reflection in the side view mirror. He inched up alongside the vehicle, alternating his attention between the silhouette inside it and the mirror.

Right when his face would've come into view, the man whipped his head back at the same time the engine roared to life. The Audi screamed backward, nearly clipping his hip when it made a sharp turn out of the stall. He jumped out of the way. By the time he righted himself, the S4 was out of reach. He didn't bother running after a turbocharged V6 engine.

But he did commit the license plate number to memory. He followed the car's race down Main Street until it rounded a corner, the taillights blinking out.

Coen strolled back to the now-empty stall. Stood in the location of the Audi's driver's seat, crouched till he had the same view as the driver had had, and peered inside Triple B.

What he saw made sweat break out all over his body and his heart drop to land between his feet.

He had a perfect, unhindered view of the botanist.

Riley.

What kind of trouble had she gotten herself into now?

26

THE SCENT OF A FRESH SPRING RAIN INTERWOVEN WITH A sultry summer night drenched the air as Coen strode down the service drive leading to Riley's greenhouse. Water dripped all around him. The rhythmic *splat, splat, splat,* combined with the *kreeeck, kreeeck, kreeeck* of a dozen insects, created an oddly soothing symphony.

Once Reid heard about the Audi Guy situation, he'd stormed back into the B and ordered Riley and her brothers to meet them at the training academy. There, Way and Reid had laid out a plan that included Riley being under twenty-four seven surveillance.

The botanist's reaction had been swift and hide stripping. She'd wanted nothing to do with more "alpha-male bullshit" because she already felt like she "couldn't take a dump without one of them checking to make sure she used the right toilet paper."

By the time she'd finished, she'd actually managed to extract a promise from each of them to stay out of her space. Coen hadn't promised, because he hadn't been asked. She wouldn't even make eye contact with him. Not after the way he'd rebuffed her help at the bar.

Rubbing his neck, he gave the greenhouse a visual sweep as he passed by. At the rear of the building, a beam of light reflected off several glass panels.

He stopped and, out of habit, pressed a forearm against his side, wincing to find it free of the heavy weight that usually rested there. Although he'd been trained to kill a person a hundred different ways, he would've preferred having his pistol within reach when clearing a building.

When Reid had dropped him off, there had been no cars in the parking lot. His pulse quickened, and a cold sweat broke out over his body, but he moved toward the threat as he had hundreds of times before.

He tested the door and found it unlocked. Drawing in a steadying breath, he slipped inside. With the new moon riding high in the sky, the interior was cast in shadow after deeper shadow.

Now he wondered if he'd been wrong about what he saw the other night. When he'd found no sign of a Peeping Tom outside the greenhouse, he'd chalked the whole thing up to a shift in wind or passing wildlife.

Spotting a heavy-duty hand trowel on a nearby workbench, he picked it up and held it out in front of him like a knife.

Light flickered against the windowpanes again, and he crept closer. Once he got within a dozen feet of his quarry, he crouched low, using a large-leafed plant for cover. He counted to three, evening his breathing, before stretching his neck to see who'd invaded Riley's domain.

What he saw made him blink, certain the fog of alcohol had skewed his vision.

A ten-by-ten office space had been carved out of the

dense foliage, orange pots of every size, and an assortment of hand tools. A small writing desk and rolling chair sat inside the square, and a worn though comfortable-looking couch sat kitty-corner. Lying on the couch, with her feet propped up on the arm, was Riley Kingston.

Earbuds snaked from her ears, and she used a flashlight to illuminate the pages of a well-used spiral notebook she had propped against her thighs. She looked more at ease than he'd ever seen her, yet concentration crinkled the edges of her eyes and the center of her forehead.

Adrenaline drained from his limbs, and he rolled his shoulders to knock out the kinks. Better than anyone, he understood her need for privacy. Except for tonight, every time he'd come across her, she had been alone.

Did she prefer her own company over others'? Or had life dealt her that hand?

On the tail of understanding, anger blew in. Anger that she valued her safety so little. Anger that she didn't trust his instincts. Instincts that had helped him save lives, time and again.

Except once.

Once, they had failed him, and he would live with the consequences for the rest of his life.

Biting back a curse, he set down his makeshift weapon and strode into her tiny office until he stood six feet away. Folding his arms over his middle, he waited.

It took a full minute—*sixty seconds*—for her to detect his presence. When she finally glanced up, the notebook slid off her lap and *thunked* onto the concrete floor. A slip of paper shot from the pages and wedged beneath his boot.

He bent to grab the note, but a feminine hand beat him to it. But not before he read the first line.

EP not ded.

Ded? Who's EP?

She ripped her earbuds out. "What are you doing here?"

"My exact question for you."

Her attention shifted to her surroundings as if looking for the answer. "I work here."

"Do you have any idea what time it is?"

"Of course." Her voice contained a heavy dose of annoyance. "But I have my doubts that you do."

"This takes the term workaholic to a whole new level."

She strode to the desk and stashed the mysterious note into a colorful backpack. The cover on the notebook read Costa Rica: Year Three, Ethnobotanical Findings by Riley Kingston.

"I wasn't ready to go home, so I came here."

"After I told you about the guy in the Audi."

"No, Coen." Fire swirled in her eyes. "You told my male relatives. Not me."

He blinked. "Are you pissed at me?"

"Wouldn't you be if our roles were reversed?" she demanded. "Would you want others deciding what was best for your safety?"

"Maybe, if they were better equipped to deal—"

"Bullshit."

Gritting his teeth, he changed tactics. "You left the door unlocked."

"Men are such master deflectors."

"The world isn't what it used to be twenty years ago. Lock your damn doors."

"No one is stalking me. I'm sure the guy was waiting for someone. Or he was an online dater asshole who likes to wait in the wings to see if the woman is pretty enough."

"If that was the case, why did he almost run me over when I approached?"

Once again, concern entered her gaze as she assessed one end of his body to the other. When she detected no bandages or favored limbs, she said, "A man of your size and bearing no doubt uses his body as a weapon of intimidation. It worked."

"Doesn't seem to be working on you."

"Then you haven't been paying enough attention."

Oh, I have. "Maybe in the beginning but not now."

"Why are you skulking about my greenhouse at this hour?"

"It's in between the training academy and my tent."

"Something tells me you didn't come here to bark at me about working late." She slung her pack over her shoulder. "You've got ten seconds to purge what's on your mind."

"It's not complicated." He dragged his fingers through his half-inch-long hair. Damn, it was getting shaggy. "I saw a beam of light through the window and decided to investigate."

"Did you think Audi Guy had broken in to steal my plants?"

"My thoughts hadn't traveled that far." *Liar.* "Seemed someone was where they didn't belong."

"What would you have done if I'd been a thief?"

"Asked you to leave."

"If I hadn't?"

"I would've said please."

"What if I'd had a gun?"

"Things would've turned interesting."

Shaking her head, she strode away. "If you ever suspect there's an intruder in the greenhouse, don't be a hero. They're just plants."

"A strange sentiment from a botanist."

"Ethnobotanist. Saving greenhouse plants isn't worth a

human life." She peered at him over her shoulder. "Even if the human's annoying."

"Where's your vehicle?"

"I parked it behind the greenhouse."

"Why?"

Her voice turned into a low growl. "So I wouldn't be bothered."

When they passed by the desk, he noticed a thick, rectangular piece of paper folded onto itself. Something so everyday wouldn't have normally caught his attention.

But the paper appeared to be embedded with... He paused and picked up the rectangle. Teardrop-shaped seeds speckled the surface.

"What's this?" he asked.

"Seed paper."

"Never heard of it."

"It's growing in popularity. Have you ever come across dung paper?"

"No." He dangled the sheet from the tips of his thumb and forefinger. "Are you saying this is made from shit?" He sniffed the paper.

She laughed. "I don't know if it is or isn't. Poop paper can be found in bookshops and specialty stores. The ones I've seen are made from recycled elephant dung."

He dropped the strange paper. "Are those real seeds?"

"They look real."

"Why do you have it?"

"A former colleague from Costa Rica wrapped it around a book she sent me."

"Why?"

"She didn't say. Maybe to protect the book during shipping, or it was a craft project."

He nudged the paper. "Are you going to plant this?"

"Hadn't thought to."

She studied his profile for so long that he finally turned to her and asked, "What?"

Dropping her backpack on the floor, she said, "Let's see what kind of plant lurks in the poopy paper."

"What do you mean?"

She unsnapped the leather case attached to her belt and pulled out a Leatherman multi-tool. "Use the scissors to cut the seed paper into several strips, and I'll show you."

He did as instructed and held them out to her.

"Nope," she said. "This is your project, not mine." She collected a large, black plastic tray, a bucket of potting soil, a water container, and a pair of gloves, and placed them on the table. "Plant away."

"I don't know anything about propagation."

"Do you know how to pour soil into a tray?"

Ignoring the gloves, he lifted the bucket. A sharp, pungent odor wafted from its depths. "What's that smell?"

"I added some fertilizer."

He emptied the contents into the tray and used his fingers to level out the lightweight mixture. It was cool to the touch, almost silken.

"Now carve out grooves wide enough to hold your strips. You'll want at least two inches of soil covering the seed."

After tucking in the strips and smoothing the soil back over them, he reached for the water container.

"Give the whole thing a good pat first. You want to remove the air pockets."

When he finished pressing down the soil, he stared at his handprints. An odd sense of accomplishment washed over him. Had it been so long since he'd made himself useful that burying a bunch of seeds actually felt like he'd done something cool? Pathetic.

Even after realizing the patheticness of the situation, he couldn't dredge up an ounce of regret. The process had felt normal. She had given him the gift of an untroubled mind.

She held out the water container. When he didn't immediately take it, she asked, "Everything okay?"

Shrugging off the strange sensation squirreling its way into his bones, he avoided meeting her curious gaze. "Yeah." He grasped the container's handle, and his fingers brushed over hers.

Awareness pulsed into the narrow space between them. A squirrel of a different color shot up his arm, arrowed through his torso, and slammed into his groin.

He almost dropped the damn water.

Neither of them spoke for several what-the-hell-just-happened seconds. The botanist pulled herself together first.

"Give the seeds a good dousing." She began cleaning up the table. "They'll need a little water every day until they sprout."

"How long will that take?"

"It's hard to say. All seeds have different germination periods. Do you need something to help transport your tray?"

"Transport it where?"

Her brows knit together. "Your campsite."

"I'll care for it here." The seed propagation provided him with the perfect cover to keep an eye on her six.

"You want to hike all this way to spend ten seconds watering mystery seeds?"

"My calendar happens to be free at the moment."

"There's no need for you to make the trek every day. I can add it to my watering schedule."

"But it's *my* project—and I don't shirk my duties."

Her attention darted all around the greenhouse, as if she watched a gang of looters trashing her sanctuary.

Lowering his voice, he said, "I'll be in and out. You won't even know when I'm here." His voice hardened. "Especially since you don't lock the door."

She lifted her chin and indicated his tray. "Other than that bit of real estate, the greenhouse and my safety aren't your concern." Picking up her bag, she pointed to a utility sink. "Better wash your hands before we go."

He brushed the dirt from his hands. "They're fine."

"It won't be fine if you get fertilizer in your eyes."

Setting his jaw, he stalked off to the sink and ran his hands beneath the water.

When he made to shut it off, she called, "With soap."

Annoyance crackled along his collarbones. But like a good soldier, he pumped a blob of orange gel into his palm and lathered up.

He pictured her angling to the left and right, trying to get a read on how well he was obeying. Such a busybody.

He was a grown-ass man, who'd routed his enemy from one deadly corner of the world to another. He could damn well wash his hands without supervision.

Something new hurtled through his irritation and peered out. Appreciation. She didn't coo over his perceived heroism or treat him like he was about to fracture into a thousand pieces. To her, he was another male mucking up her world.

Normal.

"Make sure you wash your forearms too. Just to be safe."

Coen lathered up his arms... and smiled.

27

It was official. Riley lived in Clonesville. She could find little to distinguish one day from the next.

Each morning, she hiked through Steele Conservation Area, cataloguing native and invasive plants while steering clear of Transect L and a certain grumpy soldier.

After lunch, she would head to Kingston Farms to help her parents with the store or whatever else they needed. Then around five she would head to the greenhouse to check on her plant babies.

The only pearl in her routine had been reading to Coen. Some sixth sense had sent her to him when he'd needed a distraction. He hadn't mentioned anything about it last night. Had he thought it all a dream? In a way she hoped so. Otherwise, she'd be forced to explain what had compelled her to hike through the woods in the middle of the night to be by his side.

At odd moments this morning, she'd caught herself reliving Coen's accidental touch. She didn't understand why. The contact had been so fleeting she couldn't even say if his flesh had been warm or cold, soft or callused. But that *zing* of awareness? She'd noticed every electrifying inch of it as it shot from her fingers to her toes.

She wondered how he'd measure up to her Anatomy of a Perfect Mate list. No man had ever made it beyond number five. Nick had come close. He'd leapfrogged right over two, three, and four, and landed—and ended—on cinco.

Could that be the reason she'd found the strength of mind to pull away and never go back? Had he spooked a subconscious self-preservation mechanism?

Sighing, she hopped over a narrow spring-fed creek. If a four-inch trickle of water could be called a creek. The temptation to scoop up a palm full of the cool liquid was strong. But she refrained. Even though she'd determined it was spring-fed, Britt had yet to map the watershed. Until he did, she wouldn't be drinking any untreated water, no matter how refreshing it might be.

Once she finished here, she would head over to the farm and see what needed to be done, then off she'd go to the greenhouse to putter around. Clonesville.

Dear God, she needed to have some fun. Not work fun. Girl fun.

No one would call Steele Ridge a dud town. But no one could say with a straight face that it was a happening place either. Besides, she knew everyone. Nothing unusual, no surprises. More of the same.

AKA Clonesville.

For what seemed like the hundredth time, she rubbed the ridge of vertebrae rippling down her neck. The area had hummed with a strange energy all morning.

If she were the paranoid sort, she'd be scanning the trees for another's presence. But she wasn't and she refused to allow recent events to disturb her here in her sanctuary.

She'd spent enough hours traipsing into the very core of forests, ones even more massive than this, to know that hers was not the only beating, curious heart within.

When she crested yet another hill, she lifted her gaze from the ground vegetation long enough to take in the vista below. In many ways, the scenery before her was a microversion of her Clonesville life.

More oaks, beeches, and hickories rose into the sky on sturdy, straight legs. Waxy, dark green rhododendrons dotted the understory, and giant, uprooted trees lay silent and rotting on the forest floor.

The only unusual sight before her was the group of three men in camouflage, bending over a beautiful patch of ginseng, one of the most valuable plants on the black market. Using crude digging tools that could be hidden away in the packs on their backs, the poachers stabbed at the ground, searching for the plants' precious roots.

Fury rumbled in her chest and rose up into her throat. Before logic or reason or self-preservation took hold, she yelled, "Get away from there!" She stormed down the hill, her hand going to the small canister of pepper spray she kept in her pocket. "This is Steele property, and those plants are protected, as you well know."

The poachers whipped around, bringing up their tire irons and screwdrivers and hand trowels to ward off the coming threat. Their wary eyes fell on her, then searched the area at her back.

Too far gone in her rage, she missed the warning clenching in her gut. The sight of the ragged, upturned earth and too-small roots lying in bleak, haphazard piles at the men's feet dulled all her other senses.

The medium-built man on the right, with a square jaw covered in two days' worth of stubble and cruel, narrow-set black eyes, lowered his weapon first. A predatory smile split across his face.

His friends took up flanking positions behind him, their expressions more murderous than salacious. The canister gripped in her sweaty hand felt far too small. None of these men were known to her. That meant they had to be from neighboring towns or even counties. Poachers traveled a great distance to plunder patches of *Panax quinquefolius*.

She held up her phone. "I've already texted a picture to 911. You'd best be on your way." Lord help her if they called her bluff.

Left Flank and Right Flank's concerned eyes widened before settling on Cruel Eyes. The latter stalked forward, his smile deepening.

"If you've already ratted us out, then we have nothing to lose."

"Don't come any closer." The pepper spray canister she aimed in his direction felt way too small. She jammed her phone into her back pocket. Mind racing, she considered her options. Stay and fight or run like hell.

Cruel Eyes jerked his chin in her direction, and the Flanks speared out, moving swiftly despite their beer belly bodies.

Run.

28

RILEY SHOT UP THE HILL, HOPING YOUTH AND MANY HOURS OF conditioning on this terrain would give her an advantage over male strength and stamina. Once she reached the summit, she peered over her shoulder to assess their positions.

Her eyes flared when she found Cruel Eyes little more than a car length away. Fear spurred her feet into action.

"Don't let her get away!" Cruel Eyes demanded.

Even though her heart slammed inside her chest like a caged animal, she willed calm into her mind. Her brother Way had taught her the technique on one of their camping trips years ago. If anyone knew about fear and danger and survival, it was Way.

"A calm mind can still reason, plan, and stay one step ahead. A mind in terror only knows terror."

She forced her heaving breaths through her nose and commanded her panic-stricken gaze to focus, to search for familiar landmarks. She hadn't been in this section of the forest in a while, but she had an uncanny internal navigation system.

Three pairs of boots crashed through the underbrush behind her. They were close enough for her to hear their labored breathing, their low, stumbling curses.

"You can't outrun me, girl," Cruel Eyes said, mere feet behind her. "I was a long-distance champ three years in a row."

And I was a champ at outrunning my brothers' wrath.

She pumped more energy into her limbs, praying her lungs wouldn't fail her. There, thirty feet ahead, she recognized a three-stemmed redbud that had one of the stems pointing toward the ground. She'd passed the unusual tree about an hour ago. It was amazing how much more ground she could cover when running for her life.

Calm, observe, breathe. Calm, observe, breathe.

She kept the mantra ticking in her head until the crush of underbrush behind her receded.

Following her mental map, she zigzagged through the forest until the trees opened into a short grass meadow of little bluestem, rattlesnake master, blazing star, and wild bergamot. Lungs burning and legs quivering, she flew across the open area, feeling more exposed than ever. Soon a glass dome appeared. The greenhouse didn't quell her anxiety. In fact, she considered running the extra half mile to the research center.

But the center might be filled with school kids and families. She couldn't lead these idiots into the midst of such innocents. The greenhouse would protect her long enough for Maggie to arrive.

When she reached the door, she cast another assessing look over her shoulder. The meadow behind her was empty. Had she lost them? Somehow she didn't think so.

Shouldering her way into the greenhouse, she slammed the door shut and locked it. She leaned against the fragile barrier and counted one thundering heartbeat, then two, three, four, five, before giving her knees permission to buckle. Closing her eyes, she slid down and waited, her harsh breaths filling the humid air.

"What's going on?"

Her eyes snapped open to find Coen standing before her, watering can in one hand and dead leaves in the other.

Through rasping breaths, she said, "Three poachers... chasing me... angry."

The can and weeds dropped to the ground, and he stormed to her side.

"Are you okay?"

The gentle note in his voice made her eyes prick and her throat close. She managed a nod without disgracing herself.

He lifted her to her feet. "Lock the door after me."

His command snapped the relief from her bones. "What? You can't go out there. It would be three against one."

Ignoring her warning, he palmed a knife he'd retrieved from a hidden sheath at his ankle.

"Coen, no. There are three of them."

"Lock the door, Riley, and call 911."

She squeezed into the space between him and the door. "I approached them when I shouldn't have." She shifted her attention over his shoulder, seeing nothing but her humiliation. "My anger provoked them."

With one finger to her chin, he brought her gaze back to his. In a firm but not unkind voice, he said, "Good men wouldn't have been chasing you." He nudged her out of the way. "Lock, call, now."

"Coen, no—"

He slammed the door in her face.

She opened it and found him standing in her path, arms crossed.

"At least let me go with you."

"No."

"What if something happens to you out there?"

"Nothing's going to happen to me."

"If I go—"

"You'll be a distraction," he said.

She frowned. "I'm not going to do anything stupid."

"My attention will be split between you and them." He pointed into the greenhouse. "Do I need to say it again?"

She stepped back, closed—or more like slammed—the door, and snicked the lock into place. Withdrawing her phone, she tapped 911 and relayed what happened to the dispatcher. She didn't bother putting her phone away once the call ended.

Sure enough, thirty seconds later, her phone rang.

"Did they hurt you?" a dead-calm female voice asked.

Steady, rock-solid Maggie Kingston. Big sister and sheriff of Haywood County.

"No, just scared the crap out of me." She prowled along the long row of windows from one end of the building to the other, her attention outside, seeking one glimpse of Coen's dark head and wide shoulders. She found no trace of him.

How had he disappeared when she'd looked away for only a moment?

"Anyone with you?" Emergency sirens blared in the background.

"Not right now. Coen's searching for the poachers."

"Who's Coen?"

"Reid's friend."

"What's he doing there?"

"Long story."

"I want to hear it. I'm passing through the research center's parking lot now. Be there in two minutes."

The line went silent, and a mixture of dread and relief clenched her chest.

Stupid. She'd been so stupid to approach those poachers in the middle of the forest. Their destruction of the ginseng patch had hit a raw nerve. They either didn't know or didn't care how their actions would upset an entire ecosystem.

Maybe the effect wouldn't be felt today or tomorrow or even next year. But hunting anything to extinction had a cost. All living organisms were interconnected. Take one link out of a chain—one plant, one animal, one insect, one microbe—and everything else starts to falter.

Rather than call Maggie, she'd confronted the poachers like an idiot, and that decision had now put Coen in danger.

Maggie's cruiser pulled into view, and she rushed out. She didn't run to her sister like a nine-year-old who'd lost her puppy, though she did walk straight into her sister's waiting arms.

Smoothing a hand over her hair, Maggie whispered, "Tell me everything."

Riley stepped back, slipping on her scientist's cap before sharing her story. She told Maggie of the uprooted *Panax*, of her fury, and of her challenge. She described the three men, their weapons, their intent. By the time she spoke of her flight and Coen's response, she'd angled her body toward the tree line, searching.

"He's a sergeant in the Army and here on leave," she said. "He's in Steele Ridge to get away from the horrors of war and conflict, and I've thrown him into the center of the very thing he's trying to escape."

Two more police vehicles joined Maggie's.

"We'll find him, don't worry."

In what shape? He might be physically unharmed, but mentally?

Two figures emerged from the tree line. One sported a bloodied nose and rumpled clothes, the other appeared to be untouched.

Coen shoved one of her would-be assailants into the open meadow. Not Cruel Eyes. The prisoner carried too much weight around the middle to be the leader. That left either Right or Left Flank. From this distance, she couldn't be sure which one.

Her feet began moving. In some part of her mind, she heard Maggie grumble out a command. But she dismissed her surroundings, including her beloved big sister.

Undeterred, she strode to Coen as if compelled by an invisible hand at her back. She analyzed his posture, his stride and, when she was close enough, the directness of his gaze. He appeared whole, uninjured—and was assessing her with the same frankness she'd leveled on him.

"Is this one of the guys who chased you?" he asked.

The prisoner angled his face away. But she'd seen enough of him on her approach to know that Coen had captured Right Flank.

"Yes."

"Where are your friends?" Coen asked the poacher.

"Don't have any friends."

He gave the guy a shake. "How about I help jog your memory."

"We'll take it from here," Maggie said, stepping around her. "Blaine, take him to the station."

So focused on Coen, Riley hadn't heard her sister or the deputy trailing in her wake.

Deputy Blaine grabbed Right Flank's arm and hauled him off.

"You must be Coen," Maggie said.

Riley waved a hand in her sister's direction. "This is Maggie Kingston. My sister and county sheriff."

Coen held out a hand. "Nice to meet you, Sheriff."

"Ditto. And thanks for protecting my little sister." Maggie clasped his hand. "But, for future reference, I don't advise chasing a group of pissed-off men into the woods. Nine times out of ten it won't end well."

"Let's hope then," Coen said, "that this is the one and only time."

Maggie turned to Riley. "How did the two of you meet?"

While surveying, I came across him standing in front of his tent, naked and glorious.

Somehow she didn't think even her big sis would appreciate the story.

Coen raised a brow in her direction, a glint of amusement in his eyes.

"Our paths crossed while I was conducting flora surveys." She gave him a nefarious smile as she said, "Coen's helping me in the greenhouse now."

"That's generous of you," Maggie said.

"Yes," Coen said, amusement gone. "It is."

Maggie's lips twitched, a sure sign he'd passed the sister-sheriff sniff test. "You should come with Riley to our parents' house for dinner tonight. They always make more than we can eat."

Coen's wary gaze met Riley's, and she felt a pinch of disappointment at his response.

Before he could deliver his regrets, she said, "Coen's here for some peace and quiet—exactly the opposite of what he'd get at one of our family meals." She gave her sister a conspiratorial grin. "Besides, he'd off-balance our delicate testosterone-to-estrogen ratio."

Maggie glanced between them, then shrugged. "Suit yourself, but Dad's making his famous meatballs, and I heard Mom's perfected her bread pudding recipe. Again." She squeezed Riley's hand. "See you tonight, kiddo."

"Yes."

Both women turned to Coen.

Maggie smiled.

Riley stared. "'Yes' what?"

"I accept. Your sister's invitation." Something warm and challenging and nameless entered his gaze. "Unless you have an objection."

Riley wasn't sure how she felt about Coen eating at her parents' table. But denying him a home-cooked meal after he'd helped her was out of the question.

"Why would I?" she asked. "Cash and Shep would enjoy seeing you again."

The skin below his left eye twitched, like a suppressed flinch against a painful blow.

"It's settled then," Maggie said. "I'll see you both tonight."

Before Maggie could turn away, Coen asked, "Do you know anyone who drives a silver Audi A4?"

"No, why?"

"Coen," Riley growled, "don't."

Maggie's voice turned dangerous. "What is it?"

"Nothing," she said, sending Coen a warning glance.

"Quiet, Ry."

"You're not the boss—"

"Last night." Coen interrupted. "I noticed a guy sitting in his vehicle, staring into Triple B."

Riley crossed her arms, refusing to look at either of them.

"That's not unusual," Maggie said. "The parking downtown is limited. He might have been waiting on someone who was shopping a block away and had nothing better to do than watch the goings-on in the bar."

"When I approached, he nearly ran me over in his rush to leave."

Riley peeked at her sister.

In true Maggie form, she displayed no outward emotion, though Riley caught the slight narrowing of her sister's eyes. Never a good sign.

"I moved to where the car had been parked," Coen continued, "and noticed Riley was in his direct line of sight."

"Where were you sitting?" Maggie asked her.

"Not at our usual table in the back of the bar. We grabbed a seat near the front window so that I could hear the music better."

Maggie turned to Coen. "Got a description?"

"No. He kept his face hidden."

"License plate?"

Coen rattled off the number.

"Fast thinking," Maggie said. "I'll get it checked out and fill you in tonight. See y'all then." Before she turned to leave, Maggie gave her one of those sisterly stay-out-of-trouble looks.

Gritting her teeth, Riley's attention swept from her sister's retreating back to Coen's expressionless face. "Didn't we just have a conversation about this?"

"About what?" he asked, all Mr. Innocent.

"About your penchant for discussing my safety with others. Maggie has enough to worry about without adding me and a phantom stalker onto her plate."

"She might have been able to identify the driver as a Steele Ridge resident."

"But she didn't. Now she's going to spend hours tracking down a lame online dater creep."

"Lame online dater creep?"

"Impossible." She threw her hands into the air. "You're as impossible as my brothers." She poked the air between them. "Just wait. Maggie will prove me right."

"I hope so. Until then, don't wander off by yourself."

"I don't *wander* anywhere."

His hard expression didn't give an inch.

Neither did hers.

"Should I meet you in the parking lot at six?" she asked, changing the subject after a short stare-off.

His penetrating gaze slid over her features, lingering on her mouth before slowly tracking up to her eyes. He nodded once, then strode away. Into the forest.

She dug the heels of her boots into the earth, anchoring her, stopping her from following. When she finally willed herself to turn away, she struggled to breathe around the heavy weight bearing down on her chest.

What if he was right?

29

COEN PAUSED AT THE EDGE OF THE PARKING LOT TO TAKE IN the storm that was Riley Kingston.

She was perched on the front bumper of her Wrangler, her long, jean-clad legs extended to brace her position. Her unembellished toenails peeked out the top of a pair of strappy, sandstone-colored sandals.

A coral, scooped-neck top hugged curves normally hidden beneath layers of protective clothing. Her rich, chestnut hair hung free in soft waves around her shoulders.

Everything about her seemed softer, as if she'd used a giant file to smooth out the rough edges. For him? Or was this the real Riley?

Did he captivate her in the same way she captivated him?

No matter what intelligence the sheriff found—or didn't find—Coen had no doubt about Audi Guy's dishonorable interest in Riley. The only thing he couldn't pinpoint was how far the guy was willing to go. Was he benevolent and just couldn't muster up the courage to ask out a pretty woman? Or did he intend something much darker? His instincts leaned toward the latter option.

One of Riley's legs bent, and her knee began to bounce at ninety miles an hour. If she'd been a goddess, she would've shaken the parking lot with her impatience, her need to be on the move.

A grin curled one corner of his mouth.

As if sensing his scrutiny, she lifted her bent head and turned in his direction. Her knee stopped. Was she still mad at him?

Not knowing if this dinner was celebratory or casual, he'd erred on the side of caution and wore his best outfit. Which wasn't saying much.

Dark, barely worn jeans, button-down shirt, and cowboy boots. Boring but not overdressed, considering her attire.

Standing, she shoved her phone into her back pocket and approached. Her clothing wasn't the only thing she'd altered about her appearance.

Smoky eyes and rosy lips enhanced an already beautiful face. His attention lingered on her mouth, imagined its softness. Would she taste of fresh mint or a summer breeze?

When he remained unmoving, her trek across the parking lot stalled.

"Your clothes suggest you're still coming," she said. "But your expression indicates something different." She gave him a knowing smile. "Maggie is difficult to say no to. If you'd like to back out, no one will be offended."

Her offer hit like a punch to the head. He wiped his face clean of emotion, disconcerted that he'd let down his guard at all.

"Pass up a free meal?" He shook his head as he strode toward her. "Not even I'm that much of a recluse."

"Good," she said, leading the way back to her vehicle. "With you there to distract my brothers, I can eat in peace."

"Maybe I need to rethink this."

"Too late."

When he followed her to the driver's side, she pointed to the passenger seat. "You're over there."

"I was going to get your door."

She lifted a brow. "Why?"

"Because that's what guys do."

"When they're dating the girl." She pointed to the opposite side of the vehicle again. "We're not even friends yet."

He set his jaw and hopped into the passenger seat. She was right. He'd followed her, acting on years of his father demanding that he get the door for his mama and sister.

Longing clenched his chest at the thought of his family. God, he missed them. If his sister had lived, would he have been an uncle by now?

Wrapped in their own musings, they drove away, blanketed in silence. He'd grown accustomed to not talking, to living with his own thoughts. But the scent of oranges wafted to his side of the vehicle, and an undercurrent of awareness took root. Something tangible and hot filled the air inside the Jeep.

Searching for a distraction, he considered question after question, but each one sounded like senseless small talk to his mind's ear. The silence lengthened. Buckling, he spit out the next stupid thought that came to mind.

"I wasn't sure how to dress."

She slid him a glance before shifting into fifth gear. "You look great. We're a casual bunch."

"Who will be there?" He noticed his fingers curling into fists and forced them open.

"Dad and Mom, Maggie and Jayson, Shep and Puck, Cash and Emmy, you, me."

He didn't miss the fact that she didn't say "you *and* me." Why the omission bugged him was better left unanalyzed.

"Are you sure you want to do this?" she asked. "I wasn't kidding when I said you'll get no peace and quiet at this gathering. My parents can be slightly unpredictable."

"I don't mind unpredictable." His gaze dipped down to her lips. "Keeps things interesting."

Reid's cousin. Reid's cousin.

"Our families would've gotten on well together," he said, more to distract himself than anything.

"Can you tell me about them? Your family?" she asked. "Unless it's too painful."

"They died a long time ago." *Though it seems like only yesterday.*

"Time doesn't make the loss any less significant—or painful."

He filled his lungs with air and said the words he hadn't uttered in years. "My parents and younger sister were killed during a home invasion."

"How terrible. Were you overseas at the time?"

His fingers rolled together. "Yes."

"Did the military allow you to come home for their funerals?"

"Yes."

Out of the corner of his eye, he could see her scanning his profile. "Please don't tell me that you blame yourself for their deaths."

"Why would you say that?"

"You're a protector. Seemed like something you'd beat up yourself about—for not being there."

When they needed you.

He'd often wondered if he could've altered their fates had he been home. But he was enough of a pragmatist to understand that sometimes life sucked and that no matter what he did or where he was, bad shit happened.

Rolling his shoulders, he said, "No, I never blamed myself, but I did wonder if I could've saved them had I been there."

"You would've," she said with a conviction that made him turn to her. "But you weren't." She met his gaze for a brief moment. "Instead, you saved another son's family thousands of miles away. Probably several families, if I were to guess."

The pressure that seemed forever a part of his chest eased, a little. "If you know me so well, how is it that we're not friends?"

A small grin appeared. "I have a keen sense of character."

"Is that before or after you see someone naked?"

"Afterward, for sure," she said without missing a beat.

He barked out a laugh. The sound was rusty, even to his own ears.

Before long, Riley turned down a winding gravel drive that spilled into a large, multicar parking lot. A wide flagstone path connected the lot to a medium-sized white building decorated with garden-style ironwork. Smiling yellow suns, giant green insects, and happy welcome signs greeted the visitor.

Next to the building sat a large white house with black shutters and a porch that sported a swinging chair. Colorful flowers and trailing vines overflowed window boxes and large, standing pots took up sentinel on either side of the front door.

"What is this place?" he asked.

"Didn't you see the entrance sign?"

"I guess not."

"Welcome to Kingston Farm and Market."

"Your family's business?"

"And home."

She drove around to the back, to another, smaller parking area. She slid into a spot next to a sleek black Chevy Volt. Several other vehicles dotted the area.

"This is where the family parks when we don't want to be bothered by customers."

"Does it work?"

She chuckled. "Not always."

He stood next to the Jeep and marveled at the sweeping farming operation beyond the two-acre residential plot. Two large red barns flanked a massive shop yard, replete with a fuel station. Several smaller outbuildings dotted the landscape.

To the rear of both barns, grassy fields sprawled across dozens of acres. Four large temporary fence enclosures held cattle, pigs, and chickens. The last one appeared empty.

Behind the shop yard, rows and rows and rows of vegetables and herbs lined the earth.

"Impressive, isn't it?" she asked, cradling a casserole dish in her arms. "My dad is an American success story. He turned a hobby into a successful local business in the space of a decade."

"It's... incredible."

She pointed to the enclosures. "Free-ranging livestock. The fence around them is on wheels. Once the animals eat their way through the grass, they herd the animals, with the mobile fence, to a fresh spot ready to be mowed down by dozens of eager mouths."

"One's empty."

"Not for long. We'll bring in baby turkeys a few months before Thanksgiving."

"All organic then?"

"These days, we like to use a sexier term"—she grinned —"farm-to-table."

He laughed. "Given the success of your father's business, I take it this isn't the only location?"

"No, we have two more. But this is the only one that has a store and is open to the public." She handed him the casserole dish. "Come on. I'm sure Maggie filled Mom in on your daring deed and she's anxious to meet you."

He growled.

She chuckled.

As they approached the back door, he understood why she rid herself of her breakable dish. A black-and-white torpedo shot around the corner of the house and propelled itself into Riley's outstretched arms. The force staggered her back a step, but she held on to the squiggling mass of fur and tongue, stretching her neck to avoid a saliva dump.

Laughing, she said, "Nicksie, show some manners, girl." She peered at him over the border collie's head. "Do you like dogs?"

"Yes." He let the dog sniff his hand. "But don't try to pawn that slobbering hairball onto me. I'd prefer not to walk into your parents' house for the first time with dog snot on my face."

"I doubt they'd notice. Farm smells and unidentifiable stains are commonplace in the Kingston household."

Nicksie jumped out of her arms to sniff at his boots. Then she spotted a squirrel at the base of a large oak tree and zipped away again.

Brushing off black fur and dusty paw prints, Riley headed to the back door and walked into a hive of activity.

"Hello, family!" Riley strode into the kitchen, straight to a tall, lean man who was stirring something on the stove. She wrapped her arms around his waist and pressed the side of her face to his back. "Did you miss me, Daddy?" she asked with a laugh.

He patted her arm. "Always, Riley-girl. Give me a second and I'll greet your hero."

The damn botanist snorted.

She shared cheek kisses with a woman who could be her sister—if she'd been thirty years younger. Build, smile, eyes, it was all the same, except the hair color. Where Riley was dark, this woman was light.

"How's the bread pudding coming along, Mama?"

Mrs. Kingston set a timer on the oven. "It'll be done by the time we finish dinner." She settled her attention on Coen. "Who do we have here?"

"This is Coen Monroe." She retrieved the warm casserole dish and set it on the island with several other dishes. "He's friends with Reid and has been helping me out at the greenhouse."

He held out a hand. "Nice to meet you, Mrs. Kingston."

"Call me Sandy." She shook his hand in one of those warm two-handed shakes people used to show genuine affection or respect. "I'm glad you could join us tonight. Maggie told us what you did for our Riley. Quite heroic."

Heat spread into his ears.

"Look," Riley said. "You've been in his presence all of one minute and managed to make him blush. That's gotta be a record."

Sandy sent him a concerned look. "I didn't embarrass you, did I? I only wanted to thank you. No telling what would've happened to Riley if you hadn't been there."

He slid his attention to Riley. "Your daughter is more resourceful than you might think, ma'am."

Gratitude softened Riley's eyes, and something shifted in the center of his chest.

When his gaze flicked back to Sandy, he noticed an assessing glint in her eyes.

Shit.

The last thing he needed was for a matchmaking mama lasering in on him.

He should've known this would happen. Even with the invitation coming from Maggie, everyone would wonder if there was something going on between him and Riley, especially since she drove him here.

Hell, he'd suspect the same thing if he were in their shoes. When he accepted, he hadn't considered the consequences. He'd said yes out of annoyance. Annoyance that Riley thought she knew what he wanted. And because she'd been right, he'd been annoyed even more. But once he'd agreed, something like anticipation had kicked annoyance into the creek.

But he didn't want to give this sweet lady any false impressions. Best he nip Sandy's hope in the bud before it blossomed into something dangerous.

For the second time in one day, he scrubbed emotion from his features. "I would've done the same for anyone."

The light in Riley's eyes dimmed, and he batted away the guilt that crept in.

"Is the Menace here?" a masculine voice from another room asked.

"Cash, don't call your sister that awful name," Sandy scolded.

"Is Wynette here?"

Riley closed her eyes and emitted a low growl. Sandy shook her head.

"Wynette?" Coen asked.

"Riley's first name," Sandy said.

Coen arched a brow at Riley.

"Don't ask—"

"She's named after one of our favorite singers." Mr. Kingston shoved a large hand in Coen's direction. "Ross Kingston."

"Sir."

"Ross, please. What brings you to Steele Ridge?"

His shoulders straightened under the older man's assessing gaze. "A little R and R, sir."

"What branch?"

"Army, sir."

"Rank?"

"Sergeant First Class." No need to complicate things.

"Ranger?"

"Yes, sir." *And Delta Force operator.*

"Ross, you sound like a drill sergeant," Sandy said. "Riley, take Coen in to say hello to the others."

Determination edged Ross Kingston's otherwise kind expression, and Coen knew Riley's dad wasn't finished with him yet.

Into the fryin' pan.

30

RILEY ESCORTED COEN FROM THE KITCHEN. SHE SHOULD'VE gone with her instincts and asked Shep to bring Coen tonight. Twice she'd picked up her phone to do just that, and twice she'd shoved it back into her bag.

"Is your dad former military?" Coen asked.

"Four years in the Marines prior to marrying my mom." She flicked him an apologetic glance. "I'm sorry about the questions. I'll do my best to keep him at bay for the rest of the night."

"He's doing what a good dad should do."

"Which is why I should've asked one of my brothers to drive you."

Once they stepped into the family room, her brothers engulfed Coen in man hugs and back slaps. She wandered over to Maggie and Jayson, giving each a hug and kiss on the cheek.

"What's wrong?" All-seeing Maggie asked.

"Dad's got it in his head that Coen and I are together."

"Ah."

Jay chuckled, having recently survived the inquisition.

Her sister had suffered the same Daddy Dictatorship over the years. How such a gentle, loving man could turn into a barbarian at the sight of a guy near one of his daughters was mind-boggling.

"Since you invited him, you've got to help me run interference."

"Don't worry, Ry," Jay said, his disarming quarterback smile in place. "I'll give your guy pointers on dealing with your family."

Maggie smacked his arm with the back of her hand. "Watch it, superstar."

Riley shook her head, a grin surfacing. "He doesn't need to deal with my family—just survive tonight." She narrowed her eyes. "And he's not my guy. Your gal invited him, not me."

"Only because I saw you making cow eyes at him."

"I haven't cow-eyed a guy since sixth grade."

Maggie snorted.

"What did you find out about the Audi driver?"

"The vehicle's registered to Rent-A-Car. Deputy Blaine's contacting them to see who rented it."

"I think Coen's making this into something that it's not."

"I don't want to discount his instincts, but there's still a good possibility the guy was just sitting there."

"You'll stay frosty until Maggie knows more?" Jay asked.

"I'm always frosty," she said with a straight face, "as evidenced by my lack of lovers."

Maggie and Jay howled, drawing the attention of everyone in the room. A smile hovered on Coen's lips, one she'd never seen before. If she gave it a label, it would be indulgent. The same expression had been on Cash's and Jay's faces of late.

"Dinner's ready," Mom called from the dining room.

Leaves had been placed in the table to provide enough room for up to ten people. Her mom and dad took their places at opposite ends of the table.

Emmy and Cash sat next to her mom. Puck nestled at Shep's feet, who took a seat on the same side and next to her dad. Maggie and Jay moved to the opposite side of the table. Coen hesitated, glancing between Riley and her brothers.

She placed a hand on the back of the chair between her dad and Maggie.

"Sit on the guys' side," Shep said, indicating an open chair between him and Cash.

"Hey," Emmy said, peering down the table. "What do you call me?"

"Emmy." Shep dropped his napkin into his lap and reached for the mashed potatoes.

Bless her, Emmy smiled at Shep's sometimes black-and-white view of the world.

Coen squeezed in between her brothers, looking somehow at home and uncomfortable at the same time.

They spent the next few minutes passing a large platter of meatballs and marinara sauce, a big bowl of pasta, a basket of garlic bread, and an eye-dazzling assortment of side dishes around.

The blend of aromas soothed her frayed nerves. She wouldn't let a display of male chest-beating ruin her evening. An occasion when all her siblings could share a dinner had become more and more rare.

Their family dinners often turned into a rowdy competition of "who brought the best dish," but Riley had texted everyone ahead of time, putting a kibosh to it tonight. She wanted to avoid any potential triggers for Coen.

"Is Way joining us?" Riley asked.

"No," Mom said. "He left this morning."

She glanced up to find her dad studying Coen.

"Stop it, Daddy."

"What?"

"Boring into Coen."

"He's too quiet."

"Maybe because most of us are strangers to him."

"Us?"

"Despite your assumptions, I'm only his ride tonight."

"What's he doing at the greenhouse?"

"Watering a plant."

"A plant? As in one?"

"It's a long story." She bit into a tender meatball while watching Coen interacting with her brothers. As if sensing her attention, he met her gaze. She held it for a full second before breaking away. "Don't worry, Daddy. He'll be gone soon."

"How do you feel about that?"

"Nothing." The word sat on her tongue like a pile of sand crystals. "I've only known him for a few days."

He curled one work-worn hand around hers. "I have to look out for my Riley-girl."

"I give you permission to go full tilt into Daddy Dictatorship—*when* I bring home a boyfriend."

"And when might that be?" he asked, mischief crinkling at the corners of his eyes.

Grinning, she sat back in her chair and raised her voice. "I'll let Maggie's babies tire you out first."

Around a meatball, Maggie said, "No time for babies."

Between Maggie's job pulling her across the county and Jay's taking him cross-country, who could blame them for not wanting to complicate things further. Besides, Maggie would get the ring and vows first.

"Five years, Margaret," Mom warned. "Then I want grandchildren."

Jay choked on a pasta noodle.

Maggie shot Riley a death stare.

Smirking, she mouthed, *Whaaa.*

Once the main meal was done, everyone peeled away to rinse off their plates and stash them in the dishwasher.

"Cash," Mom said, "grab our guest's plate."

When Cash made to obey, Coen waved him off. "Thanks, I'll take care of it."

It didn't surprise her that Coen wouldn't allow someone else to clean up after him while he sat idle at the table. Given his military training and his recent self-imposed exile, he'd been doing for himself for years.

Somehow she and Coen wound up at the sink together. He set his dirty plate down long enough to grab the plate she'd just rinsed. Their elbows brushed. They both did a good job of ignoring the accidental contact. But when she reached for his dirty plate, he put a hand on her arm, halting her.

Brows raised, she met his gaze.

"I can rinse my own plate."

"And I was quite capable of putting my plate into the dishwasher, but that didn't stop you from doing it." She reached across him, coming within an inch of his stomach as she grabbed his plate and silverware. His pine scent filled her nose, and she took an extra second to let it wash over her. "I'll rinse, you stash."

This time when their arms made contact, he seemed to press into her rather than pull away. A touch, not a brush.

She kept her focus on the routine task of turning off the water and drying her hands. If she peered into those beautiful eyes, she would ache. Ache for something neither of them knew what to do with.

"Do you like bread pudding, Coen?" Mom asked.

"Love it, but it's been years since I've had any."

Probably not since his family was killed.

"Well, let's see if my recipe lives up to what you remember." She cut a steaming square out of the pan and set it on a plate. With the back of her hand, she nudged a metal bowl toward him. "Homemade whipped cream?"

"Love some." Coen scooped a dollop onto his pudding.

Delighted, her mom continued slicing and dicing her dessert until everyone was served.

When he leaned in for a second spoonful, Riley cautioned him. "Um, try just the one first." She glanced at Maggie. "The cream can be... rich."

His eyes narrowed on his dessert.

"Okay, everyone, eat up," Mom said.

Rather than cutting through the pudding like butter, his spoon sank into the slice like it was cutting one-hundred-year-old cheese. She really should have warned him about her mom's cooking skills, but an inner devil clamped on to her tongue and settled in for the show.

Frowning, he glanced up to see everyone watching him. Wary now, he lifted the spoon to his nose, sniffed, and eased it into his mouth.

The chewing looked a little slow going at first, then things loosened up.

Swallowing, he smiled. "Delicious, Sandy. Did I detect a hint of peppermint in the cream?"

She nodded. "I only had a bit more left in the bottle, so I added it to the mix. You didn't find the pudding too chewy?"

"Not at all. Yours reminded me of my mom's."

"How nice. I would love to swap recipes with her sometime."

Riley's smile faded. "Mom—"

A large hand covered hers where it rested on the island counter.

"I wish you could," he said. "The two of you would've been great cooking companions. But my mom passed away several years ago."

"Oh, I'm so sorry, Coen."

Silence fell over the kitchen.

Then Coen reached for the spoon and added another dollop of cream and raised an eyebrow at everyone until they dug into their pudding.

Pinpricks of gratitude stung Riley's nose. She glanced at her dad, and as she suspected, tears glinted in his eyes.

Noticing she didn't take a piece, Coen asked, "Nothing for you?"

"Not tonight."

"Diet?"

She peered down at her slim figure. "Do I look like I need a diet?"

Taking her question as an invitation, he made a languid sweep up and down her body. "No." His low voice carried a velvety richness she'd never heard before.

The muscles in her stomach—and lower—contracted.

When he opened his mouth to ask another probing question, she strode back into the dining room. Having a conversation about why she'd decided to keep her sugar intake to a minimum tonight wasn't on her list of fun things to do.

After two rounds of Pictionary, during which the ladies trounced the guys, Riley decided to call it a night. She caught Coen's eye. "Ready?"

He nodded, and they both stood.

"Leaving?" Dad asked.

"I have an early morning tomorrow," she said.

"How are we supposed to vindicate ourselves if you leave?" Cash asked.

"Whether I leave or stay, you guys don't stand a chance. Females are the superior gender."

"Smack!" Shep said.

Cash smiled from where he slouched in the crook of the couch, Emmy snugged into his side. "Want me to drive him?"

"You both look too comfortable," she said. "It won't take me but an extra minute or two."

"Thank you for dinner," Coen said to her parents.

"Come back anytime," Mom said, bussing his cheek.

Her dad shook his hand. "Next time we'll have a different sort of chat."

She had no idea what he meant by "a different sort of chat" and, thankfully, wouldn't have to worry about it since Coen would be long gone soon.

Her mind shied away from that train of thought.

Once the car door closed, she settled her phone in the cupholder and asked, "Did you really like my mom's bread pudding?"

For that, she received the second death stare of the night. "Thanks for the warning—and for hanging me out there to sink or swim."

"You did one better than swim. You floated. Made my dad tear up."

"Because I ate his wife's dessert?"

"No, because you were kind about it. More than kind."

"They're good people. You're very lucky."

"Yes."

A familiar uneasy silence choked the air. She increased her speed. The sooner she got them to the center, the sooner she could put an end to this... this whatever it was between them. Or not between them.

Arghh!

"Why don't you eat sweets?" he asked.

She angled her head around to give him the stink eye.

"Why do my eating habits hold any interest for you whatsoever?"

"I love a good mystery—and you're proving to be more than a woman who likes weeds."

"You will not provoke me into talking about this."

"Gonna make me work for it then." He settled back in his seat and stared out the window. Into the darkness. "What do we know about sweets?"

"Coen, knock it off."

"They're delicious."

She clenched her teeth, bracing herself to ride it out.

"Fattening."

He shifted his attention to her, and dammit if her heart didn't pause to hear his next guess.

"A temporary source of energy."

Swallowing hard, she focused on the road ahead, on keeping her features neutral.

"My money is on number three." He considered her for a moment. "What sort of effect does sugar have on someone who's constantly on the move and whose mind never rests?"

"Coen, drop it."

"When did your parents forbid you to eat sugar?" he asked in a quiet voice.

"My parents would never do something like that."

"If not your parents—?"

"Please *stop*. There's nothing earth-shattering here for you to figure out."

He shifted toward her. "*You* made the decision to deprive yourself of sugar."

"*Yes, for the love of my sanity, yes!*" She whipped into the center's parking lot and slammed to a halt in front of the entrance drive, where the shadows were thick. "Do you feel a sense of accomplishment now that you've unearthed my dark secret?"

"Tell me why?"

Riley closed her eyes as humiliation burned the tips of her ears. "You're not going to drop this, are you?"

"Sorry, your curiosity has rubbed off on me."

Bahh-ling. Cracking open her eyes, she peered at the display and noticed a too-tiny-to-see image before a big hand blocked her view.

"No distractions," he said.

Dropping her phone back into the cupholder, she reached across his lap, grabbed the door handle. "End of the road, big guy." She pushed it open. Or tried to. The damn thing was locked.

Before she could straighten, he grasped her outstretched arm with one hand and used his other hand to cradle the back of her neck. Their noses were a finger's width apart. His breath fanned over her face, and where his skin connected with hers, their heartbeats thrummed together in an ancient rhythm.

The frustration and humiliation she'd felt a second ago ebbed from her body at his touch. At the heat in his eyes.

How had this night gone so sideways? Once again, she'd ignored her instincts. She should've taken Cash up on his offer to drive Coen home. But she hadn't been ready to let him go. An odd feeling of loss had crowded into her mind, as if she'd peered into the future and knew this would their final time together.

So she'd declined Cash's offer, and look where her heart had led her.

Yearning. Aching. Anticipating.

"Tell me," he whispered.

"I don't want to."

Bahh-ling. She tried to break free to look at her phone, but he wouldn't let go.

"Tell me."

His thumb brushed the fine hairs where her cheekbone met her ear. Gooseflesh pimpled her arms, her legs, her breasts.

Deep down she knew that he wouldn't leave until she answered him. Damn stubborn man.

When she tried to sit back, his hand on her neck tightened, holding her in place.

"Sugar gives me a rush."

He raised a brow.

"*Much* more than the average person. I get animated and chatty and can make an all-around fool of myself." When he said nothing and just studied her with unnerving thoroughness, she continued. "After you consume sugar, your body produces dopamine—a natural opioid for the brain. My body is very, very good at producing—"

A large finger pressed against her lips.

"You didn't want to have a reaction in front of me."

Throat tight, she shook her head.

"Why?" He removed his finger. "Why would a sugar rush bother you more than some of the other crazy situations we've been in together?"

An unfamiliar shyness took hold of her, and she fixed

her attention on the tiny whiskers starting to cover his chin. "Those other things happened before you ate my mom's bread pudding."

Something not quite human rumbled in his chest. Her only warning before he took her mouth with his. *Took.* Not captured. Not caressed. Not covered. *Took.*

She allowed her mouth, her tongue, her hands to flow with his, giving as he demanded. A different kind of urgency than the one that normally haunted her nerves tingled in her bones. The ticker tape of questions in her mind slowed to a crawl.

Both his hands came up to cup her jaw, as if it were the most fragile piece of Waterford crystal. Her body began to crave a greater connection. Crave something she couldn't identify.

When he slowly sat back in his seat, bringing her with him, the roar of an engine stopped him short.

She broke away like a guilty teenager. "Who's that?"

A low, pounding bass and howls of masculine laughter carried across the lot and through the Jeep's open windows, then the driver stomped on the accelerator.

"A truckload of trouble," he said.

The white pickup spun in a circle, its frame tilting to the right and wheels smoking.

Coen opened the passenger door and stepped out.

Bahh-ling.

She fumbled to find her phone. "Where are you going?"

"To teach a few young men how to respect private property."

"Coen, no." Her fingers wrapped around her phone as he shut the door. "They'll run you over!"

"I know how to deal with drunken teenagers," he said, rounding the front of her car.

A bottle shattered against the hard pavement, not far from his location.

Anger flared in her veins, and she jumped out and ran to his side. "Watch it, asshole!"

"Get back in the vehicle, Riley," Coen demanded.

"Those boys nearly hit you with that bottle."

"They're just being idiots. They haven't even spotted us yet."

"Why did they throw the bottle then?"

"It was tossed, not thrown."

She glanced at her surroundings and realized the tall parking lot lights didn't illuminate this end. Her dark gray Jeep blended into the landscape.

"But surely their headlights..."

Coen's stillness froze the words on her tongue. He watched the pickup for several seconds. The intensity of his observation put her technique to shame.

"Do not move from this spot," he ordered before shooting toward the revelers.

"Coen!"

He ignored her warning. Barreling toward the truck, he jumped onto the driver side running board and reached into the cab. The laughter inside ceased, and the truck slammed to a halt.

Coen's position on the running board didn't budge. For several seconds, he stood there speaking to the guys in a calm tone of voice, too soft for her to hear. He didn't seem fazed by their occasional protest to whatever he was telling them.

She itched to hear his conversation, but she remained rooted in place, unable to take her attention off his broad shoulders. When he finally stepped down, he held a carton of beer in his left hand.

How had he managed to get them to hand over their liquor? She shook her head in amazement.

Bahh-ling.

Crisis over, she peered down to check her text messages. When she pulled up the tiny image, tears sprang to her eyes.

31

COEN SHOOK HIS HEAD AT THE DEPARTING TRUCK. HAD HE
ever been that young and stupid?

Yes.

Turning back to Riley, he switched mental gears. He
didn't know whether to be grateful to those boys for interrupting him and Riley or pissed off.

He hadn't meant for things to get so heated between
them. But the moment their lips had touched, he'd plunged
into a vortex of sensation. It had been a long while since
he'd experienced such raw desire. How far would he have
taken things if the boys hadn't appeared?

He glanced down at the mostly full carton of beer.
"Guess I know what I'll be drinking tonight."

When she said nothing, he peered through the gloom to
where she stood—where he'd left her—reading something
on her phone. The light from the screen shone on her face.

On the tears streaming down her cheeks.

An image flashed across his mind's eye, blinding him for
a second. He shook his head until Riley came back into
view.

"What's wrong?" he asked, picking up his pace.

She lifted regret-filled eyes to his.

Regret.

A tremor took hold of his knees and snaked its way into his gut, chest, arms, and fingers. Glass shattered nearby. Screams echoed in his ears, blinding him in their intensity, sending him back into his living nightmare. Sending him back to the mountains of Ecuador, to a jungle-enshrouded encampment.

Crack!

The wild-eyed guard stormed over to Coen's side and screamed in his ear. "Call!" For the thousandth time, his nail-bitten thumb hovered over the phone's dial pad.

He ignored him.

With his head strapped to a high-backed chair and ropes securing his wrists and ankles, he could do nothing to help Kendra, and he sure as hell wasn't calling his commanding officer. So he stared straight ahead, at Kendra, as she regained her senses after the bastard's knock-out blow.

A lone guard remained inside the shanty after one of his comrades threw open the door fifteen minutes ago, rubbing his privates and bragging about the new truckload of *chocha* that had arrived. The room had emptied, leaving a young, pissed-off guard with far too much untrained testosterone pumping through his body.

Eyes burning, he watched Kendra slowly lift her head. It lolled on her neck as though it was too heavy to hold upright. The skin beneath her left eye was split open to the bone. Blood streamed down her cheek and neck.

The guard returned to Kendra's side, grabbed a hunk of hair, and yanked back her head. His murderous gaze remained on Coen. "If you do not call," he said, swerving in and out of English, "she dies."

Her black diamond gaze flicked to him, and he saw regret flit across her features before she turned back to her punisher. *"Spineless prick!"* she wheezed, spitting in the son of a bitch's face.

Swiping the spittle from his eyes, the guard slammed a fist into her jaw, sending her, chair and all, flying backward. He followed, delivering blow after blow after blow.

When she ceased moving, the guard paused, his chest heaving. He glanced at the door, then back down at Kendra. His anger transformed into predation, and he sent Coen a sly look before removing a knife at his waist and bending to cut Kendra's restraints.

He unbuckled his belt.

Coen's arms strained against their bindings. He could no longer feel his fingers, and a punishing pulse pounded in his swollen right eye, his split upper lip, his bruised jaw. After three days of constant torture, he'd learned not to show any emotion, any *rage,* at their attacks on Kendra.

He'd made the mistake once, after observing them burning and beating her without cease for nearly twelve hours. Rather than redirecting their attention toward him, his outburst had stoked a depravity beyond any imagining.

Bound and unblemished, he'd been forced to watch them wrestle her to a filthy pallet in the corner and, one by one, they'd violated her.

Kendra's war cry shook him back to the present. Wielding the guard's hunting knife, she attacked, murder in her eyes. The first slash of the blade sliced open his cheek in precisely the same location as the gash on hers. Her second slash laid open the contents of his stomach. The third slash nearly severed his head from his neck.

The rebel dropped to the ground, and Kendra straddled his lifeless body, stabbing over and over and over.

Coen kept his voice calm, almost soothing. "Kendra, my bindings." His gaze shot to the door, wondering how long they had before the others returned.

She gave no indication that she heard him. "Kendra, cut the rope," he commanded.

Her body spasmed, and she swung her blood-spattered face toward him.

"We don't have much time, Corporal. Release me. Now."

On unsteady legs, she strode to his side and bent down to cut through his restraints.

The door banged against the wall, and three smiling faces appeared. Then their dark gazes took in Kendra and their fallen comrade. Fury replaced the afterglow of their prior activity.

After freeing his head and wrists, Kendra whispered in his ear and launched herself at the guards.

"Kendra, wait—!"

A hand grabbed his shoulder and yelled his name. His world exploded around him.

Coen came out of the darkness of his memory swinging. His forearm connected with something hard yet fragile. The sound of a cutoff yelp snapped the line tethering him to the past.

His eyes cleared to find Riley leaning against her Jeep, holding her wrist.

What had he done?

"R-Riley." He heaved her name past a throat swollen with remorse. He stared at her wrist. "I'm sorry."

She eased away from her vehicle. "It's my fault. I startled

you." Still holding her arm to her chest, she met his gaze. "You were screaming... I didn't know what to do... I tried to—"

"I'm sorry," he said again, interrupting her explanation.

No one knew what to do for him. Not the military, not the professionals, and certainly not an ethnobotanist.

Humiliation burned his neck, his ears, his eyes. He had to get her to safety, then crawl back to his tent. Away from people.

"Let me take you to the hospital."

She glanced down at her wrist, as if surprised to find it against her chest. Fingering it in several places, she tried an exploratory rotation.

"I'm fine," she said. "Nothing's broken."

Closing his eyes, he released a low, shuddering breath. When he opened them again, she stood before him, a hand lifted toward his cheek.

He jerked away, nearly falling in his haste.

Concern clouded her features as she lowered her hand to her side. "Coen—"

"Why were you crying?" he choked out.

She blinked at his sudden change of topic. Her hand shot to her back pocket. When it came away empty, she whirled in a circle, searching.

"What are you looking for?"

"My phone. Do you see it?"

He spotted it several feet away and bent to pick it up. Cracks splintered the screen.

"Oh no." Riley ripped her phone out of his hand. *"No, no, no, no."*

"I'll buy you a new one."

Tears filled her eyes again as she looked up at him. "Do you think the text messages are gone?"

Technology guru, he was not. "I doubt it. Your provider should be able to transfer all your data to a new phone." At least he hoped so.

"I gotta go." She marched back to her Jeep.

"Where?"

"To get a new phone."

"Whoa, whoa, whoa." He caught the door before she shut it. "It's past ten. None of the stores will be open."

Her body deflated and her head dropped onto the headrest.

Crouching at her side, he asked, "Did you receive bad news?"

Nodding, she swallowed hard and squeezed her eyes shut as if speaking and seeing were too difficult.

He debated his next move. His actions had caused her both mental and physical harm. Leaving her here while he disappeared into the woods was out of the question. And she didn't appear to be in the right frame of mind to drive herself home.

"Scoot over, I'll take you home."

Without a single word of protest, she shifted to the passenger seat and buckled herself in. Alarm kicked his guilt to the curb.

They rode in silence. The same kind of thick, deafening silence that falls over the land after a mortar strikes and all the debris has returned to the ground.

Minutes ticked by, then Riley stirred. She lifted her head and squared her shoulders. Her knee began to bounce.

Her brilliant mind had broken through whatever grief had consumed her back at the center. And now it was analyzing, plotting out a plan of attack.

What had been in the text she'd received?

When he made to turn in to the farm's entrance, she spoke for the first time. "No, take me home. Please."

"Where's home?"

"In town. I'm staying at Randi's house until I find a place of my own."

"How's that working out?" His small talk skills were rusty, but keeping her talking about everyday issues seemed like a good way to keep her mind off other things.

"Take a right at the next intersection. What do you mean?"

"Living with your cousin's fiancée?"

"Randi isn't there. She moved into Britt's cabin several months ago. Once they're married, I think Randi will sell her bungalow."

"To you?"

She chuckled, though he detected no humor in the sound.

"No bank would lend me the money. Not until I get a stable job."

"Your job at the center isn't stable?"

"The third house on the left." She pointed to a one-story bungalow. "Once I finish surveying the conservation area, my contract expires."

"So make it an extralong survey."

"I've thought about it."

Pulling into the driveway, he killed the engine and exited. Determined not to make this an awkward situation, he had already planned out his next several steps. Walk her to the door, check the inside, and head home. It wouldn't take him more than thirty or forty minutes to hoof it back.

He sailed through the first step and part of the second before his plan disintegrated into ash.

32

———

THE MOMENT RILEY ENTERED THE BUNGALOW, SHE HEADED straight for her bedroom. Flicking on the light, she all but dove for her tablet resting on her nightstand. She unplugged it and went through the process to get to her messaging app.

"Come on, come on."

"Do you mind if I join you?"

She glanced over her shoulder and found Coen hovering just outside her bedroom. Although her mind was still on the text, she felt a trickle of heat work its way up her neck. If it had been anyone else, she would've teased him about his virtue being safe, but her words clung to the back of her throat at the thought of all that solid muscle entering her bedroom. She waved him inside.

With no other options in the room, he would have to sit next to her on the bed. Good. He needed to get past what happened in the parking lot. If she hadn't been stupid and touched him, the strike would never have happened. Although painful, it was a good lesson learned. She wouldn't do it again.

Keeping her attention on the screen, she waited for the bed to shift beneath his weight. The sensation never came. Instead, a pair of cowboy boots appeared in her peripheral vision.

When her list of messages finally displayed, she almost cried with relief—and renewed pain.

"Everything okay?" Coen said behind her.

"Yes and no." She could get to the last text message, but she couldn't bring herself to open it.

"You got an upsetting text?"

"Yes," she said, unable to take her eyes off the name in the sidebar. "From someone I worked with in Costa Rica."

"Would it help to talk about it?"

Yes. She wanted to share this burden with someone. With Coen. But she couldn't get his stricken expression out of her head. Seeing her tears had triggered a memory. A horrible one, involving Kendra. The same name that he'd called out the other night.

The sound—like a wounded animal—would haunt her for years. What god-awful thing had he survived? Had Kendra?

She wouldn't add her situation to the horrible weight that already forced him to live in a tent, far away from humankind.

Clicking off her tablet, she set it aside. "Thank you for asking, but I reacted from shock and then concern that the text had been lost." She gave him a tired smile. "Other than needing to replenish my body's salt supply, I'm back to my old self."

He tilted his head to the right, assessing her.

With her nerves still raw, she couldn't tell if she'd managed to wipe away the worry from her brow. She needed to change the subject. Get his thoughts off her and onto him.

"Would you say that you're a good lover?" She blinked. Where had *that* come from?

His head snapped back as if she'd slapped him. "What did you say?"

You started it, Kingston, better go with it, or he'll think you're a crackhead.

"Good lover? Are you?"

"Looking for a distraction? Or trying to shut me up?"

He had distracted her in one way or another since the first moment she glimpsed his tormented eyes and well-toned body. No boy in high school and no man in college had ever tempted her thoughts away from her studies or work long enough to envision tangled limbs and sweaty backs.

But Coen had.

Allowing herself a small smile, she said, "A little of both, I suppose."

When he didn't return the gesture, she forced out a self-deprecating chuckle and wiped her sweaty palms on her jeans before rising. Nothing like making a fool of herself in front of a gorgeous guy. Hadn't she decided he'd had enough to deal with?

He caught her arm in a light grip, then immediately released her.

She neither snapped nor spoke. She barely breathed. The ache in her heart was fracturing her from the inside out.

"Riley?"

Looking into his eyes was out of the question. God only knew what he'd observe on her face—embarrassment, confusion, sadness, fear... *need.*

"Don't lose that spine of steel now." The back of his finger caressed her face, from her cheek down to her chin. He nudged her head around until those rock-solid gemstones feathered over her mouth, her nose, her eyes. "What was in that text?"

"There's no need for you to sort through my baggage." *You have enough of your own.*

"I'm a good sorter."

Riley shook her head. She couldn't. She couldn't do it to him.

"Don't look away." He released her arm and cradled her face in both hands. "It'll take more than a text to break me."

Her eyes widened.

"Ah, so that is why you're being stubborn. I wasn't sure."

Shock gave way to annoyance. "You've made no secret about why you're in Steele Ridge. I don't want to impact your recovery."

"Recovery?"

"Or whatever you call it. I assume you're trying to work through some things—or forget them. Maybe both."

"I am. But that doesn't mean I can't help a friend."

"Didn't we establish that we're not friends?"

His thumb grazed the rim of her lower lip. "A determination you made, not me."

"You barely know me."

"I know enough to recognize you're deserving of my help."

"Do friends kiss?"

Amusement softened his eyes. "Some do."

The unexpected intimacy in the Jeep sat between them. Repeat or regret?

If she'd had a clock on her wall, she could've logged the agonizing seconds that followed in the wake of his answer.

He didn't elaborate. Just continued gazing at her while his thumb tantalized, but never sated, her lower lip.

Anticipation always destroyed what little patience she harbored. Finally she caved. "Are you going to kiss me?"

Something warm curled around one corner of his mouth. "Are you going to share your bad news?"

Emboldened, she placed her palms on his chest. "Later," she said. "Otherwise you'll have to contend with my runny nose."

Her hands skimmed over the hard planes of his pecs. *Perfection.*

As if mesmerized by her own movements, she followed her fingers while they glided up his throat and skimmed over his hair. Silken, cool strands tickled her palms.

Closing her eyes, she lifted up onto her toes, preparing to meet his kiss.

But he didn't budge. Not one little centimeter.

She cracked open one eye. "Did you forget how this was done?"

"I don't think so."

"Bad neck?"

"No."

"Foul breath?"

"God, I hope not."

"Not interested?" It was her turn not to budge or breathe or even blink.

His hands slid down her shoulders and arms, finding her waist. He drew her in closer. So close her nipples grazed his chest and his hard length nestled into her lower stomach.

"Answer enough?"

"Then what g-gives?" she asked on a shuddering breath.

"I'm waiting on your promise."

"What promise?"

"The one that ensures you'll share the details of the text that made you cry."

"It doesn't feel right." Her heels dropped to the floor, and she released him.

Strong fingers grasped her forearms, urging her fingers back into his hair. "It feels exactly right."

Unable to stop herself, she massaged his scalp, eliciting a deep, satisfied groan from him.

"Promise me," he said, rolling his head deeper into her grasp.

"Okay." She squeezed his skull. "Now kiss me."

It happened so fast. Her hands went into free fall when he dipped to claim her mouth.

His initial kiss was swift and hard. But then his mouth became more deliberate. Each movement was designed to sweep her doubt to the curb, leaving only pure pleasure behind.

When his tongue slipped between her lips, she increased the pressure of her body against his. His embrace felt like a sun-warmed blanket. She wanted to burrow deeper into him.

She slipped her hands beneath his shirt, splaying her fingers wide as she glided her palms up both sides of his back. Then she made the same movement over the ridge of his spine.

A few inches later, smooth flesh turned mottled and hard.

He stiffened at her touch, and her exploration halted. She drew away from his unresponsive lips and took in his granite-hard features, his burning eyes that refused to look at her.

Sliding her hands down to his waist, she circled him and grasped the edges of his shirt. "May I?"

"It's not pretty."

Taking his quiet words as consent, she slowly lifted his shirt until a landscape of horrific burns and jagged scars was revealed. Something shattered in her chest.

The pain. Oh, dear God, the pain he must have endured.

Her dinner began to roil and work its way back up her throat. She set trembling fingers against her lips, swallowing back the anguish, the *rage*.

Who could do this to another human being? Who could be so evil?

On a logical level, she knew such people existed. But this... This was the first time she'd witnessed the result of such malevolence in a person.

Realizing that she'd been studying him too long, she glanced up. Shoulders locked and fists hard, he stared straight ahead. Right into the large mirror that hung over her dresser. Their angle was such that he could see the horror on her face.

Steel etched into the column of his neck, his jaw, his eyes.

"Does it still hurt?" she asked.

"Not really."

"What does that mean?"

He stepped away and wrenched his shirt back in place. "It means just what I said."

Calm, calm, calm... She replayed the mantra over and over in her mind. He already struggled with memories haunting his dreams. Having her gawk at his scars probably dug up all sorts of unwanted emotions.

"I'm sorry, Coen. I shouldn't have pried."

With his back still turned to her, he propped his hands

on his hips and dropped his chin to his chest. He stared at the floor for so long. She considered going to him, wrapping her arms around his solid waist and pressing her cheek against his tortured flesh.

But she stood unmoving and unsure. She thought back to her conversation with Way. Had Coen's post-traumatic stress turned into a disorder? Isolation, nightmares, short temper, flashbacks. Symptoms of stress? Or the onset of a disorder? Or a combat soldier assimilating back into civilian life?

Was the incident he kept reliving ruling his world now? Would he be able to return to duty? Did he even want to?

"The burn scars no longer hurt," he said in a low, rough-edged voice. "But they're still sensitive and can tingle."

Had he been a prisoner of war? He must have been. It's the only thing that made sense. She wanted to ask, wanted to know who'd caused him such pain. But she'd already upset him enough for one evening.

"When you're ready, I would like to hear the story."

In the silence that followed, she knew he would never share that much of himself with her. The realization hurt more than it should.

"The text I received was from Camilla, my assistant in Costa Rica." She sat back down on the bed and opened Camilla's message. "She sent me three links... and a warning."

He scrubbed his hands over his face a few times as if to cleanse away the past few minutes. When he finally slid his attention to her, she held out her tablet.

"What kind of warning?"

"I'm not sure. Maybe you can help me decipher it."

Coen bent his attention to the message and read, "You're next. Run."

33

"What does she mean, 'You're next'?"

"Open the links."

Coen tapped the first link. An internet page popped up, then shifted to a social media account. A picture of a dark-haired man stood before a copse of towering trees. He wore a big smile and an enormous backpack.

The caption below his photo read "Earlier this week, the world lost a beautiful spirit. While hiking in the mountains of his beloved Amalfi Coast, Leo fell to his death, doing what he loved most."

He glanced up. "An obituary?"

She nodded. "Next link."

The second URL opened into an actual obituary in the online newspaper. A thirty-one-year-old female had died while tending her garden.

"Lauren did everything right," she said into the silence. "There's no way she died of a heart attack."

"How can you be sure? People are struck down by freak, unknown medical conditions all the time."

"I might have been able to accept that line of reasoning," she nodded to the tablet, "if not for the others."

"These are all death announcements?"

"Yes."

"You know them all?"

"Yes."

"How?"

"We all worked together on Project Endurance." She swiped at a tear that tracked its way down her cheek.

You're next. Run.

He opened the links again. "They all died within a couple of weeks."

"Hence Camilla's warning."

Her shoulders rounded, and her gaze dropped to her clenched hands. "They were brilliant scientists from all over the world. Now they're gone."

Handing the tablet back to her, he eased himself down onto the bed. He wanted to embrace her, comfort her. But after he'd lashed out at her, he didn't think she'd welcome his touch. So he did the next best thing. He kept vigil while she grieved.

"What are you doing?" he asked.

"Responding to Camilla." She tapped out a message. "I need to make sure she's okay and see what else she knows."

"Do you know where she might be?"

"I'm assuming she's still in Costa Rica."

"Any idea of who would want to kill your team?"

She set the tablet on the nightstand. "No clue."

"Tell me about Project Endurance."

"Endurance was my ticket to being someone special, someone who would have had a hand in helping thousands of people. And it was supposed to launch my career." She anchored the heels of her shoes on the wooden plank holding the bed's box spring and propped her elbows on her upraised knees. She dropped her head in her hands. "But all it did was paste a big F on my academic record."

The loss, the defeat, the acceptance in her voice compelled him to place a hand on her back. He made big, sweeping circles. "You're not a failure, Riley."

"You can't strip *me* from the process. Somewhere along the way, I got it wrong. The interviews, the analysis, the observation—I don't know. But at some point, I confused *treatment* for *cure.*" She steepled her fingers together and pressed them to her upper lip. "I killed my career before it ever got underway."

"Another opportunity will come along."

"Not after word of my failed project gets out. Ethnobotany is a small community."

"People have short memories. Concentrate on your survey work for the next few months, then put some feelers out."

"I'm using about a tenth of my brain."

"I thought you enjoyed surveying the conservation area."

"I do. But it's not a career or what I spent years in college training for."

"Does the work help Britt?"

"It will, once all the data is compiled."

"Then you're not a failure."

"You don't understand." She surged off the bed and prowled the narrow space between the dresser and where he sat. "I'm meant to do more than count plants."

"And you will, when the time is right." He hooked an arm around her waist, halting her. Twisting her to face him, he rested a hand on her hip. "Don't let one failed project derail you."

She placed her hands on his forearms. "Endurance was

my life for several years, then it wasn't. Just when I was starting to put Costa Rica behind me, I'm being thrown back into it. But it's a version I don't recognize."

Tightening his grip on her hips, he urged her even closer. With him sitting, she had a few inches of height on him. Yet he could feel the soft wisp of her breath on his face.

One of her small hands lifted to cover his jaw. "My world is spinning on a precipice of something I don't understand."

"I won't let you fall."

"What if I drag you down with me?"

"Not gonna happen."

She set her forehead against his; her fingers sifted through the short hairs at the base of his neck. "You don't need this. You've seen and lived through enough conflict to last ten lifetimes."

He brushed a hand over her head. "Maybe none as worthy as this one."

All it took was a slight tilt of his chin to cover her lips. He pressed his tongue into her mouth, and she accepted the invasion. Toyed with it. Heat speared down his chest and threaded into his groin. He kept the kiss slow and hot and thorough, savoring the silken texture of her tongue, the sweet taste of her essence.

Easing back, he lowered them both to the bed, never breaking contact, never letting her go. She shifted until her knees were braced on the outside of his hips. Her hot core hovered over his straining cock. The scent of her desire roared through him like an ancient call to action.

But tonight was about comfort, not taking her hard and fast until they both lay panting and sated.

Her beautiful, curious mouth swept over his cheek to his ear. She teased the sensitive lobe with her tongue and teeth, sending a clenching ache to his balls. She laved a slow trail down to his neck, where her teeth scraped over his throbbing pulse. At each pleasure point, she whispered something beneath her breath. Too low for him to hear.

His cock bucked, and his fingertips dug into her hips, mooring his control to those ten points of contact. If he touched her in the way he wanted, he would unleash on her.

It had been too long since he'd had sex, too long since he'd allowed himself to feel anything at all.

She sat up, and her bottom cocooned the length of him.

"Ah, fuck." The words burst out of his mouth as a rush of pure need speared through him. He thrust against her warm center, wishing he was deep inside.

Lust fogged his brain for several seconds, so he didn't immediately key in on her rigid stillness. When her motionless statement finally broke through the haze, he cracked his eyes open and found her staring at him, wide-eyed and... unsure.

He studied her, taking the time to settle his raging heart and to gather up the fragments of his wits. Everything crystallized into a single realization.

"You've never been with a man."

34

IF A BLACK HOLE HAD OPENED UP BESIDE HER, RILEY WOULD have jumped in, headfirst.

Coen had somehow figured out she was a virgin. Already his features were hardening back into his warrior's mask.

What had she done—or not done—to give herself away?

The book she'd gulped down last night—*A Man's Top 8 Erogenous Zones*—had sworn the scalp, earlobes, and neck were great places to get the party started. But when she'd sat up to gauge her level of success, Coen had let out a gut-wrenching noise, as if she'd hurt him.

Had she nipped his neck too hard?

Humiliation, stark and burning, disintegrated the nervous thrum that had guided her thoughts and body moments before. She whipped off the bed and stormed into the bathroom.

One look at her scarlet cheeks had her turning on the cold water and splashing it on her face. She grabbed the hand towel from the rack and blotted her skin dry.

Her arms shook, legs trembled, everything from the

inside out was vibrating. She dropped onto the toilet and forced calm into her body.

For the love of God, she couldn't even please a man without mucking it up. Not even after reading a step-by-step instructional manual. Maybe she should have watched a video instead.

She'd been so hopeful that Coen was the one. The one to break through her mental barrier that wouldn't release her to pleasure. Other than the brief glimpse she had in her Jeep, no guy had ever been able to distract her long enough to keep her thoughts on him and not on the hundred other things that sailed through her mind at any given moment. The ticker tape had almost stopped tonight until she saw the look of pain on his face—followed by his yell.

Through her self-recrimination, a foreign scent filled her nose. She sniffed, then sniffed harder. Her gaze dropped to her crotch.

When she shifted, the sharp, musky scent intensified—and that's when she noticed the moisture between her legs.

"Riley?"

Coen's low, gentle voice jerked her upright.

"I'll be out in a minute."

"I didn't mean to hurt—"

"Give me a minute."

She wrenched her jeans and panties off, tossing the latter into the wicker hamper. After cleaning herself up, she pulled on a pair of yoga pants she found hanging behind the door.

A glance in the mirror told her she'd managed to get ninety percent of her swagger back, but the pink still tingeing her cheeks shone like battle scars.

Hand on the doorknob, she inhaled a bracing breath before pushing herself back into hell.

The inferno, all two hundred plus pounds of raw male, waited for her just outside the door.

With his arms folded and feet braced shoulder-width apart, he gave her body a frank assessment with one thorough sweep up to her eyes and down to her toes.

Without conscious thought, she mimicked his stance and forced herself to hold his stare. Although not happy about how she'd killed such an amazing moment, she wouldn't apologize for her inexperience.

"Are you all right?" he asked.

"Of course."

"Things got a little... out of hand."

Out of hand. Soul-sucking heat crept up her neck again. Unable to hold eye contact any longer, she strode over to the tablet to see if Camilla had responded, before heading into the living room.

"What are you doing?" he asked.

She located her keys and purse on the couch, where she'd hurled them earlier in her rush to get to her tablet. "Driving you back to the center."

"I'm not going anywhere."

"There's no reason for you to stay."

"I disagree."

"Coen—"

"You're in danger, Riley."

Her chest heaved on a relieved breath. *This* she could deal with.

"I'm going to share the information with Maggie tomorrow."

"Which leaves you vulnerable tonight."

She thought back to the times when she had the sense that someone was watching her. All creations of her imagination? Or preludes to her death?

Either way, she wasn't sharing this space with him. The bungalow wasn't dinky, but it wasn't big enough for the both of them.

"I'll make sure all the doors and windows are locked."

"And I'll take the couch."

"No." An irrational fear took root in the pit of her stomach. She needed to get him out of her space.

"Riley, I'm not arguing about this. Your sister would blow my nuts off if I left you alone after what happened tonight."

"There's no reason for someone to want to kill me."

"What about your colleagues? Did someone have reason to kill them?"

"How would I know? Just because I worked with them, it doesn't mean I knew their secrets."

"Have any of your college friends or other colleagues— outside the Costa Rican project—died?"

She shifted her attention away, looking at everything and nothing at all. "Not that I'm aware of, but I wouldn't have known about these three if not for Camilla."

"We'll sort it out tomorrow. Tonight I'm taking watch."

Part of her, the logical part, settled at the knowledge that Coen would protect her through the night. Once she'd gotten past the initial shock of losing so many friends, her mind had stalled on what all this meant to her until Coen started picking through the pieces. Then the danger had become clear—and terrifying.

But the other part of her, the feminine part, feared Coen more than a faceless murderer. Feared how quickly things had advanced between them. Feared how much she enjoyed being near him. Feared how little time he had left before rejoining his unit.

Determination hardened his eyes, and Riley recognized that she wouldn't be able to budge him off his course. She wasn't even sure she wanted to. What a muckety-muck of a muck.

Not bothering to veil her displeasure, she marched into her bedroom and fished out a pillow, sheet, and light blanket. She returned to the living room and handed over the bundle.

His fingers brushed hers, and when her eyes flashed up to his, she knew he'd made contact on purpose. She just didn't know why and couldn't summon the brain power to figure it out.

"There's another bathroom attached to the guest room." She pointed down the hall, across from her bedroom. "Everything you need should be inside."

If it had been anyone else, she would have attempted to coax him into the spare bedroom. But he wanted the couch, so he'd get the damned couch.

"The fridge is stocked, too, in case you get the midnight munchies."

Now she was babbling. Time to split.

"Good night, Coen."

Before she could close her bedroom door, he said, "Riley."

She peered out and found him in the same place, holding his bundle of bedding. Something about the sight made her throat close.

"We need to talk about what happened."

"I know, but not tonight."

She closed the door and pressed her forehead against the cool wooden panel. A barrier. A solid barrier to stop her from running into that room, into his arms, and finishing what she'd screwed up the first time.

Muckety-muck. Muck.

35

Unable to sleep, Coen prowled the shadowed bungalow, checking windows and doors, peering around window treatments, and raking shaking fingers through his hair.

The sensation of Riley's tongue on his skin seared his mind. Every flick, every stroke, every hot manipulation made him forget all the reasons he shouldn't make love to her.

Would she welcome a casual, no-commitment relationship until he was called up for his next mission? Would there be a next mission? Would the colonel take one look at him and see the demons that still seethed beneath his flesh.

The incident with Riley in the parking lot had made him realize he wasn't going to be able to conquer the aftereffects of Ecuador on his own.

The other night, Riley's voice had soothed him, allowed him to rest, uninterrupted, for a few hours. Maybe he should give the Yoga Nidra a try. After Reid had mentioned it, he had looked up the practice and instructor. Reid had been right. Nidra appeared to be more about calming the spirit than tangling up the body.

Maybe it was time to try something new. Because the bullshit sandwich he'd been feeding himself had gone rank.

Thirty days. He'd been given thirty days to come to terms with what happened in Ecuador, yet he felt no closer to normal than when he'd hammered in the first tent stake.

Serving was all he knew. The structure, camaraderie, and sense of purpose sustained him in ways civilian life couldn't. But lately he'd felt something was missing. A missing link he'd never noticed before.

Closing his eyes, he freed his senses to take in his surroundings. Although he detected a hint of jasmine, the scent was older, less prominent than the sweet tang of orange blossoms. The muscles in his chest loosened, allowing him to take a deeper inhalation, to fill every dark pocket inside him with Riley's essence.

He should have thanked her for helping him through his night terrors the other evening, but he sensed she didn't want to discuss it. For his sake? Or hers?

Scrubbing his face with one hand, he wished he could brush away the growing ache to be with Riley as easily.

And there was the rub. He didn't want to be rid of her. In fact, the more he was in her presence, the more he wanted to be there.

It was more than his protective instincts kicking in, though they were flaring off the charts.

Long before he'd failed his team, he'd been plagued by a void he couldn't explain. A void that had been there for far too long.

When he was with Riley, that hollowness disappeared. The darkness abated.

Her fearlessness and intelligence and laughter and annoying questions—he wanted them all. Every day. Every evening. Every minute.

As the realization of what all that meant penetrated, he turned toward her closed bedroom door, heart pounding.

Shit.

36

RILEY STARED AT HER BIG SISTER, WAITING FOR THE EXPLOSION.

For ten minutes, Maggie had sat quietly listening to her tale. But a volcano of activity stirred beneath the sheriff's calm façade. Most wouldn't notice the subtle shift in her sister's features. Only those, like her, who'd tested her sister's patience on more than one occasion would recognize the signs of all hell breaking loose.

"Let me get this straight," Maggie said. "You received a text last night from your former Costa Rican assistant that provided several links. Links directing you to three dead colleagues. Colleagues who worked on the same project as you in Central America. And this assistant hasn't responded to your messages." She tapped a fingernail on her desk. "And you waited until this morning to tell me."

Riley dared not glance at the man who stood sentinel behind her. He'd tried to get her to contact Maggie last night, but she hadn't wanted to deal with this issue, especially on top of her botched seduction.

True to his word, Coen had kept watch over her last night. However, instead of sleeping on the couch, he'd made a pallet in front of her bedroom door. A fact she'd learned in the middle of the night when she'd tried to sneak out of her room to fetch her forgotten phone.

After tossing and turning and checking her text messages for hours, she'd finally called defeat and decided to get her phone to see if it was completely destroyed. All she had to do was tiptoe into the living room, grab her purse off the table, and skedaddle back to her bedroom. One minute tops.

It had been a great plan until she'd opened her door and tripped over a human boulder.

Coen had caught her before she'd face-planted into the opposite wall. She'd been so stunned by the whole ordeal that she never retrieved her phone. Using her tablet, she'd worked long into the night.

She'd only been asleep for a couple of hours when the mouthwatering aroma of bacon, eggs, and toast wafted beneath her door. The damn man had made her breakfast. It had been good. Real good.

And if all that hadn't been awkward and sweet enough, he'd insisted on accompanying her to the sheriff's department. To his credit, he hadn't said a word beyond greeting Maggie and asking about the poachers and rental car. Right Flank still hadn't given up his friends, but she'd found out that the Audi had been rented to a Vince Henley. But the clerk who'd checked him out had only been on the job two days and had forgotten to make a photocopy of his driver's license.

Since then, Coen had stood at attention near her side—spine straight, chin high, and hands clasped behind his back.

A few days ago, time could have been kept by the sameness of her life. Not anymore. Now her world's axis had tilted and swayed and damn neared toppled onto its ass.

Maggie snapped her fingers in Riley's face. "Stay with me here."

Riley rewound the last minute until she landed on Maggie's question. "That about sums it up."

"Did you get the text before or after Mom and Dad's dinner?"

"After. When I took Coen home."

"Do you see anything wrong with your decision not to call me right away? Or am I playing common sense tutor again?"

She loved her sister. She really did. Except for moments like this. When she spoke to her like a mother, rather than a sister. Coen witnessing Maggie's dressing-down made it all the worse.

"I made sure she was safe last night," Coen said into the silence.

Maggie slowly turned to Coen, one eyebrow levitating into her forehead. "I don't think I caught how you came to know my sister?"

She groaned. "Mags, no."

"It's a simple question."

"There's nothing simple about your questions. They always have a hidden agenda."

"I helped her save some trapped kits, and she's teaching me about propagation."

"And now you're her protector?"

"Yes."

"No," Riley said, cutting him a sharp glance. "He just had the misfortune of being around when I got the text. I don't want him involved in this anymore."

The boulder shifted behind her, though he directed his

next words to Maggie. "I have eight years of combat experience and nothing better to do at the moment."

Maggie's features molded into hard, uncompromising lines. All sheriff. "Why are you on leave, Sergeant Monroe?"

"Maggie," Riley exclaimed. "That's none of your business."

Her sister's gaze didn't budge from Coen's.

Silence ticked by like the echo of a second hand on a grandfather clock sitting in a cavernous entryway.

"My team's last mission went wrong. Three were killed right away, and the other two were tortured for several days before"—he swallowed—"returning to the States."

Riley peered up, studying his profile.

"I'm sorry for your loss," Maggie said.

Riley's burning eyes shifted to Maggie's desk and stayed there. He'd been tortured and witnessed the destruction of his entire team. She knew enough about the close ties service members developed with their teammates to have some sense of the depth of his devastation. Doubly so if he'd been the lead on the mission and its failure or success rested on his shoulders.

"How long have you been in Steele Ridge?"

"Eighteen days, ma'am."

"Thirty-day leave?"

"Yes, ma'am."

Maggie's assessing gaze tore from Coen and rested on her for an uncomfortable set of seconds that felt more like a hundred. Then her sister stood to address Coen. "Thank you for watching over Riley last night." A note of finality echoed in her next words. "But I'll take it from here. You go settle back into your leave."

Coen's attention leaned into her as if waiting for her to contradict Maggie's edict. She couldn't—wouldn't—try to change her sister's mind. With all the serious crap he was already trying to manage, he didn't need to add her pile on top. Thank God her sharp-witted sister had recognized that fact too.

"I'll have one of my deputies drive you to wherever you need to go."

"In case I lose it," he said, venom dripping from every word, "he'll be able to put me down like a damn dog? I don't think so."

"That's not what she meant," Riley said, twisting around.

If eyes could shoot flames, she would've been reduced to a crispy critter.

"Tell the sheriff about the note." He stalked out of Maggie's office, anger seething off him in dark waves.

Her eyes widened, and she belatedly shot out of her chair to rush after him.

Maggie intercepted her. "Let him go."

"Mags, he's been nothing but kind to me. I can't let him walk away with this between us."

"Sit down and tell me about this note."

Torn, she stared at the door; every cell in her body demanded she follow him.

"Riley, give me all the pieces to the puzzle so I can help."

Unable to sit down, she paced her sister's office while she told her about how her assistant had sent back a gift with a strange note that seemed to indicate someone hadn't died.

"Do you think she sent anything to your three colleagues who died?"

"I won't know until I reach her."

"What does *EP not ded* mean?"

"I'm not sure. DED could be phonetic for dead."

"Could EP be someone's initials? Maybe one of your coworkers?"

"No. Not even close."

"Has anyone else from Costa Rica contacted you?"

"Just Nick."

Maggie's eyes sharpened. "Who's he?"

"Nick Landry acted as a liaison between Dr. Young and Dr. Hathaway."

"And they are?"

"Young headed up the lab that conducted the experiments on the plants my team sent them."

"Hathaway?"

"His foundation funded the project."

"What did Nick want?"

"To say hello. He attended a conference in Asheville."

"Did the Audi guy show up at the same time as this Nick?"

"Yes, but I drove Nick back to the airport days ago. Besides, Nick isn't capable of murder—unless it's a woman's heart."

"Did he have anything else to say?"

She hesitated.

"If you don't tell me everything, I can't get to the bottom of this."

"Nick told me that Dr. Hathaway aborted my project for a more lucrative one."

"Like what?"

"Curing impotency."

"Curing it? As in a man can get a hard-on until the day he dies."

"Exactamundo." She crossed her arms and leaned against the windowsill. "They dumped Project Endurance and started Project Stamina."

"Are you serious?"

She plopped down in a chair. "I have no idea what they called the new project, but they brought in a whole new team for it."

"That's shitty, Riley. I'm sorry."

"Not good enough to play with the big boys, I guess. I don't know how you do it. There's so much testosterone in this building that it's a wonder you haven't grown a beard yet."

Maggie laughed. "Navigating the Steele-Kingston boys prepared me for this position more than the academy, you can be sure." She paused for a moment, then switched topics. "So what's going on between you and Coen?"

Eyebrows raised, Riley stared at her sister. "Frontal attack?"

"No sense beating around the bush. The familiarity between the two of you earlier was unmistakable."

"You're confusing male overprotectiveness for interest."

Maggie snorted. "The sexual tension was so thick I nearly gagged. Have you slept with him?"

"None of your damn business."

"You're my business, little sis. Whether you like it or not."

"Mags, I trust you with my life. But this"—she thumped a fist against her heart—"you don't get to control."

"Fine, but make sure you keep a tight leash on it, because the course you're set on is a hairsbreadth from spinning out of control."

37

At Maggie's ominous warning to Riley, Coen peeled away from the wall near the sheriff's open door, thankful her eagle-eyed assistant, Shari, had stepped away.

He stormed out of the police station, tearing up pavement to put as much distance as possible between him and a too-perceptive Maggie Kingston.

Most people would never ask a soldier why he was on leave. But Sheriff Kingston cared nothing for etiquette when it came to protecting her little sister. Protecting Riley from *him*.

Had Riley told Maggie about his night terrors and how a mere image could flip a switch in his mind and send him spiraling back into the darkest corner of his fears? A corner no amount of booze, shrinks, or self-help books could illuminate and set free.

Or did he reek of *Head Case*?

Every muscle in his body quaked to life. The tremors began in his calves and crept up his thighs, pouring into his gut, his chest, arms, hands. His fucking neck.

Sweat coated his forehead, back, and underarms. He

forced air through his nose and into his lungs, once, twice, three times. He stared at a flat, black glob of sidewalk gum while he concentrated on calming his breathing.

Thirty seconds passed, then a minute. It was a minute and a half before the tremors subsided and the sweat stopped flowing.

Why hadn't Riley shared everything Landry had told her? Didn't she trust him with the information?

He guessed the latter. She hadn't actually offered up the info to Maggie until her sister pushed for it.

The woman was going to drive him insane if his night-mares didn't beat her to it.

"Hey, Monroe. Need a ride?"

He lifted his bleary eyes to the truck blocking his path, to the blond-haired man leaning across his front seat to speak to him through the passenger side window. To Cash Kingston. Riley's brother.

Just his damned luck.

Stretching the tension out of his neck and shoulders, he said, "No, man, I'm good."

"I'm headed to the training academy for some exercise. Interested?"

Punching, lifting, or shooting something might be just the thing he needed to reset his sanity button.

"I don't have the right clothes."

"Don't worry about it. Reid keeps an assortment of tees and shorts on hand for the trainees. We'll steal something from his stock."

Climbing in, he splayed his hands over his thighs, releasing the ache from having them fisted for so long.

"What brings you into town?"

"Your sister."

"What'd the Menace do now?"

"Stop fucking calling her that name. She doesn't like it."

"You coming at me as her friend—or something else?"

"What does it matter? She's a grown woman, not a snot-nosed adolescent."

Thick silence filled the truck.

Son of a bitch. What the hell was he doing? Riley had made it clear that she didn't need or want his protection. If she heard how he'd just spoken to her brother, she'd flay the skin right off his ass.

Rubbing a hand across the back of his neck, he said, "Forget it, man. I shouldn't have said anything. What your family does or doesn't do is none of my business."

"She's got you tied in knots, huh?"

He released a tight breath and stared out the window. "You have no idea."

"Oh, I think I do. Been there myself recently." Cash's voice grew solemn. "Riley's been alone for too long. Always putting school and work before her personal needs. It would take the right kind of man to show her there's more to life than the one she's living."

Coen peered down at the temperature setting. Sixty-eight. He considered rolling the dial down to sixty-five but didn't think that would sit well with the truck's driver.

With a nonchalance he didn't feel, he swiped away a sheen of sweat above his right eye before adjusting the vents. Cool air hit his face, steadying his nerves. He did not want to talk about Riley's *personal needs* with her brother. But he couldn't leave Cash thinking he was some kind of balm for his sister.

"Look, this is awkward as hell"—he scraped his fingers through his hair—"but I need to set something straight."

"Don't try to tell me you're not into my sister. You barely let her out of your sight at dinner last night."

Had he been so obvious? Even though he didn't know Riley's brothers all that well, he'd done his part to keep the conversation flowing. They'd established an easy rhythm, sharing tales of their former adventure-seeking clients, sports, hunting, cars, best place to get a haircut.

But he couldn't deny how much the distance between him and Riley had chafed. Didn't even know it had until he'd strained to pick up pieces of her conversation, yearned to connect with those always-curious gray-blue eyes, ached for the comforting presence of her smile, her orange-blossom scent, and her heat at his side.

"I won't," he admitted. "But my leave ends in less than two weeks."

"Then make the best of the time. For both of you."

Cash turned into the entrance of the Steele Ridge Training Academy, saving him from further comment.

Grabbing his duffel, Cash led them inside and tracked down workout clothes for Coen. They hit the weights first. Focusing his attention on contracting and releasing certain muscle groups created a temporary distraction from the continuous loop playing in his mind of Riley's soft lips and her dead colleagues.

His peace of mind didn't last long.

"What's up with Riley today?" Cash asked in between sit-ups.

He finished his set of push-ups and sat back on his heels, his hands resting on his upper thighs. "She won't appreciate me telling you."

"All the more reason for you to do it." When he said nothing, Cash paused his workout. "Is she in trouble?"

"I believe so."

"Talk to me."

Coen got to his feet and swabbed his face and neck with

a white towel. "Last night, she got a text from someone she worked with in Costa Rica. The text contained links to sites, announcing the deaths of three of her colleagues."

"No shit? She must be devastated." Confusion carved lines into Cash's forehead. "What happened? Did they all die in a plane crash or something?"

"No."

Understanding flashed across Cash's features, and he jumped to his feet. "Where is she?"

"With Maggie. At the sheriff's department."

"Does she have any idea who might be killing her coworkers?"

"Not yet."

Collecting his duffel bag, Cash said, "I'm going to stop by Maggie's office before heading to the station. Can I drop you off somewhere?"

"No, I'll hang here for a while."

Reid shoved through the weight room door. "You girls up for some target practice?"

"Some other time," Cash said, storming past them. "I gotta go."

Reid's smile faded as he stared after his cousin. "What the hell's up with his ass?"

Coen shrugged. He'd let the Kingstons sort out who should and shouldn't know about Riley's situation. "I'm up for some range time."

"Got a weapon?"

"Always." He couldn't remember a time when he'd moved through life without a weapon in hand or holstered at his side. He knew a time existed, prior to his enlistment. But the memories had faded into what he called the *Before*, an otherworldly time when he'd been ignorant of the cruelty of man and the arrogance of nations. A time when he'd walked and talked and played with a freedom of spirit. A time when he didn't have blood on his hands.

"Nine mil?" Reid asked.

Coen nodded.

"I got in a fresh shipment of ammo a few days ago."

They loaded up a cart with ammo, paper targets, water bottles, and other supplies before heading outside. Reid—or rather Jonah—had spared no expense on the range.

There had to be at least forty firing points, plus a rifle range and shoot houses. A guy could spend a month here and not hit everything.

Collecting two silhouette targets and a staple gun, Coen marched downrange and affixed them to the target stand. The routine nature of the task once again distracted him from thoughts of a too-serious ethnobotanist.

"How's the fresh air working for you?"

"It's a beautiful piece of property."

"It is that. You getting that peace you wanted?"

"I've come across pockets of it."

"Up for another wager?" Reid sent him a full-of-his-own-shit glance.

"What'd you have in mind this time?"

"If you lose, I'll sign you up for our next Yoga Nidra class."

"And if I win?"

"I won't tell Riley you're in love with her."

When he opened his mouth, Reid cut in. "Save your breath." He snapped in a clip. "What I can't figure out is if she has you wrapped around her finger or vice versa."

He snorted. "The woman can hardly stand me. Part my fault, part yours."

"How am I screwing up your love life?"

"Ever heard of alpha-male bullshit?"

Reid laughed. "None of the women in our two families seem to appreciate our male instincts." He adjusted his stance. "Is it a bet or not?"

"Doesn't sound like much of a wager if I lose either way."

Tsking, Reid said, "So negative." He met Coen's eye, warrior to warrior. "Some would call it a win-win."

After a long stare downrange, he folded his arms. "One caveat."

"What?"

"Even if I lose, you register for the class too. And you have to wear spandex."

"You wanna add humiliation to the mix. Nice." He adjusted his stance to line up with the target. "Best grouping after fifteen rounds?"

Coen put on his safety glasses and earmuffs. "You first."

"Aiming for the bull's-eye."

Reid's first shot hit the mark. Barely. A tight nest of bullet holes appeared on the southeast corner of his target. At the end of Coen's turn, his grouping was tighter and dead center.

A high-pitched whistle preceded Reid's "Daaamn."

"That one goes to me," he said.

Stepping up to the line again, Reid said, "Between the eyes."

Crack!

A hole appeared where the silhouette's right eye used to be.

Coen stared at the empty space, his thoughts spiraling back, back, back. The image of a man, a soldier, his head snapping backward under the force of a bullet shot from a high-powered rifle, filled his vision. Blood sprayed out the opposite side of his head.

Before the soldier—Paul—crumpled to the ground,

Coen saw that only one blue eye remained. Even from this distance, he felt its stare. For a moment Coen thought he detected confusion and fear and pain. But the eye looked through him, beyond him, at... nothing—not his team leader, not his enemy, not the dirt road as his body collapsed.

Coen blinked, and the memory faded. Cold sweat skimmed down his neck and back.

Crack!

Another hole appeared on the silhouette.

Another image slammed into him. Freddy's body jerking, twisting, falling.

Crack!

Another hole.

Miller's body exploded.

Kendra.

Still alive.

His body slammed into hers, rolling. Bullets zinging over their heads. Crawling for cover. Trapped. No help.

Run!

She won't leave. Won't save herself.

"Coen."

Captured.

Tortured.

Pain. Gut-tearing pain.

"Coen."

Strong.

So strong.

Tears.

Broken.

Broken.

All is broken.

"Coen! It's Reid. Reid Steele. Your friend."

Coen tightened his grip.

Right arm.

Right—

"You're in Steele Ridge. You're safe."

His head twitched.

"Cash Kingston brought you here to work out."

"Kingston."

"That's right. Cash, your friend."

Kingston, Kingston...

"Riley."

"Yes, Riley. The woman you love. She asks a lot of questions."

Coen blinked against the darkness. Pushing the shadows back to the fringes of his vision.

Reid stood before him, with his hands fanned out between them. His gaze shifting between Coen's face and something lower.

Coen's hand.

And the gun pointed at Reid's chest.

38

GONE.

Riley couldn't find Coen anywhere. She'd checked Triple B, his tent, her parents' place, the research center and greenhouse, Britt's cabin, and came up with nada. Reid might have an idea of Coen's location, but his phone kept going to voice mail.

Where else could he have gone?

His handsome features had remained as unemotional as ever when Maggie asked him to leave, but betrayal, hurt, and even disgust, she thought, had darkened his eyes.

Bahh-ling. She glanced down to find a text from Cash.

Where are you?

Dammit, why hadn't she thought about her brothers? Maybe Shep or Cash had run across him.

She hit the speech-to-text button on her messaging app. "Driving."

Pull over and call me.

She frowned. Her fun-loving brother rarely used that tone with her. What had ruffled his pretty plumage?

Then it hit her. Either Maggie or Coen had gotten to him. *Perfect.*

Her sister hadn't been happy when she'd left the sheriff's department. They'd had quite a sister-to-sister argument in the middle of the parking lot over her safety. Maggie had insisted she hang with her for the rest of the day and that she move in with her and Jayson until her investigators determined if the threat was real or not.

The thought of sleeping in the same house with her sister and her new boyfriend had made her shudder. She'd never get any sleep with them banging around.

In the end, Maggie had relented, promising additional patrols in Riley's neighborhood and making her swear to check in every few hours.

So why had she involved Cash?

After swinging into an open stall in front of the Mad Batter, she hit the speech-to-text button again. "Who did you speak to, Maggie or Coen?"

While waiting for his reply, she read the bakery's sidewalk sign.

It is a truth locally acknowledged that a single woman in possession of a passion fruit éclair is in want of love.

Riley blinked, wondering who the focus of Jeanine's prophetic chalk was this time.

Bahh-ling.

Dismissing the assistant baker and her eerie signs, she read Cash's response.

Both. Why didn't you call me?

"Because we don't know anything for certain."

Wrong answer.

"Where's Coen?"

Last I saw him, he was at the academy talking to Reid. Where are you?

"I'm safe. Headed to the academy."

Text me when you get there.

"Yes, ma'am."

You'll pay for that one, little sis.

Dropping her phone in the cupholder, she backed up and performed an imperfect U-ey right in the middle of Main Street. No doubt some busybody would inform Maggie of her sister's reckless driving. *Nark on.*

Heart racing, she forced herself to walk into the training academy like a civilized human being and not one who was losing her grip on the panic bubbling inside.

When she closed in on Reid's office, his administrator intercepted her.

"Hey, Riley. What brings you in today?"

"I'm looking for Reid. Know where I can find him?"

Blond-haired, blue-eyed, laid-back Gage Barber unleashed his All-American grin on her. A grin meant to disarm and distract. One he'd used to great effect with her badass cousin Micki Steele. If Riley's nerves hadn't been teetering on a razor's edge, she would've allowed him to work his wiles on her, just for the fun of it.

"He's tied up right now. Anything I can help you with?"

"No, I need to ask him a question. How long will he be?"

Gage's easy smile slipped a fraction. "I can let him know you were here."

Her attention shifted to Reid's office door, and she knew. Just *knew* who was in there with her cousin.

"Is Coen Monroe in there?"

Understanding softened his blue eyes. "Why don't you check in with him tomorrow?"

She made to zip around him, but he swung out one sinewy arm, halting her maneuver.

"I need to speak with Coen. It's important."

"So is his privacy right now."

"Gage, let me pass."

"Can't do it, kiddo."

"I-I can help."

Regret and determination molded Gage's features. As a former Green Beret, he would have an intimate understanding of Coen's struggle. Had Coen told Reid and Gage that Maggie thought he'd blow a gasket? Or had something else happened for Gage to be so protective?

"Let me speak to him. To Coen."

"Reid's got it handled."

"He doesn't need to be *handled*."

The door opened, and Reid squeezed through the opening before shutting it behind him. "Hey. How about keeping it down."

Hair askew, hard lines etched between his eyes and around his mouth, sweat stains beneath his pits, her cousin looked like he'd pulled an all-nighter.

"I'm looking for Coen."

Reid ran a hand through his hair, glancing over his shoulder at the closed door. "Not a good time, Ry."

"I upset him earlier, and I want to apologize."

He shared a look with Gage. "I'll let him know."

"You're really not going to let me speak with him."

"No."

"Does he know I'm out here?"

"Yes. Everyone in the damned building knows you're out here."

"Did *he* say he doesn't want to see me?"

Reid's jaw hardened. "Look, we've had enough drama around here for one day. Go home."

"You're a jerk, you know that, Reid?"

She sensed more than saw Gage's eyes widen.

"If Britt or Cash were standing here, demanding to see Coen, would you accuse them of creating more *drama*?"

Reid squeezed his eyes shut. "Dammit, Riley. Give me a break. There's no playbook here."

"All I want to do is speak with him. Maybe I can help—"

"You can't!" Reid barked out. "I can't," he said through gritted teeth. "Go home, goddammit. I'll call you later."

Everything hurt. Her chest, her throat, her stinging eyes. Her every breath.

She blinked and swallowed hard, sparing the door behind Reid's big frame one last glance. Before turning away, she said, "Tell him Charlotte and Cameron are about to confront the villain. *Together*."

Reid's brows slammed into a vee. "Huh?"

Not bothering to answer the ape, she stormed out. Coen would understand her reference to the story she'd been reading to him.

The walk back to her Jeep took an eternity, and she was certain a dozen sets of eyes followed her every second of the way. She ignored them. Ignored the stares, the ache in her throat, the sadness in her heart.

Only one thing registered in her pounding mind.

Rejection.

First Hathaway and now Coen.

What was she doing wrong?

39

AFTER SPENDING THE REST OF THE MORNING GPSING PLANTS, Riley couldn't bring herself to go to the greenhouse or to the farm. Going to the farm would mean putting on a happy face, and the greenhouse reminded her too much of Coen.

Coen.

What a cluster. How does a conversation go from informational to protective to injurious, all within the space of a few minutes?

She couldn't stand the thought of him walking around in the world believing she'd thought him a head case. Someone who needed to be put down, for God's sake.

Did he really believe her to be so insensitive? Or had he succumbed to some inner demon of his own?

Fat chance of her finding out. Reid in his Katie-bar-the-door mode would sooner kick her into next Tuesday than let her see Coen. The hint of bleakness she saw on her cousin's face told her something else had happened after Coen left Maggie's office. But what?

If she weren't such a coward, she'd plant herself on his tent step and not budge until he talked to her. But she didn't know how to navigate this situation. One wrong move and she could make things so much worse.

On top of all that, his rejection still stung like hell.

Sitting on her couch with her feet propped up on the coffee table, she searched for Camilla's number on her new phone. Around noon, she'd received a text from Camilla, promising to share more details soon and reiterating her warning about going someplace safe.

Was she really in danger? She'd never known Camilla to exaggerate a situation.

As a precaution, Riley had removed the pistol Way had given her years ago from its gun case and put it in her pack, along with her concealed carry permit. Thanks to their biweekly target practice sessions at the academy, she was pretty comfortable handling the weapon, but didn't know how she felt about carrying it around.

The worry that clutched at her chest wasn't for herself but for Camilla. Would she turn to someone in her community for protection? Or return to the streets?

The phone rang three times before a mechanical voice kicked on, telling her the number was no longer in service. Riley sat forward, staring at the number on her phone's display. Her mind whirled at the reality of what that meant.

A veil of helplessness and uncertainty settled over her. Not thick enough to suffocate her but heavy enough to prevent her from seeing a clear path.

She pushed her mind to focus, to sort through the data. What reason would anyone have for killing the researchers who worked on the Endurance project?

Endurance Project.

Her eyes widened, and she rushed into her bedroom.

"Endurance Project." EP. EP not ded. "Endurance Project is not dead."

Rifling through her pack, she found the note.

EP not ded. Keep fort safe.

"Fort. Fort. Fort." She ran through scenario after scenario, then it hit her. "Fourth."

You are next. Run.

"Three obituaries. Plus me. That's four. But what am I keeping safe?"

Her back hit the dresser as her legs grew weak. Camilla had known. She'd somehow found out that Hathaway had shut down the project to start up a new lab.

But what is the fourth? None of it made any sense.

Pushing off the dresser, her eyes skimmed over her bed —and caught. She squinted at the side she always slept on. At the indentation in the bedspread. An indentation in the shape of a body.

Her breath stuck in her throat as she scanned the room for anything else out of the ordinary.

Nothing.

Then her attention shifted to the floor, to the shadowed undercarriage of her bed. With lightning speed, her mind recalled all the movies where the main character had knelt by the edge of the bed and peered underneath, into a black void, until a hand shot out...

She took three steps back before dropping to her knees and bending forward until her temple grazed the hardwood floor.

Nothing.

She rested her cheek against the cool boards for a second while she caught her breath, then pushed to her feet. Room by room, she made a systematic search of the bungalow, with her pack and gun at hand.

Besides an unlocked bathroom window, the only thing

her surveillance flushed out was an indecent amount of dust bunnies.

Now that the initial scare had passed, she returned to her bedroom, certain she'd lost her mind. She studied the bedspread from different angles and came to the same conclusion.

Someone had lain on her bed.

She moved to her pillow and bent close. A familiar scent filled her nose. She closed her eyes and concentrated, but no name surfaced.

Who the hell was sneaking into the house and violating her personal space? Had Coen been right about the guy in the Audi?

Straightening, she toyed with the idea of going to Maggie's for the night. No sooner than the thought formed, it disintegrated beneath her formidable Kingston stubbornness. She might not be able to sleep in her bed tonight, but she wouldn't leave her home.

Nothing was damaged or stolen. Who knew? Maybe Randi or Britt had stopped by and took a *siesta*.

To be safe, she would pass on the information to Maggie. But first she had a big decision to make.

She marched into the kitchen. Should she drink something to calm her nerves or eat something that would kick her brain into overdrive?

So many unanswered questions swirled around her mind. The answers for each one dangled just out of her reach.

She blew out a breath, resetting the mental chaos in her head. "Ice cream it is."

Hauling out a new quart of Turtle Tango, she ripped off the lid and plunged a spoon inside, not even bothering with a bowl. One of the many perks of being single—she could double-dip all day long and not get one sideways glance.

Cold, sweet, and smooth, the ice cream slid over her tongue and down into her stomach. She shuffled into the family room and paused by the couch, shoveling spoonfuls of goodness into her mouth. The scrape of the spoon against the container echoed through the silent house.

Flopping onto the couch, she cradled the quart to her chest and put her feet up on the coffee table. She attacked her Tango like an expert ballroom dancer.

Some people hated being alone. But she found answers in the quiet. It allowed her to think, analyze, pick at her wedgies. She didn't have to pretend to be anyone except her curious self.

But there were times when crawling inside another's embrace also appealed to her. She would love to have someone smooth a hand over her hair and croon comforting nonsense into her ear, like her dad used to do when something in Riley's world hadn't gone right.

What would it be like to snuggle with a warrior like Coen? Strong, brave, deliberate. Intense. Would his hands be rough and his whiskered chin sharp against her skin? Would the taut, ribbed flesh on his stomach be hard as stone or smooth as silk?

She squeezed her eyes shut; her glasses suddenly felt like a thousand-pound weight sitting on her nose. She flipped her glasses up onto her head and rubbed at the indents the nose guards left behind.

The Warrior and The Researcher. The title sounded like a nursery rhyme gone wrong. It was definitely not the makings of a romance. Why even start anything when he would be returning to duty soon?

She stared at the ceiling, wondering if she should just

slouch there and wallow in her own pity party or if she should ditch the ice cream and upload this morning's flora findings into the database.

"Ice cream or data entry?" For most people, the choice would be simple. But she thrived on both. Both fed different parts of her brain. Both gave her pleasure.

Three sharp raps on her door forced her upright, like a vampire rising from her coffin. Who could that be at this hour? With all the curtains closed, she couldn't peek at her visitor.

Heart hammering, she sat there, unmoving, unsure. Would a killer knock? *Yes, if he was a friend.*

She shoveled a big mound of ice cream into her mouth, recalling all the movies and news reports regarding lack of forced entry, leading to speculation that the victim had known her murderer.

Brain freeze! She pressed her fingers to her forehead and squeezed her eyes shut. "Ow, ow, ow," she whispered. Her glasses slid off her head and dropped onto her nose with a dull thud.

Another series of impatient knocks kicked her heartbeat into overdrive. Still holding her ice cream, she tiptoed to the door and set her ear to the wooden panel.

Silence.

Straightening, she stared at the door. Was she being smart or stupid?

Undecided, she lifted another spoonful of Turtle Tango to her mouth.

"Riley, it's me."

The pressure on her chest disappeared at the sound of her sister's voice.

Stupid it is.

Rotating the deadbolt, she opened the door to find Maggie in her sheriff's garb.

"Everything okay?" she asked.

"Hunky-dory now." Maggie swiped the ice cream carton from where Riley had it clutched to her chest and the spoon from her hand as she strode inside. "I always knew you were a closet sweet eater." They stood in silence while she helped herself to Riley's ice cream. "Mmmm, I needed that."

Riley shut the door. "How did you know?"

"Really? I'm the one who used to sneak you Fla-Vor-Ice bars." She dropped an overnight duffel onto the floor. "Besides that, when it was just you and me, I found ice cream sandwich wrappers in your trash."

"You went through my garbage?"

"Yep. Can't say that I ever found anything exciting. Except for that half-written love letter to Tommy somebody or other."

"Tommy? That was way before Mom and Dad moved away."

"Was it? Hmm."

"Argh! Give me that." She snatched the ice cream away.

"Touchy, touchy." Maggie eyed the television. "Do you have Netflix or Apple TV or one of those other streaming services?"

"Yes."

"You have both, don't you?"

"And Amazon Video."

"When do you have time to watch them?"

Riley shrugged. "They're available when I need them."

"Find us a movie while I change."

"Change?"

"I'm dying to get into my pj's and free my feet from these boots."

"You're staying?"

Maggie flashed her a smile. "Girls' night. Like old times."

"Why does this feel like a takeover rather than a sleepover?"

"I knew you wouldn't come to me. You've got the same reckless, stubborn Kingston genes as the boys." She picked up her bag. "I'll be back in ten. Pick out something sappy—or bloody. You decide." Over her shoulder, she said, "By the way, we identified the other two poachers. My deputies arrested them this afternoon."

"Thank you. That's awesome."

"Thank Blaine. He's the one who finally got the first poacher to talk."

Riley followed her sister's exit. Hurricane Maggie. Chaos followed by unnerving calm. A familiar volley of emotions struck Riley's already sensitized nerves—frustration, appreciation, resistance, acceptance, love.

Maggie had a habit of fixing things, big and small. She felt a keen sense of responsibility for everything and everyone in this town. It was too large of a burden for one person. But Riley knew if she tried to shut down her sister on this Costa Rica mystery, Maggie would work around her somehow.

Probably sit her gladiator ass on Riley's chest and not move until she relented.

Talk about stubborn.

Grabbing the remote, she scrolled through movie after movie until one in particular caught her eye.

Maggie returned, wearing a fitted white T-shirt with pale purple bottoms, sporting dozens of dancing dogs. She'd combed out her ponytailed hair and left it loose around her shoulders. Bare toes peeked out from beneath her pj's.

The transformation from sheriff to sleepover sister was

amazing. All her hard lines had softened, and her worries had been shoved to the background. The only visible reminder of her law enforcement status was the handgun she set on a side table.

"Expecting trouble?"

"Anticipating surprises."

She knew then that any peacefulness or softening her sister projected was all for show. For Riley. Until Maggie got to the bottom of the text messages and mysterious driver, she wouldn't be able to relax.

Maybe her sister needed tonight as much as Riley did. Especially after discovering someone had been in her house, in her *bed*. But she would save that bit of news along with the meaning behind the note until later. Tonight they would both have fun. Girl fun.

"When did you start painting your toenails? And scarlet red to boot."

Maggie winked. "When I had someone around who would appreciate them."

Pro quarterback Jayson Tucker would appreciate Maggie any way he could get her. Although they both had demanding jobs that kept them away from each other at times, they were making it work.

If they could do it, couldn't she and Coen?

Did he even want that?

"What'd you pick?" Maggie asked, folding her long limbs into the corner of the couch and hugging a fluffy pillow to her chest.

"*Sabrina.*"

"The one with Julia Ormond and Harrison Ford?"

"Yep." She ignored her sister's assessing gaze. Who could blame her if she was in the mood for a flick where the nerd transformed into a talented beauty, catching the eye of a handsome, emotionally isolated rich dude?

"Got any popcorn?"

Riley handed over the carton. "I have ice cream."

"But it's almost gone."

"Better savor it then."

Before Riley could hit Play, Maggie asked, "How's Coen?"

"I don't know."

"What do you mean? Didn't you catch up to him?"

"Yes, but he refused to see me." Closing her eyes, she dropped her head onto the back of the couch. "It's complicated."

"It always is. Spill."

"I told you, dear sister." Riley lifted her head. "This part of my life is off-limits."

"I'm not trying to direct your love life. Just lending an ear —like you did for me when I was struggling with my feelings for Jayson."

She bent her head and used all eight fingers to rub at the ache in her forehead. Would talking things through with Maggie help? Or confuse her more? Would she be betraying Coen? Would Maggie judge her? Him? Them?

"You're analyzing."

"It's what I do."

"Analysis paralysis. Sometimes you just need to let things fly and see where they land."

"But what if I land in a shithole?"

"Clean up and move on. Life is one part mistakes and one part successes. What defines your character is how you react to each life lesson."

"So I must sort out my inner being in a very public and humiliating way?"

Maggie grinned. "Builds character."

"What if the exercise breaks it?"

Her sister's grin softened. "Not you, Ry. Inside that puny frame lies the heart of an angel and the strength of a Valkyrie."

"Puny frame? I'm an inch taller than you."

"But twenty pounds lighter."

"Only because I lack your muscle mass."

"Visit the gym, and I'll help you shorten the gap."

"Uh, yeah, no. Not my thing. I'll stick to my own cardio program."

Maggie nodded. "I suspect you could out-hike, out-survive me in the wilderness anytime."

Warmth speared her heart. "A girl's gotta have at least one useful talent."

Her sister's bare foot nudged at Riley's shoulder. "Enough procrastinating. I want the goods."

"What about our movie?"

"After the goods."

She released an exaggerated sigh and decided to save the heavy stuff for later. "I saw him naked."

Maggie's eyes bugged out. "What?"

"Without clothes, in his birthday suit—"

Her sister's foot shoved harder this time, knocking her to the side. "You had sex with him?"

"No!" She frowned. "We came close once, but I screwed it up."

"How?"

"I don't know." Her hand waved emphatically between them. *Hello, sugar buzz.* "Everything was going great. My brain even stopped working for a while. Then I sat on him, and he got a pained look on his face and said *'Ah, fuck.'* Which sent me to the restroom to drown in my mortification."

Confusion scrunched up Maggie's face. "I'm not following."

"Never mind. I'm not talking about this anymore."

"Is that when you saw him naked?"

"No, I came across him while doing survey work in the conservation area." Her vision unfocused as she thought back to their first meeting. "I heard what sounded like an animal screaming. Following the noise, I stumbled upon his campsite, and there he was, standing buck-ass naked in front of his tent." Riley's attention fell on her hands, on the frayed cuticle she'd been toying with and hadn't realized it. "The screaming. It was him."

"What happened?"

The foot that struck violence on her seconds ago now made soothing swishes against her hip.

"He sensed my presence, and I bolted."

"Did he chase you or track you down at the greenhouse?"

"No. I don't know. Maybe." Her knee began to bounce.

"What'd you do, Ry?"

"I went back and observed him."

"Observed him," Maggie repeated. "Like Jane Goodall watching the chimps?"

Riley nodded, though she raised her chin. "I needed to understand."

"What?"

"Who was he? What made him scream? Why was he naked during the day? What put that vulnerable, haunted expression on his face?"

"Did he know you were there, spying on him?"

"Eventually." She didn't dare look at her sister—or the yelling would begin.

"You're keeping something from me."

"I'm not going to give you *all* the details."

"I have a feeling that the reckless side of your DNA did something stupid."

How did she do that? Her sister's ability to read people was damn frightening.

Her lips twitched. "I might have snooped through his tent. And got caught."

"Oh, for the love of—" Her sister switched from one rant to another midstream. "You went into a strange man's tent? *Were you out of your scientific mind?*"

"I observed his pattern of behavior before taking my research to the next level."

"But you got caught."

"That wasn't my fault. He forgot his canteen."

A laugh-snort escaped Maggie. "Foiled by a canteen."

She pressed her lips together and forced down the laughter that was vibrating in her chest. "It's not f-funny."

"Hell if it isn't." Maggie's shoulders shook. "He came back for his canteen while you're digging through his d-dirty underwear." A full-on laugh erupted from her sister. A girlish, free laugh that Riley hadn't heard in a long, long time.

The image Maggie painted was so absurd that her laughter broke past her self-imposed barrier.

All the stress from the past week faded into the background, leaving her with a warm sense of nostalgia. She missed these moments with her sister. Even though nine years separated them, they had always been good at talking through issues.

But once they'd both moved into adulthood, these shared moments had become few and far between.

She grasped her sister's foot. "We need to do this more often."

"Agreed."

"I'll send you a reoccurring calendar appointment."

"Excellent." Maggie stretched out on the cushions and pushed her feet onto Riley's lap.

Most people wouldn't get her need for order and scheduling and whatnot, but her paramilitary-minded sister, with her closet full of crisp, perfectly aligned uniforms, did.

Without thought, she began massaging the arch of her sister's foot.

Maggie groaned. "What happened next?"

"He helped me save fox kits from a pit, planted seeds at the greenhouse, and kissed me in the moonlight."

"Good kisser?"

"Unlike any I've ever had before."

"Which is what? Three?"

She pinched Maggie's little toe and sent her a warning look.

"You can't argue the truth."

Riley let her head fall back on the couch again. "Can I help it if no guy has wowed me enough to stop the analysis in my head?"

"You're the only person I know who analyzes a kiss to the point of being an orgasm killer."

"I'm a freak, what can I say?"

"You're not a freak." Maggie's words came out harsh, uncompromising. "The right guy hasn't kissed you yet." She cocked her head to the right. "Or has he?"

Riley shot her sister a death look. "Thanks to you, there's a slim-to-no chance of my getting another kiss."

"Me?" The hard lines of Sheriff Maggie slid back into place. "You didn't want him involved with the Costa Rica matter. I did what you couldn't."

Maggie had her back. She'd fixed the situation.

Shame washed over Riley.

Squeezing her sister's foot, she said, "You're right. It's best this way." She stared across the room at nothing in particular. "He'll be gone soon anyway."

"Riley," Maggie said quietly.

She met her sister's gaze.

"All I did was stop him from screwing up my investigation. What you do with him outside of that is up to you."

"What happens if his kiss can stop the analysis? I'll be all like, 'He's the *one*,' and then he'll leave."

"Not forever."

"He could be gone for months."

"You've waited twenty-five years for love. What are a few months?" Maggie smiled that smile women get when they've found their own life mate. "For the right guy."

The right guy.

Something exciting and hopeful and terrifying took root in the pit of her stomach. Her fingers tingled and her legs shook.

"And Ry?"

"Yeah?"

"When you sat on Coen—you didn't hurt him. You gave him pleasure."

Eyes wide. "I did?"

Maggie grinned. "Yay, you."

Hitting the Play button, she continued to massage her big sister's poor feet, a smile dancing on her lips.

Yay, me.

40

THE FIRELIGHT LICKED AGAINST COEN'S FACE AND CHEST LIKE the first rays of a morning sun.

Wearing a pair of jersey shorts, he sat in a bag chair, wondering why his mind refused to rest after the workout he'd given it today.

Although he and Reid hadn't technically finished their competition, Reid had declared himself the winner by default and called in his wager. Coen hadn't argued. Spending an hour in a yoga class had been a small penance for pointing a weapon at his friend.

Four others had participated in the practice. Rather than blocks and straps and yoga mats, the instructor brought out several blankets—some to lie on, some to use as pillows, and some to use as covers.

The instructor had guided them through different breathing techniques to help them enter a state of conscious sleep. It took about fifteen minutes for him to let down his guard long enough to give the practice a fair shake. Twenty minutes after that, he'd drifted off. Rather than wake him, the instructor had let him sleep.

Coen had regained consciousness slowly. When the instructor had encouraged them to roll into a sitting position, he'd felt... different. More centered. Relaxed in a way he hadn't been in years.

Until Reid stood up. In his spandex. It was like seeing a gorilla wearing a strip of electrical tape around his private parts.

The image was still burned in his mind.

Now he felt drained. As if he'd spent the past twelve hours calculating complex sums. But he couldn't bring himself to go lie down. Couldn't bring himself to test the yoga's effects on his night terrors.

What if the nightmares returned? What if they didn't?

Would Riley return tonight and read to him until dawn? Doubtful.

After he'd refused to see her at the training academy, she would likely never come within ten feet of him again. She'd gone head to toe with Reid and Gage, demanding, pleading to see him. To help him.

He could still hear the hollowness of her voice when she'd realized he'd told Reid to keep her away. That had gutted him as much as, if not worse than, almost shooting his friend.

But facing her after what he'd done—or almost done— had been more than he could handle. Something in his mind had cracked in the wrong place, and he hadn't been able to suppress the demons that threatened to overwhelm every waking hour.

That's when Reid and Gage had walked him through what they knew of Yoga Nidra, which wasn't much since both of them had only attended a handful of classes. They hadn't even made him lie down. He simply sat in Reid's desk chair and closed his eyes.

But the controlled breathing had helped reset his focus, allowing him to wrestle back control, one breath at a time. At the end of the session, Reid made him promise to return this morning.

Neither one of them mentioned anything about the second part of their wager, the part where Reid would tell Riley that Coen loved her. Would the bastard follow through?

No, he wouldn't dare. Not after watching Coen being consumed by his own memories. Reid would want better for his cousin.

The shuffle of leaves drew his attention to the ridge. The firelight killed his vision beyond its flickering glow.

Reaching down beside his chair, he curled his hand around his Glock. "Who's there?"

Leaves rustled, twigs snapped as the slow, measured steps grew nearer.

Sitting forward, he rested his forearms on his knees, allowing whoever approached to see his weapon. "Identify yourself now."

He hoped to God it wasn't a black bear searching for an easy meal. As usual, he'd stowed all his food in a container hanging high above. But that wouldn't stop a curious bear from ransacking his tent.

"It's me." Shadows shifted, making way for the long, sleek body of his ethnobotanist as she entered the circlet of firelight.

Everything about her looked soft and feminine and sexy. Her hair draped over one shoulder like an onyx waterfall. She wore white linen pants and a turquoise button-down shirt that rippled in the light breeze. A practical yet stylish pair of hiking shoes covered her feet, and her ever-present backpack purse was hooked over one shoulder.

"May I?" she asked, hovering at the edge of light.

Without taking his eyes off her, he placed his gun beneath his chair and rose.

"What are you doing here?" he asked.

"I've come to find out how Charlotte and Cameron defeat the villain and get their happily-ever-after."

He moved toward her. "What if it doesn't end well?"

"Charley won't let that happen. She's determined to have both—a career and Cam." She bit her bottom lip. "What she's less sure about is what Cam wants."

His thumb traced over her abused lip. "He wants the girl and to continue serving those who need him most. But his past is full of darkness. Darkness that could hurt her."

"She's much tougher than he—or anyone—gives her credit for."

All the reasons he should send her away played through his mind. Instead of delivering the harsh words that would save her future heartache, he whispered, "Brave Miss Indy."

Tears glistened in her eyes. "I'm sorry, Coen. What happened in Maggie's office—"

"Don't." He pressed his thumb against her mouth. "I'm still not happy about being shut out, but I understand honor and wanting to protect those you love." He held her face between his hands. "Let me help you."

"You've been through so much. I don't want you to hurt anymore."

"I don't hurt when I'm with you. I *feel* when I'm with you."

Her tears spilled over. With impatient fingers she flipped her glasses on top of her head and swiped at her cheeks. "Can we try again?"

"Us? Or—?" He let his smile and slow inspection of her eyes down to her mouth finish his sentence.

A breath shuddered between her sweet, wobbling lips. "Both?" she asked hopefully. "I figured out what I did wrong the other night. Or I should say Maggie worked it out. Because of my inexperience, I thought I'd hurt you, but she said I gave you pleasu—"

Coen captured the last of her analysis in his mouth. She sank into him on a deep sigh that filled his chest with male satisfaction.

He splayed his hands over her ass and brought their hips together. Need spiraled through his gut, and he couldn't stop the explosive groan that ripped from his throat into her mouth.

His reaction triggered something in her brilliant mind, something powerful. Her response turned faster, hotter, more devouring. He rode the wave of her frenzy for several heart-pounding minutes. Then he moved his exploration to her neck, dipping his tongue into the soft well at the base of her throat.

Tilting her face up to the stars, she allowed him free rein, trusting him with her most vulnerable possession. He nipped and laved his way up to her ear, drawing the soft lobe into mouth, allowing his heat to sink into her very core.

"Do you want me to tell you exactly what I'm going to do with you, my little scientist?" He flicked the shell of her ear with his tongue. "Would that help silence the questions?"

She reared back, eyes wide, breaths harsh. "How did you—?"

He removed her glasses from the top of her head and tucked them into a side pocket of her pack. "My job requires observation skills too."

Nodding, her gaze shot from his eyes to his mouth and back up again, waiting, anticipating.

"Would you like the clean version? Or the dirty?"

A familiar vacancy clouded her eyes as she began to analyze her two options.

"Don't think. Answer."

"Surprise me," she said in a rush.

A sexy, toe-curling smile appeared, and he eased her backpack off her shoulder. "First let me establish the mission goal." He leaned close, making sure his warm breath caressed her ear. "I'm going to fuck you, Riley Kingston, until you scream."

Riley's insides melted at his erotic promise. Her mind lifted its foot off the gas pedal, allowing her thoughts to slow and her body to absorb the impact of his words.

She angled her head around until his mouth covered hers. He kept the kiss gentle and measured before slipping his tongue inside to tangle with hers. Within seconds, the kiss's tenor changed, becoming hot and consuming.

Her arms snaked around his waist, and her palms slid up the planes of his tortured back. Unlike last time, he didn't stiffen or retreat from her touch. The heat of her hands inflamed his desire, and his mouth became more demanding, yet intentional.

Every contact with her skin seemed designed to push her into mindless new heights. She soared with him—until he slowed everything down.

When she opened her mouth to protest, he whispered, "I'm going to remove your clothing now so that I can see the firelight lick every beautiful inch of you."

His fingers moved to the top button of her blouse, and her rapid breaths halted in the back of her throat. She froze until the bare torso before her became too much of a distraction.

While he worked the buttons, she raised her hand to his hard stomach. She traced the smooth ridges, enjoying the contraction of muscle beneath her caress.

Her exploration continued upward to his broad chest, his dark nipple. The tip of her finger circled the outer rim, making the center harden into a mouthwatering enticement.

Coen's sharp intake of breath encouraged her to greater boldness. She leaned forward, setting her tongue on the same path as her finger.

A large hand gripped the back of her head, silently encouraging her on, while his other hand slipped beneath her waistband to palm her ass. His fingers flexed, and Riley groaned. Who knew a butt massage could be so erotic?

When her teeth scraped gently across his nipple, his body jerked and he groaned out a command. "My turn."

He took his time undressing her, admiring every bare inch he revealed. With anyone else, she would have been overcome by a mixture of self-consciousness and impatience. But standing nude before Coen brought forth every feminine instinct she possessed—from the curve of her smile to the angle of her foot.

She wanted to be alluring and beautiful and the right amount of confident. Given the throbbing action going on beneath his jersey shorts, she'd hit the mark on all three.

"I can't take my eyes off you," he said.

She closed the short distance separating them. "And you're"—she brushed a finger along the line of dark hair running from his navel down to his shorts—"hiding something from me."

A roguish grin softened the lines around his mouth. "Maybe you should help me remedy the situation." He hooked his thumbs around the elastic at his waist and lifted an eyebrow in her direction. His maneuver gave her an unimpeded bird's-eye view of his straining member.

Riley's mouth went dry. Would she be able to please him? She didn't kid herself into believing that he'd come to her with little experience. How could she make this encounter interesting for him?

"Get out of your head." He dropped his shorts to the ground and placed her hand over his smooth, hard length. "Feel. Don't think."

She curled her fingers around him. "I want it to be good for you too."

A breath shuddered between his lips. "Everything about you is good for me." He rolled his hips back, then pushed forward. "Even this."

Riley marveled at the play of flesh beneath her palm. He thrust into her hand a few more times, giving her a sense of what was to come. When she tightened her hold and began learning the rhythm, he gripped her hips and threw back his head.

The intensity of his reaction set off a pulsing between her legs. She wanted, needed— "Coen?"

Something in the tone of her voice, some ancient call to action from woman to man, had his head snapping back up.

"Hold on." Lifting her up, she wrapped her legs around his waist. The position brought her aching center into intimate contact with his member. It bucked against her heat as Coen carried her to his tent.

At the entrance, he slanted his mouth over hers, kissing her with a thoroughness that brought tears to her eyes. Then he eased her to the ground and led her inside.

Rather than stand bent over, they settled on their knees. He held her gaze in the deepening gloom as he secured the tent's flaps. The sound of the zipper sliding down was as exciting as the slow snick of a door locking.

Riley pressed a hand against her lower stomach where a colony of butterflies began to stir.

Coen snuggled up behind her and burrowed his hand beneath hers, his palm instantly heating her inner core.

"Nervous?" he asked, kissing her neck.

"A little."

"I won't hurt you."

"I know."

"And you won't hurt me."

Her smile wobbled. "I don't want to muck this up again."

"You couldn't," he whispered. "I'm going to explore you as you explored me." His hand moved lower. "Then I intend to keep my promise."

"What promise?"

"Did you forget already? Let me refresh your memory."

Coen slipped his finger between Riley's wet folds, releasing a scent that was uniquely her own. Her back arched, the movement thrusting her breasts in the air. His free hand covered one perfect mound while he slid a second finger into her.

Ignoring his bucking, demanding cock, he kept his focus on Riley. It 'bout near killed him. He wanted her with a ferocity that he'd never experience before.

She turned her head, seeking his mouth. He gave her his mouth, his tongue, his everything. God, she tasted so good, felt so right.

How would he ever get through another night without her in his arms?

She broke free. "Coen, I can't—I need—*please*."

The plea in her voice echoed the same one in his head. He eased out of her, then led her to his pathetic excuse for a bed. But it was spacious and soft.

Like a goddess, she reclined on his pallet and stretched her slender arms above her head before beckoning him to join her.

Unable to deny them both any longer, he grabbed a condom from a box near his toiletry items. Ripping the package open, he rolled it on and prowled toward her until he reached the tips of her generous breasts.

He closed his mouth around the peak, curling his tongue around the ruched bud.

"Coen, *pleeease.*" Squirming beneath him, she lifted her knees and pressed her palms into his lower back, enticing, coaxing, demanding.

Smiling, he teased, "Impatient, Miss Indy."

"Impatient?" She lifted her hips and ground into him. "I've been waiting twenty-five years for this moment."

Positioning himself at her entrance, he hesitated. "This… might be uncomfortable. I'll take it slow."

In response, she thrust her hips upward, taking in his entire length.

"Dammit, Riley," he said through clenched teeth. The feel of her heat wrapped around him nearly made him lose control. "Why did you do that?"

Her nails bit into his ass, and several seconds passed before she breathed again.

"Now the awkward part is over," she said, caressing his back. "It's time to make me scream."

After stretching his neck first one way then the other, he stared down at her. "For the next phase of our lovemaking, you're going to hand the reins back to me. Got it?"

She smiled and gave her hips an experimental thrust. "Yes, Sergeant."

He brushed his nose against hers. "You'll pay for that, Menace."

"God, I hope so."

Coen moved, keeping the rhythm slow and steady until her mischievous expression transformed into concentration, then he pushed her—them—over the edge.

Both howling their pleasure into the night.

The air stirred behind her, and Riley glanced over her shoulder in time to receive Coen's predawn kiss.

She couldn't think of a better way to greet the new day than to have a chorus of birds singing in the background and Coen Monroe next to her.

"Morning," he said, drawing her naked body closer to his.

"Good morning." She rotated her hips, enjoying the novel feeling of a man's hardness nestled against the seam of her bottom.

"Careful or you'll get more than a kiss." His lips brushed along her shoulder.

She pushed into him. "I wouldn't mind."

"Not so soon. Give your body some time, or it won't be as enjoyable."

Reaching out, she touched the cover of *Night Storm*. "No nightmares."

"Thanks to you." He kissed the sensitive area at the base of her neck.

She turned over until they lay face-to-face, the sheet crumpled at their waists. Lifting a hand, she traced her fingertips over his temple, the side of his head, under his ear, along his jaw, stopping at the crease in his chin.

"When it's time," she whispered, "will you return to your unit?"

"Yes." He kissed her forehead, temple, cheekbone. "If they deem me ready for duty."

"You seem... different this morning."

"Sex does that to a man."

She pinched his nose, drawing a chuckle from him and a nip on her knuckle.

"Not just this morning," she said. "Last night I noticed it too."

"Reid introduced me to a special kind of yoga." He hesitated. "One designed for people like me."

"People who have experienced trauma?"

"Yes."

"Do you think you'll ever be able to share what happened with me?"

His hand cupped her cheek. "I don't know. But if I ever can, I will."

Covering his hand with hers, she said, "Thank you." She leaned in and gave him a soft, grateful kiss. "When you return and get your next leave, will you—will you come visit me?"

He studied her face as if it were a fine painting hanging in the Met. "No."

"N-no?" she repeated on a cracked whisper.

"Steele Ridge is a long way away from Fort Bragg."

"I could come to you."

"What about your work?"

She nodded. "I would just need to schedule it in advance so I could let Britt know."

A smile played on his lips before it disappeared. "What happens when your contract with Britt ends?"

The dread of reality intruded on her perfect morning. Pulling away, she sat up and hugged her knees. "I don't know."

Coen rose beside her, propping one arm on a raised knee while his hand made lazy circles over her bare back.

"If your research takes you out of the country, are you allowed to make trips back home?"

"Yes. I made sure it was part of the funding when I went to Costa Rica."

"Randi will likely sell her house soon, which means you'll need a new home base."

"Mom and Dad haven't turned my old bedroom into an office yet."

"What about Fort Bragg?"

She glanced back and found a hesitant smile on his face. "You want me to spend time on base with you?"

He nuzzled the crook of her neck. "Lots of time."

Twisting around mermaid style, she caught his face in her hands. "Are we really going to do this?"

"If you're sure you can handle it." His gaze held hers. "I may not ever be free of the memories, and there may be worse ones ahead."

Kissing his forehead, she whispered, "I'll help you create more good memories to help offset the bad."

"My fearless Miss Indy."

41

"What's the matter?" Coen asked after Riley hit the Send button on her text.

"Britt. He's running behind and asked me to open the public part of the center."

Curling his fingers around hers again, he turned away from the greenhouse to head up the service drive.

"What are you doing?"

"Going to the center."

"No sense in your hovering around while I go through the process of opening." She waved to the greenhouse. "It would be a big help if you'd get started on the watering and weeding."

Their lovemaking had altered something inside him, right down to the cell level. From the first moment he saw her on the ridge, he'd felt protective toward her. But now he didn't want her out of his sight. The thought of releasing her hand and watching her walk away locked every muscle in place.

"Opening the center will be faster if I help."

"No, it won't. It's been a while since I've had to do this, so

I've got to think about it. If I also have to worry about keeping you busy, it'll take twice as much time."

When she tried to remove her hand from his, he held on. She frowned at him until understanding dawned. Brushing a thumb across his cheek, she said, "I'll be fine. If someone wanted to hurt me, I've given them much better opportunities."

Feeling ridiculous, he opened his hand.

"That wasn't so hard now, was it?"

"Do you really want me to answer that?"

Smiling, she dug her keys out of a zippered compartment on her pack, unclipped the greenhouse key, and tossed it to him. "I'll be back in fifteen minutes."

When she made to turn away, he grabbed her arm and brought his mouth down on hers, needing, aching for another taste. Another sip that was uniquely Riley.

By the time the kiss ended, they were both breathing hard.

"Go," he growled, "before I change my mind."

She laughed and sprinted away.

Coen followed her long legs and flipping ponytail until she rounded a bend and disappeared. Stretching his neck one way, then the other, he forced himself in the other direction and began ticking the minutes off in his mind.

Before he inserted the key in the lock, his sixth sense—the one that had always warned him that shit was about to go down—waved a big, red caution flag in front of his face.

He inspected the lock and found the telltale signs of tampering. Sliding the key into his pocket, he used his finger to push the door open and slipped inside. Fear and memories did not follow him into the greenhouse. Discipline, training, and laser-focused determination pushed him forward and encased him like Kevlar.

Head low, he darted for one of the high shelving units filled with plants and crouched to draw a knife from his ankle.

Broken pots, spilled dirt, and trampled plants littered the floor. The drawers of Riley's desk hung open and were emptied of their contents. He scanned the area for movement but found none.

What would've happened if Riley had come across the intruder? An image of her lying on the floor, eyes vacant and blood pooling around her, sent a searing stab of fear through his bones.

Was this connected to the texts, note, and Audi Guy?

Had to be. Why would anyone break into a greenhouse unless they thought something they wanted was here?

Pushing away from his hiding place, he swept through the structure as if it sat in the middle of a war-torn city he'd been sent to secure. Row by row of propagated plants, he searched for his enemy and their deadly devices.

The blow came out of nowhere.

Sharp, skull-cracking pain pitched Coen forward. A haze blanketed his vision. He shook it away and whipped around to face his assailant. A fist connected with his jaw, and he staggered backward.

Rage ignited cylinders that had gone dormant during his leave. When a boot slashed toward his midsection, he contorted his body to the side, evading the strike. It was then that he got his first look at the intruder. Although he wore a mask, Coen could see enough to determine a few things quickly—male, white, tall, muscular but not bulky.

Tightening his hold on his knife, he demanded, "Who are you?"

The guy dove away.

He followed, but when he got to the aisle his assailant

had disappeared down, it was empty. A scuffling noise to his right caught his attention. He tracked the sound, putting one silent foot in front of the other.

The door to the greenhouse slammed shut.

"Goddammit!" Coen took off. When he got outside, he found no sign of his assailant.

Riley.

He hauled ass down the service drive and nearly ran into her around the bend.

"What's wrong?" she cried.

"Did a guy pass you?" He peered over her shoulder.

"No, there's no one back there. Britt just pulled into the parking lot, but otherwise no one. Did something happen in the greenhouse?"

Grasping her hand, he hauled her toward the parking lot.

"What are you doing?"

"Getting you to safety."

She dug her heels in. "Is everything okay at the greenhouse?"

"There's been a break-in."

"And the burglar was still in there?"

He clenched his teeth. "Yes."

"I want to see the damage."

Tugging on her hand, he said, "Later."

"No, now." She wrenched free of his grip and ran in the opposite direction.

"Riley!"

Damn, if she wasn't fast. He caught up to her right where the service drive spilled into a small grassy area before the greenhouse.

"Hold up. Let me go first."

"You think someone's still in there."

"No, but I don't want to take any chances." What he wouldn't do to have a locked vehicle nearby. He'd feel better if she had some protection while he went inside. "Stay here. Scream if you see anything out of the ordinary."

"No way am I letting you leave me out here."

"I can clear the building faster on my—"

"Own," she finished for him. "Listen, I get that having me around isn't your preference. But I'm not going to let you go in there by yourself." She burrowed her small hand into his free one. "I'll cover your back."

A ferocious determination molded her features, and warmth spread around his heart. Allowing her into an unsecured building scared the hell out of him, but he couldn't release her hand. Instead, humor twitched at the corners of his mouth.

"What will you use to cover my back?"

"I've got a healthy set of lungs inside this body, and they're just waiting to rip free."

He raised an eyebrow in warning. "Try not to take out my eardrum, okay?"

"Do I need to get you some personal protection equipment?"

"Earmuffs would hinder my ability to hear the bad guy." He squeezed her hand. "I'll take my chances. Step where I step. Do what I say."

"Yes, Sergeant."

He squeezed her hand again. Harder.

Even though he didn't expect to find anyone or anything, he gave this sweep as much attention as the first. With Riley on his heels, all his senses were heightened, the stakes higher. If he screwed up, he wouldn't be the only one to pay.

A few minutes later, he gave the all-clear sign, the action

as second nature to him as brushing his teeth. For a second he'd allowed himself to forget that his team didn't exist.

He glanced down to find Riley's eyes wide with horror. Horror at what a stranger had done to her beloved plants.

"I'm sorry," he said, skimming his thumb over her knuckles.

Eyes full of sadness flicked up to his. His heart slammed against the wall of his chest. Once. Twice. Three times. The impact of her gaze shook him to his core.

Moving away from him to pick through the debris, she said, "This isn't just a hurried robbery. This is d-destruction. It's hateful. Who dislikes me so much?"

"Maybe it's something else."

"Like what?"

If he'd given her another couple of minutes, she would've connected the dots. But her mind couldn't wrap around what was before her.

"Searching for something."

"In a greenhouse?"

"The text, the murders, and now a break-in. My gut tells me they're connected."

"You think the other scientists were killed for something they had in their possession?"

"It's one possibility." Moving to her side, he reached out a hand, running his fingers from her elbow to her other hand. Something contracted in his chest when her fingers wrapped around his. "Did you bring home anything unusual from Costa Rica?"

"A few cultural souvenirs. Nothing special."

"Has anything changed in the past couple of weeks? Anything unusual?"

She gnawed on her lower lip. "A few days ago, Nick Landry visited me at the farmers' market. He was in town for a conference and dropped by to say hello. He worked on Endurance with me."

He recalled her mentioning Landry and a Dr. Young to Maggie in her office.

"Did he ask you any odd questions?"

"Not that I can think of." Realization swiped away her shock. "The package."

"What package?"

"The one I received from Camilla earlier this week. It contained the note and a children's book."

"I think it's time you told me exactly what kind of research you were conducting in Costa Rica."

She nodded. "During my junior and senior year of undergrad, I interned in Costa Rica. Because of the constant moisture in the area, the people who live in the more remote areas are prone to fungus and skin issues. The locals rely heavily on certain native plants to treat those issues. What I found was that a combination of three different plants appeared to not only treat but cure what we call psoriasis."

"Skin rash, right?"

"That, and so much more. It can be very itchy and unsightly. Extreme cases can cause painful swelling in the joints." She peered up at him. "Psoriasis may not be as problematic as cancer, but over 125 million people worldwide suffer from it."

"What happened after your internships?"

"I mentioned what I had discovered to my mentor at the university, and he made a few phone calls. But since I didn't have a PhD behind my name, no one was willing to invest in additional research so that I could prove my hypothesis." A small smile, edged with bittersweet, appeared. "Or so I thought. Six months into my graduate program, I received a phone call from Dr. Hathaway, asking me to return to Costa Rica and finish what I'd started."

"How long were you in Central America?"

"Two years conducting interviews with the indigenous people, one year securing permissions and additional funding for Project Endurance."

"How old are you?"

"Twenty-five."

"Did you graduate college early?"

"A full two years."

"I'm sleeping with a genius."

She looked away. "Book smart, people stupid."

He hooked a finger beneath her chin. "What's wrong?"

"I found out that Hathaway aborted Endurance after discovering one of the plants was a cure for impotency."

"A cure?"

"Happy thought, huh?"

"More profit in boners?"

"Evidently."

Sensing she needed a change of topic, he asked, "Did the package from Camilla contain anything else?"

"No, only—" Her head swiveled toward an upturned cart, to the tray of seeds he'd planted several days ago.

She rushed to pick up the tray that had thankfully landed face up and set it on a nearby workbench. From her backpack, she pulled out something small and round and positioned it over the tiny plant's leaves. He recalled seeing it hanging from her neck on that first day she stared down at him from the ridge.

"What's that?"

"A loupe or hand lens. It allows me to see tiny details on plants so I can identify one from the other."

"Plant identification is that technical?"

"You'd be surprised." She spent several seconds looking at the seedlings. When she straightened, a look of wonder lit up her beautiful eyes. "This is *Timbroma subvolanum*."

"Timbro what?"

"Picanula is the common name. It's one of the plants I was studying in Costa Rica, the one Nick said cured impotency."

"Why would Camilla send you those seeds?"

Her gaze took on a familiar faraway look. She sucked in a sharp breath.

"What?"

"Camilla's note. *Keep fort safe.*" She thrummed her fingers against the workbench. "The other night I figured out *fort* must stand for *fourth*. Me and the other three scientists, but I couldn't figure out the significance." Her fingers thrummed faster. "What if she sent all four of us seed paper?"

She locked eyes with him, and they said in unison, "To protect it."

"From whom?" she asked.

A knock on the door behind them forced thoughts of precious seeds from his mind. "Stay here." He marched toward the door but heard a shuffling behind him. "I told you to stay put."

"I am. At your side."

Strong-willed, brilliant female.

"At least stay behind me. *Please.*"

She smiled. "Certainly."

Standing to the side of the door, he opened it to find a young woman.

"*Buenos dias,* Riley."

Resting a hand on his tense shoulder, Riley said with a

smile in her voice, "This is Camilla. My former assistant in Costa Rica."

42

_____

Leaning his backside against the counter, Coen split his attention between the young woman sitting at the round breakfast table and Riley at the stove. The scent of scrambled eggs, fried potatoes, and sizzling strips of bacon filled the air in the bungalow's kitchen.

Standing in the neighborhood of five feet tall, Camilla sat with her back straight, and her dark eyes took in every detail of her surroundings. Her long black hair was secured in a bun knot at the back of her head, accentuating a pretty, rounded, teenaged face.

Upon seeing the young woman, Riley had enveloped her in a long hug. They'd spoken in rapid Spanish and inspected each other from head to toe. Then Riley had ushered them out of the destroyed greenhouse and into her vehicle.

While darting across town, she'd nattered on about local landmarks and pointed out interesting shops the whole way. He suspected she did so to keep the conversation off the ten-ton gorilla stuffed inside the car with them.

What the hell was Camilla doing in the States? In North

Carolina? Had more researchers died? Had someone threatened her?

"Your home is beautiful," Camilla said in a heavily accented voice.

"Thanks, but it's not mine. It belongs to my cousin's fiancée."

Camilla smiled, dropping her guarded expression and revealing a hint of mischief that must have been a magnet to Riley years ago. "You live with your cousin's fiancée?"

"No. Randi moved into Britt's cabin. She's letting me stay here until they figure out what to do with this place."

"So much space for one person."

"Is your family from Costa Rica?" he asked.

Her chin lifted a notch. "No *familia*, señor."

"What did you do before working with Riley?"

"I was a thief."

He shot Riley a glance, and she grinned.

"Not a very good one. We met when I caught her trying to lift my pack."

"I've improved."

Riley eyed the table. "So I've noticed."

The moment they'd set foot inside the house, Camilla had shoved Dr. Young's journal into Riley's hands and backed away, as if she could no longer stand the stink of it. The journal had sat in the center of the table like a bloodied weapon retrieved from a crime scene.

Riley placed the steaming plate in front of her guest, then returned to the stove to fix two more. "Don't wait for us. Eat while it's hot."

Two pieces of crispy bread popped up out of the toaster, and Coen hot-fingered them onto a plate holding four other slices.

"Mind if I grab the butter?" he asked, setting the mounded plate on the table.

"Not if you don't mind bringing out the strawberry preserves and peach jam while you're in there."

Despite his heightened, on-alert senses, an odd note of domestication rocked him back a step. The situation was so foreign to him that it had taken him a couple of seconds to identify the feeling.

Even though he'd spent the past few weeks trying to wind down, his mind was still locked in active mode. He patrolled the perimeter of his campsite, morning and night. Cleaned and checked his weapons, every day. Ate his food as if someone would take it away any minute.

The ease with which Riley moved around the kitchen indicated she'd spent many hours at the stove. Heat crawled up his spine and burned the back of his neck at the thought of her making breakfast for another man.

Slamming the refrigerator door, he carried the condiments back to the table and slid into the empty chair next to Riley. She shot him a concerned look before pulling a slice of toast off the plate and slathering it with peach jam.

They ate in silence, the only sounds coming from the clink of their forks against plates and the air-conditioning unit shuddering to life.

"How long has it been since you've eaten, Camilla?" Riley said in a low, matter-of-fact tone.

The young woman finished chewing her food and straightened her spine from its hunched position. "A cooked meal like this? Not since you left." She glanced down at her plate, embarrassed.

Riley slid a hand over the young woman's head. "You're here now, my brave friend. Eat, then tell us what's going on."

Gratitude sparkled in Camilla's eyes. "*Gracias,* Miss King —Riley. Everything is delicious."

When the girl turned her attention away, he slid his hand over Riley's. Her gaze shot to his in surprise, and he squeezed her fingers. A wan smile appeared before she returned the gesture.

Another silence settled over them while they finished their meal. Riley's characteristic impatience had disappeared in the wake of Camilla's arrival. He'd never seen her so calm and purposeful.

Holding up his coffee cup, he asked, "Does anyone else need a refill?"

"*Sí, señor.*"

"No thanks."

He returned to the table with the coffee decanter and filled his and Camilla's cups, then he leaned against the counter again and sipped his brew, trusting Riley to know when the time was right to extract information from the young woman. He didn't have long to wait.

"Would you like some more eggs?" Riley asked.

Camilla rubbed her stomach. "I could not eat another bite."

"Can I ask you a few questions?"

Squaring her shoulders, Camilla sat back in her chair and nodded.

"First off, why didn't you answer my texts?"

"I waited awhile for you to respond to the links I sent. When you didn't, I got nervous about having that phone on me. So I reset it and destroyed the SIM card."

"I'm sorry, Camilla. I dropped my phone after seeing your messages. It took me a while to get to another device."

Riley didn't bat an eye as she stretched out the truth of

how her phone got broken. Everything she said was technically correct. But her need to do so made his stomach roil.

"How did you get here?" Riley asked.

"I got on a plane and then requested a car."

"Just like that, huh?"

Camilla raised a brow. "Did you think I stole away in the back of a truck?"

"No, I just... I don't know. It seems a long way to travel for someone alone and who has never left her country."

"I assisted with your travel arrangements to and from North Carolina many times over the years." Her faced scrunched. "Moving through the airports was a challenge, but I always found someone to help me."

"But the expense."

"For the past three years, I have been stashing away a portion of my paycheck. I had enough to get me here."

"You used your entire savings to bring me Dr. Young's journal?"

A deep line creased her forehead as she redirected her attention to her empty plate. "No, I did not intend to burden you with that, but..."

Riley glanced at him in confusion.

"Why did you come here?" he asked.

Her glistening eyes lifted to Riley. "To protect you and beg your forgiveness."

"Forgiveness for what?"

"For putting you in danger." Camilla's gaze took on a faraway look. "Never did I think that *he* would learn where I sent the seeds." She blinked and grasped Riley's hand. "But he did, and everyone is dead but you."

Covering Camilla's hand with her own, Riley asked, "Why did you send us *Timbroma*?"

"After you and the rest of our team left Costa Rica, they

didn't close down the research center. They brought in a new group of researchers."

Riley nodded. "I heard."

"How?"

"Go on with your story. I'll explain later."

"Right away I could tell the new scientists were different. They were disrespectful to those in the village, and they brought in a crew of laborers to remove *Timbroma* from the wild."

"A crew?" Riley asked. "I don't understand."

"I didn't either and started asking questions. Soon after, they fired me."

"Did you learn anything?"

"They would not answer my questions." Disgust laced Camilla's voice. "So I followed the crew for a few days and overheard a couple of them talking."

He leveled a look on Riley. "Did you teach her how to spy too?"

Riley grinned. "I didn't have to. Camilla's observation skills were already razor-sharp by the time we met." She refocused. "What did you hear?"

"They were hired to remove every last *Timbroma* from the wild."

"Sounds like an impossible task," he said.

"It wouldn't be," Riley said. "*Timbroma* can only be found in that part of Costa Rica. Of course, it would take a while to deplete the seed bank."

"What's a seed bank?" he asked.

"In basic terms, it's seed that has been deposited and stored in the soil for years. Some can remain viable for a long time." She turned to Camilla. "Did you learn why they wanted to remove it?"

"So that they could have a—" Camilla frowned,

searching for the word.

"Monopoly," he offered, crossing his arms.

She nodded.

"Smart," he said. "They're regulating supply and demand. If they're the only company who has access to this *Timbroma,* then they could charge whatever they wanted for the drug. Competition wouldn't exist."

Tears gathered in Camilla's eyes.

Riley brushed a thumb over the young woman's wet cheek. "What's wrong?"

"I killed them."

"What are you talking about?"

"I took their store of *Timbroma* seeds and sent them to the team for safekeeping. Now they are all dead." She lifted tear-blurred eyes to Riley. "Except you."

Riley sat back in her chair and stared at her former assistant. "There has to be another explanation."

"Why did you send such a cryptic note with the package?" asked Coen.

"Cryptic?"

"The note's meaning was unclear."

Camilla closed her eyes. "Not enough time," she whispered through trembling lips. "It would have taken me all day to write something more detailed to each of you, and I could not chance the delay. I did not want to be around when he came for me."

"That's the second time you've referred to *he,*" Riley said. "He, who?"

"Nick Landry."

"Nick? Why would he come for you?"

"There is darkness in him." Camilla caught Riley's gaze. "But I think you knew that—or at least sensed it. He is a dog as well as a brute."

Riley didn't blush or send him a sideways glance at the mention of her near miss with catastrophe. Lines of concentration bunched on her forehead as she no doubt sifted through past encounters with her former colleague.

"Like every other human," Riley said, "Nick had quirks —some quite irritating, but I never picked up on a brutish quality. If I had, I would've demanded that Dr. Hathaway replace him."

"The dead scientists," he said. "You think Landry killed them?"

"I'm sure of it."

"But why?" Riley asked, clearly unable to see her friend as a cold-blooded murderer.

"He changed after you left and the other scientists arrived. He became... harder."

Riley sat back, visibly overwhelmed by all of Camilla's revelations. "I can't believe that Dr. Young would condone such behavior. He wasn't my favorite person. He cared little for those around him and everything for the research. But I'm having a hard time believing he would agree to all this."

"Money motivates people in different ways," Coen said. "For some, the accumulation of wealth—or power—is their attempt to fill a black, bottomless void in their soul. What they don't understand is that there's not enough money in the world to fill the hole."

Riley stared at him as if he'd prophesized the exact date of the next coming.

Self-conscious, he turned to the window. A red Doberman pranced alongside an elderly woman down the sidewalk. The mismatched pair made him smile, despite the serious tension at his back. He followed the duo's progress until they disappeared from his line of sight.

"Despite the danger," Camilla said, "I had to come see you to explain what happened."

"I'm glad you did," Riley said. "You'll be safe here."

"I am not concerned about me. Nick must have asked the others if they had seen or heard from me, and they told him about the package. Now he is on the hunt for the journal, the seed, me, and anyone else who knows about them."

Coen asked, "When Landry was here, did he question you about Camilla or the journal?"

"He was here?"

"Nick visited several days ago." Riley's eyes caught his. "I hadn't received Camilla's package yet. I think it had been delayed because of some damage to the envelope."

If the package had been delivered as planned, she might have shared the information with Landry, effectively signing her death warrant.

He stalked over to Riley and slid a hand around the back of her neck. "It's time to update your sister."

Dazed, she shook her head. "He's gone. I dropped him off at the airport the same day I had dinner with him."

He thought a moment. "Smoke and mirrors."

"Why do you say that?"

"Because I suspect he's Audi Guy and also the one responsible for trashing your greenhouse."

Realization lit her eyes. "He didn't believe me." Her expression flipped through emotions like a rich, page-turning story—surprise, anger, sadness, and... horror.

"What's wrong?" he demanded.

"He might have been in my house."

His grip tightened. "When?"

"Two nights ago. When I got home, I noticed the bedspread was rumpled."

"Maybe you sat on it and forgot."

She shook her head. "Making my bed is the last thing I do before leaving. It's a Kingston rule. The rest of my bedroom could've been a disaster, but my dad didn't care as long as my bed was made."

"Why am I just hearing about this now?"

"Part of me thought it may have been Randi or Britt."

"And the other part?"

Guilt streaked across her features, but she didn't apologize.

"Did you at least tell your sister?"

A pained expression replaced her guilt. "I meant to, when she was over at my house."

"But?"

"We got distracted by"—her eyes shifted from his—"by another topic."

Him.

Coen would wager his bank account on it.

Camilla shot from her chair and grabbed Dr. Young's journal from the table.

Riley snatched the journal from the young woman's hand. "Where do you think you're going?"

"Leaving." Camilla held out her hand. "Give it to me. I will take the danger with me."

"Not a chance."

"Riley—"

He stepped between them. "No one is going anywhere. After we fill in Maggie, I'll move my things here."

"I appreciate everything you've done so far," Riley said, securing the journal beneath her arm, "but I still don't feel right about your getting involved in this."

Ever his protector.

Stepping close, he used his index finger to push her glasses up the bridge of her nose. "If you think that I would walk away while a murderer who is, if not in love with you, definitely in lust with you, stalking you like prey, then you don't have the slightest measure of my character."

The worry lines around her eyes softened but didn't disappear. She rested a hand against his heart.

"I don't want you... injured because of me."

"It would injure me far worse to walk away."

She closed her eyes, fighting an inner battle. When she opened them again, she whispered, "Thank you" before lifting up onto her toes and pressing a kiss to his lips. Her kiss was tentative at first, then it deepened, lengthened, heated.

He molded his body around hers, wanting to absorb every beautiful, courageous, irritating inch of her.

A throat cleared, and they broke away.

"Sorry, Camilla," Riley said, her knuckles brushing over his erection as she turned toward her houseguest.

His stomach clenched and his teeth clamped together around a curse. She would pay for that bit of mischief.

"Let's get you settled into the spare bedroom, then we'll discuss this situation with the sheriff. I also need to alert Dr. Hathaway about Nick and Dr. Young."

"No *policía*."

"There's no need to worry," Riley said. "The sheriff is my sister. She'll protect you while helping us find Nick."

Some of the tension eased from young woman's shoulders. When Riley turned away, Camilla turned her dark eyes on him. In their depths, a question hovered.

He nodded, and a pact to keep Riley safe, at all costs, was reached.

43

"WHAT MAKES A PERSON BRAVE?"

The question had clawed at Riley's thoughts, over and over and over since they'd returned home.

After wrestling the greenhouse back into some semblance of order and having Camilla share her story with Maggie, Riley had brought her exhausted friend back to the bungalow for another hot meal and a place to lay her head. Camilla had clutched at Riley's hand until exhaustion hip-checked her fear.

Sitting next to her on a cushioned glider wide enough for two, Coen used his outstretched foot to keep the seat moving in a lulling rhythm while they watched birds flit between the feeder, birdbath, and redbud tree.

"Circumstances, self-preservation, love, fear," he said. "All of which can also make a person curl into the fetal position."

"How do you tell which type of person you'll be? Brave or coward?"

"Jump into the flames and see what happens."

"Even in the military? Couldn't a soldier's courage be gauged through training and scenarios?"

"Many have tried, myself included. But there's no way of truly knowing how someone will respond to a life-and-death situation until the shit hits the fan and they're in the spatter zone." He cut her a look. "Why do you ask?"

She ached to burrow into his side and let him rock her to sleep. It had been years since she'd indulged in that kind of idleness. Not since spraining her ankle in high school and being forced to keep it elevated for hours on end. Even then, she'd read, did her homework, or packaged things up to sell at the market.

When in Coen's arms last night, her ticker tape of questions had stopped. Vanished like a bunny in a magic act. Somewhere between his expert attention on the outer aureole of her left breast and him sliding into her damp heat, she'd lost her ability to think.

Unable to meet his eyes, she turned her attention to the backyard, marveling at the secluded paradise Randi had made for herself. A fusion of pink, purple, and yellow petunias perched in the window boxes of an adorable pale yellow she-shed at the back of the property. A high privacy fence was made less off-putting by a 3D layout of towering trees, low-clustering shrubs, and blooming perennials. Not a single prying eye could penetrate Randi's garden.

"I wonder what I would've done in Camilla's place. Fought for what I believed in? Or walked away?"

Rather than ply her with confidence-building platitudes, he angled his face away and swallowed hard.

Her attention flicked to the hand resting on his thigh. To his knuckles, where they pushed against his skin. Pushed until blood leached from the veins.

Don't ever touch him.

Way's warning ripped through her mind and she laced her fingers together.

"Don't mind me," she said. "It was a stupid question." She beamed sunshine into her voice. "There's no need for you to stick around. Maggie's going to increase the patrols on my neighborhood."

"I'm not going anywhere."

"There's nothing for you to do here."

The rocking motion stopped, and he draped an arm over the back of the glider. His warmth penetrated her T-shirt.

"I disagree. There are all kinds of things to do here." His mouth closed over hers, putting an end to the argument.

His tongue swept inside, and the heat of his erotic caress made her press into the kiss, harder. Her body followed, and she soon found herself draped over him, from torso to groin. She clung to his jaw, his neck, his head while wanting more and more from his kiss.

Large hands wrapped around her hips and lifted her. She straddled his lap, thankful for her loose-legged running shorts.

A roll of his hips brought his hardness in contact with her center, making them both groan their pleasure.

Releasing her, he scraped her T-shirt out of the way, brushing his lips over one breast, then the next, before freeing a tight, aching nipple from its silken cocoon. He rolled the bud between his fingers. Her back arched, wanting, wanting, wanting—

Liquid heat brushed against the peak, once, twice, three times before the whole of it disappeared into his mouth.

She almost came. Warmth pooled between her legs, and her inner muscles clenched around a bolt of white-hot need.

While he teased and tantalized with his mouth, his hand

skimmed along her thigh. The backs of his fingers soon met the thin barrier of her panties.

"You're so hot down here," he said in a thick voice. "I want to be inside you so fucking bad."

Like last time, his dirty talk excited her on a primal level. A wildness entered her bloodstream, and she wanted him as much as he wanted her.

"Neighbors?" she asked.

"Clear."

"Protection?"

"Pocket."

"Fit?"

He hooked a finger in her panties and shoved them aside. The cool air felt delicious, but it did nothing to soothe the inferno building at her core.

Nostrils flaring on a deep inhalation, he said, "Say the word."

She couldn't take her eyes off him. His intensity, strength, and breath-stealing handsomeness excited her. She worried that if she moved or looked away for one second, he would disappear and she would be left alone, aching and unsated.

One thick finger eased inside, and her head snapped back. Her body bowed and clenched around him with a ferocity she didn't realize she possessed.

"Say it, Riley. Tell me what you want."

Throat thick, she said nothing. She closed her eyes and concentrated on his intoxicating torture, the sensations—

His finger drew away.

The hollowness he left behind made her stomach cramp. She opened her eyes, preparing to beg him to continue.

"Say it."

Heart pounding, she stared at him with burning eyes.

"Do you want to come?"

"Yes," she whispered.

"Then tell me how I can shatter you to pieces."

When she still said nothing, his jaw tightened and he grabbed her hips as if to set her away. She dug her nails into his shoulders, preparing to fight like a cat for what she wanted. The words built in her chest, rose in her throat—

"Make the world disappear."

The fierceness left his features, and he kissed her hard, thoroughly, then more gently. "Anything for you," he whispered against her neck, reaching into his pocket and rolling on a condom.

Her fear of losing *this*—him—receded against an onslaught of sensations. When the blunt tip of him slid along her wetness, the tears she'd been holding slid down her cheeks in silent thanks.

Pushing inside, he eased into her, deeper and deeper and deeper. Their bodies sat flush against each other. The summer air caught their uneven breaths as he set an even rhythm meant to draw out their pleasure until it became an agony of unfulfilled release.

"Feel me, Riley. Take me. Take it all."

Closing her eyes, she set her mind free.

The glider sailed along with them, increasing the friction between their bodies. He broke their kiss to rub his thumb along the seam of her lips. She opened her mouth and rolled her tongue around the soft pad.

Without breaking eye contact, he used his wet thumb to find and manipulate her clit. Pressure mounted until—

Her world exploded.

She buried her cry into the L of his neck at the same

time his hips pumped one last time and a guttural groan vibrated against her breast.

How long they sat there, with him embedded inside her and their pulses clamoring for calm, she didn't know.

Memories of their lovemaking punctuated the silence that grew between them. Why did she find it so difficult to tell him what she wanted?

In no other facet of her life was she so unsure, so *Beta*. Since the moment she could toddle around on two feet and issue commands, she'd organized everything in her life to suit her end goal. Whether that be making Way tie his boots a dozen times until she duplicated his technique or nagging Cash to certify her in CPR so she could land a summer job at the pool or forcing Shep to take her zip-lining in order to overcome her fear of heights (she was still perfecting that skill) or wheedling Maggie to teach her how to drive, she'd always taken control of her destiny.

Until Coen or, more specifically, Coen's lovemaking made her want to follow his every move, his every command. In his arms, she liked to be commanded, liked the anticipation of the known yet unknown.

He skimmed his lips over her neck. "There will be no more talk of my leaving. Understood?"

Closing her eyes, she nodded, though she whispered, "But you will. Eventually."

"Not tonight." He pressed a hot, openmouthed kiss against her flesh. "Or tomorrow." His tongue burned a line beneath her jaw. "Or tomorrow night..."

Tilting her head back, she peered into the night and commanded it to never end.

44

"What do you mean you still don't have it? Didn't the girl show up?"

Nick pulled in a breath, willing calm into his voice. He hated the pompous ass, but their unavoidable connection and a generous paycheck ensured Nick's allegiance. He readjusted the cell phone against his ear. "Yes, she arrived last night."

"What's the problem? Get the journal."

"There's been an unexpected complication."

"Of what sort?"

"Riley has a protector now." Nick could barely get the words past the acid eating away at his throat. After last night, the soldier was far more than her protector.

Lover.

"Who is he?"

"Coen Monroe. Beyond that, I don't know."

"I'll do some digging around. But if he's become an obstacle, take care of him."

Oh, I will. "I can't kill everyone between me and the journal."

"Since when? You've never been squeamish about the dirty work before."

True. He would have no problem disposing of the girl and that bastard Monroe. But Riley. Riley was different.

He'd wanted her since his first sight of her hunched over a wooden bowl, merrily stirring ingredients for a poultice.

The joy on her face and the unabashed enthusiasm with which she stirred her concoction had made him hard on the spot. He'd tried every seduction technique in his wheel-house to lure her into his bed, and she'd refused him. Which only made him ache for her more.

No other woman—and he'd sampled them all within a ten-mile radius—could purge his need for Riley. She'd become essential to his existence. Like air. Only more necessary.

"What are you not telling me?"

He clenched his jaw. "I'll get the journal. But I'll do it my way."

"See that you do. The foundation's board and our most influential donors are pressing me for a status report, and the Costa Rican government has requested a meeting."

"Why?"

"They're investigating a complaint about the true nature of our research."

Camilla. If he didn't hate her so much, he would've admired her tactics.

"Has Young made any headway on recreating his research?"

"He's hit a wall, which means we're dead in the water."

"What are you going to do about the board and the investigation?"

"Stall—until you do your damned job."

Patronizing son of a bitch. One day Nick would be pulling all the strings.

"Twenty-four hours, Nick. You have twenty-four hours to locate the journal, dispatch the thief—and anyone else who knows of the journal's existence."

The few emotions he had left winked out. "I'll have it taken care of in twelve."

45

"Have you enjoyed your R and R?"

Coen's pulse raced at the undercurrent in Colonel Walsh's voice. "Yes, sir."

"I have something brewing that could use your leadership."

Rising, Coen widened his stance and squared his shoulders. "When do you need me?"

"I'll know more in a few days."

He met Riley's gaze across the worktable. "I'll be ready."

"I understand you haven't contacted her yet?"

He closed his eyes, allowing his silence to answer for him.

A stool scraped against the concrete floor, then a small, warm hand slipped over his forearm, and Riley's fresh scent filled his senses. Though his chest continued to splinter into a thousand pieces, he took comfort in her presence and strength in her touch.

"Away from the unit for a few weeks and now you think you can disobey a direct order?"

"No, sir."

"What am I missing? When we last spoke, I gave you two orders."

"I've completed one." *Sort of.*

"You sure about that, son?"

"Y-yes—" He cleared his throat. "Yes, sir."

"Take care of the other, Operator Monroe. Or don't bother coming back to base."

The line went dead.

Still holding his phone, he braced his hands against the table and fought the building panic. If he spoke to her, he'd have to face a truth he wasn't ready to accept. A truth he refused to acknowledge during his waking hours. A truth that had the power to sever the thin fiber holding him together in his dreams.

"I remember the first time I set foot in Costa Rica," Riley said, keeping a hand on his arm. "The small, twin-engine plane sputtered to a halt on what could barely be called a runway in the middle of the jungle." She rested her cheek against the back of his shoulder and rubbed calming circles over his back. "When I stepped out of the plane, the equatorial sun sprayed my face and the humidity filled my lungs." More lazy circles along his spine. "It was somehow thrilling and terrifying at the same time."

"What happened next?" he asked, his voice thick.

"My guide led me up the mountain to a tiny village where I spent the next two years living among the villagers and learning everything I could from their healer." She slid her palm over his arm, up and down, up and down.

"How did the people react to your questions?"

"Same way anyone around here would react to foreigners prying into their business. A good dose of suspicion, followed by an unhealthy curiosity, and ending with a generosity I wouldn't have dreamed possible."

He could visualize a bespectacled Riley Kingston flitting from village to village, sitting in someone's home or around the campfire, with her recorder—and notepad, because she would have a backup—camera, and treats for the kids. Despite their reservations, the people would flock to her, welcome her, share their secrets with her.

Like he did.

She kissed his shoulder. "They needed to know whether they could trust me or not."

Forcing the tension from his shoulders, he twisted to gather her in his arms. "Did you miss modern conveniences?"

"Not really, though I do love my daily shower. But after a while, I fell into a routine and had never felt so... settled before."

"Settled?"

"Content to focus on what was in front of me and not chasing the hundred things plowing through my mind."

He nuzzled the top of her head. "Thank you."

"Do you want to talk about it?"

"I wouldn't even know where to begin."

"Where it hurts," she whispered.

Anxiety flooded his chest, though the temptation to share the burden of his fears and failures had him nodding into her hair.

"Camilla," she called, threading her fingers through his.

"Yes?" Camilla poked her head around one of the large shelving units.

"Coen and I have some things to discuss. Will you be okay for a few minutes?"

"*Sí.*" She held up a tray of unruly plugs. "I can repot these for you."

"You'll get your pretty yellow dress dirty."

"Not if you let me borrow that old work shirt."

He followed Camilla's nod to a well-worn shirt draped over a stool.

Riley smiled. "I've missed you."

Camilla winked. "And I you."

"The four-inch pots are in the storage shed around back. The key is hanging by the back door. Feel free to use the utility vehicle."

Turning, Riley gripped his hand tighter and guided him to the dilapidated couch in her office. Rather than face him head-on, she sat next to him, shoulder to shoulder, hip to hip, and laid his hand on her thigh, covering it with hers.

Reaching between them, she unsnapped her leather-encased multi-tool from her belt and tossed it aside before snuggling closer. They sat in silence for several seconds; he, scrambling to collect the least appalling parts of his story and she, no doubt, practicing patience.

"What I'm about to tell you is highly classified and can go no further."

"I understand. You can trust my discretion."

"Three months ago, my unit was assigned a detail in South America." She lifted curious brows in his direction. "I can't share the exact location."

Her inquisitive expression fell.

"Bear with me, Riley. I'm sliding out on a very long limb by telling you any of this."

After a moment, she nodded and asked, "What sort of detail?"

He hesitated. Of course her first question would stab at the heart of his mission. Like many other Delta Force Operators, he'd perfected the art of evasion. It had become second nature for him to steer a conversation away from inquiries about his assignments.

How far should he let her in?

Studying their clasped hands, he realized the answer came to him much more easily than expected.

"We were sent to dispatch a bomb maker. Not just any bomb maker but one who has been linked to at least five catastrophic incidents on US soil."

"Dispatch, as in kill?"

"Yes." He glanced at her profile. "Should I go on, or have you heard enough?"

Her fingers tightened around his. "Go on, please."

The weight sinking into his chest lifted a little. "Our intelligence revealed that the bomb maker was utilizing an abandoned mine to test his masterpieces. Although he staggered the days and times of testing, he didn't alter the logistics of how he gained access to the mine."

"Allowing you to put a plan in place and bide your time."

Despite his growing sense of dread, he sent her an appreciative glance. "That's right. Like clockwork, four guards would exit a shanty at their compound and surveil the area. Thirty minutes later, three SUVs would fly up to the bomb maker's home. He and his entourage would pile in, and the convoy would set off for the test site."

"How many were on your team?"

K-THUNK.

K-thunk.

K-thunk-thunk.

His heartbeat deafened him for several seconds while he regained his equilibrium. When he was certain he could get the words past his teeth, he answered. "Five, including myself."

"You, Kendra. Who were the other three?"

"How do you know about Kendra?"

Her attention shifted away. "You've mentioned her a time or two."

"No, I haven't."

She leveled a look on him. "Then how do I know the name?"

Night terrors.

During the evenings she'd stayed with him, reading for hours, he must have cried out Kendra's name. His jaw hardened. What else had she heard?

"Paul, Freddy, Miller."

"Five against?"

"A few more."

Concern carved into her brow.

"We're trained for that exact scenario."

His statement did nothing to ease her worry. "What happened next?"

"A small stretch of the road leading to the mine provided the perfect cover for us to disable the vehicles and dispatch our target. We waited three days for the bomb maker to arrive." Moisture pebbled at the back of his neck, and a cold heat flushed his body. "As planned, our sniper took out the three drivers, halting the convoy. The rest of my unit moved in to eliminate our target. And that's when everything blew up."

"The bomb maker blew himself up?"

"No, my mission."

The muscles along his spine locked down as the scene replayed in his head. As he'd done a thousand times, he assessed and reassessed the situation, searching for the flaw in his plan. He never found one. What came next was simple, shitty bad luck.

Rather than ask him more questions, she waited for him to continue, showing her support, her encouragement, through the small, settling circles she finger-painted on his arm.

"The bomb maker had picked that day to invite a client to view his latest invention. The client's caravan of killers arrived minutes later."

"Trapping your team between the two."

The speed at which her mind processed complex, unfamiliar situations was amazing. She would make a great operator. Intelligence more than brawn was the common theme in Delta Force.

"Taking advantage of the distraction, one of the bomb maker's men tossed a grenade behind Miller." He could still see the shocked realization on his teammate's face before the blast ripped him to shreds. "My warning yell came too late."

"How long had you known him?"

"As big as the Army is, you come across the same people, over and over, especially when you get selected for and receive training in specialized units." Coen pushed back the nostalgia of better days. "The five of us had known each other for years, but when we joined the counterterrorism unit, we became an inseparable team."

"I envy that level of friendship." The half smile she mustered reflected a deep-seated longing. "I'm too much of an odd duck for most people."

He looped a finger around her chin and lifted her face up to his. "You're not odd, Riley. Driven, fearless, loyal, funny, compassionate, smart, and beautiful down to your very core, yes. But not odd."

Tears trembled in her eyes. She anchored her hand behind his neck and kissed him softly, slowly, thoroughly, clearing the darkness from his mind, his heart, long enough for him to savor the moment. To savor her.

When she finally drew away, she left him stronger than she'd found him. And he wondered if she'd given him a glimpse into her heart to give him time to collect himself, to pull himself together.

He pressed a kiss to the top of her head, marveling at the bounty of brilliance contained beneath his lips. He smiled, despite the heaviness floating in his chest.

"The blast stunned Kendra, Freddy, and Paul, giving the second convoy an opportunity to push their advantage. I leveled half their numbers, but it didn't stop Paul from taking a bullet to the head or the rest of my team from getting separated in the chaos that followed."

"Where were you when all that was happening?" she asked in a measured tone.

So she'd picked up on the nuance of his references.

"On a ridge with a sniper rifle."

"Oh, Coen. How helpless you must have felt to watch your team fall into trouble."

A long silence followed while he struggled all over again with the knowledge of how badly he'd failed his team.

"You don't have to go on," she whispered in an emotion-clogged voice, "if it's too painful."

Petal-soft fingertips sifted through the hairs on his arm, the rhythmic motion somehow easing the muscles in his throat.

He lifted her hand and kissed her knuckles, a swell of love for this woman making him speechless.

Love.

A new kind of fear socked him in the gut. Then the earthy, fresh scent he always associated with her pierced through his paralyzing thoughts and allowed him to continue.

"I eliminated several more of them before hauling ass

down the ridge. By the time I'd reached the bottom, Freddy had taken a bullet to the heart. I got to Kendra, but we were overwhelmed by sheer numbers."

"They took you and Kendra prisoner?"

An explosion of images sprayed through his mind like shards of broken glass. Squeezing his eyes shut, he fought to control the nausea rising up his throat.

Unable to sit still any longer, he surged to his feet, knocking Riley off-balance in his haste. He couldn't find words of apology, not past the swirling abyss of memories sucking him down, down, down. Memories he'd spent the past several weeks locking behind a steel trap.

The greenhouse suddenly became too confining, too close. He couldn't suck in a large enough breath to satisfy his lungs, and a wind tunnel had taken up residence in his ears.

Beyond the thick, clean windowpanes, the open meadow beckoned. *Freedom.*

"I need some fresh air."

46

FROZEN ON THE COUCH, RILEY'S GAZE FOLLOWED COEN'S rigid back. She didn't know whether she should shadow him or give him time and space to collect himself.

In truth, she wasn't sure she wanted to hear the rest of his tale. Already she'd struggled to hold back her tears, and he had yet to hit on the really terrible part. Whatever happened to him and Kendra had destroyed bits of his spirit, night after night.

Twisting back around, her gaze dropped to her discarded Leatherman where it rolled into her thigh. Absently she snapped and unsnapped the case. Was she strong enough to learn what horrific event had the power to break a warrior like Coen Monroe? The answer resounded in her head.

Bolting upright, she ran after Coen. Even if he wasn't ready to share that part of his story with her yet, she would be there to hold his hand or tell him another silly story. Whatever he needed until he realized he didn't have to fight his past alone.

The moment she cleared the door, a hand clamped over

her mouth and a strong arm wound around her middle. She craned her neck to see a pair of stunning golden eyes staring back at her.

"Hello, Riley," Nick whispered. "I think you're hiding something I want very, very much."

When she began to fight against his hold, he lifted a pistol and pointed it at Coen's retreating back. Coen stalked along the edge where the meadow met the tree line, fighting off the demons she'd forced him to dredge up.

"Calm down," he said against her ear. "Or I'll add your" —he gave her head a hard shake—"lover to my collateral damage collection." He nodded toward a tangle of lifeless limbs and a bright yellow dress, peeking out from beneath a patch of fern fronds.

Camilla.

A sob caught in the back of her throat, the sound muffled by the hand over her mouth.

"Shhh-sh-sh-sh," Nick warned quietly. "Do not draw your lover's attention, or he dies."

Her mind splintered in three directions: Protect Coen. Mourn Camilla. Stay alive. Every instinct she possessed screamed not to go with him. To fight Nick and alert Coen.

But the gun aimed at Coen kept her rock still. How would she ever forgive herself if Nick killed him? A soldier who'd survived the evils of war only to lose his life over a damned research journal. On American soil.

When Nick began backing away, she didn't resist.

47

By the time Coen reached the far corner of the meadow, his hands no longer shook and the compulsion to flee from the threat—from Riley—no longer drove him away.

He dug his thumb and forefinger into his eye sockets as if he could scrape Kendra's battered body from his memory.

"Dammit!"

All he'd needed was five more minutes. Five minutes to gut out his tale to Riley. But like every other time he'd tried to unload his story, he'd succumbed to the avalanche of emotions and retreated.

"I will not let this rule my life. I will not become a goddamn PTSD statistic. *I will not.*"

Dropping his hand, he closed his eyes, tilted his head back, and inhaled several even breaths. His senses opened, taking in the heavy mountain air, chattering birds, and whistling leaves. As always, the simple, biological action slowly reset his freak-out meter and calmed the electrical current sparking in his veins.

Glancing over his shoulder, he contemplated returning

to his campsite. How would he explain his explosive reaction to her straightforward question? Especially after she'd been so supportive and patient.

What must she be thinking right now? At the very least, she'd label him rude and unpredictable. At the very worst, she'd slap him with a disorder and consider him unstable.

Neither option set well with him.

He wanted her to see him as strong and courageous and compassionate and solid. He wanted her to laugh more, sleep more, enjoy life more.

He wanted her to sleep peacefully next to him, not be ripped from her dreams by his nightmares.

He wanted to not fear lying next to her.

Son of a bitch, he just wanted her.

Before he made a conscious decision on his direction, his feet did an about-face and headed back to the greenhouse. To Riley.

Groveling apology after groveling apology swerved through his mind like the Scrambler ride at an amusement park, each one more pathetic than the rest.

Expecting to find Riley pacing outside or toe-tapping at the door or peering out a window, he frowned at her visible absence. In fact, a malevolent stillness drenched the air, sending a stab of warning straight into his heart.

"*Riley!*" he bellowed as he tore open the door to the greenhouse. He ran down the center aisle, scanning left, right, left, right. "Riley! Camilla!"

Not a murmur or scuffle or a pair of concerned eyes. What he did find was Riley's backpack on the desk, with its contents strewn all around. From the looks of it, she'd been searching for something and, in her impatience, upended the whole pack.

What had she been looking for in such a hurry? Coen

sifted through her personal belongings and came across her wallet and keys. Opening her wallet, he found thirteen dollars and a major credit card still tucked inside. Heat pounded in his ears.

Something was off. Way off.

He glanced around the greenhouse again. Where had she gone? She couldn't be far, not without her keys. He studied the bits of Riley's life scattered across the table. What had she been searching for?

The mess before him took on a whole new meaning. Riley hadn't been the one rummaging through her backpack. Someone else had. Someone searching for Dr. Young's research journal.

Landry.

Had the bastard kidnapped Riley? What about Camilla? Terror flooded his mind, making him light-headed.

Focus, Monroe. Focus.

Whipping around, he ran down the aisle and slammed through the door. He did a three-sixty, scanning the area for Riley's brown head. His chest heaved and his thoughts splintered. Trees spiraled around him, and the whirring pulse of insects became deafening.

Focus, Monroe. Focus!

He forced himself to calm down, to dig into his training. To open his senses and begin a perimeter search. A robotic detachment took hold of him, and he operated on muscle memory alone. All emotion got shoved down into a tiny, airless compartment.

A few yards away, he spotted a narrow path of trampled vegetation cutting into the woods. When he moved deeper into the tangle of trees and found a boot scrape on the forest floor, he gave no thought to calling anyone for help. He would be able to locate Riley faster on his own.

And he wanted no witnesses to what he would do to her captor.

A little farther along the path, he heard something thrashing in the undergrowth. Slowing his pace, he crept toward the sound and found Riley gagged and bound to a tree, struggling to free herself.

The moment she caught sight of him, her body sagged with relief.

It was the last thing he saw before his world went black.

48

"Do you have the journal?"

Riley stilled at the clipped voice booming through Nick's cell phone. He sat on a stool, a few feet away from where he had her strapped to her desk chair.

After Nick had forced her away from the greenhouse, he'd tied her to a tree, then went inside to search for the journal. A few minutes later, he'd emerged enraged but not empty-handed.

With Coen's broad shoulders blocking her line of sight, she hadn't seen Nick's approach—until it was too late. She could still hear the sickening thud of the butt of her pistol connecting with Coen's head.

After ranting for a full minute about running out of time, Nick had manhandled them both back into the green-house, securing her to a desk chair and Coen to the couch.

Riley glanced at Coen's unconscious body, and a cold hand of fear squeezed her heart. How long did it take for someone to recover from head trauma?

"There's been a complication," Nick said, his tone frigid. "We've been here before. I'm done waiting."

Nick slanted her a glance. "The journal's within reach."

"Then finish it. Get rid of the obstacles and head back to Costa Rica."

She concentrated on the caller's voice. Something about it seemed familiar, as though she'd spoken to the man before.

Once again, Nick settled his golden eyes on her. A chill sprinted down her spine.

Not in all the months they'd worked together had she ever suspected him of being a sociopath. How had she missed something that now seemed so obvious?

Maybe murder was just a means to an end. Maybe he saw his victims as roadblocks that needed to be removed. A —what had he called Camilla's death?—collateral damage.

Greed as his motivation seemed even more disgusting than him being a sociopath. At least the latter could be attributed to the state of his mental health. The former seemed so common, so Hollywood-esque, so disappointing.

Other than noting a slight tightening of Nick's jaw, she couldn't determine his receptiveness to the idea of murdering her.

"This isn't a time for rash action," Nick said.

"Rash? I have been patient beyond what was in my best interest."

"I—"

"You're allowing emotion to warp your sense of priority. Give up this unnatural obsession, son. We have work to do."

"I can't believe *you're* lecturing *me* about obsessions."

At the word "obsession," her heart stuttered inside her chest. She'd been holding out hope that she could reason with Nick. After all, he was a scientist like her. He operated in a world of logic and facts. But an obsessed sociopath would be deaf to any such pleas.

"Should I send Booker to sort this out?"

"*No.* I'll take care it."

"I'll give you one more opportunity to fix this. Don't disappoint me again."

Nick jerked the phone from his ear and stared at the display. "Bastard!" He threw the phone onto the desk.

"Who's Booker?" Riley's arms ached from being secured at the back of the chair.

His features hardened into something dispassionate and terrifying. "Someone you don't ever want to meet."

In a spurt of defiance, she asked, "What makes him any more dangerous than you?"

"Booker enjoys the hunt. Takes pleasure in people's suffering."

Riley picked at her bindings. "Whereas you kill with remorse and regret?"

"I neither enjoy it nor feel the heavy weight of my conscience after taking a life. I do what needs to be done."

"For Dr. Hathaway?"

Surprise widened his eyes.

During their dinner, Nick had mentioned that Dr. Young was nothing more than a tool and Dr. Hathaway was the one who had established the new lab. Connecting Hathaway to the murders hadn't required much of a leap. She just hadn't allowed herself to make the jump until now.

The tightness around her wrists gave a little, and blood rushed back into her fingers.

"Had you not proven to be so... empathetic," Nick said, "he would've allowed you to stay in Costa Rica."

"That's why I wasn't one of the chosen few? Because I cared about the people and plants?"

"Your relentless pursuit of information made you one of

the most valuable members of the team in the beginning. But that same tenacity made you too dangerous in the end."

"Because I would've uncovered Hathaway's scheme?"

"Rather than refocusing your considerable energy toward perfecting a cure for erectile dysfunction, you would've made an issue about our methods for securing the active ingredient."

It was all too much. Too much to process, too much betrayal, too much... heartbreak.

On a shuddering breath, she said, "What a shock it must have been when you realized how badly you'd underestimated Camilla."

His jaw tightened, and something ugly molded into his features. "I would argue she was the one who underestimated me."

"*Bastard,*" she spat. "Hathaway could have avoided all this if he'd been upfront about his purpose."

"Would you have accepted the position?"

Would she have? Curing men's equipment might not be as earth-shattering as curing psoriasis, but it would have an impact. A big impact.

"Who's to say?" She stabbed him with a your-boss-is-an-asshole look. "Hathaway didn't give me a chance to decide one way or the other."

A smile played on his lips, one full of longing and understanding. "You would've picked people and plants over science and progress. Hathaway knew it, I knew it, and you know it."

Resting his elbows on his knees, he leaned toward her, fixing those beautiful, terrifying eyes on her. "Where's the journal, Riley?"

She poured steel into her backbone and didn't break

visual contact. "Safe." If he knew how easy it was to find it, he'd kill her for the insult alone.

"Nothing's ever safe."

"If that's the case, you'll have no problem locating it. By yourself." Her bindings loosened a little more. "Better yet, why don't you have Dr. Mastermind come and find it. I have a few things to get off my chest."

"Don't underestimate Hathaway." A rough, almost desperate note laced his warning.

Something nagged at the back of her mind. Something... important. She studied his profile while she rewound through their conversation.

Her search screeched to a halt, landing on a single word. "What is Dr. Hathaway to you? Employer, or—father?"

Neither surprise nor bluster met her question. Instead, he displayed his rogue's smile, the one that had curled women's toes across Central America. "There you are."

49

THE LOVER'S CARESS IN NICK LANDRY'S VOICE MADE COEN want to give up his pretense of sleep and beat the shit out of the guy.

He'd been out cold until something hard hitting the desk had roused him from a concussion-induced sleep. He'd lain on the couch, unmoving, listening to Landry break Riley's heart one word at a time.

So many times he'd come close to telling the fucker to shut up. But he'd known Riley would want to hear Hathaway's scheme in its entirety.

Project Endurance's benefactor had capitalized on her passion and used it against her.

Once again he tested the rope around his wrists and ankles. His bindings didn't budge.

Where was Camilla? He hadn't heard her voice since waking. Had she been knocked unconscious too? Or had she escaped Landry's detection?

He hoped the latter.

"You don't deny that Dr. Hathaway is your father?" Riley asked.

"Why would I? He's a ruthless son of a bitch, but I've made a fortune at his side."

"'At his side'?" She snorted. "I've never seen anyone lick their master's butt more thoroughly than you."

Slap! The sound of flesh against flesh snapped Coen upright. "Touch her again, Landry, and I'll rip your fingers off, one by one."

She sat tied to a chair, defiant, yet wide-eyed at his sudden movement. Landry, on the other hand, brushed off Coen's warning like a pesky mosquito as he rested his ass against the desk, next to Riley. The bulge beneath Landry's overshirt suggested he carried a concealed weapon.

Crossing his legs at the ankle, Landry said, "I wondered what it would take to make you break out of your pretense." He nodded to Coen's bound ankles. To the length of rope connecting his feet to the couch. "Careful. If you try any heroics, your tether will go taut and you'll land on that pretty face of yours."

A bead of sweat slid down the back of Coen's neck, and his hands curled into fists.

"How's your head?" she asked.

Like an axe cleaved it in half. "I've survived far worse."

Landry's strike had left a streak of scarlet across her left cheek. "You okay?" he asked.

"It'll take more than a daddy's boy to break me."

Lightning fast, Landry grasped her by the throat and forced her head back. "Don't you recall? I have a number of *special talents*." He brought his face level with hers, air-tracing her features with his nose. "Should we show your lover the one I perfected in Costa Rica? I wonder if he'll still want you after watching you scream in my arms?"

"Let her go," Coen demanded. Heat blurred his vision, and the throbbing in his head intensified. An image of

Kendra, bloody and screaming for her captors to stop, kept superimposing over Riley.

He fought against his bindings, the flesh at his wrists shredding beneath the strength of the coarse rope.

Even with her neck stretched to an unnatural angle, Riley spoke to him in a low, modulated voice. "I'm fine, Coen." Her attention shifted back to Landry, though she continued to address him. "Casanova won't hurt me."

Landry's fingers dug into her neck, igniting a deep-rooted trembling in Coen's gut. He blinked hard, trying to diffuse Kendra's image. He wouldn't break. Not now. Not when Riley needed him. He *wouldn't*.

Lightning flashed overhead, followed by the slow rumble of thunder.

Despite having a murderer squeezing off her airflow, Riley stared Landry down, hatred sparking in her gunmetal eyes. Landry's face was mottled with rage.

Afraid she'd pushed Landry too far, Coen tried to redirect his attention. "Killing her won't solve your problem."

"Actually, it will."

"If I had my Leatherman," she wheezed, catching Coen's eye. "I'd level the playing field with Casanova."

Slap! The taunt hit its mark.

Why the hell was she provoking Landry?

"Don't you want Young's journal?" she asked.

"Right at this moment? No. My need to purge you from my blood is much greater." With unerring precision, Landry rolled his attention to Coen. "And you're going to watch."

He surged forward until his tether snapped taut. Just like Landry had predicted, he pitched forward. With his hands bound behind his back, his head glanced off the concrete floor, scrambling his brains even more.

"Coen!"

He blinked several times to clear his vision. Lifting his head sent shards of glass into his brain.

"Consider this my one and only mercy." Landry rolled him into a sitting position and then drag-dumped him onto the couch. The action jostled something free from between the cushions.

The moment his fingers slid over the leathery surface, he knew what had literally fallen in his hands.

Riley's Leatherman.

When she'd sat next to him earlier, she'd removed the multi-tool from her belt in order to get closer to him. No wonder she'd challenged her captor. She'd been trying to send him a message.

Using his half-reclined position to his advantage, he dug the multi-tool out of its leather casing and pried open the screwdriver and bottle cap opener before he finally located the knife.

Large raindrops smacked against the windowpanes, slowly at first, followed by a stronger staccato.

"Where's the journal, Riley?" Landry asked, all hint of his lewd threats gone. He raked his hand through his perfectly groomed hair. "Give it to me and we can all move on from this."

Riley's eyes sharpened, and he knew she'd caught Landry's telling gesture too.

"Who's turned stupid now, Nick?" she asked. "Do you really think I believe that you and Hathaway are going to let us live?"

"Don't mix me into the same cup as Hathaway."

"Why? Because you're so much more ethical?"

Nick stormed over to Riley, twirled her chair around, and rolled her to the edge of the greenhouse, where a large potted plant stood. He grabbed the rim of the pot and dragged it several feet away, revealing several rain-slicked windowpanes.

Riley sucked in a sharp breath.

Coen craned his neck to see what had upset her.

Just outside the greenhouse sat the utility-terrain vehicle Riley used for transportation to and from the center. Inside the UTV, Camilla struggled against her restraints while trying to protect herself against the wind and driving rain. But with her arms stretched above her head and tied to the steel piping framing the passenger compartment and her feet secured to something below his line of sight, she had little defense against the elements.

"She's alive," Riley said on a sob.

"For how long, depends on you," Nick said.

Tears slid down her face. "How did I ever mistake you for a friend?"

He ran a finger along her damp cheek. "Our friendship was the only genuine relationship I had down there."

She leaned away from his touch, hatred in her eyes. "If this is how you treat people you care about, you're more fucked up than I realized."

"Dammit, Riley! Give me the journal, and I'll free you and Camilla."

"What about Coen?"

The bastard threw his words back at him. "He's survived worse."

"Then forget it," she said.

She showed absolutely no fear, no wavering from her current course. She would not leave someone she cared about behind. She wouldn't leave *him* behind. *Warrior.*

Landry's expression shifted from satisfied to troubled to... nothing.

The switch. That moment when someone flips from husband, son, brother, dad to killer. A moment he knew all too well. He sawed faster, not caring if flesh got in his way.

"Remember," Landry said in a quiet voice. "You chose the hard way. Not only for you"—he settled his unnerving gaze on Coen—"but for him."

The blood in his veins crystallized into skeins of ice. Landry knew. Somehow he knew about his time in Ecuador.

A smug smile appeared a second before Landry plowed his fist into Riley's stomach.

Coen roared. *"Get away from her!"*

"Lover boy doesn't want me to break your ribs. How do you think he'll react if I mar your beautiful face? Do you think he'll want to fuck you anymore?"

She didn't cry or scream or beg. His warrior arrowed curses at her tormentor's head.

"Narcissistic scumbag," she spat. "I'm glad I trusted my instincts about sleeping with you. Just looking at you makes my skin crawl."

With gut-wrenching horror, he could only watch as Landry's fist swung toward the side of her face. The blow whipped her head to the side, sending her glasses flying. She blinked several times before forcing her body upright.

Pressure built behind his eyes as the past sucked him into its void. Back to Kendra and the guards. And his living nightmare.

Before any of the three guards had time to react, Kendra cut down the center one. Divide and conquer.

With the door open, she rushed outside—leaving him behind—and the remaining guards followed, bellowing their fury. Coen hobbled over to the guard at the door and searched him for weapons. Blood oozed into the corner of his eye, and he wiped it away with impatient fingers. His ribs hurt like a bitch, but he ignored the pain.

Relief swelled in his chest when he found a pistol and serrated hunting knife. He cut the plastic tie securing his ankles, hissing in a harsh breath when he rose to follow Kendra.

A gunshot reverberated through the mountains.

No!

He skidded to a halt outside the shanty that had been his prison for the past three agonizing days. Sunlight momentarily blinded him, but he couldn't miss the ragged mound lying on the rocky ground fifteen yards away.

A line of scarlet trickled from Kendra's nose, and her beautiful unseeing black eyes stared straight at him, as if she'd held out hope that he would free himself in time to fight by her side.

He opened fire.

A fist to the gut brought him back to the present. Coen's breath *whooshed* out of his lungs.

"I wonder which one of you will break first?" Landry mused as if he were deciding on which color tie to wear. "If only you'd given up the journal. I could have spared you all this unnecessary pain."

The unexpected impact of Landry's hit made him lose control of Riley's almost-useless knife. He fumbled for it again and sliced at the rope with all his strength.

Landry took the opportunity to punch the shit out of his face.

"Monster!" Riley yelled. "Stop, Nick. I said stop it!" More softly, she said, "I'll give you the journal."

Breathing hard, Landry backed away, picking up Riley's glasses off the floor and sliding them onto her face with a gentleness that belied his bloody knuckles. "I didn't hear that last part."

The final thread gave way, and blood raced back into Coen's hands. Curling forward, he went to work on his ankles, alternating his attention between the knife and Landry.

Thunder cracked overhead, making the greenhouse shake.

"I'll give it to you." Her voice remained low, restrained.

"Where is it?"

"Close."

"Where?"

"How do I know you won't kill us as soon as I tell you?"

"You don't." He traced a finger along her jaw. "But you'll continue breathing until I have the journal in my hand."

"What about Coen and Camilla?"

His hand dropped away. "Normally, I wouldn't make that kind of promise, but I can see I won't get the location without it."

She stared at him, waiting.

"Them too."

Her chin began to tremble, and she blinked several times. One lone tear eased down her cheek.

The rigid set to Landry's shoulders softened. "All this will be over soon." He crouched to wipe the moisture away before cupping the back of her neck. "Where's the journal?"

"My vehicle," she whispered. "Beneath the driver's seat."

His grip on her neck tightened. "Clever girl."

"Not clever enough."

"My father's desire to legitimize his herbal empire in the eyes of the medical community compelled him to extremes." His hold loosened until the pad of his thumb traced a path over her lower lip. "I must admit, I was skeptical of the high praise he heaped on you every time your name came up in conversation. Until I met you." His hands roamed down her body, forcing her knees apart. "However, within a few short weeks of meeting you, I knew my father had miscalculated your character." He leaned closer. "He'd held out hope that you would eventually join the team that would secure his place in medical history." He reached for the button at her waistband. "But I knew you would never allow us to do what needed to be done."

"Damn straight." Riley's long legs swept up and clamped around Landry's neck. And squeezed.

With Landry's weight on the balls of his feet, he lost his balance. They both crashed to the floor, chair and all. Riley's shoulder hit hard, but her legs maintained their death grip on Landry's windpipe. She released an animal-like cry and squeezed harder.

"I'll"—Landry wheezed, pounding on her thigh—"k-kill you"—more pounding and squirming—"for th-this."

"Fat chance of that," she panted. "Daddy's boy." She squeezed his windpipe until his body slumped in her hold.

The rope around Coen's ankles fell away, and blood rushed back into his feet. He limped to Riley's side.

"I'm here," he said, eyeing Landry for signs of revival. "Everything's going to be okay."

"You're free," she said on a choked whisper.

When he'd released her hands, he said, "I need to check him for weapons."

"Like this one?" Landry asked, pointing a pistol at her head while scrambling to his feet. He rubbed his neck and leveled a furious stare on Riley.

Coen lifted his hands in the air and slowly rose, making

himself the biggest target in the room. "Let her leave. I'll get the journal."

A dark-haired stubborn woman stepped in front of him. "I'm not going anywhere."

He grasped her shoulder to shove her behind him. "Riley—"

She shrugged out of his grip. "Coen's not part of this. He'll be called back to duty in a few days." She took a step closer to Landry. "You and I can work this out."

"If you think I'm going to leave you alone with this—"

"Enough," Landry cut in. "Riley, get over here."

Reading his intent, she backed up a step. "I won't let you kill him."

"And I can't let him live."

Coen slid his left hand around her waist. "Even with me dead, it won't take the authorities long to figure out who kidnapped her."

Nick smiled. "Nicholas Landry's chapter in my life is almost over. Time to start fresh again." His gaze roamed down Riley's body. "Where would you like to go? Sumatra, Chile, Rwanda?"

"Are you mad?" she said in disgust. "Or a complete narcissist?"

When Landry's face emptied of expression, Coen's hand tightened around the multi-tool.

"No, Riley," Landry said, aiming the gun at her chest. "What I am is done. With you."

Coen shoved her aside and flung the Leatherman at the other man's head.

A shot rang out, and fire burned his throat.

"Coen!"

50

GLASS SHATTERED BEHIND RILEY, AND SHE DUCKED LOW, grasping Coen's hand and bolting away.

"Do you really want to die protecting formulas?" Nick bellowed, wiping a smear of blood from his forehead, where her Leatherman had hit its mark.

Zigzagging down the rows, she lifted a semiclean towel from one of the worktables and Coen swiped a trowel from another. She crouched behind a wall of *Lobelia cardinalis* and *Asclepias tuberosa,* drawing Coen down beside her.

"Where were you hit—" Blood covered his neck. "Oh my God," she whispered, pressing the cleanest part of the towel to the area.

He winced. "I'm fine. The bullet just nicked me."

"There's so much blood."

"It's normal." He covered her hand with his. "Where did Landry put my phone and handgun?" He lifted his pant leg to find an empty sheath strapped to his ankle.

"He left them in the woods."

"Your phone?"

"In his pocket."

A muscle popped in his jaw as he glanced at the trowel in his hand.

Furious raindrops stamped across the windowpanes like the march of a thousand booted feet, deafening them to Nick's movements inside. A deep gloom hung thick in the greenhouse, interrupted only by flashes of lightning.

"When I say go, you make for the exit," Coen whispered into her ear. "Don't stop until you get to the research center."

"I'm not leaving you."

"You have to. It's the only way to notify Maggie."

The logical side of her mind understood his reasoning, even agreed with him. But the side that loved him could never leave him to face this danger alone.

"The lovebirds want to play hide-and-seek?" The anger in Nick's voice was gone, replaced by cold detachment. "I do love a good seek."

So close. Riley whipped around, certain she'd find him an arm's length away. But the aisle was empty.

Coen put a finger to his lips and guided her to another plant-filled table two aisles away. "I need him to think that we've left so I can circle around and come up behind him."

"I can't leave you."

"It's better if I do this alone."

"For whom? You or me?"

His lips firmed, and Riley knew his answer.

"There's no time for debate. Neutralizing threats is what I do—and I'm damned good at it." His palm cupped her cheek. "Trust me."

"Frantic whispering," Nick mused. "What could you be talking about?"

Coen moved them again, farther away.

Fear hammered through her veins at the realization of

what he was willing to sacrifice to ensure her safety. He would die to protect her—as she would for him.

The emotion that had been hovering around her heart for days formed into something solid and beautiful and terrifying.

Love.

She loved him. Why had it taken a sociopath hunting them to make her come to her senses? She'd always had freaking bad timing.

"Please don't ask me to leave you. *Please.*"

An argument hovered on his lips until his attention settled on her face. Whatever he saw there made his words dry up on his tongue.

Nick's next words settled the matter. "Trying to figure out how to get her out of the greenhouse, Operator Monroe?"

Coen dropped his head a moment and pulled in a deep breath. When he lifted his gaze to hers, a soldier stared back. Handing her the trowel, he pointed to two large water barrels that stood in a corner. "Hide behind those. Don't come out until I give the all clear."

"But I—"

"It's either the exit or the barrels. Decide, now."

Pride snapped her shoulders straight, and she started for her corner. Without a second's thought, she turned back to Coen, gripped the back of his neck, and laid a hot, you'd-better-survive-this kiss on his mouth. The possession lasted all of three seconds, but when she broke away, her lungs burned as though they'd been deprived of air for an hour.

With their noses resting against each other and their warm breaths weaving together, she whispered, "I love you." Not waiting to see his shock, hear his response, or feel his retreat, she stole away to her safe corner while he fought to save them both.

51

Coen waited until Riley tucked herself behind the water barrels before going in search of a weapon.

I love you.

Had she truly meant those words, or had they been an in-the-heat-of-the-moment declaration?

Normally his mind flipped on a dime with each scenario thrown at him. It was something he had practiced over and over and over in selection training. But all his brain cells had caught on those three words and would not give them up. Not until the air shifted around him, raising the hairs on the back of his neck.

"Silence," Landry said. "Putting all that plotting into action now? I can't wait to see what you have in store for me."

He had suffered through enough psychological mind fucks not to be bothered by this one. But to someone who had lived a war-free life, Landry's brand of torture would be terrifying. He hoped Riley's belief in him didn't waver.

In a corner, he found a shovel. Lightning flashed overhead, illuminating the greenhouse interior and bringing shadows to life.

He focused on one longer, denser, more menacing shadow—and began to stalk his prey.

52

ANOTHER CLAP OF THUNDER ROCKED THE BUILDING LESS THAN a second after the lightning streaked across the sky.

Close, so close.

As if Riley's world wasn't brimming with enough tension, she had to also contend with one of North Carolina's megastorms.

Something clinked to her right, and her heart paused midbeat. She stared hard into the gloom, though no one materialized.

A scuffle to her left had her nerves ripping out of her skin.

She waited for Nick's face to appear right in front of her —just like in *Jurassic Park* when the velociraptor's head knifed through the jungle's underbrush—right by the game warden.

Dagblast this storm!

Peering through the small opening between the barrels, she searched for any sign of Coen. Where was he?

Sitting here, waiting for something to happen, was

torture. She needed a job, a task, a mission. She needed not to be useless. She needed to *move*.

Frustrated with her narrow viewpoint, she angled her body around one of the barrels and caught her first hint of movement. She leaned forward to discern who lurked near the table of bloodroot.

And stared at the beautiful profile of a predator.

53

Employing the stealth that had taken him months to perfect, Coen closed in on Hathaway's fixer.

Rounding a table of mint-scented, pale purple flowers, he spotted a dark figure crouched low at the end of the aisle. He moved closer, raising his makeshift weapon. When he got within striking distance, he swung the shovel at Landry's head.

At the last second, the fixer ducked out of the way and swung his arm around, aiming a pistol at Coen's chest.

As Coen dove away, he caught a glimpse of a swift-moving shadow plowing into Landry a fraction of a second before the spit of gunfire exploded toward Coen. He braced himself for the searing impact of a bullet drilling through flesh and tendon and bone.

It never came.

Above them, glass shattered, one of the windowpanes taking the brunt of Landry's bullet. The trowel he'd given Riley flew across the floor.

Fragments of glass rained down on him. He ignored the

sting of tiny cuts and scrambled toward the jumble of arms and legs and curses.

Despite Landry's greater size, Riley held her own. Until the bastard produced a large knife and slashed it across Riley's chest.

Blood bloomed on Riley's shirt as she crab-walked backward to get away. Landry pounced, grabbing a hand full of hair and jerking her upright to stand in front of him. The tip of his knife grazed her throat. A red line formed in its wake.

Unable to take his eyes off the thin, bloody line, Coen stood frozen as a roaring started in his head.

"Would you like to see her chopped up too?" Landry taunted.

The roaring became deafening, blinding, and his mind spiraled deep into the darkness of his last mission.

Crouching in the rainforest's underbrush, amid large, thick leaves and a steady, soaking rain, he waited for the guards to complete their circuit and head back in the opposite direction.

After scavenging an AR and additional ammo, a hunting knife, a pair of boots, and some food, he had circled back to the encampment where he'd been tortured for the past three days. Fear of recapture didn't slow him down. The only thing that mattered was retrieving Kendra's body. He would not go home without her.

Before he'd escaped, he'd taken down several of the guards. Several more had met their end when they'd chased him deeper into the forest.

A good twelve hours, possibly more, had passed since he'd stared into Kendra's lifeless eyes. More than enough time for the bomb maker to gather reinforcements, unless his Ecuadorian hosts felt they'd supplied their guest with enough human collateral for one trip.

Given the scant activity in the camp, he was going to call this phase of his mission a success. Then again, maybe the bomb maker was keeping his men hidden in order to draw him out.

Only one way to find out.

Inhaling a steadying breath, he left the anonymity of the trees and ran to the nearest tent. He paused for a second to listen for voices. When he heard none, he cut a small opening in the canvas with the sharp tip of his knife. Finding neither Kendra's body nor the bomb maker, he moved on to the next tent and the next and the next.

Most were unoccupied. Those that weren't, he turned into morgues. It wasn't until he'd reached the outer edge of the camp that the smell hit him. Even the rain couldn't wash away the scent of death.

The odor led him to a small clearing. In the center, three shovels stuck out of a large pit filling with water, as if the diggers had put the task off until the rain ended.

Lining the rim of the pit were bodies, two deep. Guards he'd killed in a blinding rage upon seeing Kendra dead, at her captors' feet. He waited for the remorse to come. It didn't.

Keeping to the tree line, he maneuvered his way over to the pile, bracing himself for the sight of a familiar pair of dark eyes. But he found no sign of Kendra. Rain sluiced over his face and crept into his eyes. He swiped at the water to clear his vision.

Had they taken her body someplace else? Were they holding it for ransom? Propaganda?

Bile roiled into his throat.

"Goddammit!" He made to kick a rock teetering on the

edge of the pit, when he noticed something odd about it. Bending, he pried it out of the mud and—

"*What the fuck?*" He dropped the hand and scrambled away, nearly falling on his ass in his haste to get some distance.

Wiping the rain from his eyes again, he stared hard at the hand, then glanced at the corpses. He stepped closer and used the barrel of his AR to flip the hand over, fingers up.

Female.

Recognition punched him in the gut.

Kendra was here.

His gaze slashed from the body part to the corpses to point after point after point in the clearing, searching. When his scan moved over the waterlogged pit, a prickle of unease raced down his spine.

Rain beat against the surface, sending thousands of tiny ripples colliding into each other. In the midst of the melee, something bobbed. Something the size of a bowling ball. Something caught in a curtain of long, black strands.

Kendra.

Landry's goading voice pulled him back to the present. "What? You don't want your lover to be sliced and diced like poor Kendra?" He pulled Riley's head back at an unnatural angle and teased his knife along the tight flesh of her neck.

"How do you know about Kendra?"

"Hathaway's influence is vast. A few donations in the right pockets, and he learned all about your time in Ecuador." A cold smile spread across Landry's face. "Tell me, what was it like when you realized Kendra's head and hands and feet weren't attached to her body?"

Coen stared at the blood trickling down Riley's throat. His pulse roared in his ears, and it hurt to breathe.

"How does it feel to fail your entire team so completely? You give new meaning to Last Man Standing."

"D-don't listen. To this psycho b-bastard," Riley squeezed out through her distended throat. "You. Failed. No one."

"Let her go." He forced his attention away from the shallow cut on her throat. "Riley will take you to the journal."

"I think"—Landry nuzzled her cheek while keeping his eye on Coen—"our quarrel has gone beyond the journal, don't you?"

Riley peered at him out of the corner of her eye, and Coen gave her a short nod.

"Stop drooling," she wheezed though her tight throat. "Over me. And you'll. Find out."

Landry released Riley's hair with such force that her head snapped forward. Then he plowed a boot between Riley's shoulder blades and sent her sprawling across the floor.

Bad decision.

Coen swung his shovel. The sickening crunch of shattering bone echoed through the air.

Landry's knees buckled, and he landed on top of Riley.

Her curses echoed through the greenhouse.

54

Ten minutes later, the flickering lights of two police cars and an ambulance reflected off the rain-drenched greenhouse.

"Riley!" Sheriff Maggie Kingston rushed inside with Deputy Blaine on her heels.

"Back here."

Boots pounded across the concrete floor. When Maggie reached Riley's office, her eyebrow lifted at the sight that greeted her.

Coen sat in the middle of the couch with one arm around Riley and the other around Camilla. Both she and Camilla were covered head to heel by space blankets Coen had retrieved from the first-aid kit.

"Are you okay?" Maggie asked.

Having participated in several tactical medical drills with Cash and Emmy, Riley had known what information to convey to the 911 dispatcher so that a full-on tactical response hadn't shown up at the greenhouse.

Nodding, she said, "I'm fine. A few scrapes and a little shaken, is all."

"They both need medical attention," Coen said.

"You do too, from the looks of it."

Deputy Blaine appeared. "He's dead."

Maggie hooked a thumb in the direction where Nick's body lay. "Was he alone?"

"Yes," she and Coen said in unison.

"Blaine, give the paramedics the all clear."

"Will do."

"Nick Landry, I assume?" Maggie asked.

A soaked, out-of-breath Britt stormed inside. "What's going on?"

"I'm figuring that out now." Maggie cast her best sheriff look at Britt. "You shouldn't be here. This is a crime scene."

"You can file a complaint with the sheriff later."

Accustomed to the Steele boys' bullheadedness, Maggie brushed off his reply. When the greenhouse door banged open again, her sister glanced over her shoulder and sighed. "Might as well wait another ten seconds before explaining."

Cash ran inside, carrying his med bag. He took in the situation in one swift glance, giving Britt a what-the-hell-are-you-doing-here dark look before dropping down at Riley's side. "Hey, little sis. Playing for reals this time?"

The gentle, teasing tone in her big brother's voice made her throat close and tears fill her eyes. "G-gotta keep your skills sharp."

"Emmy will appreciate your dedication to my professional development." He pulled on his nitrile gloves. "Let's see where you're hurt."

"Check Camilla first. She may have a concussion."

"No, señor," Camilla protested. "My injuries are nothing. See to the others."

"She's nauseous," Coen said.

Cash motioned to the other paramedic to have a look at Camilla.

After inspecting the shallow cut on Riley's throat, Cash folded back the reflective blanket and removed the thick pads of gauze. He froze at the sight of the gash across her chest.

Britt cursed.

Maggie steamed in silence.

"It looks worse than it feels," she said with a wry grin.

"I bet it does." Cash directed his next question to Coen. "Did you dress her wound?"

The body beneath her went taut. "Yes."

"Good technique."

At her brother's compliment, Coen's hold on her softened.

"Who's the dead guy?" Britt asked, his patience at an end.

"Nick Landry," Riley said. "I worked with him in Costa Rica."

"Audi Guy," Coen added. "You'll likely find a silver A4 hidden nearby."

"I'll have my deputies search the area," Maggie said.

"He's also the one responsible for killing Riley's colleagues."

Britt slammed a hard gaze in Riley's direction. "What dead colleagues?"

"He murdered several of the researchers I worked with in Costa Rica." She peered around Coen to give her friend a grateful smile. "Camilla came here to warn me."

Britt began to prowl the greenhouse like a caged wolf. "Warn you about what? Am I the only one in the dark here?"

"I'll explain everything later," Maggie said. "It's a long, complicated story."

"*Now* works for me," Britt said. "Start at the beginning."

"Riley's had enough—" Coen started.

She put her hand on his chest. "It's okay. An explanation is the least I can do."

As succinctly as she could, Riley told them about Camilla's packages and texts, of the imprint on her bedspread and greenhouse ransacking, of Nick's involvement and his infatuation with her, and of Hathaway's wish to legitimize his business.

When she finished, Maggie studied her for a long, uncomfortable minute. Then she said, "Did you know this Nick had been in your bedroom?"

"I suspected—later."

"I must have missed your call," Maggie said pointedly. "How connected is this Hathaway?"

"The trail leads all the way to DC."

"You know," Maggie said with a sigh, "Steele Ridge used to be a peaceful town."

"No, *Canyon* Ridge was a peaceful town," she said. "*Steele* Ridge hasn't known a moment of serenity since its christening."

"*Touché.*"

"What happens next?" she asked.

"I go hunting and you go home."

"Hathaway's too smart not to have covered his tracks."

"Maybe. Maybe not. Intelligent, slightly psychotic men, who have way too much money, tend to have weak spines and flappy jaws." She smiled. "Plus I'll tap into the Steeles' secret weapon—Cameron Blackwell."

Riley grinned. "It's so handy to have an FBI agent *and* a

sheriff in the family. I suggest someone pay a visit to Dr. Young. He's involved, but I don't know to what extent."

The other paramedic finished examining Camilla. "Whatever he hit you with left a large bump." He gave Camilla an encouraging smile. "Let me take you to the emergency room so they can do some testing and give you something for the nausea."

Camilla looked to Riley.

"They'll take good care of you."

The paramedic assisted Camilla to her feet.

"I'll be right behind you," Riley said.

Cash rose, removing his gloves. "Luckily, none of your wounds are deep enough to require sutures." He handed her some gauze and other first-aid supplies. "Change your dressings daily for the next week. Let me know if the area becomes bright red or feverish." His mouth kicked up in a brotherly smile. "Pus is bad too."

"Go save someone else."

He laughed and strode away.

"Cash?" she called.

"Yeah?"

"Thank you."

He winked and left.

Britt held out a hand to Riley. "Let's get you out of here."

She glanced back at Coen. "Ready?"

"More than ready."

Once she was on her feet, Britt pulled her into his big body for a gentle hug and kiss to the top of her head. "Go on. I'll take care of this place."

Lifting up on her toes, she kissed his cheek. "Thank you."

"I'm not letting you off the hook about why you kept all this from me. Just postponing the inquisition."

"Get in line, Steele," Coen said, threading his fingers with hers. "Miss Indy has a problem asking for help."

Britt held out his hand to Coen. "Need anything. You call me."

Coen nodded.

"The rain has stopped," Maggie said from the door. "This would be a good time to make a break for it."

"See you later," Britt said with a wave.

Shoveling the spilled contents of her pack back inside, Riley tried to keep her brow smooth and her hands steady. She glanced around the greenhouse, careful not to look at Nick's bashed-in head, and wondered if she'd ever be comfortable working here alone again.

A large, warm hand slid across her back. "Leave the rest," Coen said. "I'll come back tomorrow and retrieve anything you need."

"Let me check on the *Timbroma*." She picked up the tray from the floor and set it on a nearby worktable, still amazed they had survived the fall. Using the tip of her finger, she checked to make sure each seedling still retained good footing in the soil.

"How do they look?"

"Remarkably well, considering."

"Then let's get you out into the fresh air."

She let him guide her outside. A deep numbness had taken root throughout her entire body. She pulled in a long, moist breath of Carolina air. The familiar July humidity helped center her and remind her of who she was and where she stood.

All the events of the past hours seemed so surreal, so fantastical. Had she really faced down a killer? With nothing but her mind and body for weapons?

She rubbed her hands over the gooseflesh that popped up on her arms and turned toward the parking lot.

"Where are you going?" Maggie and Coen asked at the same time.

"To the hospital. I want to make sure Camilla is okay."

"I'll check in on her when I'm done here and let you know how she's doing."

"But—"

"No buts." Maggie laid a hand over her cheek. "Go with Coen. I'll catch up with you later to get the details. For now, do what you can to forget." Against Riley's forehead, she whispered, "I'm so proud of you."

Tears pricked the backs of Riley's eyes. She was so exhausted that she couldn't even bring herself to argue. "Thank you."

Maggie held out a hand to Coen. When he took it, she swallowed hard and embraced him. "Thank you for watching over her. I won't ever forget." She broke off and marched back to the greenhouse, surreptitiously swiping a hand across her cheek.

Love for her family squeezed at Riley's chest.

Coen's hand trailed over her forearm until his fingers laced with hers again. "Come on."

"Where are we going?"

"To my campsite."

She swallowed back a lump of gratitude. The thought of going home and sleeping in the bed where Nick had reclined made her stomach queasy. Still... "I won't be great company, Coen. Maybe I should—"

In answer, he gave her arm a firm tug and headed for the tree line. She glanced back at her sister, expecting to see concern carved into her brow. Instead, a soft smile touched her mouth before she grasped her shoulder mic and reentered the greenhouse.

Staring at the muscles rippling in Coen's back, she wondered where they went from here. He had invited her to Fort Bragg, but that offer seemed a lifetime ago. Soon he would be returning to duty, and she would—hell, she didn't know what she'd be doing.

Before year's end, she would be done surveying the conservation area. And she had no other employment prospects lined up. Lord only knew how much of Hathaway's crud would rub off on her. The ethnobotanical community was small. Very small. Who would want to hire her after word got out?

The project that was supposed to set her career on fire might have killed it without a single spark.

Coen's thumb caressed her hand as if he sensed her turmoil. Guilt elbow-socked her in the stomach. Here she was worrying about finding a job when he must be roiling in emotional hell.

How many god-awful memories had Nick's taunts forced him to relive? How does a person overcome picking up pieces of his teammate?

She closed her eyes and allowed her feet to find their own footing while she fought off a bone-deep weariness. Somehow she had to find the strength to say goodbye to Coen. Send him off to God-knew-where with a convincing smile and...

She didn't know what came after *and*.

55

By the time Coen reached his campsite, the adrenaline that had been commanding his every action and reaction had disappeared, leaving him to fend for himself. Only his concern for Riley had kept him focused on the next step and the next and the next.

He raked shaking fingers through his hair and listened for any extreme variances in Riley's breathing.

Silence. Not even the sound of a hiker's labored breathing breached the air.

She hadn't uttered a word since leaving the greenhouse, just held on to his hand with the tenacity of a baby chimp clinging to its mama. What did she make of Landry's revelations about Kendra's brutal death? About his failure to keep her—all his team—safe?

Frowning, he rubbed the left side of his chest. Something felt... wrong.

As he entered the outer rim of his campsite, his head snapped up and he froze. Riley's nose bounced off his shoulder.

"What—?"

He held up a hand, scanning, sensing something foreign, something deadly in their midst.

Drawing her into a crouching position, he whispered, "We're not alone." He pointed to a dense grouping of rhododendrons. "Wedge yourself inside there until I come for you."

"I'm not—"

"Please." He pressed a kiss to her forehead. "Go."

The expression on her beautiful face shifted from confusion and fear to determination and command. "Do not make me wait long, Monroe."

Despite the gravity of their situation, he sent her a brief smile. "Yes, ma'am."

Keeping his head low, he ran toward a large oak tree and used its massive girth as cover. Surveying the ground around him, he spotted a large rock and palmed it. The weapon wasn't ideal, but it would have to do.

Drawing in a steadying breath, he peered around the tree—and came face-to-face with the business end of a gun.

"If I were you," a hard female voice warned from behind him, "I'd set down that rock. Nice and slow."

The sharp command engaged his brain's autopilot, and he immediately obeyed. Lifting his arms into the air, he wove his fingers together behind his head. "Yes, ma'am."

"On your feet, Sergeant First Class."

He rose, scrutinizing the armed man in front of him before slowly turning to face the last person he ever wanted to see.

56

_____

SHARP, OBSIDIAN EYES FRAMED BY EQUALLY DARK WINGED brows met his with a boldness that came from decades of leading warriors with more testosterone than they knew what to do with. Even though the woman's one star was nowhere in sight, her absolute authority wasn't in doubt.

On its own accord, Coen's spine stiffened and his hand snapped to his temple. "General Delarosa."

Strands of gray marbled the thick black hair pulled into a ponytail knot at the back of her head. She wore jeans, hiking boots, and a beige T-shirt that revealed arms that still knew how to work out but not with the same intensity of a thirty-something soldier climbing up the Army ranks.

"You're a hard man to track down, Sergeant First Class."

Not hard enough. How had she found him?

"Or do you prefer Operator?" she asked.

"I'm honored to answer to both titles, ma'am. Monroe works too."

"Looks like the two of you got into a bit of trouble."

"The threat's been neutralized, and the rest is in the hands of the local sheriff now."

Some of the hardness eased from her observant eyes.

The armed man stowed his weapon and stepped up next to the general.

Coen's jaw tightened. "Colonel."

"You had twelve days to make a phone call, Monroe," Colonel Walsh reminded him. "This is what happens when you don't follow orders."

Movement to his left caught his attention. Reid bent low to help Riley from her hiding place.

He needed to have a Loyalty 101 talk with his friend. Riley jabbed a finger in her cousin's chest, and given his answering scowl, he was already well on his way to enlightenment.

Delarosa glanced around his campsite. "Tell me, Monroe, are you ready to return to duty?"

Without conscious thought, his attention drifted to where Riley idled with her cousin. As if sensing his attention, she looked up and their eyes caught. Could he leave her and return to a job that he loved? Or at least one he once loved.

For the first time in his military career, anticipation of his next mission didn't make the blood in his veins sizzle to life. Unlike some service members, he didn't have a position that would allow him to be home every evening with his family. Delta Force Operators could be called away for days, weeks, even months at a time.

Could Riley handle that kind of absence? So many operators had lost their families, not because of the inherent danger and the fear of losing a loved one but because of the incessant loneliness and doubt and hardship of being a single parent for long stretches of time. Then, when the operator returned home, everyone had to adjust to new roles and rules and expectations. And figure out how to react to the operator's mood swings, silences, and nightmares.

It was a lot to ask of someone he loved.

When Riley's supportive expression shifted into confusion, then into round-eyed understanding, he cut their visual link.

"Yes, ma'am," he answered with enough force to fool himself, if only for a few seconds.

"Glad to hear it," the general said. "Your country needs you now more than ever."

A look passed between Delarosa and Walsh. The colonel nodded and backed away.

The muscles in his shoulders turned to blocks of ice, and his heartbeat nearly ruptured his eardrums.

"You know why I'm here," the general said.

"I believe so, ma'am."

"One of the benefits of being a one-star general is my security access." She clasped her hands behind her back and began a slow stalk around him. "Or, in some cases, my access to the right people."

He kept his feet planted, his shoulders wide, and his ears open, even while his instincts screamed for him to keep the general in his line of sight.

"So I have availed myself of all the written intelligence on the... mission in Ecuador."

"Then you've made a long trip for nothing, ma'am."

"Have I?" She stared down at her boots for a long moment. "Although quite thorough, your mission report lacked the necessary detail that I require."

A small, warm hand burrowed into his.

Riley.

He should reject her comfort. Send her back to her

cousin. Away from the demons of his past. A past—and present—that could destroy everything he loved about her.

But he couldn't. Couldn't ignore how her mere touch soothed the ache in his heart or how she made him feel that he might actually survive the next thirty minutes with his pride, his sanity, and his soul intact.

"Sorry, Miss—?" the general began.

"Kingston," she offered.

"Sorry, Miss Kingston, but this is a classified conversation."

Riley's fingers opened to release him, but his hold firmed. He couldn't. Couldn't send her away, and he hated himself in that moment.

"She stays, or I go."

The general gave Riley a speculative once-over before settling her dark, commanding gaze on him. "What I want to know, Coen Monroe, is what my daughter said to you before running headlong into death."

57

"Daughter?" Riley blurted out. "Kendra was your daughter?"

The general's attention on him narrowed. "It seems you've already shared classified information."

Although he'd entrusted her with some of the disastrous mission, he'd kept the vital parts locked away. Riley wouldn't allow this woman to think that Coen had betrayed his country's secrets.

"No," she said in her most academic voice. "He screa— said her name in his sleep. I happened to be awake at the time."

Given Coen's sidelong glance, she wasn't sure if she'd allayed the general's concerns or confirmed them. She recalled too late Coen's assertions about the military and their hang-ups about mental health. *Dammit.*

The general fixed Coen with a don't-fuck-with-me stare.

Coen sighed. "As I mentioned in my report, Kendra's final words made no sense. Whatever she had meant to say came out as gibberish."

Because she had rushed to free Coen before distracting the guards.

"You didn't share her words in your write-up."

"Because they made no sense."

"Humor me, Operator Monroe."

When tension rippled through his hand into hers, Riley made tiny circles against his palm with her thumb.

The general lifted her chin, though Riley didn't miss the slight wobble. "I need to hear my daughter's final words. N-no matter how insignificant they might seem."

"She said something about the stars and her back." At the general's confused expression, Coen's face hardened. "I thought she might have been referring to a scar or tat on her back." He clenched his teeth a moment. "But she had none."

While he spoke, the general's features transformed into guarded hope. "Could she have said 'To the stars and back'?" All command had leeched from the mother's tone.

Coen closed his eyes, no doubt transporting himself back into a nightmare he'd already relived too many times. Concentration etched his brow while his strong jaw, shoulders, and back held their positions, supportive, patient, ready.

When his eyes finally opened, they held a sheen of regret. "It's possible, yes."

The general staggered back as if someone had punched her in the chest.

Coen grabbed her arm to steady her, and the general clutched his forearm as if it were the only thing keeping her upright.

Riley moved to support her other side, but the general waved her off.

"I'm fine," she whispered before straightening her T-shirt as if it were a uniform jacket. "It's just that I had h-hoped—"

This time moisture shone in the general's eyes.

"Let's take you someplace a bit more comfortable and a whole lot more private," Riley suggested.

The general cleared her throat and followed Riley to Coen's makeshift dining area.

"Grab the bag chair out of my tent," Coen said.

A few seconds later, Riley handed a water bottle to Coen and unfolded the chair. "Have a seat, General Delarosa."

With the weight of a thousand soldiers resting on her shoulders, the general plopped into the chair and used her two forefingers to massage her temples.

Coen held out the bottle of water to the general.

"Thank you." After taking a long drink, the general lowered the bottle and replaced the cap. She glanced between her and Coen. "Forgive me. I thought I had prepared myself."

"Don't apologize," she said. "I can't imagine the heartache of losing a child, especially not under the circumstances in which you lost your daughter." She noted the dark circles under the woman's eyes. "When did you eat last, General Delarosa?"

The general sent Coen a slight smile. "Does she take care of everyone like this?"

"Yes, ma'am."

"She'll make a good mother one day."

Gathering the general wouldn't answer her question, Riley dug a power bar from her backpack and offered it to her.

Rather than open the snack, the general ran her thumb over the wrapper, again and again and again.

Riley caught Coen's eye and motioned for him to do

something. When he held up his hands in the age-old I-don't-know-what-the-hell-to-do gesture, she stared down at the woman's bent head until questions began to swirl in her mind.

Throwing caution into the nearby stream, she crouched at the woman's side, as she'd done hundreds of times while speaking to the healer in Costa Rica. The position felt comfortable, like coming home after a long absence.

"Do you have a picture of your daughter?"

The general's thumb stopped its assault on the wrapper. For the longest ten seconds of her life, the woman didn't move. Then she pulled a phone from her back pocket.

She didn't even have to scroll. As soon as she hit the photo icon, an image of the general and a smiling young woman taking a selfie in front the iconic Tower Bridge in London popped up.

"Our last family vacation before Kendra enlisted."

"How many people have told you that she looks just like you?"

"I never tire of hearing it."

Coen eased down onto his log bench and stretched his long legs out, crossing them at the ankles.

"Was she an only child?"

"No, Kendra was the eldest of three."

"Did she always want to be in the military?"

The photo disappeared along with the general's soft smile. "No."

"I'm sorry. It's the researcher in me. Learning about people and their cultural uses of local flora is what I do for a living." She grimaced. "Well, it's what I'm supposed to be doing. I'm helping my cousin out with flora surveys until another ethnobotany job pops up. And now I'm rambling."

A hint of a smile appeared at the corner of the general's

mouth. "I don't mind talking about my daughter. In fact, most people avoid bringing her up in conversation for fear of upsetting me." She fixed her attention on the power bar. "But you scraped against a topic I don't enjoy."

"Your daughter's involvement with the military?"

The general nodded. "Kendra grew up wanting to be an architect. The level of detail with which she could visualize structures had always amazed me." Her thumb started rubbing against the wrapper again. "But then I got sick several years ago. Really sick. When my colleagues would stop by with food, they would regale my family with stories of my accomplishments."

"That must have made them proud."

"Especially Kendra. Thinking she was losing me and wanting to honor me, she enlisted." She opened the power bar and took a bite. "Six months before graduating university."

Riley cringed. She couldn't imagine being that close to getting her degree and then completely changing focus. But unconditional love can power one's actions in unexpected ways.

"All I ever wanted for my kids was for them to find an occupation that they loved. One that would, God willing, pay their bills and then some. War has made up the majority of my career." The general swallowed hard. "I didn't want that for my b-babies."

"General Delarosa," Riley ventured, "may I ask the significance of *To the stars and back*?"

Nostalgia filled the general's eyes, and twin tears marched down her cheeks. "A silly saying between the two of us. Something we would say to each other when *I love you* was too hard." She shook her head. "I don't even recall how or when we started using the phrase."

Risking rejection, Riley placed a hand on the woman's arm. "I've never thought about what a gift a simple phrase between child and parent could be."

The general placed a surprisingly callused palm against Riley's cheek. "Hug your mama and daddy. Every time."

She patted her arm. "I will. Promise." Tears clogged her throat, and her next words emerged in a barely audible voice. "Kendra's last thoughts were of you."

The general closed her eyes, nodding. For a moment Riley thought she would let loose her grief. But no sooner than she had the thought, the general's chest rose high on a deep inhalation and she opened her bloodshot eyes and pinned them on Coen.

58

OUT OF INSTINCT, COEN'S BACK STRAIGHTENED UNDER THE general's formidable regard. The reservoir of guilt sloshing in his gut froze into a block of ice.

The general stood. Even without the uniform and star, her bearing was that of a leader. A warrior.

He rose and stood at attention. Waited for the general to tell him the Army had no place for broken failures.

Getting to her feet, Riley came to stand at his side.

"Hearing my daughter's final words, words meant for me, is a gift that I'll never be able to repay."

Shifting his attention from over her shoulder, Coen met the general's unblinking dark eyes.

"But the gift I—and my family—will cherish the most is the gift of my daughter's body."

Riley's gaze snapped to his profile. "Body?"

Sweat coated his brow and his hand began to shake.

"At great risk to himself, Operator Monroe found my daughter after those butchers murdered her and he carried her out of that Ecuadorian hellhole."

A familiar chant began pounding in his head as the

general's words slammed him back into the past. To a mud-slicked mass grave site.

Left arm.

 Left hand.

 Left leg.

 Left foot.

Coen dove into the murky pit again and again and again. His lungs burned, and the passing of time cleaved into his skull like the blade of an axe into a doomed tree.

The rain had finally stopped, but it didn't make his search any easier. Nothing could except for him to wake up and find Kendra alive and whole.

 Right leg.

 Right foot.

 Right arm.

 Right—

Where was it? He dove again. His raw fingers scraped along the grave's bottom, searching for something soft, something not quite... right.

He surfaced again, slinging God-knew-what out of his eyes. And that's when he heard them. Voices.

Whipping around, he dove again, opening his eyes even though he knew he shouldn't. Darkness. Grit stabbed his eyes, and he blinked over and over, trying to distinguish shadows from shadows.

 Tick tock. Tick tock.

This time when he broke the surface, he did so with stealth. Scanning the rim of the pit before standing and slogging his way to the edge. The voices were much closer. Too close.

Even so, Coen paused to stare down at the macabre jigsaw puzzle spread out on a sodden canvas.

Torso.

Head.

Left arm.

Left hand.

Left leg.

Left foot.

Right leg.

Right foot.

Right arm.

Right—

The urge to dive back into the pit nearly overpowered his good sense. It was only the sound of bodies cutting through underbrush that forced him to give up the search for Kendra's other hand.

Gathering up the ends of the canvas, he slung his teammate over his shoulder and ran.

Charley hesitated only a moment longer before she picked up her instruments from the tray. Despite Cam's assurances, the next few minutes would not be pleasant for him. Or her.

The soft, melodic voice along with the warm hand making soothing circles over his brow ripped Coen out of Ecuador and plopped him back in North Carolina.

He blinked several times until his surroundings came back into focus. Craning his neck around, he found himself lying on the ground with his arms pinned by Delarosa and Walsh, and Reid secured his legs.

"Riley!" he roared, bucking against his restraints.

The soft pillow under his head shifted, and Riley's upside-down face came into view. Her fingers sifted through his hair in even strokes while she produced a tremulous smile. "I'm here." Setting down a book, she nodded to the others. "We're all here. Everyone's okay." She kissed his temple. "You're okay."

Slowly the others released him, but Coen couldn't move. Molten lead moved through his veins, pressing him down, burning him alive from the inside out.

In a guttural voice, he confessed a truth that had haunted him for weeks. "I couldn't find it." He met the general's unwavering stare. "I couldn't find Kendra's hand."

59

RILEY RESTED HER LIPS AGAINST THE TOP OF COEN'S HEAD, her heart breaking with each revelation. "It's okay, my love."

He had gathered the dismembered parts of his teammate and carried them down a mountain and through a jungle—after three days of torture and likely no food or water—all while evading his captors. The strength of will it took for him to accomplish such a feat was beyond anything she could ever comprehend.

"I couldn't find it."

"I know," she whispered, tightening her hold on him. Despite her best effort, tears clouded her eyes.

"Operator Monroe. Stand, please."

With red-rimmed eyes, General Delarosa stood at Coen's feet, with her back erect, shoulders squared, and hands clasped behind her back. Reid and Colonel Walsh had disappeared, though Riley still sensed their presence.

Coen made to rise, his movements more sluggish than normal. Words bubbled in her heart, and she grasped his face. In a low, urgent whisper, she said, "I love you, Coen Monroe. *You.*"

When he didn't blink, didn't move a muscle, she gave his head a little shake, hoping her words could cut through his grief. "No matter what she says, you're mine. Mine from this day forward. No Army, no research, no past is going to come between us." She touched her forehead to his. "Understand? Say you understand."

Rather than answer, his hand whispered over her hair as he tilted his head back and touched his lips to hers. Then he rose to face the general. When he mirrored her stance, Riley fell in love with him all over again.

To have so much pain and sorrow and still be able to stand tall and proud was remarkable—and somehow heart-rending.

"Hearing my daughter's last words and thanking you for bringing Kendra home were only part of the reason why I wanted to speak with you."

Colonel Walsh returned, standing slightly behind the general.

"And the other part?" Coen asked, his hands curled into fists.

"To inform you that after we received your written report, another two teams were dispatched to the encampment where you and my daughter were held."

"Did they kill the bastards who hurt Kendra?" Coen's jaw hardened. "Pardon, ma'am."

The colonel took up the story. "Yes, and your assessment of their plans was correct."

When no one elaborated, Riley scrambled to her feet. "Which was?"

After a long, considering pause, the general said, "They found enough bomb-making material to reduce the entire length of Fifth Avenue to a patch of rubble."

Riley's hand covered her mouth. If Coen hadn't deciphered the threat—and gotten out of Ecuador alive—how many thousands of American and foreign visitors' lives would have been lost?

"There's something else," Coen said, reading their expressions.

Once again, the colonel glanced at the general, and she nodded. "On the wall of the barracks, we found a hand nailed above one of the beds. Like a goddamned trophy." He gathered himself. "Pardon, ma'am."

The color drained from Coen's face, and his shoulders sagged. "Kendra's?"

"Yes, son."

Coen closed his eyes, and she worried that he'd be thrown back into the past. Lifting the hand that hung listlessly at his side, she threaded their fingers together and placed her other palm on his lower back.

"My baby's whole again," the general said, her voice thick. "Thanks to you."

"Thanks to the other team, you mean."

"No, you." Her voice grew stronger. "The Army would never have sanctioned reentry into Ecuador to retrieve a soldier's body part. Your assessment of the threat allowed us to save many lives—and to finish bringing a soldier home." She squared her shoulders more. "On behalf of the United States government and from a grateful mother, thank you."

Eyes glistening, Coen saluted. "My duty and my honor, ma'am."

The general and colonel turned to leave, and Coen's brows snapped together in confusion. The two officers paused and peered over their shoulders.

"I expect you back at Fort Bragg in"—the colonel's attention drifted to Riley, then back to Coen—"two weeks."

"Two weeks? What about the mission you mentioned on the phone?"

"That's the thing about Delta Force, son. There's no end to fine, capable operators." The corner of the colonel's mouth lifted. "And there's always another mission around the corner."

"You want me back after..." His attention drifted to where they'd held him down on the ground minutes ago.

"We do—if you're sure coming back is what you want."

When Coen's gaze slid to hers, she produced her most encouraging smile. "I'm not going anywhere, no matter what you decide."

He brushed the backs of his fingers over her cheek. The gentle, reverent touch made her throat close and her nose sting.

Wrapping an arm around her shoulder, he said, "I'll be there." His swallow was audible. "Thank you."

With a curt nod, Colonel Walsh melted into the forest.

The general said, "If ever you need anything, *anything,* you know where to find me." Not giving him a chance to respond, she turned away.

He stared after the officers for several long seconds, then he closed his eyes and the tension in his back eased away. When he opened his eyes and looked at her, an easiness she'd never witnessed before had settled into his features.

Running her fingertips up his spine, she asked, "You okay?"

He turned until they were facing each other. "Yes. For the first time in a long while, yes." He titled her chin up, inspecting her face and neck. "Does it hurt?"

Lifting her hand, she tested several places, feeling the sting of small scrapes and the bite of fresh bruises. "All superficial."

"My warrior." He slid a hand over her hip and drew her closer. "You love me."

"Unfortunately for you, yes."

Two fingers caressed the edge of her jaw before his hand wrapped around the back of her neck. "I'm yours, huh?"

"Unfortunately for you, y-yes." His nearness made her unsteady.

"I like a woman who claims what she wants." He nuzzled the side of her nose.

Her arms snaked around his big body until her nipples brushed against his chest. "And I like a man who's confident enough to be claimed." Lifting up on her toes, she kissed the center of his chin. "We can do this."

A crooked smile cut a dimple into his cheek. "Unfortunately for you." His expression turned serious. "It won't be easy. Not knowing where I am. If I'll return. No matter what happened here today, I'm not the man I was before entering service." His thumb toyed with her earlobe. "I will have... bad days."

"Isn't that what loving someone is all about? Enjoying the good days and working through the bad?"

His smile returned. "I love you, Wynette Riley Kingston."

"Ugh," she complained, "way to kill a moment."

"You can call me Coen Julian Monroe if it would make you feel better."

"No, it doesn't. Julian is a great name."

"Oh, for the love of God," Reid said. "Are the two of you going to kiss or what?"

Riley jerked at the interruption, but Coen simply continued to stare down at her with his I'm-going-to-eat-you-up-for-the-rest-of-your-life sexy expression.

Reid reclined on a makeshift chair near the cold fire pit.

"Go away, Coz, I got this covered." She pressed deeper

into Coen's body and was gratified by the hardness rising up between them.

Ignoring her, Reid propped his feet up on one of the fire pit stones. "I'm starving. Got any food around this dive?"

Riley and Coen both laughed and, finally, kissed. A kiss hot enough to make their unwanted visitor blush by the cold fire.

60

"*Feel the weight of your bones. Feel your breaths moving in and out of your lungs. Move your body, starting with your fingers and toes. Begin the process of engaging your muscles in whatever way is comfortable and intentional to you.*"

The soft female voice helped usher Riley out of her semiconscious state. Cylinders in her brain sparked to life as she slid her arms from beneath the warm throw. She stretched hard and rotated her ankles in wide, sweeping circles. Every cell in her body vibrated to life.

"*When you're ready, roll onto your side and acknowledge that this practice Yoga Nidra is complete.*"

When Riley turned onto her side, the sock covering her eyes slid to the tent floor. Morning's soft light pressed against the tent's outer shell, illuminating the interior.

"*Namaste.*" The streaming video on Riley's phone faded out.

Her eyelids fluttered open, and she found Coen facing her with the same peaceful expression she probably wore.

Lifting up onto his elbow, he leaned over and molded his lips with hers. He kept the kiss warm and luxuriant, steady yet thorough. His tongue brushed against her upper lip before pushing fully inside.

Before the sun crested the ridge, she'd awoken to a very male, very naked, very *ready* body snuggled into her equally naked self. Their lovemaking had been slow and sleep drugged.

An hour later, she'd reached for him, and their coupling had been hot, sexy, and fast—as if it would be their last.

She squeezed her eyes against the prickling sensation and ended their kiss. Somehow she managed to produce a teasing smile. "Behave yourself. We're already running behind."

He flopped onto his back and hooked an elbow over his eyes. "Cruel woman."

Poking him in the side, she corrected him. "Practical woman. Someone has to be the responsible adult in this relationship."

"Boooring."

"I'll take boring over late any day." She grasped his hardness beneath the sheet. "Time to get up, Operator Monroe."

Trapping her hand, he growled, "I already am," and ground himself into her palm.

The feel of him, the look of his big, toned body, and the taste of him in her mouth from their earlier encounter was more than tempting to a girl who'd gone two and a half decades without sex.

She started to rip off his sheet when she noticed his cocky smile.

"Nice try." She gave him a good squeeze before removing her hand and reaching for the set of clean clothes she'd laid out the night before. "I'll go start a fire so we can have coffee." After dressing, she pocketed her phone and zipped open the tent.

"Are you sure I can't change your mind?"

The suggestive tone of his voice alone made Riley's mouth go dry. But the flesh-and-blood man had other parts of her body going wet. Propped up on an elbow and with one knee raised, he manipulated himself with long, languid strokes.

Every cell in her body heated until her breaths grew tight, fast. She took a step toward him—and that's when her watch alarm beeped.

Coen groaned and shot off his sleeping bag to snatch her. Evading his hands, she burst through the tent flaps with a shriek. A *shriek,* damn the man!

On all fours, his upper body pushed through the tent opening. "Come back here, Wynette. I'm not done with you."

She jabbed one of their fire starter logs in his direction. "Keep it up and no coffee for you."

He chuckled and backed away, like a lion disappearing behind a wall of tall grass. The sound of his laughter burrowed deep into her heart, and she knew she'd need to bring it out and relive it, again and again, in the coming days, weeks, months.

Once the tinder caught fire and there was no fear of it being extinguished, she swung the kettle over the open flame and dumped the leftover water from the previous evening inside. Deciding she needed to boil a bit more, she headed downstream to refill the container and take care of some personal business.

After the general dropped her bombshells and left, she and Coen had settled into a rhythm most would label as *domestic.* She had taken him to all her favorite haunts, and they had visited with her family, and he'd even gone off and done manly things with her brothers and the Steele boys.

Rather than stay at her bungalow, they'd chosen to spend their nights under the stars at his campsite. At the end of every evening and beginning of every day, they practiced Yoga Nidra.

He was the same man she'd fallen in love with, but different. The edge that had always sharpened his eyes and guided his reactions had smoothed out a bit. His laughter, along with his teasing, came more frequently, and he seemed more tolerant of crowds, though for only a few hours at a time.

Only one dark mood had surfaced in their time together. They'd gone to Countryside Diner for breakfast one morning and been met with a waiting line. When Riley had tried to weave her way through the crowd to ask the hostess about the wait time, she'd caught her toe on something and body-slammed into a large, irritable man.

Rather than accept her profuse apology, he decided to be a jerk, pushing her off him and telling her to watch it. Coen didn't care for the man's reaction.

Screwing the cap back onto the water container, she retraced her steps to the campsite. Although no blood had been shed at the diner, the incident had put the edge back in Coen for several hours before she'd been able to smooth him out again.

But Coen hadn't experienced any night terrors, which meant far more to her than any slip back into ultra-territorial warrior.

Bahh-ling.

Riley dug her phone out of her back pocket and read a much-anticipated message from Maggie.

Young told all to the authorities. Hathaway is in custody. Stop by later for the juicy deets.

A pressure that Riley hadn't realized she'd been carrying lifted from her chest. She couldn't wait to tell Camilla.

After recovering from her concussion, Camilla had returned to Costa Rica. Riley had tried to talk her friend into staying awhile longer, but she had important work to do back home.

Impressed with the way she'd protected *Timbroma subvolanum* from foreign exploitation, her government had put her in charge of restoring Picanula, as it was locally known, back to the wild.

It was an amazing opportunity for Camilla, and Riley couldn't wait to visit sometime in the near future.

Once she could smell the campfire, she lifted her attention from the ground to take in their home. They'd lived simply yet fully within these arbor walls. Although she'd enjoyed having a loving family her entire life, she'd never felt more cherished than when lying naked and sated in Coen's arms.

She would miss this place.

Coen emerged from the tent, decked out in a muscle-defining T-shirt, crisp fatigue pants, and Army-issued boots. It was the first time she'd seen her warrior in his military gear. The sight finalized the moment in a way no planning or conversation could.

She would miss him.

Tears prickled her throat and eyes. This moment had been imminent, yet her awareness hadn't made its arrival any easier to bear.

When their eyes met, Riley saw the same understanding whirling in his gemstone eyes.

"The uniform suits you."

His hand swept down his body as though he was relearning the texture of being a soldier again. "Feels good, though as an operator I'm more likely to be in my own clothes than an Army uniform."

"It helps to flip the switch in your mind, doesn't it?"

"How did you know?"

"Because that's what seeing you in uniform just did for me. It's all real now."

"Regrets?"

"Not a single one." Drawing in an unsteady breath, she forced lightness into her voice and efficiency into her movements as she added water to the kettle. "No dip in the stream this morning?"

Silence whirled in the air around them, and she feared he'd pick up the thread of his previous thought. If he did, she would lose the hair-thin control she had on her emotions.

Sensing her struggle, he teased, "Miss Insatiable kept me in bed too long."

"Can you blame me?" Somehow he appeared bigger and stronger than ever before, and all she wanted to do was crawl back into his arms. "Besides the obvious, there's an added advantage of you not washing off my scent."

He moved closer. "What's that?"

Smiling, she said, "To ward off the competition."

All humor disappeared, and he cupped one side of her face. "There will be a lot of things for you to worry about, but that's not going to be one of them. Understood?"

One element of heaviness lifted from her chest and floated into the fire. She raised up on her tiptoes and pressed her lips to the sensitive hollow beneath his ear and just under the jawline. "Understood."

Coen released their food bag from the tree, and she set about making their coffee. They spoke of the farm, her mom's cooking and the greenhouse repairs, but gave their upcoming departure a wide berth.

Until the chime on her watch filled the air.

"Time to go," she said in a thick voice.

Coen nodded, and they spent the next several minutes tidying up the campsite.

Riley, along with Britt and a few others, would return later and haul everything out. He didn't like leaving her with his mess, but she'd insisted, saying she'd rather spend their time together doing other things than breaking camp.

When they could delay the inevitable no longer, he slid his hand down Riley's arm and wove his fingers with hers. "Before we rejoin the world, I want to thank you."

"For what?"

"For not running away."

Tears rimmed her eyes, and her smile wobbled. "But I did. On that first day. "

He lifted their clasped hands and kissed her knuckles. "You came back, again and again and again."

"Most people would not thank me for stalking them."

"Don't you scientific types call it *observation*?"

"That's the polite term."

"Are you nervous?"

"Why would I be?"

"Leading a team for the first time can be intimidating."

Two evenings ago, Britt and Jonah had surprised their cousin with what she had later called a once-in-an-ethnob-otanist's-lifetime opportunity. She would participate in a multiyear research expedition to East-Central Africa to study plant uses along the Virunga Massif, a massive area that covered a chain of eight volcanoes, three countries, and three national parks.

To his surprise, she hadn't immediately accepted their offer, fearing the negative impact such a long-term assignment would have on their relationship. They had spent hours sitting by the campfire, talking through the logistics and the inevitable emotional toil. By the end of the evening, they had a solid plan in place, and Riley had texted her cousins with an all-caps "YES."

It still amazed him that she'd been ready to sacrifice her dream job so that they could be together. He didn't deserve this woman, but he sure as shit wasn't strong enough to let her go.

"I had no problem leading a team in Costa Rica."

"The Virunga expedition is different and you know it. Hathaway, Young, and Landry were all pulling the strings down there. With this one, you'll be calling the shots. All of them."

The mask she'd been holding in place fell, and real fear flooded her eyes. "What were those idiots thinking?" Her voice grew louder, faster as she ticked off her limitations on her fingers. "I don't have enough experience. I don't have a PhD. I don't speak the language. I don't know the plants. I don't have the leadership skills. Oh, and there are armed, unrestrained bandits roaming the area!"

"Regarding the bandits, you and your team will have round-the-clock security. The best that Jonah's money can buy."

Her eyes narrowed. "What did you do?"

"Called a few old friends. Operators retire at a young age, yet they still yearn to protect, to serve." He squeezed her fingers. "They won't allow any harm to come to you and your team. If they do, they'll answer to me."

Appreciation glistened in her eyes. "A lot of good that will do me. I'll be dead." She snort-grinned at her own quip.

He dipped his head down and nipped her bottom lip. "Don't even joke about dying. As for the rest of your list, you can overcome every one of them."

"But at what cost to the research? And Jonah's generosity?"

"Build a team that will complement your skills. They'll help fill in the gaps. The rest of it, well, no one would go into it knowing everything." He kissed the tip of her nose. "You're far too hard on yourself."

She blew out a long breath. "I need to finish my PhD."

"You can do it."

No acknowledgment.

"You can do it. All of it, right?"

She shrugged.

"You will do it, Wynette Riley Kingston, Ethnobotanist, Slayer of Bad Dudes, Guardian of Weird Plants, Stalker Extraordinaire."

"Stop!" she ordered, laughing.

"You can do it. And we can do *this*."

"Do you really think so?" she asked. "I mean about the 'we' part. Do you really think we can build a long-lasting relationship while living on two different continents?"

"In case you haven't figured it out, I love you. That's not a phrase I throw around carelessly. In fact, I've never said those words to another woman." He traced the outline of her jaw. "So, yeah, I'm determined to make this work. Are you?"

"Yes." She placed a tender kiss against his palm, making his throat close tight.

Tilting her chin up, he captured her lips. He took his

time, savoring every second of her. When he finally pulled back, they were both panting hard.

He slung his duffel over his shoulder and picked up her bag. Lacing his fingers with hers, he said, "Let's go. We both have a lot to do."

Hand in hand, they strode into the forest, into their future, into a new life filled with a love that would see them through any obstacle, no matter the distance, danger, or demons.

"Lists," Riley said excitedly. "I have so many lists to make." She started ticking them off on her free hand. "When to see Coen, research itinerary, equipment to order, researchers to contact, greenhouse directions, what to pack..."

Together they would succeed. Miss Indy wouldn't allow it to be any other way.

Thank you for reading SEARING NEED! If you want more of the Kingston family, check out STRIKING EDGE, Shep Kingston's story.

Next in Series:

While on a wilderness reality show, adventure guide Shep Kingston and fallen music superstar Joss Wynter discover a fierce passion. But the cameras aren't the only ones watching. A deadly opponent lurks in the shadows, playing a dangerous game. And all too willing to kill for a win.

Turn the page for an excerpt from STRIKING EDGE!

STRIKING EDGE

KELSEY BROWNING

Enjoy an excerpt from Kelsey Browning's *Striking Edge*,
Book Four in Steele Ridge: The Kingstons series:

The bottle slipped from the man's grasp and hit the packed
dirt serving as the tent's floor. The glass cracked and sickly
sweet-smelling scent rolled through the tent.

Shep ground his teeth at the overpowering odor. This
was exactly the reason he didn't work inside a building with
other people. Overwhelming smells, too much conversation,
complete lack of logic. He covered his nose with his palm
and stepped away.

"Are you okay?" Joss put a light hand on his arm, a touch
that would normally be uncomfortable if not downright
painful to him. But with her, for some reason, it was…
bearable.

"I don't tolerate strong scent well." Puck sneezed and
shook his whole body as if confirming Shep's intolerance to
stuff that smelled chemically fake. Shep ducked out one of
the tent flaps, with Puck and Joss Wynter right behind him.

Thank goodness, it looked as if most of the crowd had

become bored and left. Shep took a few gulps of fresh air. The scent of pine and the hint of cool the mountains were promising soothed him. Once his head was clear again, he glanced down at the tiny woman beside him. Blood streaked one of her legs.

She was a mess, but she didn't smell like a perfume factory. If he had to describe her scent, he would call it clean and warm. She had her knapsack slung over one shoulder and the strap for a soft guitar case on the other.

"You shouldn't take a musical instrument, either."

Her mouth twisted. "I traded my extra underwear for it. Besides, it's not that heavy, and I'm sure not leaving it with someone else."

"We will be hiking up to fifteen miles a day. It will be slapping against your back the entire time. It is an awkward shape, and not necessary."

"Not for you, maybe," she said as she gazed toward the mountains humping up from the ground to the west. Although she may have been teasing the other contestant a few short minutes ago, now Shep thought she might be sad. "But this is *my* best friend."

"A musical instrument can't be a friend."

"So says the man who's BFFs with a dog." She glanced up at him, but her eyelashes didn't twitch like the other woman's. Suddenly, he realized that Joss Wynter was pretty. With her turquoise-dyed dark hair, pink lips, and tiny stature, she looked a bit like a fairy. Maybe like Tinkerbell's older sister. The one who probably snuck out at night and back-talked their fairy parents.

"What?" she asked. "Why are you staring at me like that?"

Shep tried to regain the thread of their conversation and flailed around inside his head for a few seconds. Guitar. Best friend. Puck. "That's different," he finally said. "Puck is alive."

"Doesn't make it any less sad."

"Puck makes me happy." More than that, he made Shep whole.

She lifted a hand, let it drop back to her side. "So you understand why I need my guitar."

"I have heard your music."

"Oh really?"

"I do not like it."

Her laugh was a single puff of air. "Hey, why don't you tell me what you really think?"

"I just did. It's too loud. The guitar makes my ears hurt and your voice is screechy." Just thinking about it, the strident sound of her screaming lyrics on stage or over his radio, prompted Shep to take two steps away from her.

"Good thing you're an adventure guide and not a music critic." Her voice had turned hard, harsh.

"I am sorry, though."

"Nothing to be sorry about." She turned her back on him and started for the tent. "Different musical tastes for different people."

"No, I'm not sorry about that."

"Then what?"

"I'm sorry you killed your bandmates."

Joss locked her knees to keep them from kissing the dirt again. There was a sucker punch, and then there was an emotional knockout. One word reverberated through her head: *killed, killed, killed.*

Puck trotted over to her, leaned his head against her thigh, and whined up at her.

"I said something wrong, didn't I?" his owner said.

"You... you think?" Sudden low-level nausea rocking her stomach, she shot a glare his way that should've twisted up his balls worse than her claw hold on Buffalo earlier.

"I am actually not sure. But when Puck makes that sound, it usually means someone is hurting. I didn't mean to hurt you."

She'd had some terrible things said to her and about her over the past months, but few people had the sheer nerve to outright accuse her of killing her band. "Then why did you say what you did?"

"Because it was a tragedy." He dug into his pocket and pulled out a long, slim length of paracord. "I might not enjoy Scarlet Glitterati's music, but my little sister is a huge fan. I know many more people are, too."

Joss stroked Puck's ears, but the feel of the silky fur did little to ease the pain inside her. "You think I'm some kind of monster."

"I didn't say that." With one hand, he manipulated the cord, giving it all his attention. Dammit, a person should look you in the eye when they called you a monster. "I think I stepped over some line, but I'm not sure."

What huffed out of her wasn't a laugh. It hurt too damn much to be that. "I get that guys can be clueless. In fact, I'm pretty sure I've dated every clueless one on the west coast. But I thought Southern men were different. You know— polite and all that. *Yes, ma'am. No, ma'am. Let me hold the door for you, ma'am.*"

He looked up from whatever he was doing with the cord, but he still didn't meet her gaze. His darted to somewhere around her chin and back down again. "My parents did raise their children to be kind and courteous."

"You just happened to fail charm school."

"I didn't go to school." He rubbed a hand over his drying

hair—now a sun-bleached light brown—making it stand up in electrified whirls. "That's not true. I went to school until I was ten."

"And then you just ran wild like Mowgli?"

"Mowgli did not run wild. He had two families—one wolf, one human. I only had a human family."

"My God, you are the most literal human being I've ever met."

He bent over the cord and turned his back on her. "I am not making the soup right."

That was it. After he stood up for her, she'd thought they had some type of connection, but obviously not. He was rude, insensitive, and distracted.

Devil, yes. Divine, no.

He might look like over six feet of sexiness, but Joss could not suffer this man another minute. He was either playing the most elaborate mind-fuck she'd ever encountered, or he was psycho. And she had plenty of madness inside her own mind these days, thank you very much.

"Look," she said. "It might be better if you and I keep our distance during the next few days. It's obvious you don't like me, and I don't know how soup figures into all this, but—"

"Soup is conversation."

Intrigued in spite of herself, she approached him again and Puck followed. "What?"

"That is the way my dad taught me to talk to people. It is like making soup. They put in one ingredient. You look at the ingredient and then add something else." The cord dangling from his fingers, he pantomimed dropping food into a pot. "But not like radishes to their sweet potatoes."

And there was her answer. Definitely psycho. "Oookay."

Attractive on the outside, but awful on the inside.

The man growled. Actually made a low rumbling sound

that shot through Joss's body and made her hair rise with awareness. Apparently, she was psycho, too, because something about that sound cranked up her hormones. But even a psycho knew when to edge away from danger.

"You say one thing and then I say something back that makes sense with what you said," he said, pacing a tight circle around her, preventing her from escaping. "Which means I have to listen. Hearing and listening are not the same thing."

"Well, that's self-aware. Good for you." *Keep things light and friendly.* She didn't like how intense this had suddenly become.

"I wish Puck could talk," he said so miserably that Joss's heart jolted. Puck fixed a concerned gaze on his owner and whined again.

"You would be a very rich man," Joss said as she sidled away a half-step. "I have a feeling Puck is a highly intelligent dog. I bet he could teach physics if he put his mind to it."

For the first time, she witnessed a true grin spread across the man's face. "Or neuroscience."

Okay, good. They'd apparently backed away from some weird precipice, so Joss nodded. "Why not? The sky is the limit for a dog like Puck." As if he understood every word they were saying, Puck looked back and forth between them. *Zip.* Right eyebrow up. *Zap.* Left eyebrow up.

"Can we start over?" Shep asked her.

"Do I have to get back in the raft?" she joked, even though the thought of the raft and the drop made her want to vomit.

"That would not be very efficient since we are about to start our hike."

"Of course it wouldn't."

He turned to her, squaring his shoulders with purpose

and meeting her gaze. And oh, wow. Just wow. His eyes were green. Why hadn't she noticed that until now?

Because...because this was the first time he'd looked at her eye to eye.

He held out his hand, and with the feeling that she was embarking on something life-changing, she put hers in his. The feel of his callused skin on her softer palm buzzed up her arm and settled in her chest.

"Hello," he said. "My name is Harris Sheppard Kingston. People call me Shep. I work as an adventure guide for Prime Climb Tours. Steele Ridge is my hometown. My parents and most of my brothers and sisters live here. I love the mountains, my family, Puck, my cabin, and home-made ketchup."

And damn, that little autobiography charmed her. "That would make quite a Tinder profile."

"My dad taught me to make conversation because I could never understand how to do it on my own. He told me I don't always have to look people in the eyes, but some-times, when something is really important, that it's a good thing to do. Because regular people see it as a sign of truth-fulness and sincerity. My family knows I don't lie, so I don't always have to look them in the eye."

"You're looking me in the eye." And neither of them seemed inclined to drop hands.

"Because I somehow hurt your feelings, and that was not my intention. I want you to see my apology is sincere."

Charmed? This man had gone from running a blade of burning steel through her heart to melting her into a puddle of disbelieving attraction. "Thank you. I accept your apology."

"However, it's likely I will do it again. Because even Puck can't stop me from saying the wrong things."

"You hurt people's feelings a lot?" Made sense if he hit everyone with this type of verbal whiplash.

Shep finally dropped her hand, glanced away and swallowed. Took a bracing breath and met her stare again. "I don't always understand things like body language, intonation, sarcasm, and subtext. I try, I really try, but sometimes I just... can't."

She couldn't imagine there was anything this man couldn't do if he put his mind to it. He was obviously smart, conscientious, well-read, and he loved his dog. "I've never changed a tire, I don't understand geometry, and I don't know how to ride a bike."

"Really?" he said, his eyes going wide. "For the tire, the first step is to jack up the car and... Oh, soup. You don't want me to tell you how to change a tire, do you?"

"Shep Kingston, I don't think I've ever met a man like you." And it made her wonder if she'd been missing out.

"You probably have, but you just didn't know it. Because we're estimated at one out of every two hundred fifty to five hundred people. About two to four times as many men as women. They don't really know why."

"You lost me again."

"Backstory. Yeah, people need that sometimes," he said. "When I was eight, I was diagnosed with Asperger's Syndrome. It's no longer listed in the *Diagnostic and Statistical Manual of Mental Disorders,* but once you have a diagnosis, they don't take it away. Now, it's called being high on the autism spectrum. Autism Spectrum Disorder."

What? This...this incredible man was *autistic*? "I...uh... wow..."

"Don't worry," he said quickly. "It's not contagious or anything. It just means that my brain tends to work a little differently than most people's."

Yes, she was beginning to understand that. And for some reason, it made her feel not so grief-stricken and guilty. "Shep Kingston, I wasn't sure at first, but you're growing on me. Who knows, we might even become friends."

Find out what happens next and order
STRIKING EDGE

ACKNOWLEDGMENTS

A big hug and thank-you to my family, especially Tim and Helene, for their constant love, support, and patience. I love you to pieces.

My editors, Gina Bernal, Martha Trachtenberg, deserve Editor-of-the-Year awards for wading through the early drafts of this book and pointing out its nuggets of potential and moments of beauty. *Searing Need* would not be the book it is today without you.

Special thanks to Ben Haberthur for his insight into the nuances of military life—any errors of fact or detail rest squarely on my shoulders.

Huge gratitude to our awesome, behind-the-scenes team —Heather Machel, Donna Duffee, and Sandy Modesitt— for keeping Steele Ridge (and its authors) organized, looking sharp, and out of trouble. You're all gems, and we couldn't do this without you!

Extraordinary thanks to my readers. Your support enables me to return to the keyboard again and again—and helps us keep this beautiful Steele Ridge world alive.

As always, much love to my friends, partners, and plotting badasses, Kelsey Browning and Adrienne Giordano.

ABOUT TRACEY DEVLYN

 Tracey Devlyn is a *USA Today* best-selling author of contemporary and historical suspense, often layered with mystery, romance, and environmental crime. Despite the thrilling, emotional journeys she creates for her readers, Tracey lives an annoyingly normal life in the mountains of North Carolina with her husband and rescue dog.

For access to exclusive content, new release notifications, special promotions, and behind-the-scenes peeks, join Tracey's VIP Reader List at https://TraceyDevlyn.com/Contact.